HaLF MISSING

Half Missing

Jane Lebak

Philangelus Press
Boston, MA USA

Also by Jane Lebak:

The Wrong Enemy
Seven Archangels: An Arrow In Flight
Seven Archangels: Sacred Cups
Seven Archangels: Annihilation
The Seven Angels Short Story Bundle
The Boys Upstairs
Honest And For True
Forever And For Keeps

ISBN: 978-1-942133-17-9
Library of Congress Number: 2015951105

Cover: C.K. Volnek

DEDICATION

For Caroline

one

Amber's work boots crunched over the charred carpet as she moved past a hostess station to what used to be a dining area. Flashlight in hand, she traced the length of the fire-gutted wood beams supporting the ceiling, just to be sure. The roof was waterlogged, and seven AM was far too early to die.

The firefighter at her side said, "The Chief had a structural engineer come in. It'll hold. Just don't book a wedding."

"Not a chance." While the dining room must have been gorgeous about eight hours ago, right now it crumbled underfoot and stank of smoke. Her light skittered across something recognizable as a pile of menus. Several tables were broken, their linens blackened. Amber hesitated as a chair leg snapped beneath her boot. Between the smoke and the water damage, they'd salvage nothing.

No, don't think about that. Salvage wasn't her concern. Until she proved otherwise, this was a crime scene.

"I'm heading for the kitchen. I assume that's where it started." Amber hefted her shovel and aimed toward the back of the room, choosing her steps to disturb as little as possible.

Grit clung to her jeans. Her gloves had already gotten soot on them, and when she adjusted her hard hat, ashes flurried into her eyes.

In the doorway, she bit her lip in the face of the devastation. The ceiling sagged toward the back wall, where everything was black, black, black. Awful—but, really, her job dealt in awful. "Hey Rick, do you know how long it burned?"

The firefighter shrugged. "Not sure about how long before, but say a half hour. We fought it for ten minutes, and then it hit flashover."

Amber flinched. "Everyone got out okay?" Flashover was the bane of firefighters everywhere. Any time the air inside a building got hot enough to ignite everything at once, that was just as bad as it sounded. Temperatures had to have reached twelve hundred degrees in here. Maybe more.

Rick nodded. "Yeah, we were fine. It took another half hour until we finally knocked it down. The Chief was about to call Elmira for backup."

Amber picked her way among the fallen beams and the smoke-streaked appliances. It wasn't just her imagination: this place was still warm. She scanned the kitchen again. Over there would have been a row of stoves to cook for two hundred people; those had been refrigerators; that was the walk-in cooler off the side. Utility sinks. Pans heavy enough to deck a gladiator, plus knives sharp enough to do him in if the pan failed.

She squared her shoulders. "We're good. I'll take it from here."

Behind her, Rick said, "Are you sure?"

She pivoted, cocking her head. "Come on."

It flashed across his face, the hesitancy at leaving a young woman alone at a burn site. This happened often in her two years as a fire investigator. It was her height (or lack thereof) and the slight upturn of her nose, the way her voice sounded younger than she was. Sometimes it felt like the whole fire department and half the police thought of themselves as her dad. She said, "Safety's my job."

Rick nodded, and then she was alone.

Nothing was left of the oven mitts, the linens, the sponges. Wires: melted. Fixtures dangled from wires or had already crashed to the floor. There, a set of truly amazing chef's knives, their handles scorched. But certainly the fire had started in here, so she traveled out and back again to bring her equipment, first lighting a pair of battery-operated lanterns and setting them strategically to study the burn patterns.

Based on the report she'd already had, she wasn't going to determine much on those alone. Given that the kitchen reached an internal temperature of over twelve hundred degrees, anything that could burn had ignited simultaneously just from the heat in the air and walls. Then after flashover, it had burnt for so long that everything was charred.

She checked out the windows, all double-paned and effective for keeping down the heat bill during an upstate New York winter, and equally effective for keeping heat in while the place burned. Moreover, they were still shut, so there hadn't been any attempt to release the heat by ventilating the room.

Scorched insulation was visible through a gap in the ceiling, and it was the good stuff. Again, spectacular for retaining heat, and it burned incredibly hot.

It was a shame. The restaurant had seemed nice enough, with a jazz band on Friday and Saturday evenings, and Italian food that would make you feel at home if only you could have afforded it. Plus it had employed what, twenty people? Regardless, it was a mismatch to a small town with no industry, where a hole-in-the-wall mom and pop diner (and grandpop and great-grandpop) did fine selling a three-egg breakfast special—extra toast for twenty-five cents. By contrast, a high-end Italian place was sure to fail. You just never wanted it to happen, and certainly not like this.

The building, not so much. She always looked at these square, faceless and character-free structures and tried to imagine that when the building was new, someone actually loved it. Cared for it. Didn't believe it was just a rectangle with windows and a door.

Fifteen minutes later, on a trip back past the caution tape for her shovel and some specimen jars, a car pulled up behind her. Shivering in the frost, she turned as the driver stepped out, a man in a mortal pallor.

This was the moment she dreaded: when the owner got that first look, that first whiff. But she forced herself to take note of his features, the inverted V of his eyebrows, his quivering mouth.

She rubbed her hands on her jeans as she approached. Pulling her ID from her back pocket and showing him her shield, she said, "I'm Amber Brickman, from the Tioga County Fire Marshal's office. I'm the arson investigator."

"Arson!" The man's eyes flew wide. "Someone set this?"

"I can't answer that," Amber said, "but the investigation is standard procedure, and it doesn't mean we suspect wrongdoing. The State requires I track down the source of the fire and make a determination as to the cause, whether it was deliberately set."

She could have counted down the seconds until he put it together, and how he'd react with horror because he'd know the law. An insurance company wouldn't reimburse a dime if she ruled he'd burned his own place to the ground.

Sure enough, he looked nauseated. "What are you going to do?"

She really ought to tell this guy to get out of here so she could do her job. He was only going to muck things up. Either he'd caused this fire or he hadn't, and either way, he was going to try to convince her he hadn't.

Instead she put away the Fire Investigator tone, and in a lower voice, said, "What's your name?"

"John. John DelGaudio."

"Mr. DelGaudio, I'm going to take samples from the structure, and I'm going to send them to a lab. We're going to test for accelerants." He looked relieved. "I'm going to study the burn patterns and figure out where the fire started. I'm going to interview the firefighters as to how the fire behaved while they were putting it out. And based on those cues, I'm going to make a determination."

Eyes wide, he bit his lip. "I didn't do this."

"You know what?" Amber said. "I believe you."

His eyes closed.

"But the thing is, sir, if I don't do this investigation, your insurance company will claim they don't have to pay what you're owed. So I'm going to do the most thorough study in the history of Patmos Springs. I'm going to interview you. I'm going to interview your employees. That doesn't mean I think anyone's guilty. What it means is that when I write that report, I want it airtight."

Still staring off at a collapsed wall, he nodded.

"Oh," she said, "by the way, the windows—they looked new."

He gave a rueful smile. "I replaced them six months ago."

"Along with the insulation?"

He nodded. "We redid the whole kitchen."

The guy had been pouring money into this place. That's not what you do when you want it destroyed. "I can't have you in there alone," Amber said, "but if there's anything you want to retrieve right now, I'll call the Fire Chief so one of the guys can escort you. The office toward the front was spared the worst of the damage."

As Amber got out her phone, DelGaudio said, "Did you ever eat here?"

Amber paused mid-dial. *I had reservations once, the week you opened. I ended up at my date's funeral, instead.*

She only said, "No, I'm sorry. I can tell how much you loved the place."

Once she had DelGaudio squared away, Amber went back inside with her shovel, her notebook, and a bunch of jars. Time to lock up the guesses and dig for the facts. People who burned down a building took steps to help it along. It seldom occurred to them those steps left chemical footprints.

A little after nine o'clock, in the middle of filling her seventh jar, a voice called, "What a surprise meeting you here, Brickman."

She laughed, screwing the top on the sample jar. "A total stunner, finding the Fire Marshal's office at the scene of a fire. Even more surprising than finding the insurance adjustor."

She extended a hand, and Lance Harrington shook it without recoiling from the grit on her glove.

"Not much left to adjust." He shook his head. "DelGaudio did a thorough job."

"This wasn't arson." Great. Now she'd have to fight with an insurance company. "I know you get paid the big bucks to say it is, but there's no evidence."

Harrington stuck his hands in his jeans pockets and looked around. "The restaurant was flailing. He'd changed up the menu three times in five weeks and was trying to bring in sushi and, heaven help us, karaoke. DelGaudio had one month maximum before he declared bankruptcy. So he did what any reasonable man would do and had an insurance fire."

"And I'm telling you there's no evidence." Amber gestured around. "You can speculate however you like, but my job is to prove it, and there's no proof."

"The burn pattern." Harrington swung his flashlight over the floor. "If the fire starts in the center of the floor, someone set the fire. The burn seems deepest there."

"Except the kitchen burned for well over ten minutes after flashover." Amber folded her arms. "If the kitchen hadn't burnt for that long, I'd agree with you. But given the timeframe, you expect to see the center gutted. Moreover, there's double-insulated windows and brand new insulation in the ceiling. And no venting. What other burn pattern are you going to see?"

Harrington peered right into Amber's eyes. "You mean to tell me that somehow, just totally by coincidence, a man's restaurant burns to the ground mere weeks before he'd have lost everything?"

"Yeah." She smirked. "Almost enough to make me believe in God."

She turned her back and lifted the shovel.

Harrington was too nice a guy to sound really threatening, but he tried. "If you rule it's not arson, I'll fight your determination."

"Oh, gee, it sounds like I'm going to get in trouble *again* at my job." She pivoted, and looking him in the face, she steeled herself: he would *not* take the easy way out. "I can't call something a crime when it wasn't. You're working on intuition, but you learned your trade on buildings that got extinguished before they burned too long. That's bad science. Our jobs are to protect the people, but I have to make sure we're not protecting the wrong people."

Harrington huffed. "You think you can figure out this mess?"

"Ninety-five percent of the time, the past is written in the present. Come see." Amber trudged over to a row of appliances that used to be stainless steel. Turns out twelve hundred degrees can stain it. She yanked a handle and tuned her flashlight beam onto the racks of dishes.

Clean. "Pretty, huh? Plates in this one." She opened the next. "Crystal glasses. Perfectly clean." She yanked open the third. "Lovely. Except there's smoke on these, and there isn't on the other two."

Harrington said, "And—? You just said the place burned for at least forty minutes."

She whacked a hand against the body of the dishwasher. "These babies are watertight, and the frames are steel. Nothing's getting in there. That's part of the point: they keep the water in, and when they dry the dishes, they keep the heat in. DelGaudio bought the best of everything: the best windows, the best insulation, the best dishwashers. You've got three dishwashers side by side, and two of them kept out the smoke, but one was filled with it." She slammed the door and kicked the unit. "What do you do if you're running a restaurant? Well at two AM you've booted out the last diners. Your staff has finished cleaning. You've loaded the last dishes, so you turn on all three dishwashers, and you go home." She opened her hands. "The unit is designed to produce heat when it's drying, and if one of these malfunctioned, it would burn inside that stainless steel frame until it got so hot that it spread to the floor, and then, yeah, you'd have a burning floor. No accelerants necessary. The cycle on these things runs what? Two hours? And when did the fire get called in? About four-fifteen AM."

Harrington bit his lip. Victory.

"See? The past is written in the present." The look on Harrington's face was the look of a man needing to put a value on the food in the walk-in fridge and decide whether a two-week-old karaoke machine had depreciated. "I'm getting samples, and I'm going to test the hell out of the place, but I know what I'm going to find."

"You've convinced me." He took a step, then turned back. "Okay, but now you have me curious. If a guy getting saved from losing everything by a malfunctioning dishwasher is *almost* enough to have you believe in God, what would it actually take?"

Amber looked at him over her shoulder, eyes narrow. "Raising a guy from the dead."

Harrington grinned. "I think at least one major religion has that."

"Wrong guy." She bent to get another sample. "You'll have a copy of the report as soon as it's written, even if the Old Man wants my head in a bag again."

"He'd never put your head in a bag," called Harrington as he left. "You're the reason he can stroll around checking smoke detectors rather than spending mornings out here with a shovel."

———◦———

Amber collapsed into the driver's seat of her Subaru Outback. At nearly noon, she'd already spent four hours investigating the remnants of that restaurant, and her back ached.

Two calls had come in on her cell phone while working, both of which she'd sent to voicemail. The first was from her sister Olivia. "So, um, you may want to cover up your head or run over your phone. Mom had a great idea: you need to buy a house. She says a sign went up for sale on a nice starter home on Curve Street."

Oh, yeah, the old Martin place. Three bedrooms, tiny overgrown yard with blackberry brambles engulfing what used to be a white picket fence. Mom might be in need of a hobby, but at least she'd picked a place with charm. Of course Amber would love nothing more than to snow-blow her walk every morning from November to April and maintain a three-bedroom gable all by herself for the next sixty years.

"She says there's even room to grow a garden, which I know is something you lie awake every night wishing you could do, right? Right. Well, I warned you. You can thank me later."

Amber gave that message all the attention it deserved: she deleted it. She proceeded to the second, and the number that showed made her stomach lurch.

"Hello, Amber," began the message, and then, as if Amber could ever forget this voice, "This is Carmen Mateo."

Amber's fingers tightened on the phone, and she set her jaw.

"I hope you're doing well," Carmen continued, "and I'd love to catch up with you sometime."

Of course you would. Just a regular should-have-been-mother-in-law doing a normal bi-decennial check-in with the woman her son never married. What do you really want?

"Um, this is about Rocket." A hesitation before continuing, something you heard a lot with lies. "Marcus's cat. I was thinking maybe I should let you have him after all."

Four years later? Four years and suddenly Carmen *thought she should let her have the cat after all*?

Carmen said, "So if you want him, I need you to come get him soon."

Or what?

"Call me back," Carmen said. "It will be good to hear from you!"

The whole call was a crap sandwich. Start with the buttery greeting and end with the sweet closing, and in the middle slip in an offer that Carmen should maybe give back the cat she'd stolen. And why? Maybe the cat needed chemotherapy and Carmen didn't want to pay for it. Maybe Carmen wanted to go on a month-long tour of Ecuador and found out what it costs to pay a cat-sitter.

Amber dialed the numbers she still knew by heart after four years. *You told me you couldn't let Marcus's cat go, that you had to keep him because it meant so much to you and it was all you had left.*

If this were an arson investigation, she'd already have had the chief of police on the phone, that's for sure.

It rang three times and then rolled to voicemail. Trying to avoid sounding irritated, she instead sounded preternaturally calm. "Carmen, it's Amber. I need you to tell me more about the cat."

Maureen Brickman had just enough time after sliding the lasagna noodles into the pot to mix up the cheese. Into the metal mixing bowl went the container of ricotta, the shredded mozzarella, and the grated parmesan. She added an egg, broken first into a mug the way her mother had taught her, and then pepper and parsley.

While she worked, her daughter Olivia sat at the table, breastfeeding three-month-old Charlotte. Those sweet audible gulps had slowed, and it looked like once again, a baby was knocked out by a tummy full of milk. So cute. Olivia was saying, "No, really. I don't think Amber would even get approved for a mortgage."

Maureen huffed. "They'd give a mortgage to a talking parrot these days. Her apartment's nice enough, but she'd just thrive in a place of her own."

Olivia shifted the now-sleeping baby to the crook of her arm and straightened her shirt. Maureen grinned. Yep, that baby was good and out.

Olivia pointed to the lasagna. "You know you could just use no-boil noodles and dump in extra tomato sauce."

Maureen's nose wrinkled. "Yuck."

Olivia laughed.

"There's a reason you do things the right way." Maureen glanced outside at the snow, glad for a pretty kitchen and a warm stove. The yellow curtains with their embroidered flowers couldn't quite make it springtime, but she could pretend. Within a month, those flowers would be real.

Olivia added, "I think it's funny. We're going out for dinner, but you're making dinner for one of your client-moms."

Maureen turned with a grin, holding up a finger. "One. I'm making *one* dinner."

Olivia laughed. "Still, I thought showing up at the door with dinner postpartum was the work of a mom, not a midwife."

Maureen's voice sharpened. "You need to remember you're incredibly lucky. Not everyone has her mother an hour down the road, not to mention childcare at the drop of a hat. She's young. Her husband's deployed, and she has another little one to look after. Besides," and here she didn't even try to hide her irritation, "I don't stop caring the minute I cut the cord and submit the insurance forms." Not like a doctor. Who probably never cared at all.

Olivia shrank a bit. "I'm sorry. That's not what I meant."

"No, I know. But we... Not everyone has family nearby." And not everyone lived in a town like this one, where if you needed help you could count on a neighbor to stop by with a meal. Or an offer to babysit. Or a gas card. What did new moms do without neighbors?

Well, this one's midwife was bringing her a lasagna.

Olivia excused herself from the table to lay Charlotte in the portacrib.

Her poor client. It hadn't been a difficult birth, but it had been long. Maureen had sat with the laboring mom for twenty-six hours, much of that time spent rubbing her back or letting the mom lean against her. All that time, the touches, the reassurance, leading to that moment when the mom finished her hard work by birthing her baby into her own hands, raising him to her chest, and looking up triumphant. Stunned, but triumphant.

This afternoon at the one-week postpartum appointment, though, the mom was spent, just spent. The newborn period was too tough to go alone, especially with a toddler who hungered for all your attention. So no, Olivia was right, a midwife didn't have to cook for her clients, but what did it hurt anyone to make sure a woman had a decent meal?

As Olivia returned, Maureen drained off the water and began creating pasta layers, her throat tightening. Young moms needed a tender touch, something she'd never gotten. A birth with them in control, not someone else. Again, something she hadn't gotten. She should send brownies too.

As she slid the lasagna into the oven, she suddenly felt that familiar stared-at sensation. "Hey, get the phone, will you?"

On cue, the phone rang. Olivia answered, then handed it to Maureen. "Hello?"

"Maureen! It's Dr. Jacobson."

Maureen propped the phone against her shoulder as she washed her hands. "What's going on? Have you got a referral?"

But even as she said it, she knew her tone was wrong, that he sounded too reserved for that. In general calls went from her to him, since when a woman was no longer a good candidate to birth at home, he was the only doctor she trusted enough to refer her clients to. On the occasion he'd called her to discuss a patient who wanted to homebirth, he'd adopted a mock hurt tone. "I can't believe they're rejecting me," he'd say in his dusky voice.

"But Maureen, if they're going to birth outside the hospital, I want them to do it safely."

But now, instead of "I have a woman who needs your care," he said, "I wanted to let you know I'm retiring."

Her heart thrummed. "But— When?"

"Two weeks."

Two weeks? "Why so suddenly? Is it your health?"

"It's complicated, and I'm not ill, but it's time." It's *time*? Some garbage going down at the hospital? Did he lose a patient? Did his malpractice insurance premiums go up because premiums only go up?

Maureen paced the kitchen. She avoided Olivia's probing look. "Are you selling the practice?"

"I'm phasing everyone out, over to Dr. Xiang."

Ah, Dr. Xiang, whom Maureen once overheard telling a homebirth transfer, "It's good you're in the hospital, not birthing in a barn." Did she know Maureen had given birth to Olivia in a barn? It wasn't that Dr. Xiang wasn't a good doctor. She probably was—but the system that formed her? The culture of hospitalized birth? Dr. Xiang exemplified it all.

As of this moment, Maureen no longer had a backup physician. If any of her clients had to transfer to an obstetric practice, she wouldn't have a working relationship with it.

Maureen unclenched her hand. "Well... Thank you for letting me know. I wish you the best."

"Thanks, Maureen. I'm sorry for the short notice."

She ran a hand through her hair. "Oh, wait. Before you go, I talked to Jody Errols at the hospital. Remember, the mom I referred to you with blood pressure issues?"

"As if I could forget." No, Dr. Jacobson wouldn't. Most doctors didn't have the time of day for you unless they had your chart in their hands and could bill you for the effort, but he probably went home at night and prayed for each patient by name. "I trust she's told you only good things about me?"

"I saw how well she's doing. She adores you." Maureen bit her lip. "She's going to be very upset."

"I'm planning to tell her myself tomorrow," Dr. Jacobson said. "She's a real trooper. Everyone's rooting for her."

Maureen's throat tightened. Why was it always the good ones to go? "Well, thank you. And good luck. With your retirement."

After she hung up the phone, she sat at the table, rubbing her temples and feeling as if she'd just lost an ally in a war she couldn't bear to surrender.

TWO

Amber pulled into Carmen's driveway and kept her eyes off the house. Instead she noticed the lack of hedges in her headlights. Too much had changed. On the other side should have been an overgrown maple with its roots buckling the asphalt, but it was gone as well, the ground contoured over the spot where the stump should have been. Maybe Carmen had pulled it down. Maybe that freak snowstorm last October with the really high winds had brought down a tree limb that crushed the hedge, necessitating the removal of both.

Amber liked that theory best: it answered two questions at the same time.

For a couple of minutes, she sat staring at Carmen's old car, ahead of her in the driveway. The woman was home. She couldn't get out of it now, not really. Not unless her pager went off and she had to go to a fire, but when she framed it that way, someone losing his house was far worse than her talking to Carmen. So bracing herself, she got out of the car.

She refused to look at the house while picking her way through the remaining piles of snow, but that was easy because the outside lights weren't on. She held onto the paint-peeling railing in case there was ice on the steps.

When she answered the door, Carmen looked her up and down while gushing out a greeting. Hunching, Amber thrust her hands forward in her coat pockets. Let the woman inspect her. Amber didn't owe her anything. Not an explanation. Not an apology. Nothing.

Carmen gestured that she enter, and the smell hit her as soon as she stepped into the hall. The mix of carpet, cooking, people—it might as well have been four years ago, with Marcus waiting for her in the kitchen, leaning against the counter with a can of Coke in one hand and a Neal Stephenson book in the other.

She wanted to scream for it to stop. But she couldn't back out now.

Carmen said, "You look really good! You cut your hair."

About three years prior, yeah. Amber avoided the photos of Marcus on the walls. And the fireplace mantle: was that where Carmen had kept Marcus's ashes until she finally got around to burying him? "Where's Rocket?"

In the kitchen, the cat sat on the tile floor beside its food bowls. The brown striped tabby looked skinnier than she remembered, but he still had that cute white tip of the tail, and still the huge feet. *Hi, guy. I missed you.*

A pair of baby-gates, stacked one atop the other, barred off the entrance to the dining room, similar to the ones blocking the stairwell. A grandkid? Maybe Carmen was doing day-care. The litter box was in the bathroom just off the kitchen, and now Amber could detect a strong odor of Lysol. What was going on?

She knelt on the linoleum until Rocket noticed her. Then she extended a hand, not touching. He sniffed, then picked up his head, stepped closer, and sniffed again.

Carmen said, "Do you have a cat carrier?"

"I figured I'd use yours and bring it back."

Carmen said, "I don't have one."

Amber frowned. "What do you use to bring the cat to the vet?"

Carmen said, "He's never been."

Not for the first time, Amber thanked heaven for the only silver lining in this situation: Carmen was not her mother-in-law. If everything had worked out as planned, Amber would have been the top poster at Mother-In-Law-Stories-dot-com, seconded only by Marcus's posts about her own mother. Who knows—maybe their screen names would have given each other support online only to discover they were married? That would have been a riot. Marcus would have joked forever that he was leaving her for that enticing internet buddy who gave such awesome advice,

Rather than let Carmen see her grimace, Amber crouched near the cat and let him get her scent. Did he remember her? He let her scratch his head, then stretched.

Amber said, "He's not up to date on his shots?"

Carmen said, "I never let him out of the house."

"So he's not up to date on his shots." Of course not. "I can come back tomorrow with a carrier, I guess."

"Actually, can't you just take him now? It's not a very long ride, is it? You still live around here?"

As if Carmen cared where she lived. Or had a right to know. Amber said, "I'm not sure it's safe."

"Just take him today."

Why the rush? Amber felt him all over, but Rocket didn't seem vicious or sick. Baby gates. Maybe the child they'd been installed for was allergic? But then why not say so? Then again, when had Carmen ever said anything straight-up? Other than when Carmen had been straight-up about keeping the damned cat in the first place. *Marcus was my son. I have nothing else to remember him by.*

As if Amber had that much to remember him by. Not even an engagement ring, but that was by her own choice. They'd gotten a telescope instead. She had Marcus's letters and a photo album. Oh, and the grey

Nike sweatshirt he'd let her wear home from their last stargazing trip. As for the rest? Nothing. Carmen had cleaned out the place before she'd even gotten there.

Amber sighed. "Sure. I'll just put him in the car." He wasn't a kitten anymore. Wasn't likely to jump on her shoulders or crawl beneath the brake pedal.

Five minutes later, as she settled the cat in the back seat with the blanket she always kept in her emergency kit, Amber mused whether she were breaking the seatbelt laws. She ought to call the police sergeant she bantered with on slow mornings. *Hey, Scott? What's the proper restraint system for a cat?* No, even better, she could call the folks who certified her as a car seat safety inspector last June. Except they'd be all grim and tell her not to. *In an accident, an eight-pound unrestrained cat will function as a projectile and could strike you with six hundred pounds of force.*

Carmen said, "What have you been doing?"

Amber shrugged. "Working."

She slipped into the car, but before she got the door shut, Carmen said, "Are you using your archaeology degree?"

And why does it matter to you? You as good as blamed me for Marcus's death, but now you care about my haircut and my job? I don't think so.

She shrugged. "Wherever they'd hire me. You know how the economy is." Amber pulled on her seat belt. "Thanks for Rocket."

Carmen said, "It was good seeing you again."

Amber only added, "Yeah, thanks."

She shut the door and started the engine.

Rocket yowled as she backed out onto the road, then turned toward Route 17. He slunk to the floor of the back seat and huddled in fear of the vibrations and the road noise, and when she reached to the back, he retreated from her hand.

At a stop sign, Amber tried talking to him. "You may not remember me, but you were supposed to be my cat too."

Rocket wailed. She looked over the seat to make sure he was still on the floor, and he met her eyes. "It's okay, buddy. At least we're together now."

———◦◦———

At home, Amber carried Rocket up two flights of steps to her apartment. He took off for the closest available hiding space, behind the couch. "Well, bye then."

It took five minutes more to bring up the litter pan, the half-box of litter and the bag of Meow Mix, and when she returned, the cat had left cat-poop on the rug.

"Welcome home," Amber said. Annoying, but she just filled the box and cleaned the carpet.

Also during that five minutes to bring up the kitty gear, she'd missed a call. She dialed into voicemail while saying, "You know, Rocket, you can come out now. I promise not to eat you."

And then came the message. "Amber, honey?" It was her mom—her mom, hysterical. "I need you to come over now. Right now."

Oh crud. Was Dad sick? Had the place burned to the ground?

After a dreadful silence, Mom continued, "I think you have a twin."

THREE

Amber's headlights swung up the driveway. Maureen slumped forward, face to her hands.

Breathe. She could breathe again, as if the air had returned to her now for the first time in hours. She could let go of that panic, that ridiculous panic as if she'd turn around to find the past twenty-four years had been a lie, and that ghost she'd seen on the television was a glimpse of imagination and Amber was gone too.

Amber rushed inside, wearing a lostness Maureen hadn't seen since the day Marcus died. It knifed through Maureen to realize this was bad enough to set Amber off her feet. Amber was always so strong, but right now, not even unzipping her jacket, Amber dropped to her knees in front of the couch. "Mom, what on Earth is going on?"

Olivia put her arm around Maureen's shoulder, but Maureen kept her head down. Olivia said, "After we came back from See Food, Mom and I turned on the news. There was a story about a store opening in Danbury—"

Maureen said, "It was a restored theater reopening."

Olivia continued, "—and they were interviewing people, and one of the people they interviewed looked just like you."

In Amber's eyes now: dismay. Disbelief. "Okay," she drawled. "But why is that a big deal? So someone looks like me. Unless she took every category for Ugliest Woman Of The Year, who'd even care?"

"Because I thought you had a twin." Maureen's throat closed up, and her eyes stung. "When I had you, I thought there were two. I remembered there were two. And then—"

Amber stared at the carpet. She'd heard this story before.

Whenever someone asked why Maureen had become a homebirth midwife of all things, because in the 2000s weren't Americans a little beyond the days where you pumped water from a well, birthed in the family bed and then went out back to milk the cows...? Whenever they asked, she'd always open both barrels on the monstrosity of Amber's birth, how those monsters' mistreatment turned an easy birth into a nightmare.

No, not mistreatment. Abuse. Call it by its name.

It was only a few years ago that a client said the word "birthrape," and Maureen had gasped. Twenty years after the fact, finally a name for what the doctors and nurses had done to her. She'd taken that term online and found support groups filled with women both broken and outraged, struggling under the same trauma she carried. For the first time, she wasn't alone. She hated that other women had suffered the same, but the weight wasn't hers to carry alone.

Nurses: forcing her down on her back, then despite her protests shoving a hand into her for a cervical exam. Keeping that hand in there during a contraction to force the cervix open faster. A doctor who broke her water without consent—no, against consent. Nurses calling her weak and ridiculous. Undermining her confidence. Convincing her moment by moment that she was broken, defective, stupid, jeopardizing her baby and for what, just a nice experience? Wasn't a little pain worth a healthy baby? They'd screamed at her not to push until the doctor got there, but she was in a hospital to be tended by a doctor, so why wasn't he there already? Finally after ages, the doctor strutted in, threw her husband out of the room on a medical pretense, and then... And then a nurse had slapped a gas mask over Maureen's face and put her under general anesthesia while she screamed.

She'd awakened hours later with her baby in the nursery and an episiotomy in her body. Welcome to motherhood. Your body is broken and defective, and you have no right to make any decisions at all, but now you're in charge of another human being. It's only fitting to wake up from such a gauntlet having missed your own birth.

Except she hadn't. This part of the story very few people knew: she hadn't been completely under when Amber was born. Maureen had been aware, only vaguely aware as if in a dream, of her legs shoved into stirrups. Then the doctor (she couldn't even bear to think his name) yanked out her baby with forceps. The pressure, the pulling, the relief. She'd begun drifting, but then that same thing happened all over again: the pressure, the pulling, the relief.

Next morning, dim and confused, Maureen had mumbled, "I had twins?" and a nurse taking her blood pressure had said, "No. You had a little girl. She's in the nursery being warmed up."

Maureen had said, "I felt two babies."

The nurse had patted her hand. "Oh, honey, that's impossible. You felt the placenta."

And now, today, as she told the story, Amber herself echoed the nurse's words before she even got to them. "But Mom, wouldn't that have been the placenta?"

"Everyone told me that!" The tears welled up. She'd been so young, so trusting, so stupid to believe the hospital routines had her best interest at heart, that the nurses cared more about the patients than about the paperwork. "Everyone said, *Oh, Maureen, that's the placenta!* so I didn't make a fuss, but—" She blinked a few times. "Okay, so I had Olivia fourteen months later, and afterward I thought, the placenta didn't feel like a baby. It feels slippery. It's not as big and there's no pain. But that wasn't a hospital birth, so I thought maybe the doctor yanked it out and that's why."

Amber said, "But still—"

"But when I had Brendan, I knew: it was absolutely not like a baby."

Amber's brows furrowed. "You were anesthetized. Your memories might not be accurate."

"That's what I told myself," Maureen said, her voice pitching upward, "until I saw that *placenta* talking on the TV tonight!"

Olivia said, "But even if you had twins, that might not have been her."

Maureen turned to her. "She looked and sounded just like Amber!"

Amber's brow knit. "So we would have been identical twins?"

Olivia said, "Come on. How could you even know that?"

Amber shrugged. "Don't identical twins share a placenta? If Mom delivered two babies but no placenta in between, they'd have to be identical."

Maureen surged with pride: Amber had been listening through a childhood peppered with her mother's shop-talk. But no. "I've never delivered a placenta between twins. Both babies come out first."

Amber smirked at Olivia. "Well there goes that idea."

The little things kept piling up in Maureen's head, why that baby had to be hers. The fact that red-heads required more anesthetic, and that she usually needed more numbing at the dentist—that would explain retaining some awareness during the birth. The doctor had taken the other baby, and... And what? Kept her?

Amber said, "Did they give the woman's name?"

Olivia said, "Katherine. From Danbury."

"Well, that narrows it down." Amber stood. "Can I use your computer? The news station may have the report online."

As Amber left, Maureen looked at Olivia. "Don't you believe me anymore?"

Olivia pulled back a bit. "It doesn't make sense. Don't they say strangers don't steal babies?"

But that was ridiculous. People stole babies all the time, and your children were the most precious things you had. Infertile couples got second mortgages and cashed out their 401Ks in order to have children. Why *wouldn't* someone steal a baby?

Amber returned with the laptop. "Okay, what channel was it on?" Then a moment later, "And what was the story about? A school opening?"

"A restored theater," Maureen said. "Danbury, Connecticut."

Amber got that furrow in her brow and the slight frown that meant she was concentrating. She probably had no idea how intimidating that focus made her seem, but Maureen imagined arsonists broke out in a sweat before her. Amber clicked on something, then clicked again, and then a slight roll of her eyes. "Come on," she muttered.

Maureen said, "Is it there?"

"If it ever loads, it will be." She scooted around on the carpet so her back was to the couch, then tilted the screen. "Okay, here we go."

The newscasters were a woman in her mid-twenties and a man in his sixties with a deep voice. He sounded like the guy you'd want to hear if the feds got wind of a terror plot. The woman, by contrast, was up-beat and engaging. She spoke about a restored theater in Danbury, Connecticut, something that made everyone in the downtown district happy, and then they cut to footage of people on the street, each with his own way of saying, "It's good."

First an old man with a bald pate. Then a middle-aged woman with too much makeup. And then, and then—

Amber. A tiny digital Amber on the screen on Amber's lap. And she looked nervous.

"Well, I really think it's important for Danbury to have a cultural center where we can have exposure to more than just the mass market media. I mean, yeah, the kids have a steady diet of pop culture over at the theater at the mall, but when it comes to Shakespeare or other cultural references, they've just never been exposed."

Amber's roundish face, her snub nose, her auburn hair, her freckles. It was Amber, only jittery, an Amber poised to skitter away and vanish into the world so they'd never see her again.

Katherine continued, "They get the references because we put them in the footnotes, but there's no experience. Opening this theater right in the center of town is like a doorway to a world they didn't have before."

The camera cut away from her. Fifteen seconds on the screen. Fifteen seconds and a first name.

Amber dragged the play bar and brought the woman back.

Olivia leaned over. "She really does look like you. She's a bit heavier."

"Hair's longer," Amber said. "She's not wearing glasses, but I can't tell if she has contacts."

"She sounds like you," Maureen said.

Amber's nose wrinkled. "Really?"

Olivia said, "Just like."

Amber gave a self-conscious laugh. "I'll take your word on it."

Maureen said, "She's wearing a blue coat. You like blue."

"That's getting into the realm of the ridiculous, Mom. She breathes oxygen, too." Amber leaned closer. "I don't know. How many blonde women are there with this combination of features?"

"It's too small to see well," Maureen said. "On the TV, I'd have sworn it was you."

Amber focused that intimidating look on Olivia, who said, "Well, I don't know. I mean, it did look a lot like you, but—it was so fast."

Ice-cold, Maureen whirled toward Olivia. "She's right there! Don't change your mind now!"

Amber's eyes widened. "Mom, it's just— You're talking crazy. Stealing babies? And if you were having twins, wouldn't you have known it?" Amber shook her head. "You of all people?"

"I wasn't a midwife then! I became a midwife *because* of that delivery. I would never let anyone take advantage of me again!"

Olivia looked smaller than ever on the couch, and she glanced at her own daughter in the portacrib.

Amber stood all at once, rubbing her hands on her jeans. "Wouldn't an ultrasound have picked up twins?"

"I didn't have an ultrasound! This was almost thirty years ago. They didn't do them for kicks." Maureen bit her lip. "The doctor didn't even use a doppler. He listened with a fetoscope."

"But wouldn't you have recognized two sets of feet, two sets of arms?" Amber shook her head. "Wouldn't you have carried huge?"

"I didn't know what was normal." Maureen blinked hard. It was her fault, all her fault. She was broken and defective or else she'd have known these things. "You were smaller than Olivia and Brendan by about a pound and a half."

Olivia said, "Aren't first babies always smaller?"

They were ganging up on her, and Maureen slumped into the couch. Amber with that infuriating drive for evidence she could touch. Olivia waffling because she always followed her older sister. But Maureen was a mother—mothers knew. She had to be right. She'd seen her own daughter on television, only they were hundreds of miles apart and she'd never even known the girl existed. Except she had known. And just like back then, everyone was telling her it couldn't be true and that it didn't matter what they'd done to her, just that she'd taken home a healthy baby, except now they'd been lying because she'd only taken home half.

Amber peered closer at the screen. "This is no good." She pulled her cell phone out of her pocket.

"Who are you calling?" said Olivia.

"Brendan. I think he gets his TV signal through his computer." Amber looked up. "They'll probably re-run the segment on the late-night news, and he can record it so we can see her bigger. Maybe they'll have more of her, too. That way we can rule it out, and everyone can go to sleep." She bit her lip. "I'm sorry, Mom. I just don't believe it's possible."

———◦———

It was nine o'clock by the time Amber reached her apartment, and all she could think was *This is crazy. This is crazy. This is crazy.*

Amber hadn't ever seen her mother like this. Usually Mom was the one who kept her head in a crisis. When Dad would stand there with a waffling, "Well, I don't know," it would be Mom who had the plan and Mom who kept things cool. She'd walk in and take over and you just knew everything was going to be all right.

Not tonight. Yeah, not tonight at all, when Amber had found herself protesting that a late-night drive to Danbury to knock on doors would be less than fruitful. Olivia had taken the baby and bolted like the house was on fire, leaving Amber alone with Mom, who just wanted to keep watching that clip over and over. The minute Dad had stepped inside from his late-night class, Amber had made any excuse she could think of (she'd better remember it tomorrow) and fled.

Home. It was seven minutes from Mom, but it felt like another world. Only three rooms, but she locked the door as if it were a fortress.

Amber found another gift from the cat on the carpet rather than in the litter box, and again the cat remained hidden. While cleaning the mess, she sighed. The hell with it. Yes, it was dark. Yes, it was cold. But whatever.

Five minutes later she was dressed in running gear, wearing a safety light and orange reflective sneakers. Phone in hand, she walked down the stairs while dialing.

Her landlord had the downstairs apartment, so she stretched in the light of Mr. B's living room windows. She was working on her hamstrings when Nikki picked up. "Hey, what's going on?"

"I'm going for a run. Wanna come?"

Nikki laughed. "Yeah, me and the belly." Nikki was eight months pregnant. "I thought you confined your escapades to daylight hours now."

"Yeah, well. Not tonight."

"When should I panic and call the cops?"

"I'll be home in forty minutes. Maybe less."

"Is this running therapy again?"

Amber sighed. "Kind of."

"Tell me what it's about when you get home, okay?"

Why would I do that? The whole point of running is to forget.

Amber started jogging. This late at night she wouldn't wear her earbuds, but she hungered for the distraction of music. Something to take her brain away. But if she couldn't blare out the world in a whine of senseless noise, at least she could outrun it.

She increased her pace to a hard sprint.

Outrun it. It had worked before. Only four years ago, she'd been running in the heat. When her soul felt raw and her emotions exposed and she couldn't bear to stare at the TV even a second longer, she'd forced her body to get up and run, run until her legs couldn't move and she couldn't breathe anymore, and she'd look around without knowing how far she'd gone, only that she'd have to reverse it all in order to get home again. But then she'd just keep going further. Just get away. Get away from Marcus. Now get away from this woman. Katherine.

She ran full-out. She couldn't do this for long, but she could do it for now.

It didn't make sense. Mom had always talked about the obstetrician from her birth as if he were a demon. An evil man, manipulating vulnerable women, lying to them and using force. But kidnapping? Wasn't that an unbelievable level of evil?

Yet in her own job, didn't she see how sometimes a person could engage in a degree of evil you never would think possible? Like that guy last year who came back to burn down his ex-wife's home. With his former family still inside. Amber had worked nights and weekends for a month making sure the prosecution had everything they'd ever need to padlock the prison doors for the next nine centuries. And the kicker? The dude was five foot four, a little on the pudgy side, wore glasses, and had been involved in the historical society. Not the kind of guy you'd peg for a wife-beater and an arsonist.

Evil you never thought possible. Like whoever it was that killed Marcus.

Amber had slowed, so she picked up the pace, concentrating on the interlocking rhythms of her breath and her strides. So many houses all in rows. Sam from the pharmacy: his car parked on the street, but his lights out. Someone lugging grocery bags—that woman Amber recognized from the grocery store, the one with three kids. A maroon Accord waiting at a red light—one of the fire fighters?—but when she looked closer, no, not someone she knew.

After three miles, Amber became conscious of a vehicle tailing her. She turned, then laughed. Stopping, she let the police car draw beside her.

The window rolled down, and a cop leaned across the passenger seat.

Amber smiled as she got her breath back. "Hey, Todd."

Todd said, "Show me some ID. Anyone running this late must be up to no good."

"Uh-oh." Amber rubbed her hands together. Jogging kept her legs warm, but she'd forgotten to grab a pair of gloves. "Maybe I am."

Todd's mouth twitched. "It's not safe to be jogging this late."

"We're in Patmos Springs, not the Bronx." She squinted. "Did Dennis send you?"

He chuckled. "Yeah. Nikki called him because she was worried, so he told me to keep an eye out for you."

The Fire Marshal offices were two rooms in the back of the police station, so even if one of the cops wasn't married to her best friend, she'd have known most of the guys on sight. Todd Longtree boasted heritage from the Onondaga Nation, and he'd been around as long as the Police Chief, patrolling a place so dull the cops pulled each other over for entertainment.

"Well, that's sweet, but I'll be fine." Her breath left little clouds, and she rubbed her arms. "Are you going to tail me all the way home?"

He told her to be careful, and she resisted the urge to say *Thanks, Dad*. Instead she wished him a boring night, then resumed her pace. He turned up the next street, and then she was alone.

Alone but not alone. Alone with the ghost of a maybe-twin.

Back in her apartment, Amber turned on the TV and phoned Nikki. "I'm fine. Tell Dennis to call off the APB."

"What do you expect? They haven't had a real APB since 1985." Nikki laughed. "Are you ready to talk about it yet?"

"Not yet. I'm going to call you back at eleven, and then you'll see for yourself."

"Ooh, sounds mysterious."

"In a quarter-century-old kind of way, yeah."

Amber showered, and then in her pajamas, sat in front of the TV with the remote on her lap and her phone in her hand. She called Nikki.

"Turn on channel four."

"We're going to watch TV together? How exciting." Sounds of movement in the background. A breathless, "Okay," as if it were hard to settle herself onto the couch, and a moment later Amber could hear the same commercials from the phone as from the TV. "The news? That doesn't sound good. Does this have to do with DelGaudio's burning down?"

"I wish it did."

"Dennis bet me ten bucks it had to be arson."

"I bet you ten bucks Dennis is about to owe you ten bucks."

"Really?"

"Totally. Remember how I told you not to run the dishwasher while you're asleep? It seems someone didn't listen."

Nikki yawned. "Sorry," she said. "This is a bit late for me."

Amber's mouth twitched. "I shouldn't have bothered you. You're exhausted enough."

Nikki huffed. "Yeah, because when something bothers you this much, my only concern is whether it inconveniences me."

They quieted while the opening music came on and the anchors introduced themselves. "Thank heaven," Nikki said. "I never remember whether Jack is the guy on the left or the woman on the right."

Amber chuckled.

The news came out of Albany, and they endured the first ten minutes of international crises and national crises, a fluff piece about some security threat to Facebook, and a bunch of commercials.

"Not very exciting so far," said Nikki. "Except for that toilet paper commercial. Isn't the purpose of advertising to introduce you to needs you never knew you had? How often do you meet people who've never heard of toilet paper?"

Amber said, "You're frightening me."

Nikki said, "We must live very sheltered lives."

And then they were back with, "And now we're back."

"That's a relief," said Nikki.

"Wait," Amber said as a photoshopped layering of comedy-tragedy masks and an old building façade showed in the corner. "This is the one."

The woman behind the desk began with "This afternoon, residents of Danbury celebrated the grand re-opening of the West Side Theater two decades after the last exit-stage-left."

The broadcast cut to images of a black and white film from some production or other, then pictures of a building left to ruin. Following that they cut to the man-on-the-street for some quotes. First the guy. Then the woman. And then—

Nikki whispered, "Holy guacamole."

On the large screen, Katherine looked more real than she had on the computer. They gave no last name, no more information than before. It was the same clip, the same statement about theater being important and helping revitalize the downtown area.

"Who in blazes are you?" Amber said to the screen. It surprised her when her voice broke. "Why are you driving my mother crazy?"

A map of New Haven appeared over the male announcer's shoulder. Amber pushed the power button as if firing a bullet through the TV's heart.

No, no, no. This wasn't right.

A voice came from the phone Amber had forgotten she was holding. "Who is Katherine?"

"I have no idea. But Mom thinks this woman is my twin and that she was stolen by the doctor who delivered me."

Nikki made a strangled noise. "That's— That's crazy!"

"Look, I don't know. But she's freaking out, and I've no clue what to do for her. I figured if I got a better picture of the woman off the news, it would be obvious she's not. But seeing her..."

"I'd have been fooled." Nikki sounded stunned. "If I saw her in the supermarket, I'd probably sneak up and jumpscare her and then feel like an idiot for five days."

Amber laughed. "Maybe you shouldn't be scaring me either!"

"Yeah, but okay. Her hair was longer than yours, and you're a bit skinnier because you run all the time." Nikki paused for a while. "That's just so weird."

Amber's fingertip did laps around the rubber buttons on the remote.

"But wouldn't your mom remember giving birth to two babies?"

"They knocked her out. She remembers me being born and remembers something else. They told her it was the placenta." Amber closed her eyes. No, keep steady. That's not an ache in your chest, not a burn. Just breathe. "But Mom was hysterical. She's losing it."

"Whoa. She's always so calm." Nikki paused. When she spoke again, she was forcing an upbeat tone. "Well she'd better get it together by next month. She's got to deliver my baby."

"And you know there's only one, so that's cool." Amber sighed. "Geez, Nikki. This is crazy."

Nikki said, "What are you going to do?"

"I have no idea." Amber nudged her toe against the stain the cat had left on the carpet. "I don't think there's anything I can."

FOUR

A midwife gets used to being up all night. It was one of those treats Maureen began to look forward to after her first year on the job, the late nights with a laboring mother because so many babies preferred to make their entrance at night.

And at eleven o'clock tonight she arrived at the home of a first-time mom in very early labor, a young woman frustrated that she hadn't made much progress after four hours of contractions. Maureen measured out two ounces of white wine (as if prescribing it) and told her to go back to sleep. "Ten o'clock isn't a good time for babies. Three is better." She assured the mom she'd awaken after midnight with powerful contractions to see the dawn with a babe in arms.

The mom looked nervous. "You can't leave. What if everything starts up fast?"

Maureen said, "Then I'll stay in your living room. But you need some rest." So the laboring mom and dad went to bed, and Maureen went to the living room.

It wouldn't be the first time she stayed on a client's couch with a book, patient for the times she was needed and keeping to herself for the times she wasn't.

Tonight, though, was not the night for patience. Tonight a part of herself was missing.

Katherine.

Three hours later, it was two in the morning, and Maureen needed to talk to someone before it all became too much to keep inside. But not her husband. When Raymond had gotten home, she'd shown him the video, started to explain, but he knew. The only thing he'd said was, "I'm sorry."

She hadn't asked what he was sorry for because she knew. Sorry he hadn't known how to advocate for her back when they had their first baby. Babies. Baby. When she'd had Amber, neither of them had known how much the hospital system would want them to conform to the hospital system, or that they didn't need to do all the things they were told to do. Back then it was considered progressive just to have the father in the delivery room, but by the third one, heck, Ray had caught Brendan while her midwife Sherry sat across the room telling him what a good job he was doing.

And that "sorry" might have meant he was sorry he hadn't known what to do for her in the aftermath of Amber's birth, when she became depressed and didn't know whether she could care for Amber. Sorry—really, sorry for not having the experience he had now, after having had all the bad experiences.

What to do about Katherine, though—that he also didn't know.

So instead of calling him, she texted Sherry, now her colleague. "Are you awake?"

Within a minute Sherry texted her back, but Maureen didn't feel the relief she'd hoped. "What do you need?"

Maureen texted, "Personal disaster. I'm at a birth, but I need to talk."

The father had set up the coffee maker back when she'd arrived, and it stood with red lights gleaming in the otherwise-dark kitchen, hot inside and cold outside like a woman bearing a secret.

Maureen loved the couple's house, built in 1795 and remodeled so often that scarcely five bricks remained of the original, and yet a historical society had plastered a placard on the outside. All the additions adjoined one another at weird angles so you could never walk straight through. Floors were skewed and ceilings stood at different levels. This family home felt just like a family, in other words: it grew as it would, each addition soon an indispensable part of the whole.

At the back door, she looked through the scant moonlight at a barn that used to shelter horses but now was losing boards to time and the weather. But all was quiet. Even the night insects had settled down.

Then, in the distance, an owl. The low thrum made her catch her breath to hear better: an owl who could choose silence so well when it suited, but opted now to break the quiet and call to its others. *I'm here. I'm out here.*

She set her hand on the phone, and as she touched it, it rang.

She didn't check the caller ID. "Sherry."

"What's going on?" said the older woman, her voice sanded down by time and without the rough edge given by age to some women's voices.

Maureen tried to keep the story compact, but she kept feeling crowded by the details. In the dark, lying beside a snoring Raymond, the way Amber talked to herself as a child had seemed vital. But now, with a laboring mom in the house, Maureen struggled to give only the facts.

Maybe Sherry could read her mind. "Did you ever get your records from Dr. Vilkas?"

"I transferred them to the new practice when I had Olivia, but why would that matter? He's unlikely to have written *Twins, one given to mother and nursing well,*

APGARs 7 and 10, second twin, APGARS 6 and 9, sold on the black market."

Sherry said, "Of course not, but there might have been other clues to twinning. Fundal height, elevated alpha-fetoprotein, elevated HcG. I take it you never had an ultrasound with them."

"No, there was never a need." But even as she spoke, Maureen realized what Sherry had said. *With them.*

"I know I didn't have the paperwork." No, of course not. Back then a direct-entry midwife was *practicing medicine without a license* and couldn't exactly request a doctor transfer records. "Your information would have been purged long since, and doctors aren't required to keep birth records beyond when the baby turns twenty-one." She paused. "Your best bet right now is request your records from both Olivia's birth and Amber's birth. See if by some chance either practice left them in a basement or had them transferred to microfiche. Actually, get Dr. Jacobson to request them, as if you're his patient."

Maureen gasped. In the chaos, she'd just filed it away. "I forgot to tell you. He's retiring!"

Sherry sighed. "Oh, lovely. Why is it always the good ones?"

Maureen looked up as the new father appeared in the doorway. "I'm hanging up, Sherry. Baby time."

The mother was kneeling alongside the bed, head on the mattress. Maureen noted her movements, her sounds, her smell, and the changes in her body. Very focused, she couldn't talk through her contractions. The woman seemed panicked, so Maureen made sure to sound relaxed. "What amazing progress! You're getting down to the real work. Aren't you glad you had that extra sleep?"

The woman picked up her head. "This is it? For real?"

"For real." Maureen put the birth ball on the bedroom floor and showed the mom how to sit on it.

The woman's eyes widened. "Oh! That's—that's better."

"Get those hips nice and open. Roll your hips with the contractions if you want."

Maureen sat on the edge of the bed, and the mom swiveled with every contraction, leaning on Maureen and making low "ooh" sounds. The husband stayed behind her, rubbing the base of her spine and whispering that she was doing great.

So funny, so wonderful, all the different ways women labored down their babies. The hospital staff had demanded silence, and that worked for some women, but it never worked for Maureen. With Amber's birth there had been threats, insults, shaming, and a good scolding when she moaned because "the other moms are going to get scared." She'd tried so hard to keep herself from vocalizing, but why? What did it hurt anyone if she made noise?

The mom's contraction ended, and she went still, regrouping. "How much longer?"

Maureen rubbed her shoulders. "You're doing so well."

The mother's mood: serious. The shape of her body: changed, lower as the baby had descended. She wanted her back rubbed close to the tailbone. That dusky, heavy scent of birth in the air. All these said this mother was in transition.

The mom closed her eyes and moaned, low and deep, as another contraction started.

So different from her own births. Ever since she'd seen Katherine on the TV, Maureen had been living and reliving that nightmare, the soul-stripping ways the nurses had forced compliance, with Maureen knowing all along something wasn't right but caving to their dictates because this was what you did: you went to a hospital to have a baby, and you had to cooperate because they only wanted what was best for you. And so over and over and over again, when Maureen wanted something and the nurses wanted something else, Maureen had relented.

What did she know? These were nurses who worked in a hospital, so surely they'd know if what her instincts told her was wrong and dangerous. She wanted to eat, but they told her she might vomit, so they'd kept her working hard on nothing. And later she learned there was practically no risk of aspirating unless you were under general anesthesia, and it was worse to aspirate undiluted stomach acid—and yet she had been kept hungry, hungry and in doubt of her own body.

But it wasn't like that at home. The person working hardest shouldn't also be the one to sacrifice the most. So to that end, Maureen's patients could eat, could take a bath, could wander the house. Maureen had delivered babies on the bathroom floor or bending over a hot tub, kneeling behind a mom on all fours on a bed, or sometimes a woman standing with one leg propped on a kitchen chair. And through it all, she counted it a privilege.

Twenty-four years ago, she'd awakened foggy in a recovery room with no baby. When she'd asked for her baby, the nurses kept telling her it wasn't time; it wasn't convenient; she couldn't move, and they wouldn't take out the IV. After three hours, someone wheeled the baby in, sucking a pacifier, only to have the nurse say someone else had fed the baby with a bottle. "Because she was hungry, Mother."

Maureen had picked the name "Amber" three months before the birth, but it took another three months to call her anything other than "the baby." And whenever she'd tried to tell someone how the hospital had violated her, they'd only said, "You have a healthy baby. That's all that matters."

But what about her? Hadn't she mattered at all, except as a delivery package to bring that baby into the world?

The mom made a grunty sound and tightened differently. Maureen said, "Oh good! You're feeling pushy!"

A long, long pause, and then a nod. This mom was wearing a big baggy t-shirt and sweatpants, and she said, "Do you think I should get undressed?"

"A pair of pajamas never stopped a baby," Maureen said, "but you might be more comfortable if you do."

The mom wriggled out of her sweatpants and underwear, revealing a deep purple line between her buttocks. Another sign of full dilation.

Between contractions, Maureen got off the bed and had the husband sit so his wife's head was in his lap. She spread chux pads on the floor, then got out her doppler to hear the baby's heartbeat. During a push, the rate dropped, and after the contraction it bounded right back up. Good. Everything reassuring.

According to the clock, she ought to be taking notes, but the mom needed her now, and the mom's need was everything.

For a moment Maureen remembered a nurse bellowing in her face. "You have to push again!" and Maureen saying, "But I'm not ready—" and the nurse screaming, "You have to push three times per contraction or the baby will never come out!"

She'd known it wasn't true. But she'd tried anyhow. Beaten down, tired, hungry, bullied. Bullied. That was really all there was to it. Bullied by nurses, bullied by the monitors, bullied by faceless hospital policy. They'd left behind a raw wound that she'd walled off but never fully healed because she'd never forgiven herself for giving in, and giving in again.

After all that, how hard was it to believe a doctor would steal her baby?

But no, doctors weren't all like that. Doctor Jacobson wasn't like that. For that matter, Olivia's OB hadn't been like that. At nine months, Charlotte had been transverse—neither head-down nor head-up but an undeliverable sideways. For weeks Maureen had done everything she could to get Charlotte to turn, and Olivia's OB had phoned her, fascinated. Working together, they'd done everything in their power so Olivia could have the vaginal birth she wanted, but Charlotte was stubborn. In the end, Charlotte had been born via section: a no-regret, fully-informed and necessary section. That was doctoring at its finest, perfect counterpoint to the care Maureen wanted to give at home.

The mom pushed, groaning from deep within and then getting deeper, more primal. Her water broke, so Maureen brought out more chux pads. "Awesome! He's coming. Work with your body. Push whenever you want, but don't blast through them."

The mom needed no encouragement. Her body was pushing automatically, and this time her voice was more of an Ah than an Ooh. That baby was moving

Battling tears, Maureen knelt behind her, arms around her shoulders. She murmured, "You're so strong. You can do this."

Fifteen seconds later, the mom's eyes went fierce, and her mouth set, and she pushed. The baby came down further.

The mom whispered, "It's burning."

"That's the ring of fire. Breathe easy."

Maureen kept her hands on the mom, mostly to help but a part of her in awe, as if holding the idol of a fertility goddess. The mom was all power, her natural energy channeled away from her core for the benefit of someone else. This was total giving, a selflessness that not only brought forth a new self but also gave a new dimension to her own. And the strength, the focus, the coordination: for a moment, the mom was a world-class Olympian, her body acting to perfection, and as with a gymnast whirling around on the parallel bars, Maureen was only her spotter.

The mom clenched her hands around her husband's fists, knees spread as she knelt. Down slipped the baby's head, and as the baby turned, the shoulders slid into Maureen's gloved hands. Naked, slippery, but born.

The mother gasped, and Maureen said, "Bend forward." She passed the baby through the mother's legs, who lifted him, gazed at him, no longer conscious of the pain. Just him. A baby looking right into her eyes.

Maureen blinked and realized she was crying. *Katherine.*

An hour later the mother was in her bed, snuggling a sleeping infant who had nursed and pooped and fussed but then settled, a baby boy who weighed nine pounds five ounces and who passed all the tests, whom she'd swaddled and tucked right beside his mother until he'd fallen to sleep in a strange world: without water but with gravity and chill and light. But despite all this change, he recognized a voice and recognized a smell, and these were comfort.

The mother looked ecstatic. Ten hours of labor, one hour of pushing. And now she was one hour postpartum, but riding the hormone train. Maureen left the couple to enjoy their baby while she retired to their kitchen to write her notes.

But instead, Maureen opened the door to the porch and stepped into the morning. Her breath frosted in the air and hung for a moment before dispersing, warm when a part of her and quickly subsiding to merge with the rest of the world.

Out there in the world: Amber, Brendan, Olivia...and Katherine?

She shut the door behind her and stood in a world that was cold but had just welcomed one new baby. And then, instead of watching the sunrise, Maureen found herself sobbing. What they had gained. What she had lost.

FIVE

Patmos Springs clustered all its emergency personnel in a concrete building exemplifying what Amber called the best in 1950s era shoebox-style design. It would make a great target if there really were bad guys and they really wanted to mess up a town in New York State's Southern Tier.

But first they'd have to find the place, and that was harder than you'd think, this town with three stoplights *and* three liquor stores, with a Tillman Street, a Tillman's Diner, *and* a George Tillman. A few years ago, the National Weather Service had reported a tornado spotted "about three miles west of Owego," but apparently even they didn't know the place had a name.

Otherwise-anonymous towns still need a fire department and police, and when they're housed in the same building to save money, the fire department gets the bulk of the square footage while the police get more of the offices. They also had holding cells for four people *maximum* in case the Yankees were in the World Series again and celebrations got out of control.

Finally, if you walked all the way to the back corner of the building, almost into the rear parking lot, you'd reach the Fire Marshal's office. The fire department belonged to the town and the Fire Marshals were county, but they shared a building because of some long-ago agreement no one remembered but everyone knew was convenient.

This morning yet again, Amber surged with victory: she had beaten her boss to the office.

On her first day she'd realized within seconds that the Old Man didn't make very good coffee. And translate "realized" as "her throat reacted as if she were drinking turpentine." But she couldn't very well retch in front of her brand-new boss, could she? She'd often studied his technique because, well, it was fascinating how you could make Folgers do that. Turned out the Old Man used the dump-and-pour method of apportioning coffee grounds.

That's when Amber, Amber fresh out of grad school with a Master's in chemistry, had deemed making coffee a practical use of her degree.

The next day, she got in a little earlier to beat him to the coffee maker. He beat her the day after that, resulting in undrinkable sludge. Thus began a subtle arms race of arrival times, and now on most mornings, Amber won. Everybody won, really. You could tell because they came to her office for coffee. And this morning, by the time she had the pot brewing, the Old Man was sitting at his desk, glaring daggers at her but not poisoning her.

It was a good morning.

Thirty seconds later, courtesy of an online search, Amber was on the phone with the manager of Everything Electronics, appliance retailers in Binghamton, New York. Their highway signs promised the most knowledgeable salespeople in New York State. Time to test that.

"I'm Amber Brickman, of the Tioga County Fire Marshal's office," she said, and after the manager responded with a semi-surprised acknowledgment, she continued, "I need to ask a couple of questions about a dishwasher."

She read off the make and model. "I was wondering if there's been any kind of service bulletins on those, or if they're prone to fires."

"I'm putting you on hold," said the manager.

Two firefighters came and stood in the door.

Amber fought a grin. "Make sure I get some first."

Both men nodded. Behind them, one of the police officers entered. This didn't happen when the Old Man got in first.

The manager got back on the line. "Those are commercial-grade, but they're similar to another model we have, and I can research them. Are you in the office tomorrow?"

She'd be in most days. Tioga County boasted a population of fifty thousand and formed a rough square (with a peak on the northeast corner) about twenty five miles by twenty five miles. It wasn't hard to cover that much territory. She put some mileage on her car, but when they divided up their duties, the Old Man preferred to perform surprise inspections on businesses and spend a few hours counting smoke detectors, and he liked leisurely hour-long drives while listening to Mahler. He planned to retire in the next few years, but in his heart, he'd retired a decade ago.

That left all the fun stuff for Amber. New York State required a cause be determined for every fire. Guess what she got to do?

Her phone rang, and she answered with, "Fire Marshal. Brickman."

"Hey, Brickman—it's Stadler. Your appointment is here."

She grimaced, then said goodbye to the nearly-brewed pot of coffee because by the time she got back, it would be replaced by patented Old Man Swill.

Out at the front, Sergeant Scott Stadler gestured to a couple holding an infant seat. Amber nodded to them, then handed the sergeant a styrofoam cup of coffee.

"Hey, thanks!" With a grin, Scott's roundish face suddenly transformed. "How did you know?"

"The same brilliant reasoning that landed me my prestigious position." Amber laughed. "Little hints like how you come get some every morning." She handed him two sugar packets.

"You rock." Of course she did. He gestured toward the couple. "Go save a life, okay?"

A momentary sadness flitted through his eyes. But then he turned to the coffee, and she saw only his profile, his sharp nose, his close-cropped hair.

She crossed the room to the couple. "Congratulations!" she said, gesturing to their newborn, and they showed her off. "What's her name?" Amber looked at the car seat, then said, "Hey, before we inspect the installation, let's buckle Mary in right here and check the straps."

Check the straps—as if. She'd already seen enough.

The couple set the baby bucket on the floor, then buckled in their daughter. Amber knelt behind the seat so she and the baby were both facing the parents. "Remember they're recommending extended rear-facing to age two, and some seats will keep her rear-facing to thirty-five pounds."

The father said, "That long?"

"It's safer that way." Amber was gesturing now to pantomime the car. "This way is forward, and this is backward. Now, imagine your car is hit." Amber moved her hands slowly toward the seat. "You're moving forward. On impact, the car suddenly stops. Think momentum. Which way is everyone flung?"

"Forward," said the new father.

Amber nodded. "Right. Now watch."

Without any difficulty, she inserted her hands between the back of the seat and the baby's back, gripped her under the armpits, and slipped her right up and through the closed straps.

Both parents gasped.

"That's Mary's ejection route." Amber kept her voice even, calm, and she cradled the baby against her chest. Eight pounds? Eight pounds, but it was the weight of everything. "So before we do anything else, let me teach you how to buckle the straps."

She handed the baby back to the mother and began unsnapping the clasps, then hesitated. A prickly sensation. Amber turned and discovered Scott watching her. His cheeks were pale.

Six months ago, Amber had overheard a nightmare on the scanner. A car crash. Nikki's husband Dennis had arrived first. And then over the scanner came his call for an ambulance, for two ambulances—he hadn't been making sense, but Amber began piecing together the words even as every cop lit out of the building and the paramedics rushed out with the ambulance. And then the radioed request for the coroner.

Finally another officer reported in: the driver had been rear-ended by another vehicle, and when she'd come to a stop, she'd turned to find her child's car seat empty. Buckled, but empty.

The baby had died. He'd been flung right out of the seat, and he'd died. Amber had raced to the front desk hoping to hear this was nonsense, that Dennis was just rattled and the woman had left her kid at day care, but no, one of the junior officers was manning the desk, and an hour later, Scott had walked back in with Dennis, ghost-pale and shaking.

At the time, Nikki was only twelve weeks pregnant and already had a threatened miscarriage. As Scott got back to the desk he said, "Go home, Dennis."

Dennis began saying he could finish out the tour, and Scott shouted, "Do it! No, you know what? Stay on shift, but I'm assigning you to patrol your house. And so help me, if I find you're not there, that's a write-up. Now."

Dennis had balled his fists, then slumped. "Thanks, Sarge."

As Dennis had left, Scott had sat at the desk, rubbing his temples. "So incredibly small. What's wrong with the world?"

That night Amber had gone to Dennis and Nikki's after work, bringing pizza and wings, and they watched all three original Star Wars movies back to back to back. The next morning, she'd staggered in with a headache worse than a hangover. Scott looked like death, but she handed him a half-inch thick stack of printouts about car seat safety inspectors.

He'd looked at her dully.

"We need one," she said. "A lot of cities offer free car seat inspections through the police department. You need to train someone."

Scott shook his head. "Have you got any money left in your training budget?"

The next day, Amber had gotten a signature from the Old Man. That was the most surprising perk of this job: an education budget no one had touched since Woodstock. The county hadn't at first seen the need for a car seat safety inspector, but it sounded good and they could get a federal grant. And now, thanks to the Feds and the county, Mary's parents knew not to leave the shoulder-straps slack.

Amber asked them to settle Mary back into the baby bucket, then to tighten the straps until they could slip only two fingers beneath; she instructed them to put the chest clip over the baby's sternum, "right under armpit height." In that position the restraints actually restrained the baby. "You paid a lot for this seat. Let it do its job."

The new parents looked relieved. Confused, but relieved.

Gesturing outside, Amber said, "Now let's check the base."

Half an hour later, Amber returned, her mood less rosy than her windblown cheeks. The culprit: take your pick among car seat manufacturers who didn't write legible manuals, or people who didn't read the manuals because "well, it just goes in, right?" or advertisers who repeatedly showed car seats installed wrong...

Amber sighed. Well, after that demonstration, she doubted this couple would be so laid-back. The afternoon after most ejection-route demonstrations, she'd get three phone calls from the parents' friends scheduling a seat check.

But seriously, why make such a big deal over a safe birth and then take risks driving it all around?

Back in the station house, Scott and one of the officers were playing catch with Officer Cookie, a Belgian Malinois police dog.

As Amber passed, Scott roughed up the dog, calling out to her, "Saved a life?"

"Yeah, that puts me....oh, about fifteen thousand behind you." She smiled at his grin. "Should I go into the superhero business? I could be CarSeat Woman."

He studied her a moment. "You'd look good in a red cape."

"Right until the moment I sit on it funny and strangle myself, yeah."

Scott got a thoughtful look. "You'd have to wear the spandex pants, too."

She grimaced. "Then it's settled: I'm staying Assistant Fire Marshal."

Scott patted the dog, who looked as if he'd die with joy. "My loss. Hey, come with me."

She followed him, expecting...she wasn't sure what, but it certainly wasn't to be led back to her own office by a sergeant and a police dog. She cocked her head. "Do I need an escort?"

"Yeah, last night I found a lost kid in the playground, and today I'm taking no chances." He guided her past three firefighters toward the coffee pot. Which was full. And guarded by Rochelle, one of their two rookie cops. "Returning the favor."

Amber burst out laughing.

Rochelle said, "Sir. The coffee pot was secured."

Scott said, "Thank you. You can return to your other duties."

The firefighters glared, but Scott smirked at them.

Amber bit her lip. "Thank you. You didn't have to do that."

"It's probably not as good as yours, so don't thank me yet." Scott poured some into Amber's thick ceramic mug, the one with the Avengers logo. "But since you're out saving the universe and all, I thought at least you should come back to a hot cup of coffee."

He put his hand on her shoulder, and fear shot through her. She recoiled, saying, "I'm sure it's fine. Um, thanks." She stepped closer to her desk. "Okay. Well, if you need me, you know where I am."

He seemed startled, but she busied herself with adding sugar and milk, and after he left, she struggled to breathe deep and slow.

SIX

Maureen sat with proof, incontrovertible proof, that Katharine was Amber's twin. *You knew it all along, honey. I should have seen it in you even then.*

She traced her fingertips over the childhood drawing, dated to when Amber was only six. She had just barely learned to write, her print a blocky scrawl in uneven sizes and some letters backward. With the diligence that characterized her even so young, she'd created a story at school, and Maureen's intuition had told her to save it. She'd probably kept it for the illustrations because Amber was just such a talented kid, but what made her go back and get it was the story.

She'd held it beside her at breakfast, held it when Ray went to work, and brought it with her to the birth center where she'd seen patients all morning. She'd stayed grounded just knowing the old papers were in her messenger bag, waiting. And now here she was, back in her office between patients, with them again.

Haff a Girl read the title, and from there Amber proceeded to tell the story of Jean, a girl who was only half a person. Her drawings weren't consistent: sometimes she was the left half of a girl, sometimes the right, but nonetheless half.

What a horrible thing. All her life, Amber must have sensed she was half missing.

Maureen could fit the pieces together so perfectly: the way Amber always had an imaginary friend, or the way she used to be drawn to those ridiculous "separated soul-mate" type books, where someone ordinary meets something like a dragon or a ghost, and their souls belong together.

Twins grew together, touching constantly in the womb. What a shock, to be alone after all that time.

She paged through the story, eight pages in all, the corner ripped off one. Amber seemed to think it funny that the girl could wear half a hat and half a jacket and brought half a lunch to school. It wasn't a story inasmuch as it didn't really end. It was just a list of things you could do when you were half a girl, like you had it easier in hopscotch but harder in kickball.

Maureen reached for the phone, and it buzzed under her fingertips. "Hello?"

"Maureen, I got your message," said the careworn voice of Dr. Jacobson. "I have to say, I'm a little confused."

"Confused how?"

"Requesting records from twenty-four years ago? Because of something you saw on the news?"

The conversation went through three rounds, until finally he said, "I agree you were mistreated. There was no reason to give you general anesthesia, and I understand it was traumatic. But I remember Vilkas. He wasn't a criminal."

Maureen said, "In your experience, do criminals advertise?"

"No, but you suspect. Think of how many people would have to be involved if a doctor were selling black market babies. Nurses, at the very least. Other doctors. People who referred to him and got kickbacks. Someone would have said something by now, so he'd have had to be operating alone, but Vilkas was working at a fairly large clinic."

How well Maureen remembered. Huddling in a waiting room an hour past her appointment time surrounded by posters encouraging you to take a birthing class, quit smoking, get your GED and sign up for WIC. The college health plan paid this doctor, and with that endorsement, she'd gone there because that's what you do when you get pregnant: you see an obstetrician. It never occurred to her to do anything else. She'd have been better off birthing in a ditch.

Maureen said, "Can you at least request my records?"

"I doubt they still have them. That clinic was a birth mill, and they probably purge everything on a regular basis." Jacobson sighed. "But for you, I'll do it. The hospital may have something."

After he hung up, she looked again at the video from the news site. Amber's twin, uttering sentences Maureen now knew by heart. She could mimic Katherine's inflection, but what had gone on just before and just after the camera cut away? Surely she'd spoken for more than fifteen seconds. Surely she'd given other details: where she lived, where she worked.

Then what? As Amber said, she couldn't drive to Danbury and show the video to everyone. "Excuse me, but do you know a woman named Katherine?"

But what if she could? What kinds of places would Amber's twin frequent? Amber possessed an analytic zeal to turn over a problem from ten directions and then flip it inside-out. Before you realized, she'd reversed the evidence and come up with the cause, and it always left Maureen in awe that someone so brilliant could have come from her. Raymond was smart too, just not in the same practical hands-on fashion as Amber. Could Katherine do the same? Had Katherine gone into biology, developing medicines to save kids with cancer because she could look at those cells under a microscope and see how they'd gotten started? Was she even now inventing a vaccine to inoculate a child against osteosarcoma?

Surely she was doing great things. How to track her down, though?

Maureen typed "Katherine" and "Danbury, CT" into Google. Nothing helpful, of course: pictures of dermatologists, real estate agents, but nothing that stood out. It was too big a task, too inscrutable, but too important not to get it done. Like growing a baby, if you really thought about what you were doing, cell by cell you'd never manage to put together an entire human heart, but when you left everything alone it usually worked just fine.

Closing her eyes, she imagined that spiritual connection, a tie binding Katherine to her and Katherine to Amber, strengthened by the tie between Amber and herself. Triangles were nature's strongest form, and that triangle could anchor them, pointing inevitably toward Danbury, Connecticut.

Again she typed "Danbury, CT" into the search engine, and this time she read the Wikipedia page. Danbury had 81,000 residents and, for some reason, the nickname The Hat City. Maureen paused, but neither she nor her husband nor any of their (known) children favored hats, so she let that slide. She looked over their top employers (the school system and the government, of course, but also the hospital and a pharmaceutical company—interesting) and their cultural centers. She poked around the city government website and looked at their fire department: six engine companies.

As she looked at the faces on the city website, calmness crept over her. These people were looking out for Katherine, and in their faces she could read strength, honesty, credibility.

Almost on its own, her hand reached for her cell phone, and it rang. She answered, and there was Amber's voice. Maureen relaxed even further, letting the calm settle deep.

"I have that book Dad asked me to get from Nikki," Amber said. "Are you going to be home after work?"

"Yes. Do you want to stay for dinner?"

A brief hesitation, and then, "Actually, I was going to have dinner with Nikki."

No, she wasn't. Maureen said, "I went up into the attic this morning, and I found your old schoolwork."

"Okay..." Amber dragged out the word.

"Do you remember in first grade you wrote a story about a girl who was half a girl."

Amber said, "I did?"

"Yes!" Maureen surged with triumph. "She was split lengthwise, so she had one arm and one leg, and she had to hop around the school and couldn't ride a bicycle, that kind of thing."

Amber said nothing.

Maureen said, "Don't you see? You knew, even back then. You knew you were missing a part of you—"

"No." Amber's voice ticked up, but there was a note of panic. "Mom, I can't do this. I don't know who she is, but this is nuts."

"But sweetie—"

"Don't do this to me!" That was three-alarm panic, and just like a fire alarm, it came up so suddenly it sent Maureen's calm fleeing into the dark corners. "So I wrote a funny story about a girl who was cut in half. Italo Calvino wrote a story called *The Cloven Viscount* which is pretty much the same thing—did *he* have a missing twin?"

Why was she so upset? "But you were always imagining playmates."

"You're looking for proof where there isn't any." Amber sounded desperate. "So there's someone out there who looks like me. Didn't you always say there are seven other people out there who look just like you?"

Maureen said, "But—"

"No." Amber's voice lowered. "I'm not going to have any part in this. You go find her if you want, but don't involve me."

Maureen went cold. She couldn't do this without Amber. "But what if she's your sister?"

Amber said, "And what if she is? Do we try to make up for twenty-four years? If you do find her, I hope she's no one to us, that she's thirty-five and we can forget all about her."

Heart pounding, Maureen gave a small, "Okay."

Amber said nothing.

"Okay, sweetie. If that's what you want." Her hands were trembling. "I won't bother you with this anymore. I won't ask you to look."

Amber let a moment go by before saying, "Thank you."

And then there was nothing more to say. They extracted themselves from the conversation, Maureen bewildered and wondering what on earth to do now.

———※———

When Nikki opened the door, Amber greeted her with a pizza and a bag of wings. It was hard to look Nikki in the eyes, so she just gave in and stared at the carpet. "Um...guess who invited herself over for dinner?"

Nikki ran a hand through her pixie-cut hair. "Uh-oh." She stepped back to let Amber inside with the goodies, but Amber handed her the box and picked up the grocery bag she'd left alongside the door.

Nikki said, "To what do I owe the honor? Is this the fifteenth anniversary of us beating the boys at team-tag?"

"Then I'd be over for dinner four times a week." Amber bit her lip. "Come up with an occasion. I told my mother I was meeting you for dinner, and then I felt five kinds of guilty, so here I am."

In the kitchen, Nikki turned off a pot of boiling water and inspected the grocery bag. Pre-made salad. A bag of two-bite brownies. And, wait for it...

Nikki squealed. "Where'd you find this?!" She pulled out the six-pack of Jones Berry Lemonade soda. "I'm going to kill you if you've been holding out on me!"

Grinning compulsively, Amber folded her arms. "I was relatively sure you cleared out the world's supply when you spent all your time craving it in the first trimester."

Nikki frowned. "Seriously, where'd you get it? Wegmans has been out for ages."

"I ordered it online because I wanted it for your birthday." Amber looked down. "But when I decided to crash you tonight, I brought it as a peace offering."

Nikki put down the soda and gave her a hug, in that moment Amber realized how she sounded. She closed her eyes.

Something thumped into her side. Nikki started laughing, and Amber said, "Hey! No editorial comments!"

Nikki said, "That's his or her way of saying it's a crime to let pizza get cold. Get some plates. I've got those icy mugs in the freezer. You want to eat in front of the TV?"

"As long as it's not the evening news."

They camped out (well, Nikki on the couch) with Doctor Who playing. Dennis was still on his week of evening tours, so they half-watched, half-made-fun-of the episode and traded jabs. Amber felt in her pocket: phone there, but off. She sighed, then looked up at Nikki.

Nikki said, "Okay, talk. Doctor Who got us through every high school breakup and each time someone's died, but no one's dead now. So why are you hiding from your mother?"

"Why do you think? She's still getting crazy, and I don't want to hear it!" Amber's heart hammered. "Why is she so set on chasing this figment halfway across the country who looks like me—there's no reason to believe this is really a twin!"

"Whoa!" Nikki leaned forward. "Chill! Now who's getting crazy?"

"The whole situation is crazy! My mother went up in the attic digging out my first grade schoolwork to uncover any inkling I may have had that I was missing half of me."

Nikki whistled.

"And she *found* it!" Amber had quit trying to keep her voice under control. It didn't matter that the commercials had ended and the episode resumed. "So help me, she actually found proof positive that I've been walking around all my life grieving for this sister I unconsciously knew I had all along."

From Nikki, a snicker.

Amber folded her arms and dropped back against the couch. "I'm just glad I never kept a diary, because right now she'd be psychoanalyzing every entry. *See, sweetie, you began with 'Dear Diary,' which means you were longing for someone to talk to.*"

"Okay, okay, so she's flipped." Nikki shook her head. "But I can see where she's coming from. If Katherine *were* your twin, wouldn't you want to know?"

Amber exclaimed, "No!"

They were both quiet for a moment, and Amber realized she was breathing hard, as if she'd run three miles.

Nikki said, "Really?"

"Why would I want to know?" Amber blinked hard, eyes burning. "Just let her be. I wasn't missing her before. I'm not missing her now."

Nikki's eyes widened. "She's a part of you."

"She's not part of me!" Amber shot onto her knees. "I'm not half of anything! There's no such thing as soulmates and there's nothing of me that's gone!"

Nikki raised her hands. "Hey! Take it easy. It's okay."

"I'm not out to set the world right," Amber said. "I can't fix everyone's problems!"

Nikki reached for her.

Amber yanked back. "Why hasn't anyone considered that maybe she's better off without us?"

Open-mouthed, Nikki just stared.

Amber stalked out of the living room and into the kitchen, then folded her arms and leaned against the wall with her eyes closed.

After a minute, she heard, "Can I ask a question?"

"No."

Nikki said nothing.

Breathe. Amber struggled to breathe all the way down into her diaphragm. Mom said that worked when you were panicked, and heaven only knew how often she'd heard her mom talking a frightened client through early contractions. *Let your body get its air. Your body knows what to do, so give it the fuel to do it.* Well, right now her body wanted to run. Run and keep running, and maybe stop when she reached the ocean, just run until she ran out of land and ran out of breath and no one would catch her and ask questions, just her standing there, facing into the sunset with her shadow stretched out long behind her bumping over the slats of some pier, water clucking beneath the wood and then, as darkness swelled, that shadow would fade out as if it never was. And maybe, when it got that dark and that still, maybe she'd fade out too, and the world would just keep on going.

Her eyes stung.

"I hate this."

Nikki sounded shaken. "I hate it too."

Amber looked up.

"I hate it because you hate it. I don't know what to tell you." Nikki had her arms to her chest. "I'm sorry I brought it up."

"What were you going to ask?"

"I'm not going to ask it anymore." Nikki settled herself in one of the kitchen chairs and traced a finger over the bottle of berry lemonade. "Some questions answer themselves."

seven

Amber's stomach ached, maybe from the greasy wings and the greasy pizza. They'd gone back to Doctor Who, but before it ended, Amber had excused herself to drive the book over to her father at the college. It was a ten-pound coffee-table copy of *The Making of The Empire Strikes Back,* and Dad needed one of the pictures. Nikki had been quiet. Better to let her go to bed.

Still in his office, Dad was running a film forward frame by frame. Slipping into the seat behind his desk, Amber clutched the book as she waited.

Not turning from the screen, her father said, "You're avoiding the house?"

"Why do you think that?"

"Because you chose to drive half an hour to the college rather than five minutes and leave it on the kitchen table. But," he added, "you also chose to drive half an hour rather than keep it until tomorrow, so I have to assume you're not avoiding all of us. Just your mother."

One freaking annoying thing about being the daughter of a professor: he noticed everything. Her father finally looked away from the computer. "To be more pointed, you want to tell me to stop your mother from tracking down this woman."

Yep, noticed everything. "So why don't you stop her?"

Dad gave a dry smile. "Since when has anyone ever stopped your mother?"

"That's not an answer," Amber said, "because Mom is hardly an unstoppable force. She'll listen to you, but you're letting her go straight off the deep end based on five seconds of video and something she thinks she may have remembered when she was supposed to be anesthetized."

He pivoted his chair to look right at her. "Are you done yet?"

"This isn't a birth, Dad! It's not all about going with your feelings and working with your instincts. We're talking about someone's life here."

"Yes." He leaned forward. "And that someone would be my daughter, too."

Amber's breath caught.

He leaned his elbows on the desk. "This isn't just your mother's daughter. *If* she exists, and I admit she may not—"

Amber glared at her knees. "She exists because we saw her on the news."

"If she exists *as your sister*, then yes, it's pretty important *to me* to find out, and find out now. I should think you of all people would understand that."

Amber's head jerked up. "Why me?"

Dad's eyes bored into her. "Do you want me to go on?"

She shrank back in her chair, and there it was, the thing she didn't want to hear, and he was going to say it anyhow. He didn't miss a detail, and his unspoken verdict felt like spiders crawling all over her. She just wanted to get out, run, run away, just like once she'd run from someone else.

Her father said, "Well?"

She shook her head.

Dad sighed. "I'm not going to tell what you should do. I *am* going to tell you what you should not do. You should not get in your mother's way."

Amber scuffed at the floor with the toe of her boot. "I'm sorry."

"You also should know that your mother and Olivia are going to go to Danbury tomorrow."

Amber's eyes widened. "What's she going to do? Stand on a street corner with a photograph and say *Do you know this woman*?"

"I'm not sure what she's planning." He shook his head. "Look, I wish this weren't a mess as well, but it's a mess we're in, and we've got to keep moving through it. You know how that works far better than any of the rest of us."

Amber muttered, "Like I did all that well."

Dad said, "So you do understand." He'd said what she didn't want to hear, but he hadn't had to say it explicitly. "But I think you did fine."

Amber looked up. Dad reached for her hand. "I'm sorry, honey."

About to respond, she stopped as her pager went off.

She pulled it from her belt, and oh, no. "Sorry, Dad. Gotta run."

Run she did: run through the hall, run through the parking lot, floor the accelerator and head down Route 96 until she peeled off westward, toward Waverly, light spinning on the roof of her car but the siren off except for when she shot through an intersection.

At a complex of three-story apartment buildings, one flared orange, light reflecting from the smoke overhead. The worst of the smoke spewed from a ground floor window. Fire crews were already working, hoses blasting at the outside while two others disappeared in the back door.

Amber sought out the Fire Chief, let him know she'd arrived, and then retreated.

The blaze was centered at the rear of the building. Amber snapped photos, then circled and took more, noting where the fire seemed to have originated, how it spread, and how the Fire Chief had decided to attack it.

Beside two ambulances, paramedics were assessing the evacuees. This was the part Amber would never get used to, not for as long as she did this job. The way the families watched their homes burn, the frantic ones who didn't know if everyone had gotten out, the people in shock, the people in tears, the people either clutching their pets or agonizing over pets still in the building, the people screaming in anger at no one. *Why can't they put it out?* Why can't they? Why did it start in the first place?

And her role in this scene: come to these frightened, shocked people and ask questions. What happened? Where were you? Where was the fire when you got out?

A firefighter came over holding a cat wrapped in a towel. An elderly man rushed for him, gushing thanks, and the firefighter gently pressed the bundle into the man's arms.

Amber showed her shield to the nearest bystander. "I have a few questions."

It really was only a few questions, and fortunately most people could answer on autopilot, even those being triaged. She wrote their answers, noted developments, returned to asking questions, and already a report took shape in her head. There were four identical buildings in this apartment complex. She'd need to tour one of the whole ones afterwards.

A firefighter rushed over holding a child, a boy not yet in his teens but clutching a stuffed animal and with tears pouring down his face, his shoulders jerking as he struggled not to give in.

The firefighter called to the paramedics, who gave an okay. Then he returned, and the boy kept standing there. Staring.

The paramedics were busy. Amber took a step toward the boy and showed her shield. "I'm a fire marshal. Are you okay?"

The boy said, "Where's my brother?"

She said, "They're going to get him out. That's what they're doing."

"Where is he?" The boy turned to her. "It was so hot, and they took me, but where is my brother?"

The boy started sobbing, and Amber hugged him. She sat on the ground and held him in her lap while he sobbed in jerking gasps, and she wondered where his parents were or how she could say to him it would be all right when it might not be. His home was being consumed right in front of him, and maybe his brother.

So she stopped being the junior Fire Marshal and just held this boy, waiting, silent, wondering, too far to choke on the smoke but too close to breathe freely. She ought to get this kid away from here, but he wasn't going to leave, not without his brother.

Amber said, "Where are your parents?"

The kid said, "Mom works nights. I don't know about my father."

"How old are you?"

"Eleven."

She said, "Your brother—how old is he?"

"Sixteen."

Amber frowned. "He was supposed to be watching you? And you couldn't find him?"

"The alarms went off. Alan was supposed to be with me. But he wasn't. And when I went in the hallway it was burning, so I went back inside, and—"

The kid choked up again.

Amber kept him on her lap until a paramedic took the kid by the hand. The kid made two steps, then turned back to her. "You'll find my brother? Please?"

Amber blinked back tears. "They're going to do their best."

The building had sprinklers: that was in its favor, and everyone agreed the sprinklers had gone off at the same time the alarms started. Still, the blaze was tremendous, and it took another hour before they declared it out. The incident commander went back inside, then called for Amber.

"Let's check the laundry room first," she said. "Everyone who escaped from the bottom floor agrees that's where it started."

The laundry room was a disaster, the floor soggy and the walls still radiating heat. She shone her flashlight around and looked inside all the dryers: four of them, all empty. In the corner, a trash can had melted into the floor. She started taking pictures.

In front of the dryer were beer cans. Burnt, but still recognizable. Time to take a picture. She swung the light over the floor, then looked between the dryers, between the washers, behind them all. Come on, it had to be here. She needed more to go on.

She opened the first dryer and pulled out the lint trap. Clean. The second dryer: clean. Third and fourth: clean.

She looked up at the incident commander. "I'm going to need the police for this."

He pursed his lips. "I figured you would."

"I'm looking for at least one sixteen-year-old boy," she said. "One's named Alan."

It didn't take all that long. When the police began evacuating the residents to a hotel for the night, that eleven-year-old's brother showed up right on cue, and Amber had Dennis cull him away from the group (and away from his younger brother) for questioning.

"I didn't get a chance to speak to you before," she said, eyeing him. The kid looked nervous. Not stressed and upset, but nervous. She asked a few generic questions to get him used to answering her, one of the tricks she'd learned during training. Things she already knew, like "So your parents were out tonight? You go to high school?" And then, "You were baby-sitting your younger brother?"

He nodded. She said, "When he woke up and the alarms went off, he was scared because you weren't there."

He looked at the ground, and he hesitated before saying, "I— I went into the hallway to see what was going on."

"Don't lie to me, okay? Actually, don't answer me at all." Amber wanted to look him in the eye, but he was just staring down. "You were supposed to be baby-sitting, and instead you went into the basement and hung out with your friends. You were smoking cigarettes in the laundry room."

The kid folded his arms. "No, I wasn't."

"I told you not to lie to me." Amber took a step closer, right into his personal space. He reflexively took a step backward. "You were drinking beer. One of you got the brilliant idea to pull the lint from the dryer lint traps and set it on fire because you heard it would burn like crazy, only it exploded, and you ran."

The kid was shaking his head. Beside her, Dennis stood with folded arms.

"I told you not to lie to me, Alan. And I'm pretty sure you weren't alone."

The kid said, "Even if I did any of what you said, why would I rat out my friends?"

Amber opened her hands. "You left your brother to die."

Three minutes later, Amber sat on the sideboard of one of the fire trucks, staring at her notes, while Dennis had the kid in the back of the squad car. *Stupid kid. Stupid, stupid kid.* He probably hadn't meant to burn the place down. Being stupid shouldn't be a death sentence, except it could have been. And yeah, it was quite a look on that eleven-year-old's face when Dennis had read the older kid his rights.

In the morning she'd have to write a report. The cops and the DA would take over from there, and then a judge would get the case. Afterward—who knew? Maybe community service. The kid had been stupid, and he recognized it. It wasn't really attempted arson, and any judge should be able to figure it out. Criminal mischief? It was too late to think clearly. Too late and too smoky and too much work left to do.

The incident commander came to her. "You never want that to be the cause."

Amber nodded. "I have to go back in for more evidence. In case this goes to trial, we have to be sure."

The incident commander folded his arms. "And he just left his brother in the apartment." He huffed. "What kind of jerk wouldn't risk everything to get to his own family?"

Amber stared at the ground. "Yeah. I've been wondering that myself."

The birds were still calling out sunrise when Maureen raised the garage door. She put her travel mug in the cup holder, slipped into the driver's seat of her Jeep, and spread a map on the passenger seat. She'd pick up Olivia and Charlotte in Ithaca, and after that, Danbury was a four-hour drive. She'd make it there by lunch. She had photos and a notebook for taking down directions.

She started the engine...and stopped when she realized the driveway was blocked.

Amber's Subaru.

What on earth? Maureen already said she wouldn't involve her! Wasn't that enough? Did Amber need to stop her from doing it on her own?

Maureen shut off the engine and stepped out, jaw clenched. Amber had no right, no right whatsoever. Whether it was jealousy or hard-headedness, Amber could make decisions for herself, but not about what everyone else did. And yet there she'd parked, blocking the driveway. And she was still in her car, staring through the windshield.

Fists clenched, Maureen stalked down the driveway and yanked opened the door. "What are you doing here?"

Amber looked pale even in the pinkish light, her eyes shadowed. "I'm saving you and Olivia a lot of heartache. You're not going to find her this way."

Maureen's throat tightened, and her anger evaporated: Amber wasn't giving off a fighting vibe. She smelled like smoke.

Amber went on. "All that effort is for nothing if you don't organize it first. You need a plan rather than just showing up with your daughter and a baby in a city of a hundred thousand and asking around."

Maureen kept watching for cues. Amber's fingers fidgeted with each other, and she was staring at her steering wheel. Was this capitulation? Or was this just an attempt to stall so Maureen would never go? She slipped into the front seat. "What do you want me to do instead?"

"I want you to think about this." Amber turned, and she really did look awful. She had circles beneath her bloodshot eyes and a soot smudge on her cheek. "I'll help you find her. But we've got to plan it so that when you dive in, you've got the best chance of success."

Tentative, Maureen said, "What kind of planning?"

"Mom, we live in the information age. I bet we could turn her up if we just knew the right criteria to search for. Then once we have that, we can narrow down our target and block it off." Amber raised her hands, an L between thumb and forefinger, then flipped one hand to meet the other and make rectangles. Amber blocked out areas of the air before her until Maureen could see ropes plotting out a grid on an archaeology dig. "We're bound to find her because she'll have left her fingerprints all over the world. It's just a matter of knowing what to look for."

Maureen said, "What have we got to go on?"

"We've got a name and a city, and we've got an age range. I'm betting she won't turn out to be anyone we care to know, and it will be obvious." Amber's voice sounded bitter. "Maybe she's five years younger than me. But whatever it is, she's got to be out there leaving clues. Comments on weblogs, membership on some kind of forum. We can suss her out that way."

Weaving her fingers, Maureen stared out the side window. "You went from telling me it's impossible to telling me this."

Amber shook her head. "The past is always written in the present. You just need the index."

Maureen closed her eyes and tried to be conscious of where she was: here in Amber's car, with Amber's discarded coffee cups, hearing her daughter saying she'd take the wheel and bring to bear a mind trained to reverse-engineer the present. And this change of heart— why? But did it matter?

Maureen reached over to squeeze her hand. "Speaking of the past written in the present, you look exhausted."

"Because I'm exhausted." Amber shook her head. "I don't know what to think right now. But it needs to be done, so let's do it right."

EIGHT

Four hours of sleep was more than enough. Amber would keep telling herself that for as long as it took to get home, and then she'd drop into bed at 7:30pm like a little kid. She could do anything for twelve hours, right?

Almost immediately, Scott paged her to the front, and he accompanied her into a deposition room off to the side of the lobby.

Just inside the door stood a woman, enraged. "I want my son back. Now."

Amber blinked. Trying to get her balance—because she knew who this had to be—she went for more time. "May I ask who you are?"

The woman said, "I'm Felicia Hernandez, and last night you framed my son for arson."

Yes, of course. Amber stepped toward the woman, right into her personal space, and it worked. The woman stepped backward, and now Amber had enough room to get past her to the desk. With not a little relief she saw Scott remained by the door.

Amber took a seat. "Your son was not questioned last night because we wanted to make sure he understood his right to legal counsel."

"And I'm definitely going to get legal counsel! We're going to beat any charges you make up." Ms. Hernandez stood with her hands on her hips. "You'd better not have hurt him or exposed him to career criminals."

"He was put alone in a holding cell and probably got a good night's sleep." More sleep than she'd had, digging through the charred basement-level apartments. And what kind of career criminals lived in Patmos Springs, for crying out loud? Anyone that awful outclassed their little lockup. She looked toward Scott. "Do you know if he's had breakfast?"

"He asked for Pop Tarts, so I picked some up from the MiniMart." He was trying to look somber, only his eyes gave it away. "But then I got him an apple and a carton of milk too, because I think we're supposed to make sure they get some kind of nutrition, especially a minor."

She looked back at Hernandez before Scott's smirk made her giggle. Awesome. If this woman had the slightest inclination, she'd hand her lawyer the Pop Tart box and charge them with chemical warfare. *Your honor, can you even pronounce half these ingredients? Isn't that ninth one a key component of plastic?*

Amber said, "We can certainly escort you to see him."

"And you'll let him right out of there, too!"

Amber said, "Not before he's been questioned and we get a judge to rule on bail. This is a criminal investigation."

Hernandez said, "He's not a criminal!"

"He's been charged with criminal mischief and arson," said Amber. "We have reasonable cause to believe your son and two of his friends were the culprits."

"My son is a good kid."

Amber said, "While I don't dispute that, your son was drinking beer in the laundry room and burning laundry lint."

Her voice went plaintive. "That's not arson. That's just fooling around."

"He was playing with fire." Amber narrowed her eyes. "The building burned. There may be thousands of dollars in property damage—"

"My son wouldn't do that!"

"Your younger son needed to be rescued. Alan left him in a burning building."

The woman's face tightened. "I said, my son wouldn't do that."

Amber looked at her, exhausted. No, this woman's son wouldn't do that. No one's son would do that, except someone's son had.

Well, time to stop appealing to her non-existent sense of reason. "New York State requires a cause be determined for every fire." Her voice was low, steady. She needed coffee in the worst way. "I've got enough evidence to determine a cause, and the evidence says your son was part of the cause."

The woman leaned forward, her eyes watering. "Look, I don't have a lot of money. I'll get him a lawyer and we'll beat this, but I don't know how we're going to pay for all this. The kid can't help that he doesn't have a father and I've got to work second shift because it pays more. I'm doing the best I can. You're going to destroy my family."

In her mind Amber could recreate the real destruction: the hallways blackened, the carpet incinerated, the neighboring apartments with water and smoke damage. Some stupid mistakes you walked away from, and some...well, some ended up in the station house. But this was what mothers did: mothers fought for their children.

Hernandez said, "Find the cause as faulty wiring. He's never been in trouble. He's going to finish high school and go to college and get a decent job and move to the city. You're going to ruin his life if you say he did this, but you could just say one of the dryers malfunctioned or the fuse box sparked."

Amber's shoulders dropped. "You know I can't. My job is to serve the public by keeping everyone safe."

"How does it keep people safe when you ruin a kid's future?" Hernandez charged the desk, and Scott took a step into the room, but Amber didn't move. She kept her gaze steady. Hernandez said, "What about his friends? What happens to them?"

"If your son cooperates by giving us their names, he gets a lesser charge." Amber narrowed her gaze. "Maybe only probation. He's a juvenile. I know how the DA's office works around here. He'll get charged with arson, and then the DA will suggest that if he pleads guilty, he'll get a suspended sentence on condition that he keeps his grades up in high school. The judges love that kind of arrangement. Believe it or not," Amber added, "we don't want to ruin his life any more than you do. What we want," she said louder over Ms. Hernandez's protests, "what we want is to keep everyone safe, and we need to drive home that three bored teenagers playing with fire...is arson."

Hernandez let off a huff and stared at the carpet.

"Why don't you go talk to him," Amber said. "See for yourself he's fine. Even if Sergeant Stadler did give him Pop Tarts."

"Blueberry Pop Tarts," Scott added. "The kind with the swirly frosting."

Hopeless. She said, "And then after you've seen him, we'll hook you up with the public defender. You don't have to pay for a lawyer when everyone wants the same thing."

Hernandez shook her head.

Scott moved toward the door. "Would you like to visit your son now?"

He guided Hernandez to the lobby. Amber sat at the desk, rubbing her temples. Caffeine. Now she'd pour it into her body. Oh, right, and look for her twin because she'd promised her mother, and that's what mothers did: they fought for their children.

Five minutes and one bitter, disgusting, overwrought cup of Old Man coffee later, Amber sat at her desk looking at the work before her: a phone call to return from an appliance store in Binghamton. Two letters from an insurance agency. A letter from Waverly Middle School's DARE coordinator (those programs were always fun) and the usual stack of reports to be filled out after a major fire.

She opted against the paperwork and began the search for her twin. And here was where Google became her best friend.

Within ten minutes, she decided Google was her worst enemy.

Soon after, she was accessing every kind of public record imaginable in the state of Connecticut.

She jumped when a hand landed on her shoulder. "Earth calling Brickman. Come in, Brickman."

Amber pulled back, and Scott was right there. "What?"

He snickered. "I've been trying to get your attention, only you're staring holes in the laptop screen." He got a worried look. "Are you still upset about Hernandez? She's calmer after seeing the kid, and the public defender is stopping by in two hours. At three PM."

"Really? It's that late?" She turned back to the computer and realized abruptly that she wasn't hungry. Given the time, she should have been famished. "Nothing's working."

Scott sat on the edge of the desk. Amber was about to tell him to get the hell back to the front when she looked around. The Old Man was gone. The coffee pot was empty. She'd been here the whole time, but obviously she hadn't been. "Why are you here? I don't have someone waiting, do I?"

"No, but I tried to call and you didn't answer."

Amber tensed. "I'm sorry." She looked down. "That's totally uncalled for. I won't let that happen again."

"Not a big deal. Someone had a question about smoke detectors. I told him I'd call back." Scott folded his arms. "They've been talking about the Hernandez fire, and man, that kid's just lucky. The Fire Chief says it's a miracle the insulation didn't ignite. Oh, and then they pulled apart the laundry room walls. Oopsie. No firewalls between the apartments."

Amber's head shot up. "No firewalls?"

Scott nodded. "The Old Man is already pulling up the original inspection certificates and getting a very heavy, very annoying mountain of paperwork ready. Personally, I'm looking forward to a lawsuit where everyone sues everyone else. Some contractor somewhere is already in touch with his attorney, and whoever signed off on the initial inspections is in for a world of hurt." He sighed. "But yeah, the kids are pretty damn lucky they didn't torch everything."

Amber shook her head. "So stupid. I can't even imagine what they were thinking."

"I can totally imagine what they were thinking because I was a stupid kid myself." Scott rolled his eyes. "*Hey, laundry lint will like explode if you set it on fire! Wanna see?*" He shook his head. "At least they didn't ignite each other."

Amber grimaced and stared off to the side. "I thought you cops like it when the street cleans itself."

Scott's voice leaped half an octave. "What?"

Amber said, "When a drug dealer gets shot and the cop says, 'Just the street cleaning itself.'"

His eyes went huge. "Did one of *our* guys say that?"

Tracing a circle on her desk, she said, "Binghamton."

"Well, no, I don't lie awake at night warm with thoughts about how the street cleans itself. I've never even thought that. We're in Patmos Springs and the streets are already pretty clean." He took a seat opposite her. "Talk to me. What's got you so worked up if it's not the Hernandez kid?"

Amber's mouth twitched. "Do you like mysteries?"

"I love mysteries. I should have been a detective. Oh, wait, I am." Scott grinned, and it brightened his whole face. Amber caught herself smiling too, and she looked away. "Does it involve a dead body in the study with a lead pipe?"

"Actually, it involves a live body stolen from a hospital." Amber took a deep breath. "You really want to hear this? Because it's crazy."

Scott rested his elbows on his knees. "Can't be crazier than the guy I pulled over last Tuesday. He told me he was on his way to teach violin to Antonio Vivaldi, and he'd already passed Rome, NY, so which way was Venice?" When Amber chuckled, he said, "Lay it on me."

Struggling not to feel like an idiot, Amber told him about the news broadcast, her mother's conviction, and how she'd gotten roped into the search. When she snuck a peek up higher than his knees, she found Scott looking right at her, not battling laughter or disgust. "Go on. What have you done so far?"

"What have I done? Let's see." Amber counted off on her fingers. "I've Googled whatever I could think of. I searched those people-searching websites and went through the DMV records for Danbury. We don't have her last name, so I need to search based on things like what street corner it looks like she's on, or where she might live. I've turned up twenty-five Katherines in Danbury, but when I can find pictures, they don't look like her. I searched the Twitter stream out of Danbury.

I've searched sites I never would have thought of, and I keep watching the recoding of that damn broadcast looking for something I might have missed, even if it's her earrings or someone walking by in the background."

Scott squinted at her. "Why are you doing this online?"

"Because the clues have to be out there somewhere. She's moving through the world. She's leaving fingerprints."

"The thing about prints is you need something to match them to," Scott said. "Can I see the broadcast?"

Amber brought up the video on her laptop. She made sure that when Katharine first showed up on the screen, she was watching Scott. His eyes went wide. One more check mark in her mother's column.

Scott said, "This is all you have on her?"

"Yep."

"Have you contacted the news station?"

Amber blew at her bangs. "I can't get through to the newscaster. They'll only take a message, and that's it."

"That's garbage. I'll get you some answers. Come with me."

Amber said, "I need to call someone about smoke detectors."

Scott shook his head. "Ma'am, police business. Kindly allow me to do my job."

Scott brought her to the booking room and unlocked a drawer with a camera. "Here, hold this." He gave her a sign with a random booking number. "You look terrific. I wonder what you've been arrested for. Stand over here." He turned on the lights and shone them right on her. "Now do me a favor. Look annoyed. Actually, no, look…" He stopped. "Look sad."

Amber said, "Sad?"

"Yeah. She seemed sad, on the broadcast."

Amber stood there, wondering what about Katherine made her seem sad to Scott, only she couldn't come up with anything. That woman shouldn't be sad. That woman lived in Danbury, Connecticut, and probably pulled down six figures a year with a pharmaceuticals company. What was there to be sad about that?

Scott shouted, "Brickman!" and when she started, he snapped a picture.

"You're insane," she said.

"You look awesome when you're pissed off." This time the flash coincided with her filthy look. "Especially when you want to beat me with my own baton." He laughed. "Okay, you can quit being arrested now."

He loaded the photos into the computer, then out at the front desk, he called the station, introduced himself as Sergeant Stadler of the Patmos Springs, NY police department, and asked to speak to the news anchor.

Amber said, "And what are you going to do? Arrest her too?"

He gave her a tolerant look as he continued talking to the main receptionist. "It's about your March 14th broadcast. I'm conducting an investigation, and one of the individuals interviewed may be a person of interest in an unsolved case."

Amber's eyes went wide. "You can't do that!"

"Thank you, I'll hold." He looked at Amber. "Why can't I do that?"

"Because that's an abuse of authority!"

"Oh, gee." He widened his eyes. "I hope no one tells the sergeant! I'll get in so much trouble. ...Hello, Ms. Kingston?" His voice dropped back to a professional timber. "Thank you so much for taking my call. I'm Sergeant Scott Stadler of Patmos Springs, New York."

While Amber stood beside the desk twisting a tissue into a toothpick-thin stick, Scott described the woman, again lied about her being a person of interest, and then asked for the full name she was going under currently, and if the news station had an address and a phone number for her. There was some tense back-and-forth while Scott declined to mention the nature of the investigation, and then his promise that if the investigation bore fruit he would talk to her first. Finally, "Ms. Kingston, may I have your email address?"

He typed it into the desk computer while repeating it back, then hit send. "You should be receiving an email with a photo."

Amber held her breath.

"Yes, she certainly does. Her hair is a bit longer, but yes." He gave Amber a thumbs up, and she shrank. "Thank you. When can I expect to hear back from you?"

Amber folded her arms on the desk, then laid her forehead down on her wrists. Oh, goodness, how long had it been? Late night, all day—the Hernandez fire. An angry mother. Katherine, somewhere on the end of a phone call and maybe looking sad even though Amber hadn't seen it herself, and information. Scott, pretending to investigate. It was too much.

"Hey, are you okay?"

Amber lifted her head and let out her breath. Scott had ended the phone call, but she said nothing.

"It's no big deal. She's going to talk to the reporter who did the interviews and have him get back to me." Then he hesitated. "Do you need to sit?"

"No." She bit her lip. "You lied to her about police business."

"She's your evil twin. Of course it's police business."

Amber folded her arms.

"Oh, wait, maybe you're the evil twin?" He reached under the desk and pulled out a clipboard with a blank report and a pen attached to it. "You want to make it police business?"

He handed them to her. Wide-eyed, Amber took a step backward.

"Kidnapping is a Class A felony. There's no statute of limitations on it in New York State." Scott's brow knit, and his eyes grew sharp. "If your mother is right, someone should go to jail."

———⊷∘⊶———

She didn't care if he found the name. Amber didn't care, and she told herself she didn't care, but she had to go through the lobby several times that day for other reasons. A trip to the supply closet, a discussion with the public defender, and a walk down the block to Tillman's Family Diner (Breakfast Anytime) to grab a salad for a late lunch. It wasn't as if she went through the lobby more times, but it didn't matter. Scott wasn't around, probably out on a call. She checked her cell phone often, but only because she wanted to make sure her mother was all right or that Nikki hadn't had her baby.

She didn't care if Scott found the name, but she left her phone beside the bed that night because bad things came in threes, and that meant a higher than normal chance of a fire tonight. Tired as she was, she didn't want to risk sleeping through a page.

And because she didn't care if Scott found the name, she was not disappointed, not even a little, when she woke up at seven with no missed calls, no texts, no email.

When she walked into the station house, Scott didn't even say hello. "I'm calling her back later this morning."

"It's not a big deal," she said, even as her mouth went dry and her stomach felt like a rock. "Whenever you hear back is okay."

There were reports to be filled out, reports to be faxed to Harrington, the insurance adjustor, and John DelGaudio, the soon-to-be-very-relieved restaurant owner. Also a letter to a dishwasher manufacturer (following up on a phone call) recommending a recall on a specific part. A discussion with the Fire Chief about the apartment blaze, followed by another discussion with a public defender, plus a phone call from someone who wanted to know if her oven was still safe after she'd set a pan of chicken on fire.

When Scott came into her office, he was grinning. He held up a sealed envelope.

Amber clutched the armrest. "You have it?"

"I have it." He sat on the corner of her desk, but he snatched back the envelope as she reached for it. "And now you owe me dinner."

She shrank back in her seat. "I didn't say anything about dinner."

"Oh, I must just have thought about it." Scott looked at the envelope, but pulled it back again. Amber hadn't gone for it, though. "Regardless, I think you'll agree this is worth dinner, so what time do you want to meet, and where?"

"Never, and nowhere. They work for me." Amber arched her eyebrows. "May I have the envelope, please?"

"I'm not sure why I should turn it over to you without a guarantee of repayment."

Amber said, "I've no guarantee you actually have the information."

Scott frowned. "That's a good point. Well, there's a full name and a home phone number, which I would think is enough to win me a rain check."

Amber said, "Other than the fact that I didn't agree to the dinner in the first place—"

Scott held up a USB drive.

"—and you told me it was police business anyhow, so it's like your public duty. You should pay *me* for the honor of a job well-done." She frowned. "Okay, what is that?"

"Nothing much." His eyes crinkled. "Just the rest of her interview."

Amber gasped. "You mean—?"

"I mean they interviewed her for about three minutes before calling it a day."

Her voice was thready. "What else did she say?"

"I didn't actually watch it," Scott admitted. "I copied the file to the thumb drive and brought it to you because she's not my sister, and I figured you'd want to see her first."

It sounded weak when she said it. "She's probably not my sister either."

"No, but that's what you're here to determine. For all you know, she holds up a copy of her birth certificate and says she was born on live TV in Lithuania in 1980, but whatever she says, it'll be more information than you have now." He held it up again. "So...dinner?"

Amber looked at her lap. "Not giving me that is aiding and abetting a kidnapping. I'm sure that's a felony."

"I hope no one tells law enforcement." He sounded amused. "Bribery is also a crime. So, dinner?"

"You must be totally starving." Amber took a long breath. "Why?"

"Because you're so eager to dine with me, obviously." Scott laid the envelope and the thumb drive on her desk. "Fine, I know when I'm beat. Page me if you want to open an investigation."

"Thanks." It sounded lame. She knew it, and she didn't know how to make up for it. "My mom will really appreciate your help."

"I'm sure she will." There was a little too much emphasis on the pronoun as Scott walked to the door.

Amber trembled at her desk, taking the envelope in her hands. He'd sealed it, and she left it that way, flexing the paper in her hands. Then, shaken, she reached for her phone. "Mom, I'm coming over tonight."

Nine

Maureen was so distracted while making dinner that she might actually set fire to a pot of boiling water. She knew it was possible because Brendan had done it once (thank heaven she didn't know all the details of his college life,) but she'd rather not have it happen tonight.

In the living room, Raymond was analyzing a movie in French, taking incomprehensible notes on a yellow pad. How he could work right now, Maureen couldn't imagine, but working he was, or at least a good facsimile thereof. Maybe he was staring at the screen, wondering how she could be cooking, except that cooking was supposed to be something she enjoyed and maybe he thought she'd find it relaxing.

Maureen had forgotten to start making tomato sauce, but before she got the can open, she realized the phone was about to ring. It would be Olivia. She ought to get that.

It rang, and she answered. "She isn't here yet."

Olivia said, "Oh, I was hoping she'd gotten off work early."

"I'm more hoping she doesn't have something that keeps her late." For a few different reasons, not the least being that *working late* might mean someone's house burnt to the ground. "I'll let you know what happens as soon as I can."

"It's great that she got the police to help. I mean, she works in the same building with them, so it makes sense." Olivia sounded far less tense than Maureen felt, and she wondered momentarily whether Olivia thought the matter would be settled. "Did she say anything about what he found?"

"She didn't look at it." That much Maureen couldn't understand. Amber hadn't wanted to drive it right over, hadn't been willing to read it to her, hadn't wanted anything to do with it. She... She just didn't want it.

Maureen had seen that before. It happened sometimes with her clients. Rarely. Rarely, because a woman choosing a midwife had considered her pregnancy enough to do something countercultural, and therefore she was thinking about it. Maureen imagined you'd see it more often in an obstetrician's office, a place American women went on autopilot.

When it happened, the woman looked normal enough, but she seemed oddly distracted. She'd look at you and respond but not react, and Maureen could never pin it down. "And how are you feeling?" *Oh, I'm fine.* How was her nausea? *Fine.* Has your husband been supportive? *Yes, he's fine.*

She wanted to wake them up, warm them, do something for them, but against their flat affect she felt so helpless. What caused that kind of damage? And who's to say that in the face of the same, she herself wouldn't have shut down?

And then during the birth, sometimes these women asked to transfer to the hospital, not because of any distress but because they wanted the epidural, because they couldn't do this, and now during labor when they had to be *here*, when they had to be *now*, they didn't want to be in the here and now. It was the worst, the moment Maureen saw all their feelings come home to roost because she hadn't been able to revive the women's feelings before they crashed. Then the women wanted to escape the pain, and then Maureen knew for sure that all along they'd threaded an epidural right through the backbone of their emotions. What would happen to them when at the end of the birth they were handed a baby and told, "He's yours"?

Two times, she'd succeeded. Twice a woman like this had broken down during transition, sobbing into Maureen's shoulder that she didn't deserve a baby, one because of a long-ago miscarriage and the other a long-ago abortion, and now each woman had to look her loss dead in the eye at a moment she needed to say hello to a brand-new person. Someone who was hers and someone else who could no longer be, confronting her at the same time. So Maureen had let the women cry, comforted them, stroked their hair, told them to breathe out the grief and breathe in a new wholeness, envisioning themselves as powerful woman who could carry this forward, rather than remaining forever blocked.

Amber hadn't been flat, not always. It was the worst thing in the world to hold both images of her side by side, her now versus her back then. But grief will do that, and maybe the way she'd handled Amber's hadn't been the best way. It's just that in the teeth of a loss so unfathomable, you want to give shelter to a broken heart, but you can't. You just can't.

So when Olivia said, "Oh, I guess she wants you to see it first," Maureen only said, "Yes, probably," and not, "No, Olivia, Amber doesn't want to admit a part of herself is missing."

She asked about Charlotte, and Olivia chattered for a while. So amazing, her little one having a little one, and it was the first confirmation Maureen had that maybe she'd done okay as a mom. If your own daughter could be an amazing mom, you hadn't ruined her, right? So every day it was like a treasure chest opening, even if Olivia joked that her mother only wanted to see Charlotte, when in reality, it was Maureen wanting to see Charlotte being mothered by Olivia.

But after the phone call, Maureen remained subdued. The dinner formed up in front of her: the sauce simmering, the pasta water at a boil. The salad as she sliced and chopped. The place settings as they grew around the table piece by piece. She thought not about Katherine, not even about Amber, but rather about Marcus.

He had been such a good addition to their family. Soft-spoken, polite, a little sarcastic and prone to seeing through nonsense. Oh, and a hard worker. Marcus and Amber had met at a stargazing group in Owego, although they'd gone to schools an hour apart, and while she finished up her undergrad degree in archaeology, he was in Binghamton earning his degree in business. He'd moved to a lousy part of town to save money, and they'd planned a back-yard wedding and a relocation to New Mexico. She'd work at an archaeology dig; he'd find a job; they'd stargaze in the nation's clearest skies.

And then...that night, the feeling like a bomb in her heart followed by a terrible phone call. Maureen had flown up route 96 to get Amber because she was in hysterics. Marcus: dead, a single gunshot to the temple. Ruled a suicide by the police, but how could it have been a suicide? He and Amber had been together just that night, stargazing. He'd made plans to see her the next week, only she'd gotten back to her dorm to find out he'd been killed. Days later, Marcus's mother had stripped everything out of the apartment, leaving Amber with pretty much nothing of him. Memories and a telescope.

Amber had stumbled through her finals—Maureen had no idea how, but somehow she'd made it to her graduation day, which she'd shuffled through like an automaton, blank-eyed and silent. In the days after graduation, she'd sat there on the couch. No, Amber mustn't move to New Mexico now. She'd backed out of the archaeology dig and watched endless reruns of *The Muppet Show*, eating when Maureen reminded her. Maureen told her to get out of the house, so Amber started running every day and logging five thousand hands of computer solitaire every night. At the end of that summer, Raymond had called in a favor, and just like that Amber was enrolled in the graduate program in chemistry, previously her minor. She rode to campus with her father, did classes or lab work until evening, and then rode back home.

It probably wasn't the best way to handle things, but Maureen hadn't known what else to do. Amber needed a focus, and the grief counselors only said, "Don't make any major changes the year after a death." Moving to New Mexico meant a major change, and she wouldn't have been with her family. A Master's in chemistry bought her two years, two years longer to remain a child and not have to change anything.

Except for all that Maureen tried to keep everything the same, Amber had changed.

Well, the same personality was still there, only amplified. Amber had always tended toward the more serious and thoughtful, but now she did so much processing in her head. The job of fire investigator was a natural for her in that respect because of how much time she spent reassembling puzzles (remember the puzzles? Maureen would come home at three AM to find Amber with a new thousand-piece puzzle, assembling it across the breadth of the dining room table, every piece sorted and categorized, one square at a time rebuilding the world,) but Maureen sometimes wondered if it catered to a trait Amber ought to have suppressed. Because there wasn't any longer a trace of the young woman who'd dreamed of unearthing ancient civilizations (well, there she'd been reassembling puzzles too) and instead was someone who never stargazed, never daydreamed, never made long-term plans other than dutifully contributing every month to her 401K and a college fund for Olivia's baby.

Maureen had even brought Amber along on a couple of births, and instead of reacting to the breathtaking entrance of a human being into the world, Amber only focused on answering the phone and bringing juice for the mom. She gave excellent back rubs and never held a baby, and Maureen backed off. Amber had rejected any suggestion of being at Olivia's birth (which Olivia echoed). Although Amber would be at Nikki's. Maybe she'd crack a smile then.

When the doorbell rang, Maureen got it so Ray didn't need to leave his computer, where he appeared to be measuring the angle of a shadow against a doorway. Some symbolism or other; if he got a paper out of it, more power to him, but Maureen had to admit most of his articles left her baffled. If the film directors were inserting these things, it made sense to pay attention, but Maureen wasn't sure why.

At the door she found both Brendan and Amber, Brendan lugging a laptop bag and Amber a step behind without any noticeable baggage. Maureen kissed them both while Brendan crowed non-stop about how awesome that his mother had finally realized they weren't in 1850 and might want to view TV through a computer for once.

Amber said, "Our father is in the other room with three thousand dollars in video equipment."

Brendan said, "And our mother is three thousand miles away from knowing how to turn it on."

Maureen said, "Fine, fine, make fun of your mother."

Amber said, "She's got a system that works for her."

"Yeah, old VHS tapes." Brendan picked up one and held it to his ear. "Wow, I think I can hear the tape rotting away."

Maureen went back to the kitchen. Amber said, "Do you want to see the video now?"

Maureen's stomach tightened. "Dinner is just about done." Yes, she wanted to see it now, but still... "It will take your brother some time to set up everything."

Brendan opened his laptop on the kitchen counter. "Here we go. Set up."

Maureen looked at them both. Amber wore a poker face.

For a moment Maureen tried to imagine eating dinner without having seen the video, tense and expectant, and then she tried to imagine eating dinner after seeing the video, and whether the tension would be higher before or after.

Amber handed Brendan the thumb drive, and he began clicking. A video player opened. "Say the word."

Maureen turned off the stove. He pressed the triangle.

Ray had come up beside her, so they all four saw the image at the same time, Amber's clone looking a little nervous but smiling at the camera. And wonder of wonders—a toddler in her arms.

A blond-haired boy, maybe two years old.

"You say hi to the camera," she was saying to the boy, who buried his face in her shoulder. "Oh, you're so silly." She looked obliquely at the screen, as if at the cameraman alongside. "Should I just put him down? Okay? Here." She bent and slipped the child out of her arms, then raised her hand to her hair to straighten it after the wind. She wore a wedding ring. "I think he'll stay put."

Some sounds from off-camera, and she looked down at the child again (was that why she glanced down during the interview? The child clinging to her leg?) and took a deep breath. "What do you want me to say?"

Behind Maureen, Amber laughed. It wasn't a mean laugh, but she didn't sound surprised either.

The reporter's voice sounded muffled, "Tell us a bit about why you think this is important."

Katherine said, "Well, I really think it's important for Danbury to have a cultural center where we can have exposure to more than just the mass market media. I mean, yeah, the kids have a steady diet of pop culture over at the theater at the mall, but when it comes to Shakespeare or other cultural references, they've just never been exposed. They get the references because we put them in the footnotes, but there's no experience. Opening this theater right in the center of town is like a doorway to a world they didn't have before."

The reporter said, "Go on."

"I'm thinking about the kids who go home and do sports and maybe watch TV after dinner. Once this theater opens, there can be class trips. Or think about it, the Girl Scouts or church groups. It's not that hard to organize something like that, and with it being right here in Danbury, it's not expensive to bus them, or really for the surrounding communities either. You know how they say a kid has to be exposed to a food seven times before he'll eat it?" She laughed, and her eyes crinkled up. "Well, over the course of their public education, I bet we can get them in here seven times."

The reporter said, "Why live theater?"

Katherine's eyes lit up. Why hadn't they chosen this part for the broadcast? She was alive, so alive. "Live theater is immediate. How many people will pay hundreds of dollars for concert tickets to a group they already own all the albums for? It's not because they like wasting money. Having a performance right in front of you is an entirely different experience. This theater being right in the center of town will be like a breath of fresh air, and I think it will be a mutual thing. The theater will bring customers to the businesses, and the businesses can give exposure to the theater."

From offsides, the reporter said, "You aren't in marketing, are you?"

She laughed and glanced down again. "No, not at all."

The reporter said, "Do you plan to go?"

She looked like a "Hell yes!" but instead she said, "Well, it depends on what production they're doing. We used to go to the theater when I was a kid."

"Here?" said the reporter.

"No, in Greenwich, and I know I loved it then."

"I can tell," said the reporter, and then, "Thank you. This will probably be on the evening news tonight."

She smiled. "I did okay? You're not going to ban me?"

"You did fine," said the reporter, and then the clip ended.

Maureen realized her heart was racing. Her ears started to ring.

Brendan snorted. "She does look like you, sis. In fact, maybe she *is* you."

"Yeah, like I ever went to the theater."

"No, but Dad does." He laughed out loud. "You know how they say the apple doesn't fall far from the tree? Well you not only rolled away from the tree, but across the highway too."

"Shut up, Dorkface." Amber folded her arms. "Well, even without her name, we'd have her. I could track her down with that, no problem."

Maureen flushed. Amber could. If anyone could, it would be Amber.

Brendan said, "Overconfident much?"

"I've reconstructed fires with less information." She extended the envelope, and Maureen took it. "Well? You want this?"

Maureen opened the envelope, and written in blocky print was a name and a phone number. *Katherine Woodson.*

Maureen murmured, "We can call her."

Amber's voice was flat. Final. "No. We do not call her tonight. The first thing we do is internet stalk her to find out more. After that we call her, or maybe we write her, but we do not call her tonight, and we do not drive over there in the dark hours so we're sitting on her front porch when the sun rises."

Brendan said, "Actually, the first thing we do is eat dinner."

"Actually, the first thing you do is copy that file and then give me back the USB drive."

"You're so picky." Brendan was already doing it, though.

Maureen managed to get dinner on the table, somehow, although come to think of it, Amber and Ray may have done most of it. She did tasks like hunting in the fridge for parmesan cheese only to discover it already out.

And eating. Somehow that happened too, but subdued. There was some talk about Katherine with Maureen always unable to put into words what she wanted to say—that little boy at the beginning, a grandson? Could hoaxes get this elaborate? Were hallucinations so thorough? Or could it be as she'd known all along, a second daughter, a life divided, and a life lived fully with all its antecedents. Children. A husband. A job. Hobbies.

Childhood. Someone had taken her to the theater in Greenwich, Connecticut. Someone had shown her the arts. And now, was she an artist? An actor? No, she'd have mentioned that. But the way she'd talked marketing and economics...

Amber too seemed subdued.

Brendan said, "What's eating you? How your evil twin got on TV but you didn't?"

"That's why people have evil twins." Amber smiled wickedly. "To go on TV so they don't have to."

Brendan said, "How'd that cop get all this?"

Amber rolled her eyes. "Actually, I'm the evil twin. He sent the reporter my mug shot."

Maureen looked up. "Who?"

"Scott Stadler, the police sergeant." Amber looked annoyed. "He said it was police business and she was a *person of interest*." Brendan laughed out loud, and Amber said, "Yeah, abusing police authority is hilarious."

Brendan said, "You need to remove the stick up your butt. *Abusing police authority?*"

"Okay, if it was kidnapping, it's a class A felony, and there's no statute of limitations." Amber still looked annoyed, but a chill ran up Maureen's spine. Kidnapping. That changed the whole game. They could nail that doctor and lock him away forever. "But he wasn't doing it for that. He was trying to get me to go out to dinner with him."

Maureen sat up straighter.

Brendan said, "Is he really ugly?"

Amber exclaimed, "No!" even as Maureen said, "Brendan! What a thing to ask!"

"Just trying to figure out why any guy would be that totally desperate."

Ray said, "Brendan." It was flat enough that Brendan shrank a bit and muttered a chastened apology to Amber.

Maureen said, "That's a lot of effort to go through for dinner, though. Is he nice? Have you known him long?" She brightened. "Do you want to invite him here?"

"Don't imagine him as some starving waif." Amber chuckled. "He said he likes solving mysteries, and he's got a heart as big as Binghamton. It's just—he put pressure on me afterward to take him out, and I don't appreciate that. He shouldn't have tried to bribe me."

No, but he sounded like his heart was in the right place. "Where will go you?"

Amber said, "I'm not going."

Nothing further.

About to press, Maureen felt a sudden urgency, an awareness of the new moon and that she had two mothers due in the next two weeks. She looked at the phone, and when it rang, she knew it would be one of her clients, just not which.

She took the call in the living room, abandoning discussions of police sergeants and missing twins, and she focused only on the pitch of her client's voice, asking questions to keep her talking through two contractions (four minutes apart, but she could still talk through them) and weighed it all in her mind: client's first baby, her family history, and that sense inside telling her how much time she had. Not that she fully trusted the last. She'd run red lights if that sense told her a baby was coming far faster than anticipated, but she wouldn't delay just because she felt birth was eight or ten hours off. Which now she did. But she never trusted that she wasn't acting on prejudice rather than instinct because who knew where instinct came from? Even when it was right so often, Maureen wouldn't wager a mother's birth experience on it.

So she told the mother to relax, watch a funny movie, keep her mind off the contractions, and call anyone she wanted to be at the birth. She promised to get her bag together and be there in less than half an hour and agreed cheerfully that it sounded like the real thing (another contraction, and the mother could still talk through it).

Back in the kitchen, she kissed Ray on the lips and reminded him of the pudding in the fridge for dessert. "I'll be out all night unless she's so early I decide to come home for a few hours."

Brendan said, "How many men let their wives stay out all night after a mysterious phone call?"

Amber said, "Gee, you've only used that joke for ten years now. Maybe it'll get funny in another five." She turned toward Maureen. "Do you want me to keep looking for traces of her online, now that we know her name?"

Maureen nodded. "But you're right. Don't contact her yet." When Amber looked up, Maureen sighed. "First let's get to know who she is."

ten

Katie Woodson sometimes wished you could grow an extra arm for each kid you had. It made sense, really—one hand to keep on the kid, one hand to lug the extra groceries, and that last to bring in the mail, the diaper bag, the purse, and the toy the kid had insisted on bringing but then handed over as soon as you got where you were going.

Instead, she had her hands full, only two. And maybe it was better this way because people would have counted too many arms, and then people would have asked too many questions.

"Come on, sweetie." She held the door and tried to be patient as Daniel climbed the front steps one stair at a time. The grocery bag strap bit into her hand. "Just a little bit further."

Five minutes later, she was unpacking groceries in the kitchen, glad not to be sick but still wondering why she had picked some of these foods. But never mind. If they didn't get eaten, they'd just go into the bin for the next food drive at the high school. Mike would roll his eyes, but Mike didn't mind. If she apologized—*when* she apologized, because she knew she would—he'd just tell her no harm done, and if a few cans of some weird soup were what she needed, then she should have it, even if its only medicinal value was being available.

Now her Mom—well, Mom would have expected her to keep everything, especially something she bought for herself. Even if the food she found soothing on Monday only nauseated her on Wednesday. Even if it was loaded with salt and the obstetrician told her to lower her salt intake. *You might need it someday,* Mom would say. Never mind that someone would eat it, someone from the food pantry who maybe appreciated the food. *Oh, but tomato soup is much cheaper—you could have donated ten cans of that.*

Katie sighed, then looked at the phone. Welcome to one of the reasons she made sure to visit her parents during the first trimester rather than inviting them over. Mom with those sad comments *(I thought I raised you to appreciate things)* and Dad looking into the pantry *(Why do you need five cans of Campbell's Manhattan clam chowder? You don't like Manhattan clam chowder.)*

The phone rang. Caller ID: her parents. "Hello?"

It was her mother. "Hi, sweetie! I was wondering how you're doing."

"Pretty good." She checked her watch. Either Mom had been calling every ten minutes, or she had worked out exactly how long it took between the doctor and the grocery store. Or maybe both. "Everything's looking good."

"Did you have an ultrasound?"

Katie started putting away the rest of the groceries, head cocked to keep the phone in place. "Yep. Good strong heartbeat and everything's the right size and in the right place. I'm sixteen weeks now."

Mom said, "How was your blood pressure?"

"Fine." Three different kinds of milk. Whole milk for Daniel, skim for herself, one percent for her husband. At this rate, they'd need a second refrigerator.

Mom said, "And how much did you gain this month?"

"A pound." Mom should just come with her to these appointments, as involved as she was. Maybe she'd come into the bathroom with her to get a proper clean catch urine sample.

"Did you tell the doctor about the nausea?"

"He said it was just fine. I was sick until fifteen weeks before, you know." Katie decided enough was enough of the medical details. "Daniel was so cute. He's gone to enough appointments now that he starts making woosh-woosh sounds when the nurse gets out the blood pressure cuff. He says it's going to give my arm a hug."

Mom laughed. Katie fished for something else. "Oh, and I got a couple of pictures from the ultrasound. I'll email them to Dad and you can see them too."

Mom said, "Is that wise? I mean, it's medical information. You shouldn't be emailing things like that if it's not secure."

"It's not a HIPAA violation to mail my own stuff, and besides, what will they find out if even if someone does intercept the email?" She paused. "That I'm pregnant? Big secret."

Mom said, "Maybe you should just show me tomorrow."

Katie sighed. "Fine. If you feel better that way." Mom had already made her promise not to show ultrasound photos on Facebook because some crazy stalker might wait until she was almost due and then kidnap her and cut her open to take the baby. It had happened once about five years ago, and Mom had begged her, in tears, not to post the pictures, even though everyone else on her support groups had posted photos.

Mom said, "You don't know how technology is going to change. Years from now, someone might be able to use that ultrasound photo to deny the baby a job because of a health risk we can't detect now but will be detectable then."

Katie frowned. "What?"

"Or someone might try to scam the baby. They might even use you medical information to access your credit cards and steal her identity."

Katie sighed. "If someone wants that badly to be a high school teacher in Connecticut, they're welcome to it."

Mom snapped, "That woman on the news went mad and cut another woman's baby out because she'd lost a baby!"

Katie raised her voice. "So maybe you should tell everyone on the internet to take down *their* photos because I might steal their babies!"

Mom gasped, leaving Katie feeling three inches tall. "I only want what's best for you."

She'd gone too far. "I'm sorry," Katie said, because if she didn't, Dad was going to get between them again and tell her to quit being so selfish and worrying her mother. It was easier just to apologize now, so she did, and did it again, and then reassured Mom that she knew Mom only was looking out for her safety.

And then, while Mom continued to fret, Katie thought of inconsequential trivia to talk about.

After another five minutes, Katie extracted herself from the conversation not by claiming she needed to pee (hey, Mom wanted to know her business) but rather by saying she needed to put away the groceries she'd already finished putting away. Goodbye, I don't want the fish to spoil, yes I know how to cook it, yes it was on sale, no that doesn't mean it's about to go bad.

Eventually she went to the door and rang the bell. "Oh, gotta go. Someone's at the door."

Mom: "Someone you know?"

Katie, staring into the foyer mirror: "Pretty well."

Finally unleashed from the phone, Katie checked on Daniel. He was playing with his wooden train set, clicking the cars together with their magnetic attachments, sending them around a course she'd worked hard to make reversible. So often you'd get the railroad tracks hooked up only to realize that once the train got off the main track, it could never get back again. Daniel didn't care. But a train ought to be able to go back to where it came from, darn it. A mistake shouldn't leave you locked into one little circle forever.

Daniel was quiet, so Katie looked again at today's ultrasound photos, the spot she'd learned to recognize as the beating heart, the curve of the skull, the string of pearls for the spine. Everything good. Everything on track.

She put them into the front of the album she hadn't fully assembled yet, a baby book of sorts, just blank pages for now but ready to be filled with all sorts of things—her conception chart, her pregnancy test, the receipt for the copay at her first prenatal appointment, the ultrasound photos from five weeks, nine weeks, twelve weeks, and now sixteen weeks—finally past the time she'd consider the danger zone for early miscarriage. For the next five weeks the danger was late miscarriage, and then it became preterm delivery.

She closed the cover, then hesitated. But Daniel was still pushing trains on overpasses, so she picked up the other album, the one with little blue letters that said Kieran.

Kieran, her autumn baby.

She flipped through the few dozen photos. So few, so few. A photo of him alone in the hospital bassinette, black and white because the color photos looked so—well, harsh. Photos of him wrapped in the pink and blue hospital blanket with a stuffed bunny at his side. A photo of his face, of his little hand, his tiny feet. Why didn't she have more photos of her holding him? Kissing him? Why hadn't the hospital turned up the lights? And then the photos of the funeral, a casket barely larger than a loaf of bread, and Daniel wearing sneakers with his suit because no one thought to buy him dress shoes while she was still in the hospital. There was a photo of Katie and Mike at the gravesite, and Katie knew she'd been leaking all over that day: her milk had come in the morning of the funeral as she'd tried to fit a postpartum body into her only black dress, and she'd still been bleeding, still crying. It wasn't fair.

And the last photo in the book, Kieran's gravestone with a tiny Christmas tree. They'd gotten the stone in just before Christmas. Not fair at all.

She looked down to find Daniel at her thigh, looking up. "What, sweetie?"

He seemed worried. She said, "Do you want to go outside?"

It was chilly, but not especially. Katie bundled up, and out they went. He got onto his swing set and she pushed him, gentle and smooth strokes that set him moving like a pendulum. *Higher, higher, faster, faster*, he'd say, and she'd say, "Do you want to break the clouds? No stinky feet on the clouds!" and he'd laugh, and it was good.

He got off the swing and ran to the back fence. Katie called, "Stay away from the branch!"

A tree limb had come down during the blizzard in January, and Mike had said he'd take care of it once it wasn't frozen to the ground. But then he'd never had time, and when Katie thought about it, she really didn't want him using a chain saw, so she didn't push the matter.

Daniel ran straight for the branch, and Katie shouted, thinking of branches poking out his eyes, or the jagged edges of wood, or if there were beehives in the dead limb. She marched over to the branch. It wasn't that big after all, so she hefted the broken end that lay near the tree. It strained her abdomen, but she lifted anyhow. When she gave a tug, it moved.

Good. No chain-saw, and no poked-out eyes. She dragged, and the tree limb followed.

Daniel laughed out loud, a big belly laugh that made Katie giggle too. "Is the tree following Mommy?" And then Daniel laughed even louder.

The branch fit beneath the deck. Daniel never went under the deck anyhow, and she could forget all about it.

"Come on!" She patted Daniel on the head. "I'll push you again."

This time Daniel climbed onto the plastic horse suspended by chains. "It never goes anywhere," he said.

Katie chuckled. "No. But you have fun doing it."

Amber marched into work the next morning and tried not to look Scott in the eyes. It should have been easy: he was tossing a ball over the desk to the police dog. Officer Cookie, who only played when he wasn't wearing his police vest, was making the most of the game.

"Well?" Scott called as she walked past. His voice was loud enough that the dog and the K-9 handler both turned to see who'd gotten that tone. "Brickman? Answers?"

She turned in place and took three strides back to the desk. She reached into her back pocket and handed him a gift card to the Olive Garden.

He didn't take it. "What the hell is that?"

"Dinner." She offered a confused look, hopefully more convincing than the look at least one arsonist had tried on her. "You said I owed you dinner."

His expression was well worth the $25. "Are you kidding me?"

"You said dinner." Amber pushed the card toward him, and he retreated like a vampire before a full-spectrum bulb. "This should cover a dinner, and I know you love Italian."

The K-9 handler had slipped away with Cookie. Amber should have thrown the gift card because at least then the dog would have caught it.

Scott folded his arms and leaned forward. "Brickman—"

For a moment, Amber flushed. He flailed for a way to tell her she was an idiot, and that was ideal because if she was an idiot, he'd leave her alone. Judicious stupidity was a lovely thing. She could be just a shade too dumb to hold his interest. But during her momentary revelry, he caught his breath—darn it, she'd let it show. He said, "Dinner, Brickman, that involves *you*."

"Involves me?" At least she'd nailed the mystified note she wanted. "I had no idea."

Turning aside, he waved away her and her gift card. "You'll have to try harder than that."

Amber shoved the card into her pocket. "Fine."

"It's a huge ego boost the way you fling yourself at me." Scott turned back. "So, our mysterious Katherine? Is she, or isn't she?"

"She *is*," Amber said. "Who she is, I still don't know. But next up, we're going to cyberstalk her and piece together anything else that might be out there."

Scott said, "Let me know if you need any more help."

Amber said, "If I do that, you're going to want lunch too."

Scott said, "Or breakfast."

"Don't push it."

At the office, Amber consoled herself that at least she'd beaten the Old Man and could make the coffee herself. As it brewed, she retrieved her voice mail. A call from Felicia Hernandez, who still wanted her head in a bag. A call from Harrington, salivating for her report on the Hernandez kid. And finally the Old Man had left two messages even though in the next ten minutes he was going to be sitting like a toad at his desk, reading a report. It would have totally killed him to tell her in person. Whatever.

The pot finished brewing, and Amber waited for the parade of firefighters and police officers who came in to ask her or the Old Man a question as a coffee-excuse, usually something inane but businessey, and yes, Scott came through too. Then after Amber heard every bit of firehouse news for the morning, she made sure to get to the pot in time to brew more.

She looked over the calendar. The Old Man had inspections today, scheduled all over the county. Good.

At ten, he left. Amber picked up the phone and called Nikki.

"Great timing!" Nikki sounded chipper. "I'm seeing your mom in two hours."

"We found her. That woman."

Nikki squealed so loudly Amber dropped the phone. When she got it back again, Nikki was saying "—have to tell me how you did it!"

"Scott Stadler called the news station."

"Oh my goodness, he's so hot. Don't tell Dennis, but he totally is. Dennis wants to set him up with you."

"Dennis needs a hobby that doesn't involve me." Amber tapped her pencil on the desk. "Her name is Katherine Woodson."

"Did you spend all night Googling her?"

"I found a few things. She teaches the sciences at a private high school, or she did. I found an address. She went to University of Connecticut in Storrs."

"Really? Who do I know who went there...? Oh! Kelly Carroll."

Amber rolled her eyes. "The cheeriest cheerleader of them all!"

"Do you have a graduation date? Because she totally didn't mention meeting your evil twin at our five-year reunion."

"Doesn't surprise me. She probably mentioned herself at the five-year reunion."

"What about her birthdate?"

"Nothing."

"Facebook page?"

Amber huffed. "If the one I found is her, I can't tell. It's locked down tighter than Fort Knox."

"Try friending her," Nikki said.

"Am I on Facebook?"

"You should be." Nikki paused. "Okay, so here's the plan. You get on Facebook, go out with Scott, and I'll see your Mom at noon."

"Sounds like a plan," Amber said, "except for the Facebook thing and the Scott thing." She sighed. "Thank you. For talking sense to me."

"You're the sensible one." Nikki chuckled. "It's just that sometimes you need someone's permission to go ahead with the nonsense."

Eleven

Nikki opened her front door about five seconds after Maureen knocked. Maureen gushed, "There's my thirty-six weeker!" Nikki grinned, and she added, "You're in the homestretch now. One more week until you're cleared to birth at home."

"I'd better stand on my head until then." Nikki brought her inside, showing just the beginnings of a pregnant waddle. Maureen smothered her smile—this was a real change from the tomboy eight-year-old who dragged Amber out onto the soccer field during third grade, but it was a good sign: her joints were relaxing in preparation for birth. Nikki didn't show any pain as she moved, another good sign, and she didn't drop the last four inches when she sat on her couch.

Maureen settled on the opposite side of the couch. She remembered Nikki as practically a baby, and now Nikki was going to have a baby of her own. "How's the little one moving?"

Nikki described a typical pattern of kicks and stretches. "I think I felt a somersault the other night." She laughed. "And now I'm getting big kicks up here." She rubbed the spot just under her ribcage on the right side. "Maybe there's a foot-rest on my ribs."

"I bet the baby's gone head-down. Let's see."

Nikki lay on her couch, and when she raised her shirt, Maureen pressed her hands on Nikki's abdomen. "I'm sorry if my hands are cold."

"They're fine."

Nikki was wearing those under-the-belly maternity pants that made no sense whatsoever. Maureen had delivered in the era of over-the-belly pants paired with underwear that functioned postpartum as a tent. Maternity clothes were so cute nowadays, although everyone told her they were flimsier. One mom of four, showing already at her first prenatal, had griped, "They don't even last five months."

Nikki said, "Do you like my racing stripes?"

"Your stretch marks aren't too bad. You have nice elastic skin." Maureen concentrated on her hands as she mapped the baby's position: the head, a shoulder. "I've seen some beautiful stretch marks. At her postpartum appointment, one mom had a silver star on her stomach."

"Cool," Nikki whispered.

Maureen finished palpating the baby's position and gelled up the doppler. "You ready?"

She positioned the wand over where she'd located the baby's chest, then turned it on, and immediately the baby kicked. Maureen laughed as the room filled with a regular, *Whoo, whoo, whoo…* "He didn't like that, did he?"

Nikki laughed. "Best sound in the world!"

Maureen got the number for the heart rate, then turned it off. Next she measured the fundal height with a tape measure ("Thirty-six. Excellent.") She got Nikki's blood pressure, then had her check her urine for protein. "I'm afraid you're perfect. You don't need me at all."

Nikki laughed. That was a good sound—the sound of a woman who thought of pregnancy as normal and something you live rather than a medical crisis to fear. You watch, you monitor, but when it goes right, you encourage it to keep going right. And when it starts to go wrong—then you bring your medical interventions to bear.

Maureen sat back. "Show me where you want to have the baby, and we'll evaluate what needs to be prepared."

They had two weeks to get the home ready for the birth. It was always better to assume the baby would arrive at thirty-eight weeks than plan on setting up at forty and not be ready.

Nikki showed Maureen her bedroom, the master bath with a shower, the regular bathroom with a tub. Maureen asked about the garage, and Nikki showed her. It was on the same level, so it would be easy to get a stretcher in if she needed transport to the hospital. There was cream-colored carpet in the living room, so Nikki was sure to deliver there, not on the brown bedroom carpet or the hardwood floors. Babies loved late nights and white carpet, but cream would do in a pinch.

Sure enough, Nikki showed her the box for a portable labor tub. Where would it be set up? In the living room.

"Do you use the fireplace?" Maureen asked, and when Nikki said yes, occasionally, she asked about getting it cleaned. Yes, Amber had insisted. Maureen asked about pets.

"None," Nikki said. "Although Amber has that cat now."

Maureen paused. "What cat?"

"Marcus's cat."

"Marcus's mother took him."

"Well, she gave it back out of the blue." Nikki shrugged. "She probably forgot to tell you after that whole thing with Katherine."

"Maybe." Maureen needed to go over the birth supplies handout, but Marcus? Why was Marcus popping back into Amber's life at the same time as a mysterious twin? Poor kid. It was no wonder she was so stressed. All those ghosts in the corners.

She and Nikki went over the birth supply list, Maureen stressing the bottle of hydrogen peroxide. "Full," she said. "New."

Nikki said, "To keep things sterilized?"

"To get blood out of a carpet." Nikki laughed. Maureen pointed. "And a shower curtain. Really."

"I think I can get one for two bucks. And a bottle of olive oil? What's that for?"

Maureen told her. Nikki's eyes widened. "Oh-kay."

They went over the other prep, all of it a bit more complicated than packing a bag for a hospital birth, but in other ways so much less complex. To be in your own home, with your own food, your own germs, it meant freedom. If you wanted to watch your favorite movie, you didn't need to have thought of it before, and if suddenly in labor the only thing you could think of was having someone read you *Watership Down*, it was right there. Well, right there in a box of books in the basement. But still: there. And you didn't have to worry about the woman in the next room overhearing it.

Maureen finished up the list. "And now you can go shopping. Any questions?"

Instead of saying, "Why two shower curtains?" Nikki said, "Katherine—is she legit?"

Maureen shivered. "We don't know."

"That's Amber talking, and I love her, but we both know she doesn't have an imaginative bone in her body."

Oh, but she used to. She used to live in those books about ancient civilizations, and so many times she'd shown Maureen a picture of some fossil and said, "They said this is a cooking tool, but this would be perfect for making cloth." Then she'd give this amazing explanation that left Maureen feeling like a Paleolithic mother, needing to skin rabbits and spin fiber, awed by the worlds her daughter could see.

Nikki said, "All I'm saying is, I thought nothing scared her. She runs into half-burnt buildings before they're cold and starts to dig." Nikki frowned. "But Katherine scares the daylights out of her."

Nikki was...fishing for information? Fishing for information about *Amber* from *Amber's own mother?* That took guts. "I'm not sure what you want me to say."

Nikki said, "Well..."

"Because you know as well as I do where she's coming from, and if you don't, I'm still not wanting to break my daughter's confidence."

Nikki brightened. "So she's talking to you about it?"

Maureen hefted her bag, yanked on the zipper, and started shoving equipment back in. "As a mother, I know my daughter. And I would suggest you back off."

Nikki stayed silent while Maureen kept packing.

"I'm sorry," she finally said.

But Maureen didn't answer, the anger still thrumming like a violent thing ready to claw its way out rather than be birthed in calm and order. She shouldn't get angry at a client—it wasn't professional—but Nikki was more than a client. She was a friend much closer to her daughter than even Olivia.

Although if Nikki was digging for information, that meant Amber wasn't confiding in her either.

Nikki finally said, "Look, she should be curious. I've never known her not to want to solve a mystery, but this she didn't even want to touch. She's scaring me. I don't know what to do for her."

Maureen said, "You be supportive. You support her choices, even if you disagree with them."

"Even if she's being stubborn?"

"Especially then." Maureen sighed. "She needs reasons."

"But you think Katherine is the real deal?" Nikki pursed her lips. "Legit?"

The little boy at the opening of the video—he looked so much like Brendan at that age. But the woman's unfamiliar mannerisms, the sheer chance of finding one another this way... How could she say yes?

Maureen said, "We still don't know."

Staring down, Nikki bit her lip. "I may be able to help you out a bit. I'm going to make a few phone calls."

———◦———

Katie hadn't gotten all the way in the door before Mom was taking her bag out of her arms. "Don't carry that! You'll hurt yourself!"

Katie let her do it, but muttered, "I carry Daniel. He's thirty pounds."

"You shouldn't!" Mom's voice ticked up. "Don't the doctors tell you not to lift?"

Katie said, "Did the doctors tell you not to lift anything when you were pregnant with me?"

Mom said, "That's not the point. *You* can't take any chances this time."

Katie bristled. *So you're saying it's my fault? You think Kieran died because I carried the diaper bag?*

No, no, breathe. Mom would start pouting. *Oh, baby, I'd never think that, but you don't know what did it, so you can't chance anything, and blah blah blah.* Then she'd call Dad, and Dad would say, *You're too sensitive, Katie! Why are you always worrying your mother? Just leave the bag in the car if it makes her feel better.*

Instead Katie said, "The ultrasound photos are in the side pocket if you want to get them out."

Mom rooted through the diaper bag. "Is Daniel eating these fruit snack things? You said they weren't good for his teeth."

Katie grinned. "They're neither fruit nor snack."

Mom looked at her blankly.

Katie shrugged. "He likes them, so I got him a box." Three boxes, actually, all fruit gummies in the shape of cars. Hey, Mom, I'm munching a Corvette!

Mom said, "Oh, okay. I thought you were doing that healthy stuff."

"I do, but you know, I was sick for so long. That was the time for convenience food."

Mom said, "Are you still that sick? Vomiting? Every day?"

Katie reached past Mom's hand and pulled out the ultrasound photos. "Here we go! That's the cause of all the trouble!"

Mom asked about all the light and dark spots in the grainy photo: *What's that? Why didn't the doctor order a 3-D ultrasound?*

After the tour of the photos, Mom brought her a cup of the weakest decaf tea she'd ever seen (because decaf coffee had chemicals, and decaf tea might too, and herbs could be bad for you) and offered her shortbread cookies (normal Lorna Doones, thank goodness). Daniel grabbed one before going back to the TV.

Katie said, "The morning sickness is better now, but I don't want risk my stomach getting empty."

Mom pushed the cookies toward her. "Have some more."

Katie took another. "One of the woman on my forum gets sick the whole nine months. It's not quite bad enough to treat her for, but she's miserable. Can you imagine?"

Mom said, "Has she tried saltines and ginger ale?"

Cutting edge wisdom from the 1920s. "Does that ever work?"

Mom said, "That's what I always gave you when you got sick."

"But when you were morning sick?" Katie waited a beat. "See? It might work if you get a stomach virus, but not if it's because your hormones are all out of whack."

Mom said, "Well, I wouldn't know. Your father's the doctor."

Katie leaned forward. "But you're the woman. Dad knows a lot, but it's all from books."

Mom said, "Oh, and your father was telling me about a new kind of weight-loss surgery."

Katie nodded. "Is he going to start doing it?"

"He's taking a seminar on it. He might or might not, depending."

"Like if it's safe."

Mom nodded. "Or if the malpractice insurers won't cover it, or if the hospital won't allow it—although they're talking about this being an out-patient procedure."

"What?" Katie's jaw dropped. Well, she hadn't been sick until this moment. "Even I know bariatric surgery is dangerous."

Mom shook her head. "Your father wouldn't do anything dangerous. That's why he's taking this seminar."

Daniel came in to grab more cookies, but Katie intercepted his hand. "Two more, and that's it."

He said, "Five more!"

Katie shook her head. "Two."

He laughed out loud. "Ten!"

Katie said, "One."

He laughed even harder. "One!" and lunged for a handful. Katie pulled away the package and handed him two. He handed one back. "One."

"Okay, one."

Daniel walked away while Katie wondered how he parsed what just happened, or if she was a bad mom, or if he felt cheated.

Mom said, "He's not going to learn to count if you keep doing that."

"He's here all day, so you know he can already count to twenty." Katie shook her head. "He's just being silly. He'll be back for the other cookie in a minute."

Mom said, "You're teaching him to be pushed around. He's going to be easy prey for scammers. What happens the first time he gets one of those Nigerian Prince emails? He'll be sending them all his money in no time."

Katie glared at the table. *Or maybe I just won't worry about that until Daniel learns to read.*

While Mom got up to make herself more tea, Katie thumbed through her email on her smartphone. "Oh," she murmured. A message from the faculty mailing list: the senior year students had been recognized with a community service award.

Mom said, "Is something wrong? Did your phone get hacked?"

"My seniors won an award!" She grinned. "That's neat. They worked really hard for this."

Mom looked around. "What did they do?"

"Remember all the flooding last year? They fund-raised to help out that halfway house up near the hospital, and then they bought supplies to rebuild the fence, resurface the yard, and landscape it."

Mom shook her head. "They shouldn't have been doing that."

Katie shrugged. "A couple of parents are gardeners or contractors, and they supervised so no one got hurt using the tools."

Mom said, "But a halfway house—someone might have taken advantage of them."

Katie opened her hands. "You'd rather the halfway house *not* have a fence?"

Mom paused, and Katie fought a smirk because that would make Mom feel bad.

Mom only bit her lip. "Well, I guess if they were supervised the whole time. I just wish you didn't still work at the school. On your feet all day."

Katie texted her husband. *Let's see: have the same argument for the thousandth time? Sure!*

Mom was saying, "Standing on your feet all the time can cause prematurity."

"Prematurity didn't kill Kieran," Katie said. "My doctor said I'm fine to work."

She glanced back at the phone. Maybe Mike would text her back with important news that would require her presence at...oh, a presidential flyover? And she'd have to take Daniel and leave Mom to fret about fruit snacks, gravity, and halfway houses.

Mike texted back, *Hang in there.*

She texted, *You're talking sense. You must be trying to scam me.*

Mom's conversation shifted to another topic, which surprisingly enough was something she should avoid because it worried her mother, and while Mom talked, another email came in, notification of a Facebook friend request. She didn't recognize the name. She'd deny it, just like she always did.

Mom was saying, "The world's just such a dangerous place. You can't be too careful."

Except for the times you could be too careful. The times your past kept you pegged in tragedy and didn't allow you to move into the future. You might as well be dead.

She looked again at the friend request. A normal-sounding name, Kelly Carroll. And now there was a message from her too. "Hi! I saw you on TV last week! I went to UConn too! I think we were in History 101 together."

Just then, Mike texted her again. *You've gotta live, Sweetheart.*

And at the same time, Mom said, "You understand, don't you?"

"Yeah." With a smirk, Katie clicked on *Accept Friend Request.* "I understand what you want."

———————◦◦———————

It was almost 5pm, and Amber wanted to scream.

First issue: she'd gotten two phone calls from local papers about the Spice Hills Apartment fire, the first totally business and the second suspiciously slanted. Really? A kid playing with matches is arson? What makes you so sure? What will this do to his future?

Amber never knew if she should say "no comment" or just tell them off. Whipping off a string of profanity struck her as bad press, especially in a place as small as Tioga County. You didn't really want the public wondering if they needed both the Old Man and the New Kid. Granted, job security wasn't her primary concern (she loved her job, and it loved her back) and she didn't mind whom she pissed off, but she didn't think *doing* the job the public paid her for ought to piss off the public. "It's a matter of public safety," she told the reporter. "I can't speak about this specific case, but teens experimenting with fire can jeopardize everyone's safety."

That quote wouldn't make it into the article, of course. Not unless the reporter was friends with the apartment complex owner. No, more likely the reporter knew the mother or one of the kid's friends, and Amber would get lambasted. But you lived with that in a small town. Your choice of paper was either the free rag that printed happy sunshine in order to sell advertisements or else the nearest big-city paper that loved sniffing for scandals and found so precious few real ones.

Second issue: Scott kept checking her out all the time. It had gotten to the point where she hesitated before using the copy machine, in case she'd pass him in the hall, and that was beyond ridiculous. She worked here. She had a right to be in this building. He was delusional if he thought he could coerce her into a date, and for a minute she wondered if she should talk to the Chief of Police about a hostile work environment.

But...he wasn't hostile. He wasn't even pushing. He'd be beyond shocked if she called it sexual harassment, because it wasn't. He just thought he was attracted to her, and he was really friendly, and...and what?

Well, he did take no for an answer. He'd backed off about dinner, after all. She'd been the idiot who kept things going by giving him the Olive Garden gift card. For all she knew, he might never have mentioned dinner again.

It wasn't a crime to be flirty. It was just...why did he want to be flirty with her?

A year ago, Amber had been new on the job and the Old Man told her to go interview someone about a fire; she hadn't thought twice when he gave her a hospital room number. The doctors had said sure, the interviewee could talk for a few minutes, and into the hospital room she'd gone with a notebook and a naiveté unparalleled in its stupidity.

She'd never considered what a burn victim looks like or sounds like or smells like—and the reality left her in no way capable of conducting an interview because she ached to pry that man out of his body and put him back in a body that was whole.

He wasn't in agony. He was actually in good spirits, although drugged. Amber apologized, saying she didn't want to disturb him, and she wrote on the form that she couldn't question him. But that image never got out of her head: skin burnt off so raw that even the air hurt. Nothing but pain medication between him and the damage, and if you took that away, what would happen?

She'd traced the cause of the fire to a wood stove, one of two in a home heated with wood. But most baffling to her had been that this man—this man who admitted the treatment hurt just as much as the burns—this man had rebuilt his home and reinstalled the same two wood stoves.

"He's nuts," Amber had declared, to which Mom only replied, "There's nothing wrong with the stoves, and new stoves are expensive."

But even so—would you trust them again? Sleep in the home with them burning in your basement and your living room?

Mom had pointed out that oil furnaces and gas furnaces also caused fires, and Amber only replied, "I'd rather freeze," because it was obvious, obvious, obvious that once a system fails with a thirty-percent-of-your-body kind of failure, you don't go back to that system.

Amber shook her head. *Quit that.*

The point right now was Scott: Scott, a very nice guy who'd had great conversations with her about whether Iron Man 4 would stink as badly as Iron Man 2 *("I can't see how.")* Someone whom she'd joked with about paperwork and questioned about crime scenes—always friendly but never someone she'd considered a friend.

So why now? Why this?

Whatever. The third irritation of the day was the distressingly small internet footprint of Katherine Woodson. Katherine turned up on the kind of websites where you couldn't help but be listed if you'd lived and breathed. Alumni donors, scores from an ages-ago swim team meet. And other than that? Nothing. No Twitter account, and only that Facebook account with no profile photo and a perpetual, "You don't have permission to view that page."

It would be so easy, so easy and so impossible, to pick up the phone. Dial the number. *Hello, I'd like to speak to Katherine Woodson, please.* But then what? *I'm not a telemarketer. You see, I saw you on the news and you look just like me, and you're driving my mother crazy because she thinks you're some lost part of her, only I don't think she has a clue what it means to lose yourself, or to lose just enough of yourself that you wish the universe had gone all the way and disappeared you completely.*

She rested her hand on her cell phone, but no more. Just the warm plastic meeting her fingertips. No. Don't.

The phone rang, and Amber laughed out loud, the first time she'd heard her own voice in an hour. "Maybe I'm my mother's daughter after all," she said, and flipped over the phone to find her sister's number on Caller ID.

"Hey, Olivia." Amber cocked the phone against her shoulder and began shuffling paper. "How's my niecelet?"

"Good, although I'm waiting for her to get bored and start shrieking." Clicking noises in the background, and then baby music played. Amber grinned. "I haven't had a chance to ask you about Katherine on that video."

"Oh. Did you get to see it?"

"Brendan did it as a private YouTube thing." She paused. "So, you think this is for real?"

Amber stopped. "I thought *you* did."

"I don't know anymore. I mean...yeah, I don't. She's— She's a lot like you, but she's not, you know? I looked at you a lot for like eighteen years, and she's not the same."

"I'm pretty sure even identical twins aren't the same." Amber went back to straightening her desk. "What's on your mind? Are you still pissed that I stopped Mom from taking you to Danbury in the dark hours?"

"Yeah, that would have been kind of weird. I just don't know."

A long silence on both sides, as if Olivia was taking care of something and just letting the silence dwell. Even the baby music had stopped. Amber returned to the file in front of her.

"Would we be Irish Triplets?" Olivia said.

"I guess so." Three babies fourteen months apart. "With two of me, Mom and Dad wouldn't have had you."

Olivia said, "That had occurred to me. Would she have gotten my name?"

"I don't know. Dad got to name you after Olivia de Havilland because Mom got to name me, right? So he'd have picked something complementary to Amber, like Audrey after Audrey Hepburn."

Olivia said, "There's a Katherine Hepburn too, you know."

Amber hesitated. "You'd better not tell Mom about that. She'll tell you about the universe's sympathetic vibrations."

"Are you kidding? I'm totally telling her about that, and then you'll be the one she's dragging to Danbury tomorrow morning at Oh-Dark-Thirty."

Olivia laughed, but Amber could only flinch.

Olivia continued, "The thing is I think one of us *should* be there tonight, just in case, you know? Because Mom's Mom, and I keep waiting for a call from Dad asking where she is because she just took off, and now that she has Katherine's address..."

"Yeah." Amber recalled parking her car across the neck of the driveway a few nights ago. "I can't take her keys."

"No, but you're like seven minutes from her. And she cooks better than you, so maybe you should go get dinner there or something, because she listens to you."

Amber said, "You're the one she adores. You made the baby and you bring her over three nights a week. It's like her dream come true."

Olivia made a snorting sound. "Whatever. Just—keep an eye on her, okay?"

"Yeah, yeah."

So when Olivia got off the phone, Amber dialed Mom's cell.

"I'm worried about you," said Mom.

"It's okay," said Amber. "I'll see you tonight, and we'll make more plans then."

twelve

Maureen wasn't sure what to expect when she got home. She'd gotten a text message from Nikki asking if she could come over, but when she arrived, it was Amber's car at the curb. They must have come together.

Two guests for dinner wasn't a big deal. She'd pad it out with an extra big salad and some rolls, a small price to pay for having both girls over. Nikki was such a good friend for Amber, and Maureen loved watching them together.

She hung up her coat and purse, then looked around for the girls. Neither Amber nor Nikki was in the living room or the kitchen. Sounds came from the laundry room, though, and it was there she found Amber lying on her stomach with the front off the dryer, armpit-deep in the bowels of the machine. The shop vac stood at her side, plugged in and ready to whirl.

"What are you doing?"

"I should ask the same of you." Amber sounded unamused. "Have you cleaned this thing since I was twelve?"

"We got it when you were eighteen," Maureen said, "so I'm going to guess no."

"I can tell. You were a month away from a major fire."

They taught that line in school nowadays. Maureen had heard it from her auto mechanic, from the boiler guy, and from an electrician. Amber couldn't see the look on her face, and it was just as well.

"Look in the trash can."

Maureen took a peek. "Wow." The whole thing was full of dryer lint. "That came out of the tube?"

"I haven't even gotten to the tube. This was clinging to the engine. You know, the thing that dries your clothes by making heat?"

Maureen said, "Well, thank you for cleaning it out."

"I had to. It would be a professional disgrace if the Fire Marshal's parents' house burned down."

Maureen stifled a laugh until she could get in the kitchen. Fortunately the sound of Amber's shop vac drowned it out.

Maureen checked on her every so often, watching the dryer go through various stages (pushed away from the wall, vent detached, vent getting cleaned out, and Amber's object lesson where she showed how the tube was a quarter its previous diameter because of all the lint.) Afterward, the tube got fitted back into the wall, the panels went back on, and Amber hauled the shop vac into the garage.

She returned, looking dusty. "Thank you," Maureen said again. "But where's Nikki?"

Amber rubbed her hands on her jeans. "Nikki's coming? First I've heard."

Maureen said, "Then why are you here?"

"Because I needed to save your life and my career. Oh, and also because you're my mother, and I thought we were solving a mystery together or something." Amber grinned. Now that the lint was gone, she was all better. At least until she got a bug to resolve some other fire hazard. "But why would Nikki come?"

"She said she would. Maybe I left something there this afternoon." Maureen tilted her head. "She has a really nice house. I'd never been there before."

"It'll be even nicer if Dennis paints it the way he's been promising since, oh, Abraham Lincoln was president."

Maureen went into the kitchen. "Well, I'll get started on dinner, and if she wants to stay, she can." She put a pot of water on the stove. "You didn't tell me you had a cat."

Amber snorted. "I *don't* have a cat. I have an animal that hides behind my refrigerator and craps on the carpet when I'm not home."

Maureen frowned. "Is it angry at you?"

"It sure seems that way, but I haven't had time to make nice with him yet. I'd like to pet him, but I can't even get near him. I only know he's there at all because the food disappears and he leaves poop all over the place."

Maureen said, "What kind of poop?"

"Mom!" Amber laughed out loud. "Seriously?"

"Seriously, there's nothing wrong with discussing bodily fluids. Maybe the cat's not mad. If it needs something in its diet, or if it needs something removed, you can tell by its waste."

Amber said, "Fine. It's runny."

"Try fish oil." Maureen reached into a cabinet over the stove. "Just poke a hole in the caplet and squeeze it out over the food. The cat should like that." She poured a handful of the caplets into her palm and put them in a plastic bag. "See if that helps."

She looked up to find Amber blank-faced. "Okay." As if she didn't believe but would try—or maybe as if she believed despite herself.

The bell rang, and Amber got it. In came Nikki, pink-cheeked and chilly, eyes bright.

Amber said, "So what's up?"

"Have you got your laptop?" she said.

Maureen turned from the stove because Nikki sounded about ready to jump out of her skin. "It's on the desk."

"Cool! Start it up." Nikki hadn't even removed her coat, but she pulled out her cell phone and called someone while Amber got the computer started. Then, after some preliminary greetings, she held the phone toward Amber.

Amber gave a puzzled shake of her head.

"It's Kelly Carroll."

Amber's eyes flared. "You didn't!"

Maureen had no idea what was going on. Nikki, so thrilled. Amber, refusing to take the phone. Nikki said to the person on the other end, "Hang on. I'll give you her mom instead."

Maureen took the phone, warm against her fingers. "Hello?"

The person on the other end sounded thrilled just to be alive. "Hi! Is this Amber's mom? This is *so* exciting about a twin! I think it's great!"

Maureen looked at Amber, who'd folded her arms and fixed a furious glare on Nikki.

"It turns out Katherine Woodson and I went to the same college!" The voice sounded even more elated, if that were at all possible. "So of course I wanted to help! I felt so *bad* when I heard about Marcus and all, and I know Amber didn't even go to our reunion, but maybe this is even better! So I sent Katherine a Facebook request and she accepted! You can go look at her profile!"

Maureen said, "I can?"

"Totally! You're going to login as me, and then you can see everything! Her wall, her pictures, her friends—that's like everything."

Maureen's voice broke. "Thank you."

"Nikki knows my login name, and my password is tea for two. But like with the letter T and 2 just regular, and *for* spelled out. I know you won't mess with my account or anything."

Nikki had the laptop open and mouthed at her, Type it in.

She typed Tfor2 and hit enter. Kelly talked her through the next couple of steps, and suddenly she was on Katherine's personal page. Photos. Statuses. Everything.

"Thank you." Maureen's voice came quiet. Reverenced. Those pictures. Dear heaven, there were pictures.

She handed the phone back to Nikki, who signed off. As soon as she did—

"How could you?" Amber exclaimed.

Maureen stepped back even as Amber got right into Nikki's face. "How could you do that to me?"

"But—"

"This is a tiny town! Everyone's already up in everyone else's business!"

Nikki looked scared. "Kelly doesn't even live here anymore! She lives in Horseheads!"

Amber's voice rose. "And that matters? Her mother's here—her friends are here! She's probably already on the phone! Everyone's going to know!"

Maureen's jaw locked, and she turned her gaze on Nikki.

"But—" Nikki's eyes watered. "We've got information now."

"It's not *we*. It's not *your* problem to solve." Amber grabbed her coat and keys off the couch. "I can't believe you did that. You had no right."

She stalked out the front door, slamming it at her back. Maureen darted out after.

Halfway down the drive, Maureen called, "Amber?"

Amber got into her car and started the engine. Maureen didn't pursue.

At the front door, Nikki stood, face blank and tears on her cheeks. "I didn't... I thought it would be okay."

Maureen couldn't speak. If she started to speak, she'd start yelling, so instead she walked to the stove and snapped off the gas. She glanced at the computer. Katherine's profile, purchased at too high a price.

She turned to Nikki, ghost-white in the entryway. "I think you'd better leave."

There. That emerged without anger. It emerged without anything.

Nikki said, "I'm sorry."

"I understand." Maureen wasn't sure how long she'd be able to keep from saying the things she wanted to. Amber didn't give free passes to betray her a dozen times. But to start saying that was never to stop, so she just repeated, "I think you'd better leave."

Nikki left.

Maureen stood at the stove battling tears, but she tracked the motions, the sounds. A door thumping shut, an engine starting, headlights reverse-dancing across the ceiling.

The bubbles slowed in the pot. She returned to her computer.

Katherine. Katherine, and everything she'd ever told the world.

———◦———

Amber slammed the apartment door loud enough that Mr. B would still be complaining about it three rent-checks from now. The lights went on, and there in the kitchen were two gifts from the incontinent cat. "Stupid animal," she snapped. "What good are you?"

In the middle of cleaning, the phone rang. Mom. Amber took the call. "What?"

"I sent Nikki home. She may call you soon."

"She's already called. I'm not interested." Her tone iced over. "And if you put her up to that—"

"I put her up to nothing. I don't even know how Facebook works." Well, that was true enough. "Don't be hard on her. She wanted to help."

Amber huffed.

Mom said, "Do you want me to tell you what's on the Facebook page?"

"Isn't that being an accessory to treason or something?" Amber pursed her lips. "Katherine gave Kelly permission to see her stuff, not us. And since she locked it down, I figure she meant it."

"It's not that personal," Mom said. "Nothing I'd consider private or sensitive."

Amber deposited the paper towels in the trash. She washed her hands. And when she felt like she had a grip: "Go ahead."

Mom started at the top, not reading as much as summarizing. "She likes her students," she said. "Dinner. She's tired. Doctor appointment—I wonder if she's pregnant."

"And you'll drive to Danbury to deliver the baby in her outdoor hot tub?"

Mom laughed out loud. Amber laughed too because if *she* could make Mom laugh, it wasn't that bad, and they'd get through it. Whoever this woman turned out to be, they'd get through it.

Mom kept scrolling through, giving tidbits, the minutiae of anyone's day according to Facebook. "She doesn't really post pictures," Mom said. "I thought that's why people use Facebook. To see faces."

"Like I'd know."

Mom chuckled. "She likes chocolate."

"I'll alert the media."

And then...silence. A silence that persisted so long Amber finally said, "Are you still there?"

"Yeah. I..." Mom sounded small. "Her baby died."

For a moment Amber heard nothing at all, and she felt herself suspended in place, the world far away and the sound muted, the light dim, and when she finally began to think again, she noticed movement in the corner. A cat's tail vanished behind her couch.

"Say that again?" she whispered.

"I still don't know," Mom said. "She made an anniversary post. I'm looking, looking, okay, here. A boy. Last October or November, I guess. The anniversary post is from December."

Amber's voice was raspy. "How did he die?"

"I haven't found it yet."

Silence. More silence. Then finally, "Stillbirth at thirty-eight weeks."

"Damn it." Amber's pulse pounded in her throat. Beating there, life so fragile. "Damn it, that wasn't supposed to happen to her."

Mom said, "It's not supposed to happen to anyone."

"It wasn't supposed to happen to *her*!" Amber closed her eyes to get the world on a stable axis. "*She* was supposed to have the perfect life. *She* got raised in Greenwich and went to the theater and got married. She was supposed to have everything."

Mom said, "Everyone has tragedy."

"You think I don't know that? I walk through smoldering houses for a living." Amber blinked her eyes tighter, but no matter what, Mom would hear the tears anyway, even if she shut up right now and said nothing else. Mom would know she was crying, and Mom would know why, and Mom would maybe say just the right thing that would hurt like hell going in but maybe she'd have a point.

Mom only said, "His name was Kieran."

Amber managed to get to the kitchen table and put her head in her hands. "What the hell kind of name is Kieran?"

"It's maybe a name you choose when the baby you just gave birth to isn't breathing, and the name you intended doesn't seem right anymore." Mom sighed. "Or it's Irish. Take your pick."

Amber tried to breathe out the tightness in her throat. "I thought the luck of the Irish was a good thing."

"They never specified. It could be either." Silence. Mom must be clicking backward through the Facebook timeline. "There isn't a name before he died, so who knows when they picked it."

But Amber didn't answer, because Amber didn't care about the name, and she waited while she thought about what it meant to give birth to a dead baby and all the rotten-awful stuff you had to go through, and how it was all over before it even began, but everyone would know. That huge baby belly, gone but no baby. Thank heaven she'd never had an engagement ring, she realized with shock. Because someday, she'd have had to take it off.

Everybody knew anyway. But they couldn't see.

She glanced outside. It was late to run. But she'd run later than this.

Mom said, "Are you okay, honey?"

"I'm okay." Mom had known she was crying after all. "My head is reeling."

"Don't go out for a run. Go to bed."

Amber chuckled.

"Promise me."

"I won't sleep."

"Take a half glass of wine and a hot shower. Get yourself together." Mom sounded bolder. "Tomorrow night, let's give her a call."

THIRTEEN

The next morning, Amber used the back door to reach her office, then set up everything she needed so she could get it out front in one armload. With any luck, Scott would be on the phone.

As she headed to the lobby, one of the rookies stopped her. "I need some help." Her name was Rochelle. "Um, with Scott."

Amber frowned. "Can it wait?"

"No, it's a good time. You know those nameplates they put in the front desk?"

Amber nodded.

Rochelle held up eight plastic placards. "Did you know you could just order them?"

Amber choked on a laugh. "What?"

Rochelle flipped through them. *Captain James T. Kirk. Sergeant Smartmouth.*

"This is awesome," Amber said. "You need me to distract him?"

"I need someone not in his chain of command to slip one in the holder."

"Ah." Amber held out a hand. "I'm on the job."

Rochelle handed her *Grand High Poobah,* and Amber headed out.

Scott had someone at his desk, ranting about an RV parked on the street in a dangerous and there-oughta-be-a-law way that required immediate police intervention. Amber entered the desk area and set down a crock pot, plugged it into the power strip, then left a loaf of Italian bread and a bag of salad alongside. Finally, she reached around the front of the desk and effected a name change. Perfect.

Scott turned. "What are you doing?"

She slipped his nameplate into her back pocket. "I owe you dinner, remember?" She gestured to the crock pot, white with tasteful blue flowers, a blue crock, and a glass lid so you could see the delicious interior. "And we've already established you love Italian."

RV Guy stared openly. "You make dinner at the station?"

Scott looked at the spread. "What is this?"

"Crock pot lasagna. On the low setting it'll take about six hours to cook. Don't open the lid until then." She smiled. "That should fulfill your requirements. You specified it had to involve me."

Dennis came out of the locker room, and Amber decided to bolt. "Well, enjoy."

"Hang on." Scott turned his back on RV Guy and moved toward her, even as Dennis came from the other direction.

Dennis said, "Hey, I need to talk to you."

"Take a number," said Scott.

Dennis halted. "Yessir."

Scott took a deep breath. "You," he said to the RV guy, "fill out the form and I'll be with you in two minutes." He turned to Dennis. "What do you want her for?"

"Nikki has sent..." He looked at his phone. "...ten texts telling me she's ruined everything and Amber will never forgive her. I was wondering," he said to Amber, "if maybe you'd reconsider the eternal hatred thing, because she's really upset."

Scott said, "Ten?"

"Well, ten spontaneous texts. There's a lot more if you count the conversations." Dennis quirked an eyebrow at Amber. "She gets that she overstepped her boundaries. But I told her I'd talk to you."

"Awesome." Amber folded her arms. "Consider your mission fulfilled. You've spoken to me."

Scott said, "You're really into minimalism, aren't you?" He pointed to the crock pot. "That's dinner?"

"It's a dinner that involves me, and it'll probably be like two or three dinners."

Dennis's eyes lit up. "Is that a crock pot lasagna? Any for me?"

"Sure," Scott said. "But it doesn't count."

Amber smirked. "I need to see the letter of the law on this one."

Scott grabbed a clipboard and a sheet of blank paper, and on it he wrote, "I, Amber Brickman, do solemnly promise to go out to dinner with Scott Stadler in exchange for his heroic work in tracking down my potential sibling."

Amber said, "You don't have my signature."

Scott signed her name to it.

"That's beautiful," she said, looking at it upside-down with the clipboard between them, "but it'll never hold up in court."

"You'll need the police to investigate the forgery charges." Scott held it at arm's length. "It looks real to me."

Dennis said, "You brought Italian bread, too!"

"It's got six hours to cook," Amber said. "Go home to your wife and tell her to quit self-flagellating. It's bad for the baby."

He nodded. "Should she call you?"

"I'm still pissed, so no."

"Fair enough." Dennis tore off the end of the Italian bread. "Thanks for breakfast," he called as he left.

Scott rolled his eyes. "Come on. Place and time. Name it."

Amber looked around for a rescuer, but the only other person was RV Guy, who said, "Pitchfork and Knife. They got decent steak."

Oh, good grief. Why hadn't that place burnt down instead of DelGaudio's? "Wild horses couldn't drive me there."

The man said, "Szechuan Garden in Waverly has a buffet."

"Done," said Scott. "When?"

Amber looked at the floor. "Scott, I—" She shook her head. "I don't know."

"Probably not tonight," he said. "I have this lovely lasagna and three-quarters of a loaf of bread."

Amber said, "And you'll want to check how badly the papers skewered me before you're seen with me in public. I rob children of their futures."

"Bummer." Scott went back to his desk. "Dinner tomorrow, then."

RV Guy looked up at Scott. "You're the Grand High Poobah?"

Before Scott got a chance to see his name plate, Amber slipped out of the lobby. And the whole way back down the hall, she tried not to think. Yeah, that had been a colossal failure.

Atop her desk, reports lurked with the patience of a torturer at His Majesty's dungeon (take your time—I'll wait) while skulking behind it were two firefighters.

"Did you make me coffee?" she said, her voice a little too tight. They both shook their heads. "Then get out. I'll get to it when I get to it."

The Old Man came into the office at her back, and at that point, she wasn't getting to it anymore. He went straight for the pot and filled it, dumped "one wrist-twist" of coffee straight from the can, and proceeded to turn water into oil. Alchemy at its very best. Worst.

Whatever. The Old Man looked a little too pleased with himself.

In her inbox, Amber found information to thoroughly disappoint some unfinished paperwork plus the contact information for higher-up dudes at a dishwasher manufacturer. No, you do not screw with the Fire Marshal's office. The State of New York would follow up for her if she got blown off, but yes, this safety concern would get investigated.

Half an hour later, when she had a lack-of-caffeine headache because no one would touch the midnight-black stuff in the pot, she looked up from her nearly-ready report to discover the Old Man had taken off. The calendar said something about conducting safety inspections at a meat-packing plant. Better him than her.

She glanced at her paperwork knowing the Old Man was probably thinking the same. He'd better not retire.

Coffee would be welcome. There was no reason to leave that undrinkable sludge on the burner until it left a black crust for the cleaning staff to scrape out, one grain at a time. But she hesitated, then opened her web browser.

Doctor Anton Vilkas, Obstetrician. He turned up right away, practicing in Cortland although no longer with the multi-doctor women's clinic her mother called Cattle Car Obstetrics. This practice had two doctors. It also had a pleasant website in relaxing colors with comforting text about being there for you during this exciting time to bring to bear all the most modern science that medicine had to offer—but with a human touch! Prenatal testing to offer peace of mind and all the drugs you'd want to deliver easily, painlessly and safely.

On the "Meet Our Staff" page, Amber got her first look at Dr. Vilkas. He was younger than she expected, and good-looking. About the same age as her dad, although who knew how dated the photo was. Glasses, a trim haircut, a lab coat over a button-down shirt and tie, hands hooked into his pockets to relax his shoulders and make his neck seem longer.

As for his bio, he gave it as a list. College here, medical school there, residency there, and then "Over twenty-five years of experience in the Southern Tier," but not listing the clinic where she'd been born. His first private practice opened about six months after Amber's birth, and although he'd changed locations a few times, he'd been in private practice ever since.

Amber peered into his eyes as if a building had burnt to the ground and he were a prime suspect.

Scott would have been able to analyze his face and say, "Dude's guilty as Hell" or say "This guy never even takes the little pencil home from mini-golf." If Mom were right, this guy made money selling other people's kids. He'd made a decision that changed Katherine's life.

Or could have changed hers.

That was the thing, wasn't it? The guy could just as easily have left Katherine with Maureen and Raymond Brickman, and then Katherine would have been their Amber, and Amber would have gone to be Katherine. Maybe then Katherine wouldn't have gotten pregnant with a baby who died, and maybe then Amber would have married the man she loved instead of burying him.

Would Katherine have loved Marcus? Would Marcus have loved Katherine, as if hearts were so easily interchangeable?

You'd better not have, Amber thought at Marcus's memory.

What about the other future-that-didn't-happen, the one where Maureen and Raymond came home from the hospital holding a baby apiece, girls raised together, sharing a room, sharing secrets and chicken pox and crushes, forming up each other in the longest relationship either would ever have, from first heartbeat to final breath. If only Vilkas had said, "No, this isn't right."

She saw no guilt in the photo. But uneasy as she was looking into his eyes, she couldn't be sure what she saw. What could you really tell from a publicity headshot?

Don't think.

She lifted the phone, dialed the number. "I'd like an appointment with Doctor Vilkas," she said. "No, I'm not a patient of the practice." She hesitated. "My name is Nikki Ferrara."

***

Katie sat against the desk as the bell rang and the students settled down. "It's that special time of year," she called, and their sounds changed from socializing noises to getting-ready noises. Pens coming from bags, notebooks opening. She walked across the front, handing out a stack of papers at the head of each aisle. "In fact, my favorite time of year."

One of the kids got a look at the paper. "Science fair?"

Mr. Parker, head of the science department, joined her at the front. "Science fair! Now, if you'll look at the information packet, you'll see a bunch of suggested projects, although you're encouraged to devise your own. And of course you'll be demonstrating for all the lower classes, so you'll want to make sure to do your best."

Katie glanced at Mr. Parker: while in his sixties and a solid teacher, he was not in command of the students' attention. There were so many ways to jump in and get them excited, but instead he droned on. "This will be an interdisciplinary assignment, so it will involve math and statistics, writing for the report, and of course some area of science."

Katie still had a classroom of bored kids, their primary science question that of how little work they could get away with. Mr. Parker said, "Any questions?"

No one had any.

Katie wasn't so much older than her students that she'd forgotten the monotony of the school day and the hateful formlessness of an open-ended question. Even though she'd been accelerated one year (her father's idea, not her mother's) she'd still felt like the only kid in her class who even thought the science fair would be fun, but she'd managed it. Boy, had she.

Katie stepped in front of the class. "Of course, the science fair isn't *just* about twenty percent of your grade." (There. That got their attention.) "It's about becoming your own research lab! It's about getting knee-deep in a question and leveraging the scientific method to pull up answers you didn't think you could get."

She moved into the center row, and the faces followed her. "You can study anything. That's what makes a science fair so exciting, and that's why two of our students even went to Nationals last year. If there's something you always wondered about, something where the answers your parents gave just never seemed to line up—you question it. What happens if lightning strikes an airplane? Why do we preheat an oven?" More kids were looking up, and she pointed at them as she asked questions. "When a seed grows in soil, does it take as much weight out of the soil as it makes in leaves? Why do some fish live in fresh water and others in seawater? How much do preservatives actually preserve your food?" She opened her hands. "Then you come up with a guess at an answer. Maybe wrong and maybe right—but you have to figure out how to test that answer. You covered all this in freshman year, guys!" She laughed. "You can even work in teams, but seriously, it's got to be incrementally better if you do. If all of you collaborate, I want a working prototype of a solar-powered air car and someone piloting it across the Atlantic."

One of the kids shot up a hand. "Did you have to do one of these?"

"Of course I did." Katie grinned. "It's why I went on to teach science."

A girl in the front row said, "What did you do?"

"Two of my friends and I decided to come up with a way to recycle type three plastic. Most places won't recycle it, so we came up with a hypothesis of how you might be able to do it better, and then we asked one of my father's friends to let us use the lab in the hospital."

A boy in front said, "And they *let* you?"

"You'll be surprised what people are willing to let you do for a science fair project." That had been fun, using real equipment rather than the student-grade stuff. Her father was worried, but the girls had been so careful that the hospital said it was a pleasure to have them. "We came up with a pre-treatment for number three plastic that made it behave more like number two, and then you could recycle it using the same techniques that work on number one and number two. Do you think you guys could do that?"

Lots of heads shaking *No*. "You can!" Katie beamed. "We went to the Statewide competition and based on that, DuPont gave scholarships to all three of us, and I even interned for two summers in college."

Katie wrote out a chemical formula on the smartboard. "That's a kind of plastic. So the idea was to turn this into this..."

She bracketed the important part of the compound, then started explaining the process of breaking it down. "We wanted to mimic digestion," she said, "as if you could put all these plastics into a giant stomach and dissolve them."

That whole semester had been so fun, with college applications already completed, the project absorbing her afternoons, her father bringing her into the lab where she could show off her friends and be shown off by her father. And the day when the testing paid off and they had it down, and they could go back over the lab notes and repeat everything, and it worked again. And again.

Nothing ever came of it. The process was too expensive, and most municipalities would rather throw it out than pre-treat it at an extra cost. But still. So exciting.

When the bell rang, she looked up from the smartboard, filled with information, and the kids were still firing questions at her. Katie wondered if it were a mistake, but no, the clock said time, and the students were packing up, and she hadn't gotten to her lesson plan at all.

Mr. Parker was still standing there, arms folded. "Now that was a sight."

Katie realized she'd grown breathless. "Really?"

"I've never seen you fired up like that."

Katie put her laptop into her bag. "Well...it was an exciting project."

She turned off the lights and followed Mr. Parker down the hall to the teacher's lounge. He said, "What I don't get is why you're teaching. Why didn't you go to work for DuPont?"

Katie shrugged. "They just gave me that scholarship because it looked good for them. I guess they felt sorry for me."

Parker barked out a laugh. "No one does that!"

Katie hesitated. "Well, they knew my dad through the hospital. Maybe that was it."

"Mrs. Woodson," he said, "I assure you, the executives of the DuPont corporation are all paying tuition for their kids. They don't just write checks to colleges because they know someone who knows someone."

Katie shrugged. "Well, I went into science education rather than any of the sciences. It was—it didn't work out. It's better this way."

Better. She'd spent those two summers interning, but Dad said... she just didn't think it would work out. She hadn't made it to the national finals, after all. DuPont had wanted to get in good with the hospital, and Dad knew how hospital politics worked, and he and Mom had told her it wouldn't be good for her to go working all the time with chemicals, having to deal with the stress of traveling and getting grants. Mr. Parker was nice, but he was a different generation even than her father, and her parents knew about things like that. They wanted what was best for her, so when they guided her toward an education degree, that's what she'd done. And anyway, she liked teaching.

Parker said, "Regardless, I bet you have a lot of kids coming up with questions more interesting than what happens if you water a plant with Coca Cola."

Katie nodded. "That's what I like. They need to open up their imagination and learn just how much they can do."

Fourteen

At 4:45, Amber looked up to find Scott standing at her desk. "It's time."

"Time?" She squinted. "For what?"

"Dinner. You and me. Szechuan Garden."

"I distinctly recall a crock pot lasagna." Amber shook her head. "You, my good man, are a day early."

"Unfortunately, the entire force has been scoping out that lasagna ever since lunchtime, when it began smelling amazing." Scott looked crestfallen. "We...I mean, they, have consumed it. Besides, I know a flight risk when I see one."

"Looks like me, huh?"

"Just like."

"There's this woman in Connecticut," said Amber, and Scott laughed.

"Come on. Out. Now."

She went for her jacket, and he sat in her chair.

"What?"

Scott opened his hands. "Your purse is in here, right? You're planning to forget it, then run back to get it and flee for the hills."

She sighed as he opened the bottom drawer. No bag. "Okay, where is it? This is the only drawer big enough."

"You stink as a stalker." Amber picked up her backpack. "My wallet's in here. That way I don't have to keep track of two bags."

He poked through the drawer. "Diva?"

"Huh?" Oh. Oh no.

He leaned over. "You've got a little purple bag that says 'Diva.' You're the least Diva-like woman on Earth."

"You don't want to touch that."

Scott looked up, aghast. "It has flowers on it, too."

As he reached for it, Amber jumped forward and put her hand on his arm. "You really don't want that."

He stopped mid-reach. "Is it some kind of woman-thing that robs a guy of his manhood?"

"Like a buzz-cut to Samson."

He sat back, eyes wide. "Well I've got to hear this, then. And don't worry, I grew up with a mother and four older sisters, so I've heard it all."

Amber folded her arms. "And your dad?"

"Dad took the dog and ran as fast and as far as he could to escape the estrogen poisoning." He pointed back to the drawer. "What's in the diva bag?"

Well, at the very least, this would get her out of dinner when he fled screaming, in pursuit of his erstwhile father. "It's a menstrual cup."

He puzzled at her. "A cup?"

She nodded. Five seconds until he fled. Start the clock. "Right. For bleeding."

Instead of fleeing, he looked as if he suddenly comprehended. "Oh! You put it up there like one of those little cotton bullets. And then what?"

"You empty it out every so often." This was unexpected. "No icky garbage in the landfill. And it's latex, so no toxic shock syndrome. No chemicals."

He looked intrigued. "So you're big into saving the environment?"

She shrugged. "Not especially. I just don't want to have to depend on the store. So I have these. This is my backup, in case I get surprised."

Ah, but she'd been surprised after all because Scott was still in the chair. He said, "My Mom always hated that it was all disposable stuff. She'd have loved one of those."

"I could get her one if she still needs it," Amber said. "In fact, I'll drive over to Whole Foods in Binghamton and get one for her now."

He stood and took her arm. "Nah-uh. The roads are icy enough that we've had four accidents today alone. Dinner. Now."

So, Chinese tonight. She'd have to text Mom to let her know they'd call Katherine later than planned.

In the lot, Amber said, "We're going in my car?"

"Unless you want to go in a patrol car. I walk to work." He chuckled. "I call shotgun."

"Makes sense. You're the one with the gun license."

In the car, Scott exclaimed, "Hey, wow! It's like a reunion in here!" He started a puppet show with the empty coffee cups. "Great to see you, Uncle Dunkin! Do you remember me, your nephew Starbuck? And have you met my friend Tim Horton?"

"Are you quite through?" She waited until he buckled in before starting the engine. "Remember you're the one crashing my party. I would have cleaned out the car before tomorrow night."

"Of course you would." He smirked as she put it in gear. "I see how you keep your desk."

"Not so messy that you couldn't find a lasagna."

"Touché. It was delicious. I actually turned it to high and no one waited past lunch."

"Not my fault." Amber idled to a stop at a light. "I provided dinner. The fact that a bunch of starving law enforcement officers devoured it—"

"Starving," said Scott.

"—and you couldn't even defend your own food...what kind of sergeant are you?"

"A starving one," he said, looking cute. "I must be fed soon, or I'll perish. Fed Szechuan noodles in peanut sauce."

"You poor thing." Amber fought a grin. "Crab Rangoon won't do?"

Before Scott could respond, sirens screamed behind them.

"Oh, no." Amber pulled to the side as first one fire engine blew through the intersection, then another. She flipped on the scanner, and Scott grabbed the handset. "Stadler here. What's going on?"

Amber's heart pounded as she watched the rear view mirror for more lights. They appeared. An ambulance followed, howling past.

"Car accident and a gasoline spill on Union Street," said the dispatcher.

Scott looked at her, and she nodded. "Go," he said.

She floored it through the intersection, pulling out the emergency light and flipping on the siren. The engine shuddered up to top gear as she caught up to the ambulance.

She expected a snarky remark about whether her tires were rated for this. Instead, silence.

A few miles out of town, where trees towered with their crowns interlaced over the state route, they came on the scene. Amber slammed on the brakes and pulled over, narrowly missing the drainage ditch. She flew out the driver's side door. Scott was already out the passenger side.

She ran until she found the incident commander, showed her ID, then turned. In the ditch, one car lay on its side, the front staved in. Nearby an SUV lay on its roof, straddling the center line with its side crumpled. The whole area stank of gasoline, and the firefighters were already spreading sand on the spill.

"Hit a deer," one of the firefighters said.

"Oh." Amber sighed. It was semi-dark, with the brush growing right up to the side of the road on this stretch. It was one of those things you could never anticipate, but afterward you said "Of course." Now that she knew to look, she could make out a mound of brown hide between the vehicles. A white-tailed deer.

Based on the damage, the SUV had swerved to avoid the deer, hit it on the side, flipped over, and hit the sedan head-on before sending it into the embankment.

Amber ran back to get the camera for accident reconstruction. Scott was already on the road, directing traffic to turn around.

The ambulance crew was taking stock of who needed help. "We need another ambulance," the paramedic was saying into the radio. Meanwhile, the firefighters were taking care of the gasoline.

"Watch it!" yelled one of the firefighters, and Amber turned just in time to see the deer launch to its feet and lunge two steps before collapsing. The firefighter moved toward it, but the deer hefted itself again, hooves flailing on the slick roadway, scrambling and kicking. You couldn't get close to that. One hoof to the head and you'd die.

"It's hurt," she whispered. "You've got to do something."

The Fire Chief was standing beside her. "The internals will finish her off. Her hip's broken."

Amber gasped again as the deer flailed on the ground, nearly nailing one of the paramedics. A doe. Please God, let it be too young to have a fawn waiting in the brush for a mother who'd never return.

Scott turned from directing traffic on the far side of the deer. Amber watched him square his shoulders and approach, and she gasped because that those flying hooves could nail him.

In the distance, a siren called as a second ambulance approached.

The Fire Chief tapped her shoulder. "Don't watch."

"What?"

Scott drew his gun. The deer flailed again, Amber tensing because it looked so close to him. Then, as the deer paused, came a flash and a bang.

Amber's ears rang so much she couldn't hear. *I will not cry. I will not cry.* She rolled her eyes up the way she'd learned to do as a kid, and rolling her eyes trapped the tears and kept her from crying.

The deer didn't move. Scott stood, shoulders slumped.

Amber wanted to go to him, but she couldn't move. Her ears kept ringing, and then as the ring faded, Scott turned his back. He walked back up the road, and he seemed to Amber smaller than before.

A child wailed in the wake of the gunshot, and as the paramedics rushed to the pickup in the ditch, Amber headed to the SUV on its roof. A firefighter named Rick crouched beside it, calling to the crying kid. Amber got down beside him. The driver seemed to be a woman, held inverted by the seat belt. Motionless.

"The roof is crushed," Rick said. "We need to extract the driver."

"Hey, buddy," Amber called, "can you unbuckle?"

"Stuck!" the kid shouted. "Stuck!"

She steadied herself. "Well, here we go."

Rick said, "Really?"

"Really." She pulled off her jacket and laid it across the shattered glass at the window's edge.

The firefighter pulled his off too. "This is better protection."

Amber dragged herself through the narrow entrance into the SUV's back seat. "Hey, buddy. We're in a cave."

It was cold, but not so cold she could see her breath. The kid was crying, held upside down, and begging for his mother. Amber groped in the dark for the woman, then stripped off her gloves to feel for a pulse at the neck. Slow, but there. If she had to guess, she'd say concussion but no internals. Maybe. Dear God, please. The deployed airbag hung across the dashboard like a curtain. Amber tucked it back from the woman, the only thing she could do for someone held upside down by nothing more than a seat belt across her thighs.

"Is she alive?" called Rick.

"I've got a pulse. Respiration seems slow, but I'm not sure. She's unconscious."

How could she sound so clinical? There was a terrified kid here. A dying woman.

"Okay. Get out the kid so we can extricate her."

On her knees, Amber groped for the seat. Please, please, please let this be a one-handed release. "Here we go, Ace. I'm going to get you out. Anything hurt?"

"I want my Mommy."

"Of course, Ace." She felt along the straps and identified it as a five-point harness. She separated the chest clip. "I'm going to open this, and you're going to fall onto me. I've got you, okay? Put your arms around my neck." She was face to face with him as he cried. "Hold tight. Tighter."

She opened the lap buckle, and the child dropped onto her. She edged him around until he was sitting on her lap, but he lunged toward his mother.

"No, buddy. We've got to get you out first. Then we'll get her." Amber wrestled him to the broken window. "We're going out that way. Pretend you're in a cave."

"Mommy!"

At the window, Rick grabbed him under the shoulders and hauled him out.

"Stay in there," he called. "We need four people."

On either side of the vehicle, firefighters slid a board through the front windows, and Amber guided it under the driver's thighs so her entire weight wasn't supported by the seat belt. Behind her, the car shuddered, a teeth-clenching metal-on-metal that left her seeing stars. "I'm going to talk you through," Rick called. "Recline her seat as far as it goes."

Amber reached between the seat and door until she felt the lever, then clicked it and pushed up with her shoulder to move the seat back. The woman remained dangling.

"Get the head rest out of the way."

Amber found the catch. "Done."

Behind her, a firefighter said, "To your left," and she slid to the passenger side, then guided another C-board until it was beneath the driver.

"Make sure her airway stays clear." Rick's matter-of-fact instructions kept Amber focused. She guided the board until the woman was lying on it face-down.

Behind her, firefighters removed the hatchback door and pulled out the back seat.

"Make sure she's fully supported," Rick said. "Then unbuckle the seat belt."

Amber undid it. "I think her arm's through it."

On the other side, they sawed through the belt. "Get clear." The firefighters slid out the crosswise board, then drew the woman out the back of the ruined vehicle.

Amber sat breathing hard, for the first time registering what was left of the car: doors cut off, rear cut off, glass smashed, wheels in the air. Whoever this woman was, she must have been delighted with this car when she first got it, and now it was just the metal frame and a car seat on a bench chair by the roadside. But the kid was fine: that car seat had done its job.

She tucked her hands beneath her armpits. She hadn't noticed the cold before. Careful for the glass, she picked her way out of the wreck.

Four firefighters were loading the woman, still prone, onto a stretcher. Rick was holding the child over by the ambulance.

She shook out her jacket to free any remaining glass. If she inhaled deeply, she'd smell not only the odor of gasoline, but also gunpowder. And in the back of her mind, she imagined smelling blood.

———❖———

One hour, two tow-trucks and one pickup truck later (for the deer carcass) plus another pickup to remove the gasoline-soaked sand—at that point, Scott returned to stand beside her.

The first fire truck pulled away. Amber watched the red tail lights moving along the road.

What do you say? What makes sense? Well, nothing.

So instead, she waited for Scott to speak, and he too stayed silent until they got into her car. That's when he said, "You'll do anything to get out of dinner, won't you?"

She offered a pained laugh as she started the car. "Do you still feel like eating?"

"Not really." He reached over to the GPS and pushed the button for Go Home.

"What are you doing?"

He laughed. "You won't have to drive. It'll just go home."

"You're punchy." She shrugged. "It leads back to the station house, though."

He said, "A comment about your working hours?"

"If someone steals my car, I don't want them to find where I live. If they ever steal my mother's car, they'd push Go Home and get to her driveway and push the garage door opener." She rolled her eyes. "At least Dad let me reprogram his. His directs you to the MiniMart."

Scott hit the cancel button. "Well, bring me to the station house anyhow. I discharged my weapon, so I need to fill out the paperwork."

She recoiled. "Really?"

"Hell yeah. I'll send a copy to my dad. 'Hey, your son finally shot a deer.'"

"You ever go hunting?"

His mouth tightened. "I actually like animals. I have no problem with other people hunting, if only so the cars don't go hunting, but it's not for me." He stared out the window. "But even the seasoned hunters won't shoot a doe. It's not sporting."

Amber said, "Why not?"

Scott sounded bitter. "You'd have to ask my father."

Amber let it drop. As they hummed along the road, she watched both sides for glittery lights. Deer eyes. They wouldn't be out this late, but still. Watch for them on the road edges, and be ready.

Scott sounded exhausted. "You were great in that car. The guys were talking about it. But don't do that again."

"Someone had to get in there. The opening was small, and I have car seat training."

"I'll put that on your gravestone when a piece of metal rips you down to the bone, okay? No gear, no go. The Fire Chief's going to tell you the same thing."

Amber huffed. "I'm sorry. I'll track down the mom and apologize for getting her kid out so they could save her."

"That attitude gets rookies killed. You know what to do at an actual fire. Well, now I'm telling you what to do when there's not a fire. Don't be the second victim."

That sounded like a catchphrase. "What does that mean?"

"Google it."

And that sounded irritated. Amber bit her lip.

Scott sighed. "Okay, so this is going to get me in trouble, but I just shot a frightened animal while she looked me in the eye, so I don't care right now." He waited a moment, as if gathering himself. "Are you lesbian?"

Amber started. "What?"

"I don't care if you are, but if I'm wasting my time, let me know. I'll respect your wishes and leave you alone."

He shifted in the seat. It was too dark to see him even if she turned, but fast as her heart was pounding, she made sure not to turn anyhow. "Is that the only reason a woman would want not to date you?"

He laughed out loud. "Wow, that does sound egotistical! I guess I should say something else piggish to follow up, but I'm afraid I can't top it." His laugh was so genuine that Amber found herself smiling. "It's just that I'm usually good at reading people, and I can't figure you out."

Amber was about to say, "I'm pretty easy," but then she realized she couldn't figure herself out either, so she said, "I'm like the Rubik's Cube of women?"

She stopped at a light and looked at him. He was grinning. "That's what I mean. You're not turned off. You're relaxed. You joke around with me even if we're having a serious conversation, and believe me, despite what you may think of my ego, I do turn people off, and some women do dislike me, and I leave them in peace. Their loss."

She chuckled. "Okay, then."

He pointed to the light. "Straight ahead on green is permitted in New York State."

"Thanks, but actually, no." She flipped on her turn signal and headed up Main Street.

"Serves me right for being a smartass." He sighed. "Kidnapping?"

"Worse. Poisoning."

She pulled into McDonalds, the one and only drive-through in Patmos Springs. At the speaker, she ordered a quarter pounder value meal, then turned to Scott. He murmured, "I'll have what the lady is having."

She said, "I thought I wasn't a real lady."

"Then I'll have what the Diva is having."

She groaned as he smiled. "I'm never going to live that down."

"Ma'am?" said the drive-through speaker box.

"Make it two of those," Amber called.

"$10.48 at the second window."

Scott muttered, "Diva *and* a spendthrift."

"Speaking of," said Amber as she pulled around the building, "would you mind reaching down in the seat and groping for dimes?"

He was still laughing as she handed a twenty to the sixteen-year-old at the window. They made a great picture, reeking of smoke and unable to place an order. With her luck, the manager was calling the cops for a suspected DUI. "Two pot-heads with the munchies. Should I detain them?"

But no flashing lights appeared, and two value meals did, so Amber handed them to her passenger and drove the four blocks to the station house. She parked near the front door.

He started separating the contents of the bags, but she said, "I'll eat with you. The paperwork can wait five minutes."

"You make a man feel like a king. Here." He handed her a straw and some napkins.

The scent of the fries was alluring, but Amber forced herself to take a bite out of the burger first. Then, with the light off and the heater puffing, the fries steaming up the window and the scent of smoke in her mind, she said,

"I'm not lesbian. Four years ago, I was engaged to be married."

Scott visibly straightened. "He left you?"

"He died." Amber looked out the driver's side window at the light-polluted sky. No stars were visible. "So yeah, he left me. His roommate in Binghamton found him shot, and the cops ruled it a suicide. Which was garbage." Wow, that sounded more bitter than she intended. "He was the least suicidal person I knew. He couldn't understand depression or suicide, and... Yeah, not him."

Scott said, "Do you understand what makes someone want to commit suicide?"

"Of course I do." Amber's mouth tightened. "Just after he died, for a little while I wanted to go and be with him. I got all the way down to the Susquehanna River before I told myself no, it's not like that. He's gone forever, and there's no one to be with anymore." Her mouth twitched, and she blinked hard. Stupid tears. "But that wasn't Marcus. Life could hit Marcus like a train and he'd keep going."

Scott said, "Was his place looted?"

"No." She balled her fist in her lap. The fries smelled repulsive. "So are you going to tell me it had to be suicide? Just *the street cleaning itself*?"

"They said that to you?"

"I overheard it. They didn't spend five minutes investigating. Then his mother came and took everything, even his cat, and that was it. Dead, cremated, case closed, and..."

She couldn't go on. She closed her eyes, then rolled them back up in her head. Doing that stopped the tears. Stop them now or they'd start again and never stop.

Scott said, "They should have looked out for you."

"I wasn't law enforcement back then."

"Well, gee, here I stupidly thought law enforcement existed to protect the innocent." He huffed. Amber dug her nails into her palm. "I'm sorry they did that to you. You deserved better."

"Marcus deserved better."

Her voice broke again. She stopped.

"Marcus deserved better." His hand rested on her arm. "Four years?"

"Four years this May."

He squeezed and then let go. She put her hands over her eyes.

"I didn't know about that." His voice sounded soft.

"I figured everyone knew. Dennis knows."

"I don't pump Dennis for gossip. And three years ago, I was still in Syracuse." A long hesitation. Amber turned toward him, and he handed her his napkins. "I didn't mean to upset you."

"You didn't. It's just... It's all wrong. I should be digging for artifacts in New Mexico, that other life I never got to live. And this is a good life too, but sometimes I think it's not me, like the real me and Marcus are out in New Mexico at an archaeology dig, and he's out at night with our telescope, and I'm not really here getting kids out of car seats and ordering tests for accelerants."

Scott said, "Four years, though. That's a long time."

Her eyes narrowed. "Are you telling me to get over it?"

"I'm asking you if that's it, you put all the chips on the wheel and your number didn't come up, and you'll never play again."

"That's what marriage is." Amber rolled the tip of a napkin in her fingers. "It's going all in. You're committed."

"Would he want that for you?"

Amber muttered, "We'll never know now, will we?"

A pause, and then Scott said, "Have you heard from him? Since then?"

If Scott had asked whether she owned flying reindeer, he would have made more sense. "How? Madame Futura's psychic shop went out of business."

"You'd think she could have predicted that." Scott grinned, and Amber's heart melted. A bit. Just a bit. "No, I mean dreams, signs, things like that. Your keys moving to a candy dish on the table every night. Finding random pennies with his birth year."

Amber said, "Aren't you a police officer? Evidence, dude."

"Not everything real is evidentiary."

Amber rolled her eyes, and this time it was real. "If there are signs, his mother took those too."

"Well, keep an eye out. Maybe they're there, but you're not open to them."

"You sound like my mother."

"Your mother sounds like a genius." He gave her an innocent smile, and she smiled back. "Thanks for dinner." He started gathering his stuff. "And thanks for the explanation."

"This fulfilled the obligation?"

"Well, no." He hesitated, then took his hand off the door handle. "Where do I stand? And be honest. Is it okay to joke around with you?"

Amber said, "Yes."

"Yes, but...?" He waited, and she realized he was right. Yes, but.

That's all, though.

"Yes, but I'm a Rubik's Cube?"

He said, "I'm asking if you want me to leave you alone. I'm not going to try changing your mind if you tell me no, you're done with guys forever, and you're all out of chips and you can't even ante up. That's fine. I'll respect that. But..." He hesitated. "But I don't think you are."

Amber stared at the Subaru logo on the steering wheel.

"So, can I try to convince you I'd make a good boyfriend?"

Amber said, "You're asking permission to court me?"

"When you put it that way, I should have asked your dad."

She snorted. "He'd say yes."

"Then I'm in!" Scott sounded thrilled. "One courtship coming up. I'll see about renting a lute. And maybe a lute player, too, because my own mother wore ear plugs to my first grade recorder concert." He stepped out of the car. "Thank you, my lady. With your blessing, I must venture forth now to battle the mighty terror known as the paperwork."

Amber watched him enter the station house, wondering what had just happened and how she was going to explain this to herself.

FIFTeen

Amber let herself in to her parents' house, a little cautious as if even as an adult she'd get scolded for being late. Of course that was ridiculous. Mom looked first surprised, then pleased. "I didn't think we'd be able to do the call tonight. Did everything work out okay at the accident?"

It figured. Amber's mother was one of those people who could legitimately call the police on a regular basis regarding the whereabouts of her daughter. "A woman got injured, I don't know how bad, but her kid was fine, and another driver is getting checked out at the hospital. No fire, fortunately. Scott had to shoot a deer."

Mom's eyes widened. "Oh, the poor thing!" The deer or Scott: it could have been either. "That's so frightening. Your father drives those roads at night, and the idea terrifies me."

Amber pulled off her jacket to hang on the pegs by the door. "They're most active at dusk, actually. Coming home in the dark, he should be safe."

"I'll tell him he didn't pass a deer in the other lane at 10PM last Friday," Mom said. "Good to know."

Amber shrugged. "Maybe the deer was on California time?"

Mom chuckled as she went to the kitchen. "Well, you must be starved. I'll heat something up for you."

"Not really. I did McDonalds."

Mom gasped out loud. "McDonalds? Oh, honey!"

"They had a drive-through. Look—" She raised her voice over Mom's protest. "No, it's not organic-grass-fed-cage-free beef..." (Mom started to grin) "...flash-frozen at sea. I get that. It was cheap, and it was there, and Scott just shot a deer. I didn't think it was time to mill our own corn."

By the end of all that, Mom was laughing out loud. "Fine, fine. Once isn't going to kill you." She paused. "If once did kill you, something else was bound to get you anyway."

Mom went to the table where she had a bunch of index cards. "I've been working on what to say to Katherine."

Amber took a seat cater-corner to her mother. "You're serious? You wrote a speech?"

Mom nodded. "I wanted to make sure we got right to the point but weren't too blunt."

Good idea. How do you even introduce a subject like this? *Say, did you ever wonder if you were stolen, like a changeling baby? Hah hah, yeah. So, about that...*

But as she glanced at the cards, Amber's apprehensions melted. With a midwife's touch, Mom had refined the unthinkable into easily-digested bits of conversation, the phrases gentle, the explanations not too much at once but building into the whole.

They were even organized, the question at the top and the answer beneath. Mom, so free-form and unscripted in life, had put on each card an answer for every likely question, each the verbal equivalent of a reassuring touch.

"I arranged them in the most likely order," Mom said.

It had never occurred to Amber that Mom's formless intuition actually had a very organized format. She'd never seen it laid out like this before.

Amber blinked. "I want you delivering my babies."

"Fine with me." Mom looked startled, but she returned the serve. "I'm old-fashioned, though. Date someone first."

"Yeah, I guess you'll have to content yourself with Olivia." Amber looked over the cards again. "There's no way I can memorize all this in the next half hour."

"No, no, you read them. That way it sounds natural and you're more relaxed. By the time you reach the end of the third card, you're going to be warmed up enough that you'll go off-script regardless. The cards are just here as a crutch."

Amber looked across the table at her mom and met her eyes. This was huge. They were trying to bridge what might be a quarter-century gulf with ten index cards. It was like the outline of a jigsaw puzzle.

Mom laid a hand on hers, and Amber bit her lip. Mom's grip felt so strong. "Are you ready?"

Amber shook her head. "Not in the slightest. Am I supposed to be?"

Mom handed her the phone. "If she's your twin, you were born ready."

Ready or not, Amber tried dialing four times before she got all the digits in the correct order. And it took an act of will to push the green button to talk.

It rang three times, and then the first thing went wrong: a man answered. "Hello?"

"Hi." Amber's voice came a little too hesitant. "I'd like to speak to Katherine, please."

The man laughed out loud. "You want to try that again, honey?"

In a panic, Amber looked at her mother, who was listening on the other line with the speaker muted. Mom had gone white. "What?"

"You dialed home and asked for yourself." The man chuckled. "Is the PTA meeting that awful?"

Mom's eyes widened. Amber said, "Is this Michael?"

"What's going on?" He sounded confused.

"Um...my name is Amber Brickman." Her voice came soft now, slow. "I'm calling to speak to Katherine. And...I guess I sound like your wife?"

"Yes, exactly. Strangely enough. What do you need?"

Unreal. He still thought it was Katherine.

Amber said, "Can I have her call me back when she gets home?"

"Seriously, what's going on?" Michael sounded cautious, no longer amused. "Who are you?"

Mom handed her the first card, and Amber took a steadying breath. "I understand this is going to sound strange, but I saw Katherine" [she had to change the pronouns] "on TV, and she looked exactly like me. And I guess she sounds like me as well, as you've figured out," she added.

Mom was nodding.

Michael said, "Go on."

Mom handed her the second card.

"I agree this sounds strange. But I was separated from my twin at birth. When I saw her on TV, I hoped it might be her."

Michael said, "She wasn't adopted."

The third card. "This would not have been a legal adoption."

Michael said, "Are you serious?"

Card number four was in Mom's hands, but Amber was ahead of her. "I was born on September 29th, 1991."

"You could have found that information online," Michael said. "Do you have Skype?"

Mom used it to see Olivia and her baby. "We do," said Amber.

"I want to see you."

"Fair enough."

She gave him Mom's user name while Mom got the computer set up. Michael put down the phone to do the same, and Amber hit the mute button. "I can't use index cards on a video chat."

Mom looked unconcerned. "You'll do fine."

Amber's mouth tightened. "I'm not going to be able to sound like you."

"Don't be ridiculous," Mom said. "I know how you talk. I wrote out all those cards specifically to sound like you."

Before Amber could reply, Michael was back. "Okay, I'm trying now."

Even as Amber un-muted the phone, Mom said, "I've got him," and Amber went to stand behind her. The call connected.

Amber shifted over so both she and Mom were visible on the screen, and she waited while Michael studied her, frowning.

Mom said, "Can you hear us okay?"

"I hear you fine." His mouth twitched, and Amber sat without saying anything because the moment she saw him, she recognized the look of someone who dealt with untrustworthy people. She was being tested. What had Mom said he was? A judge? Not a cop. Maybe a lawyer. So just stay silent and let him assess, and don't act guilty.

Michael finally said, "You're a passable copy."

Amber surprised herself by smiling. "I'll take that as a compliment."

It was hard to tell what part of the screen he was studying, harder still to remember that he was looking in the eyes on the screen and that's why he appeared to be looking down rather than at her. Amber forced herself to look right into the webcam rather than the monitor. "All I saw of her was on a TV screen too," Amber said, "so we accept this is a long-shot."

"Well, you've got the same soft palate thing going on, but that can be faked as well. Your mannerisms are different," he added. "You couldn't pass for her, at least not with someone who knew her." He folded his arms and sat back, his gaze still disconcertingly low. "Do you have ID?"

Amber pulled her wallet from her back pocket and held her driver's license up to the camera, then said, "hang on," and held up her Fire Marshal ID so the shield and her photo showed.

"Fire department?"

"Fire Marshal. Assistant. I'm actually the fire inspector. The Old Man doesn't like climbing through rubble any longer, so they make me go out with the shovel and the plastic containers."

Below the desk, Mom squeezed her hand. Amber stopped talking.

Michael fell silent, studying the screen, and Amber realized he'd just switched windows to Google her. "There you are. Charged a high school kid with arson, did you?"

"That's generally what they call it when you toss a match into a can full of dryer lint." She paused. "Off the record, of course."

"I heard nothing." Was that a tiny smile twisting his mouth? "I notice when you're on the record, you generally say 'No comment.'" He looked up. "Okay, so you seem to be you. Now whether the rest of the story is true, that's another matter."

"Agreed." Amber nodded. "Two people who look like one another is not a lot to go on. That's why I'd like to suggest we do a genetic test."

His eyebrows shot up. "You think she'd agree to that?"

"It's up to Katherine." Amber shrugged. "But it's the most conclusive way to find an answer."

"I've performed them before," Maureen said. "I use a lab in Vermont that will keep the results private to only you and us."

Michael's eyes narrowed. "You've tested other potential twins?"

"I'm a midwife." Mom sighed. "Unfortunately, I've had to perform paternity testing."

He offered no follow-up question. Then, "You understand that I don't trust you."

"Nor should you." Amber left that one alone. "My mother and I can submit genetic material to the lab of your choice if you have another preference. And we'll foot the bill in advance so there's no cost to you."

Mom added, "It's very easy. You get a swab like a Q-tip, swirl it around your mouth, and mail it back in a container they provide. It's less invasive than brushing your teeth."

Amber said, "At no point would we have access to your information."

Michael said, "And if she was stolen? Then what?"

Amber looked down. "I don't know. I haven't thought that far."

Mom said, "I'd like to play it by ear."

Michael said, "Think about what you're asking. You'll destroy her relationship with her parents."

Beside Amber, Mom stiffened. Amber said, "Only if it's true."

"Can you be so sure?" Michael said.

Amber kept silence because what she wanted to say would sound cruel: what kind of parents would destroy their relationship with their kid over just a few questions? Like Mom had said about one meal at McDonalds—if that would do it, it was doomed anyhow. Hadn't her job shown her that if you loved someone, you'd always believe in them? Katherine's parents would love her despite any questions she might ask. That only made sense.

Mom said, "Is it really so fragile?"

There was hesitancy in Mom's voice. That was no good.

Mom added, "We can back off. She's safe and secure. You're obviously a good man, and I don't want to hurt her. If this is going to destroy her family—"

Amber said, "Mom!"

Michael said, "I'm going to leave that to her, but I have my own opinions, obviously." He smiled. "For that matter, how do we know Amber doesn't belong here? What if you stole her? I could send you to jail."

In the monitor, Amber caught her mother's smile. "They'd still be sisters," Mom said. "Wouldn't it be wonderful to reunite them, at any cost?"

Katie shut the door behind her and paused with her coat half-off her shoulders. She heard voices. Specifically her own voice.

Odd. Mike didn't usually watch their family videos. She'd never been a good enough mother to magically intuit to turn on the camera for the first steps or the first smile. But she had a few, including a first birthday party (which you could, after all, predict was coming). Maybe Daniel hadn't gone to sleep and Mike was entertaining him with videos until Katie got home to tuck him in. Lovely. Tomorrow the kid would be overtired and grouchy.

Coat off, she followed the voices into the den, where Mike looked up from his seat on the couch. He wasn't watching TV. "Come here," he said, interrupting whomever was speaking on the computer. The voice stopped when he looked up. "I need you to see this."

Katie dropped her purse on the end table and approached, unnerved by his studied blankness, an expression that came in useful in the courtroom. Your honor, may I approach the bench?

She settled on the couch, and pivoted the laptop screen.

"Hi," said the person on the other end, tentative. Guarded. And then waited.

Katie realized the woman, the younger of the two in the picture, looked like her.

"Katherine?" said the younger one. The woman forced a smile, but she looked terrified, and she kept glancing down as if she expected to find a teleprompter. "My name is Amber Brickman, and, um, well, I already explained this to your husband, but I think I may be your sister."

"What are you talking about?" Katie frowned. "Who are you?"

The woman repeated her name and her job title. She mentioned she came from some town in New York. She showed her ID to the camera. Fire Marshal? What did those do? But as Amber talked, the more Katie's heart raced and her vision spotted. Sister? What the hell was this all about?

"I don't expect you to believe me right away," Amber added.

"I don't believe you at all." Katie thought she might vomit. "My father would never cheat on my mother."

"I wasn't saying—"

"Moreover," Katie said, louder, yanking away from Mike's hand on her arm, "moreover, my parents were married for ten years before they had me, so if you expect me to believe you're some youthful mistake of theirs, you're a decade too young." She stood up, shoving the computer back at Mike. "And you're talking to them? You knew all that."

Mike said, "Katie, honey, you need to listen to them."

"I'm not sitting here while they insult my father."

173

Mike said, "No one said a thing about infidelity. They think you're her *twin*."

"What?" Katie stepped back. "How could that be?"

"We don't know how," said Amber on the computer. "But it's easy enough to rule out. Please, just listen. I'm not asking for anything."

Katie stared at Mike. What was he thinking? This was a scam, a scam like she'd been warned about all her life. Stranger danger. The news. Fraud. Her parents' warnings.

On the screen, the older woman was staring at her lap. Katie glowered at her. "And is that supposed to be my real mother?"

The older woman looked up. "The woman who raised you is your *real* mother. But I may be your biological mother. I'm Maureen Brickman."

Katie folded her arms. "Go on."

Maureen began telling a story, an ages-old story that brought a haunted shadow to her eyes, about being forced down in a hospital, a gas mask slapped over her face, and a vague recollection of two deliveries, but then in the morning, only one baby.

Katie said, "That was the placenta."

Maureen's eyes narrowed. "I know what a placenta feels like."

"The point is," Amber said, "when we saw you on the news, we wanted to make contact and rule it out. We can do a DNA test and have the results sent to you if you like. It's just a cheek swab, and we'll pay for it."

Katie said, "What are you going to do with my DNA?"

Amber gave a really convincing look of confusion. "Match it against mine and hers."

Katie said, "And then? Make a clone of me?"

Mike said, "They can't do that."

"Not now they can't. But they might be able to do that someday." Katie shook her head. "And in ten years, or twenty, you'll still have my DNA."

Dear heaven, this was way beyond scamming. Scammers wanted your money. These people wanted a part of her body! Was this identity theft? Could they maybe turn Amber all the way into her? What if they already had something of hers?

And if she said no, would they break into her house and maybe steal her hairbrush to get DNA that way? Maybe she should start flushing her hair down the toilet.

Amber raised her hands. "Look into it, that's all. It's the fastest and most accurate way to get answers."

"Answers? But I don't have any questions." Katie shook her head. "It's not like you're saying they mixed up the babies in the hospital. If they gave your twin to my parents, they'd still have an extra baby around somewhere. Do you think the L&D Unit chucked it in the Lost And Found, and now it's wandering the hallways like a feral child?"

She froze. Froze solid.

Katie's hand went to her abdomen. She thought about the times her mother had been so scared for her when Kieran died, how Mom hadn't even wanted to talk about Kieran because "You don't do that." Her mother had been so surprised that they'd named Kieran and held him, photographed him, given him a funeral.

Oh God, no. What if it had happened? What if her mother's baby had died, so in order to cover up their negligence, the hospital had taken a twin from someone else who didn't know she'd had two?

Amber said, "Are you okay?"

Katie looked at her lap. Especially since her father was a doctor, the hospital would have been desperate to avoid the appearance of negligence. But then again, these women were probably lying. They wanted something else from her. They wanted part of her body in a test tube, mailed off to someplace in Vermont where there weren't any state regulations, right? Or was that New Hampshire? And they were from New York. Wasn't New York full of criminals?

"There's no rush," Amber said. "I want you to think about it before doing anything. If there are answers to be found, they'll still be out there in a week, a month, six months."

Katie twisted her wedding ring on her finger, and Mike took her hand. She needed to stall them, make them think she wasn't onto them so they didn't come and try to get a sample some other way. "Before I even think of giving you anything, I want information from you." She spread her hand on her abdomen, over her baby. "As much information as you have."

sixteen

Amber awoke the next morning with her jaw aching from grinding her teeth and her heart aching with a regret-hangover. Too much sharing. It was the distinct discomfort of having sent someone the equivalent of an Identity Theft Care Package.

There'd been no way around it. "We have to be vulnerable if we want their trust," Mom had said, and she hadn't replied when Amber said, "But then we're vulnerable."

Six-thirty. She found her running clothes and drank water, grabbed her iPod, and went outside.

Scott stepped out of his car. "Ready?"

She stopped in her tracks. "Ready...for what?"

He wore sweats and a light jacket, his breath visible. "I figured if you're going to run away from me, it should at least be literal."

"You're crazy." She folded her arms and shifted back her weight. "Why did you think I'd be running?"

"Because you told me you run at six-thirty in the morning on the street rather than at Jim's Gym."

She frowned. "I did?"

Looking earnest, he nodded. "It was a whole conversation with me and Dennis about why you've never run a marathon."

"Because I'm not a runner," Amber said. "I just run."

"Exactly what you told Dennis. So today, I'm avoiding the treadmill, and I'll run with you."

Amber frowned. "What if I hadn't gone running this morning?"

Scott mimicked her expression. "Then I'd have felt like an idiot. I prefer this way."

She started stretching. "You realize running outdoors is harder, right? So I'll have to slow down for you."

"Ouch!" Scott watched her stretching. "Did you call the twin last night?"

Amber concentrated on her hamstrings. "She... She took it well. I guess. She doesn't believe us, and I think she wants me dead."

"Imagine if she'd taken it badly."

"Maybe she did and there's a report on your desk right now. Oh, and I looked up the 'second victim' like you told me to, and I assume you mean when someone gets hurt and you rush in to save them, only you get hurt too."

Scott nodded. "Then when the EMTs come for the first victim, you've made yourself the second victim."

Amber bounced a bit on her toes. "I'm not wired to just let people die."

Scott said, "No one is. The key is responding the right way to catastrophe and making sure not to protect the wrong person at the wrong time."

"It's too early for philosophy." Amber cocked her head. "Ready?"

Amber set a light pace, just to get warm. She'd always run alone, so no one had ever noticed her thick knitted mittens or the bare spots on her sweat pants. Now she was unbearably self-conscious, wondering whether she made too much noise or if her breathing was too hard.

"You're overstriding," Scott said.

"You're not helping."

"You're coming down on your heels," he said. "A few years of that and you'll wreck your calves. You should know that."

Amber kicked up the pace in the hopes he'd be too breathless to offer more advice. "I told you I'm not a runner."

He kept pace but didn't comment further, and Amber found herself even more tense. She lowered her arms to a more natural swing and picked a song to think in her mind, anything other than feeling Scott running alongside. *I'm not a runner. I just run.* And run. And run some more.

Four years ago—almost four, almost—it had been Marcus at her side. He was dead already. They'd never run together, but since she'd never run before he died, in effect she'd never run without him. It was the cruelest blow, how he'd have been the first person she'd have called to get through any crisis, and then when tragedy struck, she couldn't lean on him.

"You have to get out of the house," Mom had begged, and one day Amber had walked out the door, and then she jogged, then walked, then jogged. She ended up out far on some farmland, staring at the calf-high corn stalks, realizing that for the first time she'd been focused. It was June, not May anymore. School was over. She was home, here, in the Southern Tier. The wind carried the sound of church bells, and she'd turned back to jog all the way home. Because while she struggled to run, nothing else came into her head.

Every day a new route. Faster. Longer. Harder. Up all night? Get out of bed and run anyway. Run long enough and she'd forget. Maybe she'd forget forever.

One morning before Mom was awake and after Dad had left for the college, she'd wandered into the kitchen and paged through an issue of *Midwifery Today*. She'd came upon an article titled, simply, "Stone Baby." At first she thought it was a fossilized baby from a grave, but no, this baby had been excavated from the uterus of an otherwise-healthy thirty-seven-year-old woman in Zaire.

She told doctors she'd been pregnant decades ago but then "the baby never came out." And when they operated, out came this calcified baby body, a six month fetus where you could still see the head, the curve of the elbow, the bend of the knee.

Amber had dry-heaved, staring at this artifact, this relic of a human life. The potential, the future, the love, all turned to stone.

She ran to her room, yanked on the shorts and sneakers, and fled. She bolted out onto Oakview Avenue, then sprinted further up, and further, and she'd never checked the weather so she hadn't realized how hot it was. Mid July, the cicadas shouted in their crescendoed calls, and the purple heads of the loosestrife stood still in a windless oven as the road reflected heat. But she kept pelting away from that image of a person turned to stone and carried hidden in the body of the only person who ever loved him.

When she first started cramping, she ignored it, but within a quarter mile she was staggering. She slumped over at a fence post, head to the sawn-off wood, gasping and dizzy. She tried to walk, but pain shot up her legs and through her chest. She lurched only as far as the roadside before she dropped to her knees, and there she curled up. Nauseated. Dizzy. She didn't even have her cell phone. Wait. Just wait until she could get up.

Cars pulled through the intersection, stopped, then started again. In a few more minutes, she'd get up. Just a few. A while. But it hurt. Her arms hurt. Her legs hurt. Couldn't think. Just stay down. Stay down.

And later—how long?—a car pulled over, and cool hands touched her skin. She looked up and couldn't comprehend...a grey SUV parked on the grass, facing the wrong way. An old man helped her up, his shoulder under her sweaty armpit, and forced her to walk. He pushed her, clammy, into the back seat, then reached into the front to crank the air conditioner. The chill blasted her, and she shivered, knees curled to her chest on the bench seat. Her limbs locked up. Everything ached.

In her hands, a bottle. Water. When he held it to her mouth, she tasted salt. On the carpet were torn paper packets from McDonalds. She sucked it down. He opened another bottle and sponged her neck, her face, her arms.

Eyes closed, she finally whispered her address. The car shifted into gear, and she melted into the road noise and the roar of the air vents in the tight quarters of the back seat.

At home, a panic-stricken Mom took her from the car and gushed thanks to the man, and Amber finally focused on him long enough to recognize the Fire Marshal.

Mom cried and forced home-made sports drinks down Amber's throat to restore her electrolytes, spiced up with occasional rants about Amber trying to run herself to death. But for the rest of the day, in their only air-conditioned room with a DVD of *The Muppet Show*, Amber kept tasting salt and thinking of a man who lifted her into his SUV. Two years later, she'd gone to the county and applied for a job in his office.

Behind her, Scott gasped, "Hold up."

Startled by how fast she'd pushed her pace, Amber turned. Scott's breath was heaving—no, he was wheezing. She stopped, and he sagged against a tree.

"Are you okay? You can't breathe?"

He shook his head, barely able to get air in and out.

"Crap. Oh, crap—what's going on?"

"Asthma," he gasped. "Cold air."

She put her arm on his shoulder. "Walk it off."

They kept it to a really slow walk, but he struggled even with that. Finally he said, "Awesome. Thought I... outgrew that."

Amber said, "I'm sorry. I always figured I'd run myself to death. I didn't want it to be you."

"Didn't kill me," Scott said between gasps. "Made me stronger."

He tried to chuckle but broke up coughing. Amber slowed a bit more. "Do you have an inhaler?"

He shook his head. "Haven't needed one. For years. It's the cold."

"Great. Keep walking."

Attuned to that telltale whistle in his breath, Amber had her hand on the phone, but who would she call? She could get an ambulance, but he was breathing for now. Maybe Nikki could send Dennis over with a car. Instead she pulled off her scarf. "Wrap this around your neck and mouth. It'll warm the air."

If he thought it would make him look like a dweeb, he didn't say anything. But it did seem to help, and by the time they reached her house, his breath still whistled, but he looked steadier. She fished out her key. "I'm sorry. I really wasn't trying to show you up."

He winced. "It would put an end to courting you if you killed me." He coughed. "Maybe I'll stick to scarfing down French fries in your car."

"Come upstairs." He looked awful. "I don't want you out here suffocating to death."

"I'm okay," he said. "But you ought to know I'd never turn down the offer."

Upstairs, she opened the door to the smell of cat poop. Muttering nasty things about the stupid cat, she located the mess and gathered the cleaning supplies.

Scott sat at her kitchen table. "I didn't know you had a cat."

"I *don't* have a cat." Amber huffed. "I have a ghost that makes messes on my floor and then hides during the daylight."

Scott said, "Marcus's?"

"Of course." Amber huffed. "That's the only reason I keep it around."

He was quiet so long that she wondered if he'd keeled over. When she looked up, Scott's eyes were wide. "What?" She paused. "I'd never hurt it."

Scott looked stunned. "Marcus's ghost?"

"Marcus's *cat*." She shook her head, and Scott relaxed. "This is the cat my mother-in-law-to-be stole from his apartment and wouldn't give back to me because," she drew a deep sigh and made her voice a little lilty, "*It's all I have left of him.* At least," she muttered, "until suddenly it was okay to let him go."

Scott was breathing a bit easier now. "Have you taken it to the vet?"

Amber's nose wrinkled. "The vet's going to encourage it to poop in the box?"

"The vet might figure out if the cat's sick. Our dog got sick once, and that was how we knew."

Mom had said the same thing. Up until Scott said it, though, it seemed obvious the cat was mad at her for taking him away from his home, and this was his version of a telegram. But she considered the bleach smell of Carmen's home, and the double baby gates. "You think maybe that's why she found it in her heart to relinquish *all she had left* of her son? That figures." She washed her hands. "Do you still own a dog?"

"I'd love to." He took a shallow breath. "Wouldn't be fair to the dog." He shook his head. "I'm gone so long. So Cookie's it for me. For now."

She turned toward him. "You're breathing again."

"I'm not quite at all-systems-operational," he said, "but at least it doesn't hurt." He tried taking a deep breath and ended up coughing again. Finally he said, "Did you really want to run yourself to death?"

"If it happened, I was okay with it." She opened the tap, then went to the cabinet. "Seemed as good a way to go as anything else, and I'd have been with Marcus. But I've got my job now, so I have to stick around."

She brought him a glass of water. He held it at arm's length. "Doctor Who?"

"Of course. I drove to a different Burger King every day until I got the whole set." Her shoulders ached; she'd wrapped her arms too tightly about herself. "I had to go all the way to Cortland to find Jon Pertwee."

Scott coughed again after drinking the water, then rolled his eyes at himself. He said, "Does Katherine really want you dead?"

"Well, she'd rather I disappear." Head down, Amber took a seat on the opposite end of the table. "She hasn't agreed to do the test, so we're in a holding pattern. She refused to comment on any of the information we had, or give any of her own."

"Keep me posted."

That was his "law enforcement" tone, and Amber looked up in surprise. It was a steadier, deeper timbre for addressing someone in a panic. Maybe they learned it in police academy. Maybe some people just had the knack.

She said, "You're still thinking of the kidnapping angle."

"Damn straight. Her DNA matches yours? Then I'm getting warrants within twenty-four hours." He wrapped his hands around the glass. "That newscaster in Danbury wanted a story. I'll give her one."

"But..." Amber wrapped her ankles around the chair legs. "What if her parents were innocent? What if they didn't know?"

"It's not your job to decide if they're guilty. You only have to report a crime. Then everyone else's job comes into play." Scott shrugged. "Why would you protect them?

"It's..." She shook her head. "My mother's worried this will destroy her family."

184

"A family that shouldn't have been in the first place?" Scott fixed his eyes on her. "Down it goes. Let them figure it out afterward."

"She's loyal to them," Amber murmured.

"I'm loyal to the law." Scott didn't look away from her. "You keep me posted. I'll know what to do."

That ferocity, that strength. Her heart pounded, so she got up from the table and went to the stove. Her voice came unsteady. "Do you want some tea? Maybe that would help you breathe better."

"I'm breathing fine, actually." He sighed. "I'm sorry. You want a shower and there's this strange man in your apartment." He finished the water and handed back Doctor Who. "Thank you, my lady, for running me into the ground. Now that my lungs are better, my Achilles tendons will be next to cry your name. Or maybe just cry."

He smiled and went downstairs. When he left, she realized he wasn't the only one breathless.

seventeen

The problem, Katie decided, wasn't too little information, but too much.

She drove to her parents' house, twitchy from a sleepless night and a caffeine megadose. The baby liked it, at least. All day she'd detected joyous somersaults and something that felt suspiciously like the fandango.

But tension could do that too. Stress hormones crossed the placenta, so maybe the baby knew. You couldn't really avoid stress while pregnant. Katie awoke every day afraid this was the day she'd start to bleed, making sure to note every kick in case it was the final one. This time if, God forbid, it happened again, she wanted to know which thump was the baby saying goodbye.

Last night's call ushered in a whole new category of stress, though. Lying awake last night, she'd gone over everything again and again and again, replaying every word she remembered of the conversation, every verbal tic, every detail Mike had told her of their previous talk.

That she might be adopted. That they might be scamming her.

Neither made sense. Scammers asked you for something. Amber and Maureen only wanted a few cells from the inside of her cheek, unless what they wanted was far more nefarious. Maybe they wanted to learn all about her so they could kill her and replace her with Amber. Then Amber could go through Katie's life as Katie, married to Mike and raising Daniel, and live what

Katie had to imagine was a really good life. Mike had a great job. He kept the family pretty comfortable.

Because think of all the things DNA could do. DNA was all the information it took for your cells, mindless little things, to build an entire person. Packed into every cell was a thread a mile long, folded around with instructions on how to build a new you. What could you do with that? Could they examine it and figure out she'd tried marijuana once in college (and hated it—it just made her paranoid) and then make her lose her job? What if they could design a virus that would target only her DNA, then release it in the school so the next time the common cold came around, bam! everyone else got the sniffles but she'd be dead?

But even worse, what if she wasn't the real target? What if they wanted Daniel, and once they had her DNA, they had a window into his DNA? Especially if they could somehow get Mike's DNA too—but even without it, they could maybe just grow more of Katie's DNA in petri dishes all over their house and then show up and kidnap Daniel, and if anyone complained, Amber could just whip out some of Katie's DNA and say she was Daniel's mother all along.

Or since they were talking about stealing babies, what if Katie gave birth and they stole hers?

They were evil. This was an evil world, and people did horrible things.

At least Katie hadn't given them anything. She tried to take a deep breath and grasp at that flimsy little straw. For now and forever, the information flowed toward them rather than away, only there was too much of it and not enough important data. They'd sent Amber's birth certificate and a copy of her driver's license, assuming they weren't fake. Those documents had been faxed to Mike's office, so she hadn't seen them, but two dozen childhood pictures had gone to her email account, plus photos of the parents and a rough outline of a family history. In the flurry, Katie could no longer trace what wasn't there.

Last night, an hour after they should have been in bed, Mike had shaken his head. "It's all circumstantial. It might maybe be enough to get a warrant, but not enough to convict."

Katie had said, "The DNA, then. That's the evidence?"

And Mike had replied, "Not even that. The DNA might tell them who you were, but not how you got here."

The scientific method was no help. If you had a hypothesis, you had to devise a method to test it and measure your tests against the expected outcome. Easy-peasy, except how do you hypothesize about a human being?

Specifically, her parents. Because even thinking about it...wow.

Mom would cry. She'd sob and gasp and no matter what, it would be *You're going to leave me!* Hadn't it been all that (and worse) when she'd married Mike? Enough that Mom had convinced Dad to move to Danbury from Greenwich (a thirty-five minute drive) just to be closer?

Dad, iron-firm, would just remind her she had no right to upset her mother with fancy stories concocted by internet scammers. She'd end up apologizing for even bringing up the question, and her mother would give her the silent treatment for days, even while still expecting to be her day-care for Daniel.

Go back to the scientific method. Hypothesis: they're innocent. They'd react exactly that way because they were hurt and shocked. Of course, if your hypothesis was that they knew she wasn't theirs, then they'd react that way to shut her down because it worked. The third theory, that the hospital had replaced Mom's dead baby without their knowledge, that kind of fit as the first category.

You could make it more complicated. What if Katie was Mom and Dad's child, but that other woman seduced Dad and produced a sister? That would explain why Amber resembled her and how the woman had known to find her. Maybe this was a jilted lover's revenge, twenty-four years in the making.

But really, the most likely scenario was the most obvious: these women were criminals, and they wanted to blackmail her against releasing information they didn't even have.

She pulled into her parent's driveway and edged herself out of the car, unsteady. Her shoulders were tense and her hands trembled. Three cups of coffee had not been a good call, even if it did keep her ready and able to face five classes of high schoolers.

She saw a wave from the living room window. Daniel, beaming. She waved back, and he disappeared with a ripple of the curtains, his face reappearing between the privacy curtain and the windows alongside the door. Warm inside, Katie unlocked it and was greeted with a giant hug and a "Mommy!" followed by a steady patter about dinosaurs and which was the biggest and which the fastest and that oviraptors ate eggs. He'd been watching the Eyewitness Videos again.

Katie looked up to see her father in the kitchen, and that put paid to any idea of talking it over with Mom. Still, she could pick a hypothesis, and then test it sidelong. "Early day today?"

Dad hugged her, then took her bag and brought her to the kitchen. "We rearranged a few appointments, and I'm home."

She joined Mom at the table, and Mom patted her hand. "You look exhausted, honey."

"Yeah, my students keep me on my toes." She smiled. "They're getting ready to begin their science fair projects."

No interest from either, but that was fine. Time to begin her own science fair project. Question: Was she her parents' biological child? Hypothesis: she was biologically theirs, and they knew it.

Time to test. "One of my students was upset today. I guess he found out he was adopted."

Mom and Dad both nodded. No gasp, no furtive glances. "How old is he?" Mom said.

"Fifteen. Apparently his parents never intended to tell him."

Mom shook her head. Dad said, "How did he find out?"

Katie indulged in a thought she'd often wondered about, since her curriculum forced her to play with fire once a year. "One of the biology assignments, for the genetics unit, is to compile a genetic family tree. You know, how two blue-eyed parents can't usually produce a brown-eyed child, or how parents who are O positive and B positive can't produce an A-negative kid? Well, bad luck there."

Mom said, "That must have been a shock."

Dad said, "Why didn't he assume his father wasn't his biological father? That makes more sense."

"I know he argued with the teacher," Katie said, "and the dean got involved. I think the school counselor had to call the parents and it came out there, although obviously I'm not privy to the details."

They still weren't acting at all guilty. Perfect. Time to go further. "Adoptions aren't considered shameful nowadays. Why wouldn't they just have told him?"

Dad sighed. "People are strange. I come across all sorts of ridiculous things from my patients. What can you say?"

190

Mom added, "I hope the poor kid adjusts all right."

See? Mom was concerned for the kid, not the parents. Exactly what you'd assume if she were innocent.

Dad leaned forward. "I had a patient who found out at age seventy-five! Boy, that was a shock for him, but he took it great. He was laughing while I was checking him over for something else. He started with, *Doc, remember that family history I gave you? Well, forget it.*"

Katie chuckled. Dad said, "I asked further, to make sure he didn't need to talk to a counselor, but he really didn't seem to mind. Said it explained a lot."

Mom told her about Daniel's day (pretty much the same-old-same-old) and then, inevitably, Mom asked how Katie felt. Perfect opening for the next test, a slantwise attack on the pregnancy. "I've been feeling a shooting pain in one hip. I think it might be the sciatic nerve."

Dad said, "You need to stay off it if you can. That happens a lot during pregnancy."

Katie nodded, then looked at Mom. "Did you ever have that when you were pregnant with me?"

Mom thought for a moment. "No, I don't think so."

"It's a pretty distinctive pain. You'd probably remember it."

Mom just shook her head.

"Oh, I forgot before." Katie pulled a notebook out of her bag and opened to a blank page. Hah, lab notes. "The obstetrician was asking about my family history. I weighed a little under six pounds, right?"

Mom nodded. "Five pounds ten ounces."

"And did you have any problems during delivery?"

Mom shook her head, so Katie added, "Blood pressure problems?"

Dad said, "They'll monitor your blood pressure regardless."

"Yes, but he might want to see me more often." Hah—Dr. Shapiro already wanted to see her more often. Nonstress tests twice a month in the third trimester, for one thing. "How long was your labor."

Dad answered, "Twenty-four hours."

Katie jotted it down. "Did you have an episiotomy?"

"Everyone did back then," Dad said. "Katie, these are ridiculous questions. Why would Shapiro want to know that?"

Oh, yeah, Dad knew Dr. Shapiro. "The nurse asked that one. It might mean there were problems during the pushing stage." She looked at Dad. "Were you allowed in the delivery room, then?"

Dad said "Yes" without hesitation. Awesome. He wasn't making this up on the spot. He'd have had to keep double-checking a made-up story.

"Was I doing okay after I was born, or did I need oxygen?"

"You were fine. Pinked right up."

Katie looked at her notebook. Okay, more. Involve Mom. "Did I move a lot in utero? Did I get hiccups?"

Mom said, "I... Why does he want to know all this? Sure you moved."

"She only ever had you," Dad said. "How would she compare moving a lot versus moving a little?"

In that moment, the world made sense again. This was all a lot of playing games, questions she really knew the answer to all along. She'd been born Katherine Hayward, never needed to be anything else. Mom was Mom, Dad was Dad. Those women were scammers: brazen, bold, and not her relations. Liars took all forms. This was where Katie belonged.

And now with her answers, she owed it to her parents to stop pushing, something Dad had seen from the start. Mom might feel hurt if she kept asking questions, and *How could you do that to your mother?* was the endless mantra of her childhood, the threat that kept her on the straight and narrow during her teenage years. For Katie, it was never *My mother's going to kill me* as much as *My mom might get upset.*

And with good reason. Didn't Mike protect Katie herself? What if she cracked the way Mom had? Did she want Daniel and the new baby growing up with the same guillotine poised to drop at any moment?

Those women in New York had no right to disturb her mother. It was over. She'd call tonight and tell them to leave her alone. Or maybe have Mike do it. Maybe even call the cops. That would shut them down good.

Katie said, "You know, I'd like a cup of tea. Do you have any of that decaf still? Would you like some?"

She busied herself with the tea kettle, keeping her eyes down. What was she even thinking? Mom could never hide a secret so big. It would have come out any of the times she was hospitalized for her anxiety. Dad always said Katie was just as anxious as her mother, and Katie knew too well that compulsion to apologize for anything and everything. Those times she'd sat with Mom in the ER, waiting either for admission or to be sent home with a new medication, when Mom had sobbed her fears of being a terrible mother, it always had been "for putting you through this" and not for taking someone else's baby or having an affair.

Mom said, "Did Dr. Shapiro want to know anything else about the family history?"

"No." Katie reached of the box of tea. "I have everything I wanted to know."

At home, Katie found Mike already starting dinner. She kissed him, then helped Daniel out of his jacket and boots. "Smells great."

"Glad to hear it." He smiled. "If your mother taught me nothing else about cooking, it's to fry up an onion first thing so the house smells good."

She followed him into the kitchen. He said, "I've been thinking about Amber and Maureen, and I've pored over all their information." He checked on the stove, then turned to her. "I'll run you down on the most interesting stuff."

He removed a faxed birth certificate from a folder. Placing it alongside Katie's actual birth certificate, he said, "The birth date is given as one day apart, and although they're both New York birth certificates, they're from separate hospitals."

Katie nodded.

Mike gestured to her birth certificate. "The doctor of record on both certificates is the same doctor: Anton Vilkas."

Katie frowned. "Okay..."

"Well, that actually lends credence to what they're saying. They wouldn't have access to your birth records, although I guess as law enforcement Amber might possibly have been able to obtain it outside normal channels."

Katie folded her arms. "She's law enforcement and she's pulling this kind of crap?"

"That's my point. She may think there's reasonable cause. By the way," he added, "I've researched them both on the web. Amber's in a visible position. Small county, small department, and her name comes up in the papers. People either love her or they hate her, but reading between the lines tells me she's darned good at what she does. She's thorough and doesn't show favoritism."

Katie's mouth twitched. "How so?"

"She's getting pressure right now for pursuing arson charges against a high school student who nearly burned down an apartment complex. The parents and the PTO and the high school are rallying around the kid and saying he's such a good boy. The kid's mother is a home health attendant, and ninety-nine-year-old ladies are writing letters to the editor saying it's a crying shame what Amber's doing. But she isn't caving. If you go back a bit, though, she seems to have cleared someone in a case that looks to the world like financially-motivated arson."

Katie scowled. "She's taking bribes? The kid can't pay, so down he goes?"

Mike said, "You aren't maybe a bit bitter, are you?"

Katie huffed. "Go on."

"Maureen Brickman has a website. She is, of all things, a homebirth midwife." He nodded. "Yes, even though we're no longer in the 1800s. Her website says she does it to give women more choices *after two unsatisfying hospital experiences, one unassisted birth, and one midwife-attended homebirth.*"

Katie said, "That's insane. What if something goes wrong?"

"You'd have to ask her," Mike said. "But her clients love her."

"The ones who survive."

Mike was quiet for a few minutes while he took care of things on the stove. Then, "Katie, I'm investigating this to help you. You're making it difficult for me."

"My parents aren't liars."

"Based on a cursory examination, neither are the Brickmans. I'd hire a private investigator to look into them before we went any further, but so far, so good."

Katie folded her arms and watched him pour rice in a pot and lower the heat. "Where does that leave us?"

"I looked into black market adoptions. Like it or not, that's what they're alleging." Mike looked up. "The easiest and most common method of managing a black market adoption is for the doctor to fill out the birth certificate as if the adoptive parents were the birth parents. There were doctors and midwives who did it exactly this way for dozens of babies every year, to spare teens the shame of being unmarried mothers, and to spare the couple an adoption fee. The adoptive parents could be paged to the hospital, escorted to a special room, and given the baby before signing a birth certificate. The birth mother would leave, and no one was the wiser."

Katie frowned. "But—"

"Bear with me here," Mike said. "If you take a baby from a woman with undiagnosed twins, then she leaves the hospital with the one she expected to have, and the other family leaves with the other. She doesn't know."

"But the adopting family would know," Katie said. Then paused. "Unless they don't. If one baby died, the hospital could avoid a medical malpractice lawsuit by giving away the other baby. Then both families would leave with one and no one's the wiser."

She thought for a moment, then sat at the table. "It's... Wow."

"So even if it's true," Mike said, "your parents may not suspect."

Katie said, "We can't tell them this. My mom would fall apart. I can't do that to her."

"No, I suggest not mentioning it at all unless we're certain." Mike shrugged. "But how did your parents end up in upstate New York? I thought they lived in the city before moving to Connecticut."

Katie drummed her fingers on the table. "Dad did his internship and residency at NYU Hospital, and then for about five years he worked as a hospitalist at New York Presbyterian. When Mom became pregnant with me, they decided there was no way they could raise a baby in the city."

Mike started turning chicken pieces in the pan. "Lots of people raise babies in New York City."

"Yeah, but Mom had already been hospitalized two or three times with anxiety, and it got to the point where she couldn't ride the subways or even talk to people. She was always afraid of getting mugged or kidnapped. Dad was working crazy hours at the hospital, and he couldn't be home for Mom, so he decided to become a specialist."

Mike nodded. "Go on."

"He got a fellowship for graduate medical education up at SUNY Upstate, and he moved with Mom to a place where it would be quiet and she could relax during her pregnancy and not be stressed."

Mike said, "And being the wife of a medical student isn't stressful at all."

Katie smirked. "Not as stressful as being the wife of a hospitalist. Anyhow, she had me, and after he finished his gastroenterology certification, he found a job in Greenwich."

Mike said, "So that explains why they were up there to have you. But that also means during her pregnancy she wasn't near family. And they don't really have long-term friends."

Katie said, "Because it's really hard for Mom to talk to people. It gives her panic attacks. But it should be easy enough. Photos, right?"

Mike pointed to her. "Good idea. Look through her photo albums. Find a picture of her pregnant and you've as good as got proof she's innocent."

Katie shook her head. "The burden of proof should be on the accusers. I have a birth certificate. The State of New York says I'm their child."

Mike nodded. "Fair enough. Shall I get a private detective?"

"Do it." Katie squared her shoulders. "Let's nail them for the scammers they are."

Amber looked up from her desk to find Scott with an armload of gladiolus. "Oh, for goodness sake!"

"Don't get excited," he muttered. "Someone beat me to the punch."

"Huh?" She crossed the office to take the flowers from him. "Where'd they come from?"

"Delivery service," he said "Sort of. The delivery person is still out front."

Amber slid the flower tag from the mini envelope. In neat printing it said:

Amber, I'm so so so so so so so so sorry. Please don't hate me. ♥ *Nikki* ☹ ☹ ☹

Amber sighed. "Is she really out front?"

"Yes, and crying a river. If you don't go talk to her, I'm going to have to arrest someone for disturbing the peace."

Amber waved a hand and turned away. "Call Dennis."

"Dennis conveniently says he's in the middle of a very important investigation that absolutely cannot be interrupted for...oh, three hours." Scott gestured to the door. "It'll be fine. Just pretend you're walking into a burnt-out building."

"Usually I have a structural engineer clear it first." Amber sighed. "Escort her to a soundproof room. I'll be out in two minutes."

For one of those minutes, Amber fussed over the flowers, ignored the glare of the Old Man, and then braced herself.

Perhaps thinking it a joke, Scott had not escorted Nikki to the soundproof room after all. She rushed up to Amber, red-eyed, and then stopped just before hugging her. "Can we be friends again?"

In the face of how sad Nikki looked, Amber's nasty responses evaporated. Of course that would happen. Half the reason she'd avoided Nikki was she knew she'd never be able to keep up a good 'mad' in her presence. All the canned sentences, like "Oh, were we ever friends in the first place?" flew away like sparrows.

"I only wanted to help!" Nikki bit her lip. "I called Kelly and begged her, and she promised she wouldn't tell anyone else—"

Terrific.

"—and I'm so sorry."

Nikki stepped forward, and Amber accepted the hug. Then the baby thumped her in the gut, and Nikki laughed. Amber said, "No input from you, small fry."

Nikki tried to smile. "Is it okay?"

"I need to talk to you." Amber looked around. "Let's see..."

Scott called from the desk, "I can free up an interrogation room for you."

"Or you could mind your own business."

"Ooh," Scott said. "Minding it now, My Lady."

Nikki's eyes widened. "My Lady?"

"Somewhere else." Amber grabbed Nikki by the hand. "Now."

They hadn't even gotten to the street when Nikki cried out, "You don't have a coat! Let's go back. At least take my scarf," and Amber was saying, "I'm fine, I'm fine, I'm really fine."

Amber strode right for Tillman's, a diner in business since 1938 but truly blessed in 1955. That was the year the town council voted to put the police/fire station right next door. Cliché or not, within twenty-four hours Mr. Tillman Senior had added donuts to the "breakfast anytime" menu, and they'd thrived ever since. The one time some guy had attempted a holdup, he'd been warming a bench in the lockup within ten minutes.

"Amber," the owner said as they walked in. "Nikki! Had that baby yet?"

Based on the glint in Nikki's eyes, the only reason she didn't scream was that the man was ninety-two years old. "No, Mr. Tillman. When I do, you'll be the first to know."

He laughed out loud, already clanking thick ceramic mugs on the counter. "You promise? Gracie hated it every day when people asked when she was gonna pop." He poured two mugs of coffee. "Can I interest you in a muffin?"

"No thanks." Amber pulled out her wallet.

Mr. Tillman said, "Sorry. It's on the house."

Amber stuffed the five into the tip jar and grabbed the mugs.

Mr. Tillman said, "Oh, and I just heard about your sister. I didn't realize you had a twin."

She froze. "What? I don't."

Tillman frowned. "Someone told me she was kidnapped."

Nikki waved a hand. "Don't believe everything you hear. This is a small town, remember?"

As if any of them could forget. Amber fumed as she took the mugs to a table.

Nikki murmured, "Yeah, I'm really sorry about that." She leaned across the table. "Okay, talk. What's with the *my lady* stuff?"

"Hang on." Amber frowned, and Nikki pulled back. "First off, I didn't say I forgive you and it's all sunshine and roses. Everyone knows my business right now, as you already saw. You betrayed me."

Nikki nodded. "But here's the thing. When you say all those five-dollar words like *betrayal of confidential information*, all that means is we're both well aware I screwed up and you're trying to convince yourself to stay mad."

Amber said, "I don't do that."

"You totally do." Nikki shrugged. "You do just what you're doing now, straightening up and holding your

200

head like this…" (she tilted it a little and pulled back her neck) "…as if you're trying to keep your distance in your body when you don't want to in your heart."

Amber tried to relax her shoulders. "I do not!"

"I've seen you do it with Scott, too, only he can't translate your body language yet. So…*my lady?*"

Amber rolled her eyes. "He thinks he has permission to pursue me."

Nikki gasped. "That's terrific! Why does he think that?"

Amber bit her lip. "Maybe because I told him he could."

"Well, I can see how he'd read between the lines and reach that conclusion." Nikki beamed. "What's it going to take?"

Staring at the coffee, Amber shook her head.

"He's not Marcus," Nikki said. "He's a good guy anyhow."

"Then why's he interested?"

"Because opposites attract?" offered Nikki.

Amber nodded. "And if you look in the paper, they've got my headshot on page two under Cold-Hearted Jerkface of the Year, so it makes sense."

Nikki said, "Have you found out more about Katherine?"

"Some." Amber sipped her coffee. Gosh, Tillman did it well. After being in business a hundred years and training his son and two grandsons, he'd had enough practice. "We talked to her."

Nikki gripped the sides of the table. "Really? Is she it? What do you think? Have you met her?" Then, "Wow, you really did want to punish me, doing that when we weren't talking."

"I did it just to spite you, yeah." Amber shook her head. "And the answer is…I don't know. Her husband thought I was her on the phone, so then we did a video chat, and, well, we sent information to them. Records, dates, IDs. That was last night, so heaven only knows if she's even seen it yet. We're going to talk again and see if they're willing to do a DNA test."

Nikki said, "Why wouldn't she be willing to do that?"

Amber grinned. "She puts the *uh?* in *Paranoid*. It's really tough to convince her we're not scammers."

Nikki sipped her coffee. "What would convince you? If positions were reversed, I mean?"

Amber looked out at the street as a car passed, and after a moment, she realized...nothing. The answer was nothing.

EIGHTEEN

A cup of tea with Olivia was the best thing Maureen's day had going for it. "Better put two tea bags in that." Olivia was jiggling Charlotte on her knee while looking in her eyes. "Extra strong."

Maureen smiled as she poured the hot water. "I'm used to those hours."

"Delivering babies, not delivering documents."

Maureen laughed.

"Well, Charlotte kept me up all night, so put the extra one in mine." Olivia switched to a baby voice, putting her face right in Charlotte's. "And I can't believe Amber let you send her birth certificate. My sister's loosening up."

"She knows it's important to me. That's the only reason I got her to go along with it. With clenched teeth." Maureen sighed as she set the kettle on the stove. "She probably woke up this morning with her jaw aching." She paused. "Have you heard from your friend? Nancy? How's her baby?"

Olivia cuddled the baby against her chest, ear to mom's heartbeat. "Doing great. She had a rocky start breastfeeding, though. She thinks she doesn't have enough milk."

"Have her call me." Maureen nodded. "I can check her latch and look for a tongue-tie, and if nothing seems wrong, I'll prescribe some Reglan if her doctor isn't helping."

Olivia's nose wrinkled. "Really?"

"Why not?" Maureen wrapped her hands around the warm mug. "I'll see her for a consultation, bill a dollar so she's technically my patient, and write the script."

"I thought you could only prescribe medications for labor." Olivia chuckled. "I should have had you renew Andrew's medication last month when the pharmacy mixed up the refills."

"Nope. Only women." Maureen held up her hands. "Don't even get me started. I can prescribe for a man if I'm treating an STI, but only if I'm also treating his female partner. Otherwise men are outside my scope of treatment."

Olivia rolled her eyes. "That makes no sense."

"Part of being an LM. I'm fine with it." Maureen shrugged. "Remember when it was illegal for me to carry drugs at all?"

Olivia grinned. "My mom, the drug dealer."

Maureen shook her head, looking down. If any of the kids had gotten into drugs, she would have blamed herself, and she knew it. "I still kind of feel privileged being able to administer Pitocin rather than calling an ambulance and pretending I'm the woman's sister." She squeezed the tea bag dry.

Ah, the years when she could have been arrested for transporting a mom to the hospital, and the fun of finally practicing in the open. She'd needed to take a pharmacology course and then, hilarity of hilarities, intern in an accredited program. Working for free for a hundred births—but it was worth it, entirely worth it to bring midwifery to the state. Nowadays she was one of the county's four licensed midwives.

Since tonight was Ray's late night, Olivia said, "Do you want to pick up a pizza? My treat."

Maureen's heart thumped. "I think Katherine's going to call tonight. I want to be here."

Maureen had kept Skype on and reset the energy-save settings so it wouldn't go to sleep while inactive. That sense of anticipation kept revving and then backing off, like an engine with a bad starter. *Come on, Katherine. The evidence is all here. Call us.*

Amber wasn't coming. Just as well. Katherine and Amber hadn't built much rapport on the call, although that was mostly because Katherine was too defensive to develop a rapport with anyone.

When the shock died down, though, when Katherine had a chance to look at the paperwork and consider, the rapport would come. It had to.

Maureen stood to pace, came to a stop in front of the computer, and reached for the keyboard.

Skype chimed. Incoming call from Michael Woodson.

Olivia rushed in, the baby on her hip. "It's her?"

"Let's find out." But something felt wrong. Maureen tapped to open the connection.

Olivia stepped back to where the webcam didn't capture her but she could see the screen. Maureen sat at the desk and adjusted the laptop window until everything lined up, and while she was doing that, Michael appeared in the window.

"Michael!" She smiled. "Good to see you."

No, actually, it was lousy to see him. Lousy because in every good scenario, it was Katherine talking to them herself.

Michael said, "Hello, Maureen. Is Amber with you?"

"She's at home."

Michael's brows knit. "I was hoping to catch both of you at once."

"We might be able to get her on Skype for a three-way chat. If you want to try, she's AmberBrickmanFire."

"Thanks." He jotted that down. "Hang on." Then a minute later, "She's not responding."

"I can call her," Maureen said.

"Actually, I'll just talk to you," Michael said. "Katherine and I don't want to move too quickly on this. What you're suggesting is beyond belief, to be honest."

And yet he wasn't telling her no, or that they had indisputable proof she was wrong. Hope sparked: they hadn't ruled it out.

Maureen said, "Of course you need to take time. Shall I try you again on Saturday?"

"Maybe longer," Michael said. "Remember you've had days since you saw the broadcast to think about this. And for you, it doesn't change all that much."

Maureen's heart quickened. "It changes everything!"

"Not as much as it would change for her."

Out of view of the camera, Olivia nodded. Maureen bit her lip, and it hurt to speak. "Well, I suppose. I'd want it settled, if it were me. One test and no more wondering."

But of course you'd only decline the test if you thought it would give you information you didn't want. Why else?

Didn't want...or planned not to act on. How many of her clients declined prenatal screening on the grounds that "It wouldn't change anything"?

Maureen said, "No matter what she finds out, she doesn't have to act on it."

Michael squinted. "What?"

"Even if she discovers she's Amber's twin, there's no need to change anything. She would never need to tell her parents, wouldn't have to meet us, nothing like that. She doesn't need to change her whole world. It's just one piece of information."

Wouldn't Amber say that? *Information isn't scary, Mom. It's ignorance that scares me.*

Michael's eyes flickered up and to the side, and Maureen realized Katherine was standing like Olivia, just out of view of the camera.

Maureen said, "But what it might do is provide Katherine more information about her background, her family medical history, and so on. You'd want more accurate information for any children you may have."

Michael looked over again. Then, "In what way?"

His eyes had stayed on Katherine while he spoke to her.

Maureen said, "Well, I could tell you my mother gave birth to one premature baby, or that she had two miscarriages. Did you realize identical twins are a birth defect? A wonderful, glorious, amazing birth defect—but they're a defect in cell division, and it might point to other genetic issues you should look out for, like maybe Katherine would want to supplement with extra folic acid."

Olivia's eyes had widened when Maureen said twins were a birth defect. Michael looked startled, but he kept it under wraps. "I could have her ask her doctor about that."

"Absolutely," Maureen said. "Genetic history doesn't replace good medical care, of course. An obstetrician or midwife or pediatrician will be screening for these things anyhow. But," she added, "there's a reason they take a family history. It's important to have the right one, not only to screen for likely issues, but also so they don't waste time preparing for issues that aren't likely after all."

Michael glanced at Katherine again, then back at the screen. "That's a good point. I'll have to talk about it with her." Then he said, "Could you...um, could you send that anyhow?"

Maureen said, "I'm not sure I feel comfortable doing that."

Michael forced a laugh. "What? That your grandfather might have had hypertension?"

"It's not my grandparents I'm concerned about. You're in effect asking me to share the medical histories of my three living children and my grandchild." She shook her head. "That's not fair to them. I'll tell you all about myself, and with Amber's permission I'll share her information, but I don't want to share their—"

Before she finished, Katherine had pushed her way into the camera view. "Wait, back up. Your three *living* children?"

Relief flooded her at seeing Katherine, relief mixed with tension because of the anguish on Katherine's face. It felt like seawater clogged with crude oil.

Olivia's eyes were wide, and she was open-mouthed, looking at Amber's clone. Her own sister. Well, maybe.

"But your website said four," Katherine blurted out. "Four births. Two bad hospital experiences, one unassisted, one midwife-attended."

Maureen blinked. And then, "Oh—"

"Because I'm pregnant now," Katherine said, and then as she went on, her voice caught, and the tears welled up, and she choked on her own words, "and six months ago, my second baby died. And they didn't know why. And he was stillborn. But he was so perfect and so tiny..."

Michael put his arm around Katherine's shoulder. Maureen leaned forward, as though she could touch Katherine through the screen. Olivia was clutching Charlotte hard enough that it was a wonder she didn't cry out.

"But if you can guess why," Katherine stammered, "if your baby died of something..."

"I'm so sorry." Maureen could barely see through her own tears. "I'm so sorry."

Olivia slid a box of tissues nearer her. Maureen grabbed one. "No, it wasn't like that. I had a bad experience with Amber in the hospital. Even if you weren't there, it was a horrible nightmare. When I had Olivia they were doing all the same things—holding me down, forcing me to have cervical exams, threatening to break my water—so I snuck out of the hospital, and I delivered unassisted in an English adjunct's barn."

Katherine stared. "That's dangerous!"

"Not as dangerous as staying would have been." Maureen crumpled the tissue in her hand. "So that one counted twice. Both a bad hospital experience and an unassisted birth."

She nearly said, "I'm so sorry about Kieran," but then remembered she wasn't supposed to know, so she only said, "What was the baby's name?"

Michael said, "Kieran."

Maureen said, "Do you have photos?"

Katherine looked up, mouth trembling. "You want to see him?"

Maureen nodded.

"No one ever asked. Not even on Facebook." She got up. "Wait here."

Michael watched her go. Maureen said, "That must have been so awful."

Michael said, "It was worse for her."

Katherine returned with a silver photo album, flipping through. "This is my favorite picture." She held it up to the webcam, but her hands were shaking. "He looks so sweet in this, so normal."

The photo was black and white, a trick Maureen knew eliminated any mottling on the baby's skin.

"Oh, look at him," Maureen cooed, and she ignored Olivia's expression of horror. "He must have been such a little fighter. How big was he?"

"Six pounds two ounces," Katherine choked out. "Here, I love this one too."

This photo had Katherine looking like she'd been hit by a train, stunned and exhausted, forcing a smile and holding the baby in a blanket. "You poor thing," Maureen said.

Katherine showed another photo, Kieran's hand resting on two of Michael's fingers.

"Were these by a professional photographer?"

"Yeah, the hospital has one on call, when a baby dies. He did them for free." She stopped and bit her lip. "I'm sorry. I shouldn't—I mean, you deliver babies all the time."

"That's how I know it's a tragedy," Maureen said. "How many weeks were you?"

"Thirty-eight." Katherine shook her head. "That's why this time my doctor's going to section me at thirty-seven weeks."

Beside her, Olivia put her hand over her eyes. Maureen exclaimed, "What?"

"So it doesn't happen again."

"But thirty-seven weeks isn't even full term." Maureen straightened in her chair. "What if your dates are off? The doctor could cause him to be premature! And why a section? Why not a cord-imaging scan to rule out problems with the placenta and umbilical cord?"

Katherine said, "It's safer that way."

"It most assuredly is *not* safer." Maureen leaned in toward the screen. "C-sections are more dangerous for both the mom and the baby."

Katherine folded her arms. "Oh, so all those moms and babies should just die?"

"Of course not! When they're necessary, thank God we have a surgical option! My own granddaughter was saved by a necessary cesarean section!" Maureen's cheeks burned, and she vaguely realized she should stop, but she couldn't resist adding, "I'm saying it's not risk-free to have major abdominal surgery. It makes sense only when the birth itself is high-risk."

Katherine's eyes narrowed. "Mine is!"

"This won't help." Maureen shook her head. "What kind of a doctor would recommend unnecessary vaginal bypass surgery?"

Katherine exclaimed, "I demanded he do it!"

Maureen's jaw dropped. "Then he had a moral obligation to tell you no!"

Michael said, "Calm down, both of you, this isn't about her delivery –"

"Just because you squatted out your kid in a barn doesn't mean every woman in North America has an evil doctor!" Katherine's eyes were livid, and Maureen shrank back from the screen. "And just because Jesus was born in a barn doesn't make you the Madonna who did it God's way!"

Olivia was motioning with her hand, palm-downward. Cool it.

Katherine wasn't cooling it. "You don't know what it's like! You never lost a baby! I'd do anything to never let that happen again!"

Maureen said, "You're right, Katherine. I'm sorry."

"Katie. It's *Katie*." She stood. "I'm done with you. I don't care if you're my biological mother or if you had an affair with my father or if you sold off your newborn on Etsy. You can go die."

She reached toward the screen, and the connection cut.

Maureen closed her eyes, and somehow she managed not to scream when Olivia touched her arm.

Vaginal bypass surgery?

Katie stormed around the kitchen slamming cabinets as she emptied the dishwasher. Damn that woman. Damn her attitude, her smugness, her birth-nazi mentality. *Vaginal bypass surgery?* What's next? Asking if she'd circumcise the kid and then calling her a penis-whacker?

She shouldn't have gotten on the line, should have stuck to the freaking plan, let Mike do all the talking and not deal with that woman until Katie darn well felt like it. Maybe in December. Of 2034. Yeah. Because someone who boiled hot water to deliver a baby in the living room totally knew more than a board-certified surgeon.

The argument kept cycling in her head, and the kicker was, she had no one to vent to. Mike had gone into his office to catch up on the work he'd missed while chasing this stupid wild goose, and he was the only one who knew enough to get why she'd be so furious. She couldn't tell her parents, and none of her colleagues would care.

Oh. Yeah, wait. There was someone.

She stalked to the computer. There was definitely one person she could yell at, yell good and loud, who'd both know what was going on and would deserve every minute of it.

Mike had jotted Amber's Skype ID on a Post It note, so she pushed the button to send a recorded message, but actually...Amber was on.

Well. Wasn't that just perfect? She clicked to connect a call.

The baby kicked, and Katie rubbed her abdomen. *Sorry. I'm too angry right now. I hope the stress doesn't hurt you.*

And then, on the screen was Amber.

"Well, hello, Mrs. Woodson." Amber looked cautious and a little puzzled. "I didn't expect to hear from you, and I really didn't expect you to have my Skype ID."

"Your mother," said Katie, "is the most obnoxious, overbearing, know-it-all hypocrite I've ever met!"

On the screen, Amber's picture was jerky because of the connection, but abruptly she wore a knowing smile.

"Ah, so you've talked to her for longer than five minutes?"

"What the heck gives her the right to tell me how to live my life? She gave birth with the cows and the sheep looking on." Katie rolled her eyes. "I don't care what all this is really about. I'm blocking her and I never want to talk to either of you again."

"Makes sense." Amber leaned back and folded her arms. "What did she do?"

Getting closer to the screen, Katie spat out the story, one sentence at a time, her eyes boring into Amber's and making sure she mentioned *vaginal bypass surgery*. And all through it, Amber kept nodding, sighing, rolling her eyes at the 'vaginal bypass,' and finally shaking her head.

"I'm done with you," Katie said.

"I'd be done with us too." Amber huffed. "I get the same treatment, only she *is* my mother, so it's always, 'Oh, you had cramps? Drink this red raspberry leaf tea infusion.'" Amber shrugged. "I'm sorry that was your introduction to it."

Katie said, "It's just obnoxious."

"Of course it is. Look," said Amber, and then she stopped. "I'm sorry. About the baby. That's just..."

Amber looked for a moment like she was going to start crying, but the screen glitched, and when it came back, Amber was biting her lower lip and staring at her lap. "That's got to be worse than anything I've gone through. You didn't deserve that."

Katie said, "Um... Thank you."

Amber still wouldn't look up. "Do you... What was his name?"

"Kieran." Katie's throat tightened. "Kieran Joseph."

"That's a good name." Amber looked up, but the screen froze even as her voice continued. "Do people avoid talking about him?"

213

Katie melted back into her chair. "You know... No, they act like he never existed, and if I mention him, they get this deer-in-the-headlights look, and they wait, and then they change the subject."

Amber's frozen photo said, "Yeah. I've been there."

Katie's voice went shrill. "Did you lose a baby?"

Amber's motion returned mid-word. "My fiancé. Six weeks before we should have gotten married, someone murdered him."

Katie's hands went to her mouth. "What happened?"

Amber shook her head, and she rolled her eyes. "No one knows. I figure his low-life neighbor came around again to bum something off him and Marcus didn't give it so he shot him. I told Marcus the guy was an addict, but he was like no, I'm just going to be nice, go along to get along." Amber rolled her eyes again and her mouth tightened. "Yeah. That worked out well. So no babies for me."

Katie groped for something to say, but the only things that came to her were all the false comfort people had offered her, the "You're young and can try again" when trying again was the last thing she wanted. You can't try again to have the same person.

So instead she said, "Do people tell you you're young, and you can find someone else?"

Amber forced a smile, and its familiarity was like a knife to the gut. Katie glanced at Kieran's photo album, open to the picture of her holding her son.

Amber said, "Not anymore they don't."

Katie said, "How long ago was it?"

"Four years." Amber shrugged. "And before you ask, no, I'm not interested."

Katie looked again at herself holding Kieran. She teetered on changing the subject, but no. Twice in one night people had wanted to talk about Kieran. Wanted to talk, listened to what she said, didn't spout platitudes about *it's so much better this way* and *there was probably something wrong* and *God needed another angel.* But at the same time, Amber's grief scared her. Heavy but with the sharp edges worn off.

Somehow Amber had gotten through it. Alone. Katie and Mike had gotten through it by leaning on each other. Who would have been there for Amber to lean on?

"Thank you," Katie said. "For asking about him."

Amber said, "Did you ever want a t-shirt that says *Ask me about my dead baby*?"

Katie burst out laughing. "What?"

"But it needs a flap," Amber went on, her voice sharper, "so you can pull it down and it says *Don't* for when you're having a crap day and you don't want to deal with it."

"I couldn't wear something like that. I already feel like I'm marked." Katie shook her head. "I'm the baby-killer."

"And I'm the Black Widow." Amber paused. "You didn't kill Kieran. Nothing you did could have caused this."

"If I'd done kick counts more—"

"Babies don't die because you forgot your kick-counts," Amber said. "And let me guess: a glass of wine in your second trimester, and a manicure before you knew you were pregnant..."

Katie flinched. "Well, not quite that bad."

"And Marcus didn't die because I was ribbing him about not buying me an engagement ring or because we were going to move to New Mexico. Sometimes the world just destroys you."

Katie squared her shoulders. "But that's why I want a C-section at thirty-seven weeks. Give the world less chance to get me again."

"Your choice. Just make sure you're not controlling the wrong thing." Amber took a deep breath. "Look, here's the best way to deal with Mom."

The edge returned to Katie's voice. "She's not my mom."

"No, she's *my* mom, and I call her Mom. Sorry." Amber leaned toward the screen. "The best way to deal with Maureen Brickman is to have your facts in a row. And I know you're not going to talk to her again, but still. Go on Pub Med. Look up articles and studies and get numbers. *Are* C-sections less dangerous? Is it less dangerous at thirty-seven weeks than at term? Are there other options? Because in your shoes," Amber added, "I'd want hourly ultrasounds and a nurse living in my spare bedroom."

Katie chuckled. "Insurance won't pay for that."

"But really, look at the risks. Know your facts. Then when some natural birth junkie says, *You only need to take evening primrose oil,* you can say, 'Actually, I read a study that recommends exactly what I'm doing.'"

Katie bit her lip. "But I'm not going to talk to her again."

"For yourself. For every other busybody who knows it all." Amber grinned. "You'll do fine. Either way. But really, what my mother likes best isn't necessarily an unmedicated childbirth as much as a woman who researches the heck out of everything and practices informed consent."

Katie said, "So when I inform you guys that I don't consent to talk to you again—"

"—she'll be sad," Amber finished, "but she'll respect it."

Katie waited. Nothing else followed, and there should have been something. A huge emptiness stood between them, so she ventured with, "And you?"

"I'll be sad too." Amber's shoulders tensed. "Besides, my job is solving mysteries. I don't like leaving them unsolved."

Katie said, "Like the way Marcus died?"

Amber nodded.

"Or the way Kieran died."

She nodded again.

Katie shook her head. "I don't know. I just..."

Amber raised her head. "Look, Katherine—"

"Katie." She leaned forward. "Please. I know you found me in a phone book, but call me Katie."

A grin spread across Amber's face, and Katie found herself smiling too. "Okay, *Katie?* Can I offer a solution? Don't make me dead to you. I'll answer if you call, but I won't pester you, and I'll tell my mother to leave you alone. Take a few days, weeks, months, and think about it. I already ordered a DNA kit for you, but nothing triggers until you send back the sample."

Amber sounded so darned sensible. Did nothing rile her up?

Katie muttered, "I could send someone else's DNA. It'll say we're definitely not related, and you'll go away."

Amber said, "I have no choice but to trust you, but you don't have to do it at all, so there's no reason to trick the system."

"True." Nothing really did rattle her. This was so strange. Why wasn't Amber screaming? For that matter, why wasn't Katie herself screaming? "I'm going to try getting more information, and maybe in a week."

"Sounds good." Amber shrugged. "Contact me in a week, either way. Or sooner if you decide sooner."

Katie reached for the disconnect button, and as Amber's picture blinked out, she tried to reach for the outrage and found instead something she'd never expected to feel. Hope.

Hope?

Such a strange flavor in her heart, hope that there was a real connection to such a level-headed, sturdy person. Hope that her world would be upended and shaken out like a dusty rug. Hope that after all, the worst might be true.

NINETEEN

*O*kay, *then, smarty-pants. Reverse the hypothesis, and this time, no confirmation bias. Hypothesize that Amber and I are sisters. How to test that?*

Not that Maureen was her mother. Maureen was a self-righteous know-it-all and the question wasn't about being her mother. But Amber being her sister—that Katie could do.

A Fire Investigator. So cool.

But first, at a computer station in the teacher's lounge, Katie Googled "C-section safety."

She found two major categories of websites to avoid. Every obstetrician website said C-sections were perfectly safe and used only when necessary. They made her feel good, but she was trying to conduct science, not feel good. On the other end were the crunchy granola moms with their hemp baby slings who lauded Maureen as their Empress. *Vaginal bypass surgery?!* These types ranted about the evil "Medical Model" and how hospital labors were harder, even as they supported one another and soothed and shared links to all sorts of alternatives. From these sites Katie also learned the term "unnecessarian."

The top hits were mostly of the first variety and some of the second, and they all had a bizarre assortment of statistics proving both that C-sections were perfectly safe and that they were perfectly dangerous, and that C-sections were only used when necessary as well as drastically over-used. So next Katie tried "relative safety

C-section vs vaginal delivery" and finally added "studies." That's when she hit paydirt.

An hour later, she nearly missed getting to her 4th period class, and her brain was on the ten studies she'd bookmarked to reread later.

She began class with, "Despite what I've told you about the scientific method, sometimes the answers aren't clear-cut."

Maureen was still a jerk. But now Katie had actual risks to balance against one another, and new questions about how to alleviate one set of risks while not increasing the rest. Plus she had a twenty-page document open right now about high-resolution umbilical cord scanning. Albertus Magnus would have been proud.

Fly through the day. Drink herbal tea so as not to end up screaming at strangers over Skype. Pick up Daniel and find Dad had worked a normal day this time. Have another cup of tea with Mom.

Hypothesis test:

"Mom, I hate maternity clothes." {Noncommittal response.} "Did you hate maternity clothes too?"

Lovely and non-charged. Complain about the fashion industry: even Dad would find nothing to object to.

And Mom's answers—Katie tried to listen like a reporter rather than a daughter, and the details weren't there. Mom mentioned about styles back then, but not anything specific. If Katie asked a question, it was agreement without elaboration. Didn't you hate maternity bras? *Oh yes.* And how your boobs changed size each week? *Katie! We didn't talk about things like that.* Did you wear your underwear over the belly or under the belly? *I don't remember.*

Katie said, "You do have pictures of you pregnant right? So you could show everyone how big you got?"

Mom shook her head. "I hated how I looked. I wouldn't let your father take pictures."

Test? Inconclusive. Either Mom was being evasive, or Mom was being Mom.

Driving home, with Daniel in the back chattering about his day, Katie decided she needed more data. Real data.

And who kept data? Amber had the right idea. Doctors did.

———◦———

It had been a week since Amber had spoken to Katie, and contrary to how it felt at the moment, she had not spent it all in an OB/GYN waiting room.

No, the week had been filled with all sorts of joy. Begin with the joy of Mom pumping her for every last bit of information about her conversation with Katie, and continue with the joy of blowing up at Mom for picking a fight about someone else's elective C-section.

Oh, and then the texts from Olivia ("If you're an identical twin then technically you're a mutant or something") and more from Brendan ("Mom says you're defective!"). Those just coaxed the family joy to a fever pitch.

Add in the fact that half the police department and two-thirds of the firefighters had come down with strep, somehow, in the last weeks of winter. They all staggered around coughing and looking ill, and both rookies were overheard muttering to one another that if you got arrested this week, you might accidentally contract the death penalty.

But not Scott. Despite doing a week of the overnight shift, Scott kept showing up in the early AM to go running with her. Scott and an extra inhaler that belonged to his sister's kid. "You can't do that," Amber had said, and Scott only replied, "I can't get in to see my doctor for two weeks. This is just as good."

"What's the point of a doctor you can't see when you're sick?" Amber said. "Do you just make appointments for a couple months out and hope those are the days you'll have problems?"

An unrepentant Scott had used the inhaler, saying, "Wow, that feels just like third grade again." So she made him tuck the scarf over his mouth and run. But his stamina improved every morning as they ran around snowbanks that shrank and grew blacker as the dirt on top drew closer together. Soon they'd be flat black patches on the ground, and the first rain would smell dusty but wash it all away.

Or at least, that should happen. The news was predicting a monster of a snowstorm. In other words, it was late March in upstate New York.

Scott still had the nasty habit of being totally confident he'd win her over. For now, she'd just let him think it. Plus, he also thought he could lure out the cat on the day she needed to bring it to the vet.

"You know those grants we get from the feds?" he'd said. "They bought us a tiger cage," and she'd muttered, "Thanks. Thanks a lot."

The cashier at the MiniMart and the bank teller had both talked about her stolen twin, which was just lovely, and she'd told them both there was no such person. But that was still better than the people who wanted her burning in Hell for doing her job. The newspapers were having a field day about the Spice Hills apartment fire and the Hernandez kid. The more airtight Amber's case, the more the mother hyped it up. She'd convinced the high school to hold a legal defense fundraiser. Waverly Middle School had suggested she not talk for their DARE program after all. And some yahoo with more food than brains had egged the police station. All in the name of justice. You had to love that.

So that was her week, capped off by a glorious stay in this stale-smelling waiting room. Amber kept her nose in *The Birth Partner* by Penny Simkin.

The last time she'd been in a waiting room, it had been with Nikki. Before her first prenatal appointment, Nikki had visions of ultrasound photos, a cozy chat with the doctor...all that. But Dennis had to work, so it was Amber she called, singing out "I just peed on a stick and guess what? You're coming to the doctor with me!" followed by the inevitable, dreaded, cringe-inducing, "And I want you to be there for the birth, too!"

Amber had tried to punt. "I think you and Dennis need to share that moment together," and Nikki had said, "Look, half a hospital will be staring at my girly bits. And besides, you were at Ellie Grant's birth."

Amber shuddered. Yes, she'd doula'd for Ellie Grant, one of Mom's misguided schemes for bringing her back to life after Marcus died. She remembered nothing of it, only that it was such a success that Mom never again brought her to a birth.

"I wasn't really there," she said, and Nikki insisted, "But you'll be at mine." And when Nikki had gone to the midwifery side of the channel, that made it more a given.

A nurse called, "Nikola?" And after a pause, "Nikola Ferrara?"

Amber started when she remembered that was supposed to be Nikki. She got up, dropping her backpack, then gathered her things and followed the nurse, feeling flustered.

The nurse chuckled. "There's no rush."

"Sorry," said Amber. "I'm not myself."

The nurse weighed her, took her blood pressure (a bit on the high side for her, but in the mid-normal range for anyone else) and then left her in a little room with crinkly paper on the exam table. "Strip from the waist down. Dr. Vilkas will be in shortly."

Amber tossed the paper gown onto the chair and returned to her book.

One chapter later, after a light knock, Dr. Vilkas arrived.

Amber's whole body tensed as he entered the room. He greeted her in a thin voice, and he was older than his photo but still handsome. He said, "And what are we here for today?" while looking at her chart.

"This is a preconception appointment," Amber said. "I had some questions about my cycles."

She pulled a sheaf of charts out of her bag. Dr. Vilkas said, "Is your cycle irregular?"

"Yes." Watch for that incoming train in three... two... one... "It's usually every twenty-eight or twenty-nine days, but I'm ovulating late, and my luteal phases are very short." She handed him the charts. "I have about six months' worth with me."

These were Nikki's *Fertility Friend* charts from last year. Mom had glanced at them and said, "You need to take B6 and eat one large carrot every day, plus make sure you're taking lots of folic acid. See? The cervix patterns and temperature patterns aren't lining up with one another." Nikki had followed directions, and two months later announced to the world that "Amber's mom made me pregnant."

Amber had carefully trimmed the "intercourse" line from the charts, more than a little horrified that Nikki would post that kind of thing for every rocks-for-brains internet user to access. But then again, Nikki had also thought nothing of walking into their high school homeroom and announcing to the teacher, "I'm sorry I was absent yesterday. I had diarrhea."

Vilkas frowned at the charts. "This doesn't tell you anything. Are you bleeding regularly?"

"My ovulation is all screwed up, and my luteal phase isn't long enough to sustain a pregnancy," Amber said. "I was wondering how to fix that."

He handed back the charts. "You can't tell when you ovulate."

Amber showed him her copy of *Take Charge Of Your Fertility*. "The book says this temperature rise means I've ovulated in about a forty-eight-hour window. But it has to stay up for eight or nine days to sustain a pregnancy, and I'm only getting six."

Vilkas shook his head. "Do you want the Pill to regularize your cycles?"

For a moment, Amber realized how frustrated her mother felt. She wanted to shake the guy, and she wasn't even sick. Why should she have to know more about healthy female hormones than a doctor? Why, for that matter, did a gynecologist not know how to pinpoint ovulation? She'd always thought it was Mom doctor-bashing when Mom went off about this stuff. "How will the Pill help me conceive? I just want to fix what's wrong."

She studied him while they argued about whether she could get a hormone panel. He had no time for her—this she expected, since Nikki had gotten the same brushoff from her own doctor. That plus, "You're young—you shouldn't worry about having kids yet."

But despite how she wanted to put his head into the wall, Vilkas didn't seem a criminal. He had no use for the proper functioning of a female body, but nothing painted him as a baby-thief and record-falsifier for tens of thousands of dollars a pop. His clothes were neat but not privately tailored. He wore a Timex, not a Rolex.

He said, "Let's do your pap," and then stopped. "Didn't the nurse tell you to get undressed?"

"I don't want a pap until I get my health insurance straightened out," Amber said. "I can't afford it right now."

He sounded incredulous. "But you want a hormone panel?"

She nodded. "I'm not worried about HPV I *might* have when I can see there's an estrogen dominance I *do* have."

He shrugged. "It's not necessary. There's nothing wrong with you. If you don't get pregnant after a year, come back to me then."

He stepped toward the door, and Amber said, "Wait!"

Because...no, she'd come all this way. She couldn't tell just by seeing him, listening to him. So she leaned forward and said, "A friend of mine needs your help."

He said, "She can make an appointment."

"Can you get rid of her baby for her?" Amber said. "Not an abortion. But she doesn't want to do a legal adoption. She doesn't want any record of the pregnancy at all, so there can't be a birth certificate that might be unsealed someday. It has to *never* come to light."

Vilkas said, "She needs to talk to social services."

"She needs a doctor to put another couple's name on the birth certificate so the child can't ever track her down." There we go. No backing out. "Just hook her up with a childless couple who maybe can't afford the adoption fees, and they'll all be happy. She won't ask any questions. She just needs the child to disappear."

Vilkas's face went white. He shut the door, then stepped toward her. She braced herself, but it was hard not to cringe. "You're talking about breaking the law. The reason no one does that is it's illegal. And it's wrong. She needs to talk to social services, or if her need for secrecy is that great, she needs to terminate. But this scheme is insanity. She needs counseling. And so do you."

Push him. "It's just a piece of paper."

He got right into her personal space. Thank heaven she hadn't stripped. "Who are you? What do you really want?"

Don't speak. See if he hangs himself.

"Whatever you're after, no." His eyes narrowed. Amber could smell Italian salad dressing on his breath, and his hand crumpled the edge of her file folder. "Whatever fantasy you're chasing, take your charts and your birth certificates and leave. Do not come back to my practice, and don't ever contact me again."

Amber kept her spine straight. "Are you throwing me out?"

"Absolutely I am." He opened the door. "I want nothing to do with your conspiracy theories."

He stalked into the hallway, and before Amber could even gather her coat and books, a wide-eyed nurse appeared in the door. "The doctor asked me to escort you out."

Amber smiled. "I need to pay first."

The nurse couldn't argue with that. At the desk, Amber pulled out a handful of twenties. Well worth it. As the receptionist drew up a receipt, Amber said, "I was wondering how I could obtain medical records. Really old ones."

The receptionist said, "Those get stored in a microfiche facility in Syracuse. How old are we talking about?"

"Twenty-four years," Amber said. "Dr. Vilkas delivered me, and I'd like my records."

The receptionist laughed. "Oh! Then you're the perfect person to answer a question we all have! Did that suggestion run in a magazine or on the radio?"

Amber squinted. "Why?"

She chuckled as she filled out the receipt. "Oh, we see mini-trends all the time whenever a pregnancy magazine makes a quirky suggestion. We'll get five calls about whether it's safe to drink grape juice, and then two weeks later one of the patients shows us an article saying *Ask your doctor about grape juice during early labor.* That kind of thing."

The nurse behind her said, "You're the third person this week to ask about medical records that are over twenty years old."

Amber tensed. "What?"

"Actually the second one today." The receptionist handed over the receipt. "Whatever happened with that second one, though, Dr. Vilkas was furious. I heard him yelling." The receptionist turned to the nurse. "Then he called in Claudine and started reaming her out too."

The nurse said, "Probably in a lousy mood because that patient stiffed him and then wanted her records," and both women laughed.

The receptionist shook her head. "Whatever, though, those records are gone by now. We're only required to keep birth records twenty-one years, so he called the facility a couple of hours ago and ordered a purge of anything older than that."

But Amber had already strode away from the desk, shoving the receipt in her pocket and pulling out her cell phone. Katie. Oh no. Katie.

Katie hadn't even gotten out of the car before Dad stalked down the driveway. He flung open the door, tearing the handle out of her fingers. "What on Earth do you think you're doing?"

"I'm getting out of my car." She scrambled in her head to piece together what she'd done to make Dad so angry. "What's wrong?"

"What's wrong? You're destroying your mother, that's what's wrong!"

Katie opened her hands. "How? What's going on?"

Dad had stormed out of the house without a coat and he folded his arms in the cold, now brittle in advance of tonight's snow. Katie took the opportunity to get out of the car, leaving her bag inside and the door unlocked. She probably should have left the engine running, too. But Dad stood between her and the house, and that put him between her and Daniel. "Did she have a panic attack? What's wrong with Mom?"

"It's not what's wrong with your mother. It's what's wrong with you. I told you to leave matters alone about her pregnancy. It was a difficult time and there's no reason to go asking her about it."

"What have I asked her?" Was this about the maternity clothes? Was Dad really this worked up about horizontal stripes?

Dad said, "Then why did you request her medical records?"

How'd he find that out? "Mailed to *me*. Me. Not here. Mom didn't have to know. I didn't even give them her address, so how would she find out?"

"Because the doctor called me," Dad said. "He wanted to know what was going on that she was requesting her records from a quarter century ago—and then we find out it's your address, not hers, so you even forged her name to that letter!"

She sighed. "And you told him gee, my grandson *died* six months ago and we'd like some answers."

"No, Katie." Dad stepped toward her, and Katie inched back. "Those records aren't going to tell you a single thing about Kieran. But I did call Dr. Shapiro to find out why he was telling you to harass your mother, and he told me," Dad's voice dipped to a dangerous whisper, "that he wasn't asking you anything of the sort. So now I want to know, what's going on?"

Katie backed toward the car. Dad stepped forward again. "Well?" Looking right into her eyes. "What's going on?"

Katie looked at the ground. It was so cold. The wind tore at her.

"Then let me hazard a guess." Dad was barely audible. "There's a woman in her late forties who's putting you up to this."

Katie folded her arms. "Are you sure you want to confess to your affair right here on the driveway?"

"With her? Not hardly." Dad snorted. "She's...well, she was, a delusional girl who made all sorts of outlandish accusations against a friend of mine, the doctor who delivered you. She was obsessed with him, and when he turned her down, she spread all sorts of rumors."

Would the private investigator turn up something like that?

Dad said, "I have no idea how she tracked you down, but she's a dangerous woman."

Katie said, "What would she do?"

"She's not well." Dad shook his head. "She might try to take your baby."

Katie's hand went to her abdomen. "But how? She's not even around here!"

How far away was Patmos Springs? An hour? Maybe two?

Dad said, "She was unstable then, and if she's still pursuing him, she's unstable now."

Katie said, "Then we need to call the police!"

Dad raised his hands. "Don't over-react, Kitten. Just cut contact with her. Most stalkers will back off if there's no contact for six weeks. She'll lose interest."

"You just said after twenty-four years she'd try to steal my baby!" Katie's voice broke. "If that's true, then we need to call the cops!"

230

"Well, maybe I overstated it." Dad's mouth tightened. "Just don't talk to her. Don't listen. She's got a grudge."

Katie would have rather had Dad admit to an affair. Then at least she'd have Amber as a sister. A half-sister. That would be just fine. But now, with this—Amber wouldn't steal a baby, would she? To make up for not having a baby with Marcus?

Although, come to think of it, what *would* Amber do? Katie said, "But where's the evidence?"

Dad spread his hands. "What evidence?"

"You're telling me this lunatic somehow tracked down the daughter of a patient of a doctor she had a crush on two decades ago in another state." Katie shook her head. "How can you prove that?"

Dad's eyes narrowed. "Why should I have to prove it? What did she tell you? Can she prove whatever she said?"

The wind alone didn't explain the sudden shivers, the multiple urges to run in the face of Dad's stare. And inside: a surety that telling Dad was the last thing she should do. She wanted to run, run, run as fast and as far as she could. But she couldn't leave Daniel.

Pull Amber from her back pocket again. "I'm just thinking about evidence. Data."

"What does your mother's pregnancy record have to do with evidence?"

Katie shoved her hands in her pockets. "Records are evidence. That woman's working as a nurse or a midwife or something. She said *she* has proof that Vilkas committed medical malpractice against Mom, and that's why she's so anxious all the time."

Dad did a double-take.

"She said the doctor gave Mom post-traumatic stress disorder." Her voice broke with the lie, but whatever. Let Dad think she was crying. She looked off into the wind, and that brought tears to her eyes. What had Maureen said they did to her there? "Forcing her down and making her have cervical exams, breaking her water against her will. That stuff. And Mom couldn't leave, but everyone protected the man. But... But yeah. That."

Dad said, "Katie?"

"And you all said it was a tough time for her, but if we could only get proof the doctor mistreated her, she'd be okay!" Katie looked back at Dad. "Don't you want Mom to be okay? You said the doctor was your friend, but isn't Mom more important?"

Dad's eyes were really wide now. "That woman had no right to say that!"

That woman. Did he not even know Maureen's name? Dad said, "Dr. Vilkas treated your mother so well. We drove over an hour just to deliver with him. He wanted everything to be right for her, just like I did!"

"I hate that woman!" Katie exclaimed. Real tears came, and she didn't even need the wind. Her chest heaved, and she groped in her pocket for a tissue that wasn't there. Hated Maureen. Hated her for making Katie lie to her own father. Hated the questions, hated that she'd made Dad angry, hated that she might hurt her mother's feelings. "I wish she'd never called me. I just want to know what really happened."

Dad reached for her, and Katie tensed. But he only handed her his handkerchief, and Katie wiped her face. "I want to know the truth about my mom. And I want to know the truth about Kieran."

Dad hugged her. "Honey, your mother will be fine. That doctor didn't hurt her. You mother was sick even before we moved out there."

"I know. I know." Katie shook her head. "But I'm being safe. Mike got a private investigator."

Shocked, Dad said, "What? Really?"

Katie nodded. "To check her out. To make sure she wasn't deranged. Or dangerous. Like you said."

Dad sounded cautious. "Do you have the report yet?"

Katie shook her head. "It'll take a while."

"Well, I want to see it when you do." Dad frowned. "Now stop this nonsense and come inside."

"I can't. Mom will see I'm upset."

Dad hesitated. Then, "Just go in and wash your face. Tell her you did an experiment in class that was smoky and made your eyes water."

As she walked up the steps, her phone rang in her pocket. She pushed the button to send it straight to voicemail, then turned it off. In the privacy window she could see Daniel, watching with large eyes from behind the curtain. She ducked her head against the first snowflakes.

TWENTY

Up later than she cared to be, Amber found herself playing Words With Friends with both Scott and Nikki (and losing to both) while watching for a Skype call.

A message from Nikki: *Why are you still awake?*

She replied, *In case Katie calls.*

Nikki: *You worried?*

Her reply: *Yes.*

Not that Amber was the best judge of character, but Katie didn't seem the type to bear the weight of the world with a tragic stoicism. If that scheming doctor got on the phone screaming at her, she'd crumple. Or worse. What if he decided to protect his livelihood by taking them all out? It wasn't a far step from stealing babies to killing a witness.

If he came for her: fine. Amber wasn't irreplaceable. If Marcus could die, anybody could, and nobody would miss her if she disappeared. But Katie had a kid. And Mom. What if that jerk went after Mom?

She texted Scott. *Could you have them do a drive-by on Oakview Avenue tonight? That doctor scares me.*

Scott: *I'm on it.*

Asking favors. Yuck. It only increased his sense that he'd get her to date him if he just persevered long enough. Ask for a movie and drinks, and then...and then what?

He messaged her again: *Jogging tomorrow?*

She replied, *In a foot of snow?*

He replied, *I'd do it for you.*

Amber found herself smiling. *I wouldn't do it for me.*

It was late, though, and staying up wasn't going to make Katie call, so first she would put the computer to sleep, and then she would put herself.

In bed, Amber closed her eyes, and after thirty seconds decided this would be one of those nights she spent looking at the clock, only then she wasn't anymore.

On a hill, she wrapped her arms around herself because of the breeze, and she looked over her shoulder. Marcus was calibrating their telescope.

He seemed sad. "You don't look at the stars anymore."

"There are no more stars." Amber took a step toward him. "Why are you setting that up?"

"This is ours. I want you to see the stars one more time."

"Where have you been?" She began shaking, and she couldn't move any closer. He met her eyes, and she struggled to reach for him. Touch him. Feel that solidity, smell the musky scent of his skin, put her lips against his neck. Get his arms around her. "What happened to you?"

She couldn't unlock her limbs, and in the next moment, she found herself in her bed on her back. No stars. No stars.

The silence ached all around her, as if the air had congealed into a prism with her at the center and the world at a distance. She didn't dare move. She stared at the dashes of light across her ceiling where the streetlamps seeped around the corners of the window.

After ten minutes, she realized it stank, so she got up. The horrible cat had messed up the carpet again. She cleaned it, but the cat remained hidden. At that point, good and awake, she figured she might as well see if it was her turn on Words With Friends.

In her email was a message from Katie. "I don't want to contact you again," it began, followed by a paragraph of rambling, circular reasoning Amber didn't care to parse right now. Sure, why not. It made no sense anyhow.

The time stamp said only half an hour ago. Hm.

Skype opened right up, and Amber clicked on Katie's ID, figuring that if Katie would Skype her to say she was never talking to her again, and then email her to say she was never talking to her again (along with two hundred words of explanation) then it was a good shot she'd also answer a call to explain why she wasn't talking to her ever again. This kind of thing was annoying as anything in a friend, but useful now. Was Katie trying to flounce out the door, or was she so invested in everyone thinking she was a great person that she couldn't bear to leave without justifying herself?

"Because frankly," Amber whispered while the computer tried to make the connection, "if I'm leaving someone behind, it's because I *don't* care what they think." And the worse they thought of her, the better, that way they didn't try to contact her again.

Sure enough, a message appeared with "Connecting," and when the call established, Amber got a view of Katie holding a toddler.

Amber's throat ached, but she forced a smile. "Well, hello there."

Katie looked wretched. "I told you I don't want to talk to you anymore."

Amber didn't have to force the sad look. Actually, on the monitor, she looked awful herself. "I don't get why. Did I offend you by leaving you alone for a week? Isn't that what you wanted me to do?"

Katie sighed. "Look—"

The toddler started coughing, a wracking cough that came from deep in his chest. Amber flinched. "Ouch. That sounds lousy."

"Yeah, he can't sleep, so guess who else is awake?" Katie pressed his head to her shoulder. "This is Daniel."

Daniel picked up his head and looked at the computer screen, although Amber figured he was mostly interested in seeing himself. He sat forward, then gave another chesty cough.

"Poor little guy. Has he got strep? Half the town is down with it now."

"I don't think so, but who could sleep through that?" Katie said, "And really, I don't want to talk to you anymore."

"Did you get my message?"

"Yeah." Katie sighed. "I found out first, though. The doctor called my father, and my father laid into me."

Amber straightened in her chair. "He hit you?"

"No, I mean he yelled. He's furious." Katie frowned. "Okay, so he told me your mother was delusional and wanted revenge on Dr. Vilkas because she was a jilted lover."

Amber choked on a laugh. "What?"

"Look, I'm just telling you."

"And I'm telling you I was glad to find out this guy was practicing in Cortland because if my mother ever ran him over with her car, I wouldn't have been sure it was an accident."

Katie glanced at Daniel. Oops, probably shouldn't joke about homicide in front of a toddler. "Well, neither of us was there, so we don't know. Your mother hates him, sure. Why? Well, that's her story."

Amber said, "Except you can solve it for us. One cotton swab to the mouth and we're done."

Katie grimaced. "My father forbade me to have any more contact with you."

Amber couldn't fight the smile. "And you're going to do what he said?"

Katie looked up, brows knit.

"Probably the fastest way my parents could get me to give you *my* DNA," Amber said, "would be to forbid me to do it."

Katie looked miserable. "It's more complicated than that."

Daniel coughed again, deep and raspy.

Amber's mouth twitched. "Do you have any Vicks Vapo Rub?"

Katie said, "He hates it. He says it stinks."

And it follows that as the adult, you let the child dictate his medical treatment? "Hey, buddy, is it funny to have stinky feet?"

Daniel grinned, then coughed.

"Mom needs to give you stinky feet medicine," she said.

Katie said, "What?"

"Put the Vicks on the soles of his feet." Amber shrugged. "Then put his socks over it."

"What's that going to do?"

Amber in the monitor looked somber. "It will give him stinky feet."

Daniel giggled.

"Go on. Try."

Katie got up, leaving Daniel at the computer. Amber watched the boy watching himself on the screen. Did he look like Katie? Maybe a bit. Maybe Kieran looked like Katie too. Maybe when Katie looked at Daniel she saw the Kieran that could have been, the same way maybe the Amber and Marcus living in New Mexico might have had a baby by now. Maybe two. His dark eyes and rich hair, his sly smile.

Stupid reality.

Katie returned. "Okay, Daniel. Let's look at those piggies."

Daniel coughed and held his nose, but Katie rubbed his feet with the gel and then pulled on his socks. "Feels funny," said Amber. "But not as stinky?"

He coughed, and Katie put aside the jar, then took him back on her lap.

Amber said, "You're the adult. If your dad forbids you to send off your DNA, what's he going to do? Take away your TV privileges?"

"Mom is childcare for us while I'm at work," Katie said. "He might stop her from doing that."

"Pay for daycare," Amber said. "Free childcare isn't free if it has all those strings. They don't get to run your life just because they watch your kid."

"But my mother likes having him," Katie said. "She'd be upset."

"Then your Dad couldn't very well cut you off."

"It's complicated," Katie said. Yeah, yeah, everything was complicated in their family. "If he found out, it would get ugly."

Amber said, "You never learned to be sneaky."

Katie tried to smile. "Did you?"

Amber grinned. "As sneaky as I had to be."

"What was it like growing up there?" Katie rolled her eyes. "No, wait, I bet Maureen was all over you all the time, telling you everything you needed to know."

"And I ignored her, like all good teens since the stone age, yeah." Amber shrugged. "Mom had a crazy schedule, and Dad worked late a lot. They juggled us pretty well."

Katie smiled weakly. "Why are you up now?"

"Nightmare." Amber shook her head. "I figured the computer was as good a distraction as any."

"What did you dream about?"

"Marcus." Amber stared at her ring finger. "I guess it wasn't a nightmare. He asked me why I don't go stargazing anymore, and I told him there were no more stars."

Not until she said it did she realize she'd been speaking the truth: in the dream, if she'd looked up there would have been none. The sky would have been empty, an eternal unbroken field of nothing.

Don't think about it. Don't. "By the way," she pointed to the screen, "he's out cold."

Katie looked down. "Whoa! I had no idea that would work."

"Camphor on thin skin. It's not the smell that makes it work." Amber nodded. "That's my mom's trick. So you can see she's not totally insane."

"Maybe only partly." Katie looked up. "You guys used to go stargazing?"

Amber nodded. "That's how we met. The night he died, we'd been on a hill looking at the *eta aquarids* meteor shower. Actually, he was irritated at me because he wanted to look at stars and I wanted to see the meteor shower, but I won and we put the telescope back in my car. The telescope was our engagement present to each other, instead of a ring just for me."

"Oh," Katie murmured. "So you haven't gone out with it since?"

Amber tried to nod and ended up shrugging. She couldn't meet Katie's eyes, so she stared at the webcam instead, which ironically would make her appear as if she really was looking Katie in the face. "I said something about this being the biggest engagement ring any woman ever had, and he said, you told me it was fine you didn't have a ring. I shot back that a mounting ring didn't count. He acted hurt, but I didn't think he really was. He said, 'I'm going to make you sorry you said that,' and I joked back, because I thought it was a joke, 'You've got the rest of your life to make me sorry.' And he kissed me. So I thought it was fine. I didn't realize the rest of his life could be measured in hours." Don't cry. Roll back your eyes and stop it before it starts. "That night he died and they ruled it a suicide. So, yeah. He made me sorry I said that."

Katie did have tears on her cheeks. "But you were joking."

Amber wove her fingers together. "Did he know that?"

Katie said, "I'm sure he did. Was he mad at you in the dream?"

Amber's mouth twisted. "What does that matter? It's not like it's really him."

Katie shrugged. "Maybe and maybe not. Was he mad?"

Amber shook her head. "More like sad. But I was scared because he didn't realize there were no stars."

Katie said, "Do you dream about him often?"

Amber looked down. "Only a handful of times. Not for a year at least."

Katie's voice sounded quiet. "I don't usually dream about Kieran either. But I like to think he's watching over us. Praying for us. That maybe in Heaven I'll find him still a baby and get to raise him there."

Amber said nothing.

"Maybe Marcus is waiting for you."

"I don't believe in Heaven anymore." Amber's hands clenched. "I'm glad you do. You're comforted by it. I'm not into that. He's dead. It's over."

"Oh. Sorry."

"No need."

Katie said, "But I think you need to make amends with Marcus."

Make amends with someone who's dead?

She went on, "Do you ever visit the cemetery?"

"Not since they buried him." Amber glared up. "My stupid future-mother-in-law had a closed-casket funeral and then had him cremated, and she kept him in her house like just another knick-knack, so I couldn't have gone and visited even if I wanted. Then like a year later, her parish priest told her oh, by the way, Catholics don't keep dead bodies in their houses, the Church says they have to bury them. So she called me one Saturday morning and said, hey, can you come here in an hour?" Katie choked, but Amber kept going. "So yeah, I ended up out there once, standing on top of a hill watching them put this little box in the ground, and that's not Marcus. There's nothing left."

A few weeks later, she and Nikki had watched a Doctor Who marathon, and the Master had gone up in an explosion. Nikki had shouted at the Doctor, "Don't be an idiot! If there's no body, he's not dead!" And for a minute Amber hadn't registered anything on the TV. No body, no death. Maybe Marcus was alive somewhere. In New Mexico. Out under the stars digging with the Amber who could have been his wife.

Katie whispered, "I'm sorry. I just thought you might like to go there sometime."

Amber narrowed her eyes. "You think I'm heartless for not?"

"Not a big deal." Katie didn't look judgy or anything. "The grief counselor told me that when it comes to cemeteries, there are 'goers' and 'not goers,' and both are just right."

"It's not like he's there."

"Right." Katie nodded. "But I find it comforting, so I go and leave things on the grave."

Amber smirked. "Grave goods."

Katie looked puzzled. "No. Wind chimes, a pinwheel, Matchbox cars. Stuff like that."

"That's a carnival." Amber chuckled. "But that's what grave goods are. When you're working at an archaeology dig, sometimes you find these things that people buried with their dead. It's because we don't want to let go, and it feels like one of the most human things we can do is to *have* something, so we show love by giving. All sorts of cool things got buried with people."

Katie looked irritated, kind of the way she'd looked about the vaginal bypass surgery thing. "So I'm human?"

Amber nodded. "I'm afraid you and I are exhibiting behaviors."

Katie squinted. "What's your behavior called?"

"Being a jerk?"

Katie grimaced. "I'm sure there's a more academic term."

Amber laughed, and Katie cracked a smile.

An awkward silence, and then Katie said, "Well, thank you for the stinky-feet trick. I'm going to put Daniel back to bed now."

"Are you still discontinuing contact?"

Katie sighed. "I... Geez, I don't know. My mother is so fragile. This would kill her. One way or the other, she'd break down. I should wait until she dies of old age and then call you back."

Amber said "Why?"

"She has anxiety. She has since forever, and she's always afraid she'll lose me. It dominates her." Katie shuddered. "So if she suspected I wasn't hers, or suspected I wondered if I wasn't hers, or thought I felt like she thought I wasn't hers...she'd fall apart, and it would be all my fault."

Forget what she'd said earlier about Katie not being able to bear the weight of the world. Clearly she'd been bearing it all her life. Amber said, "So you figure whatever happened, she's innocent. Either she had you, or someone convinced her you were hers?"

Katie nodded.

"What do you think happened?" Amber said. "For real."

It stunned Amber how often that gave her the real answer. Ask outright and you'd get three rounds of "I have no idea," and finally the person would say, "I don't know, but if I had to take a guess," and then bam, out came this whole incredible story. You'd investigate and suddenly the information would be there.

Katie did the "I don't know" twice before saying, "But I think my Dad knows more than he's letting on."

Amber said, "You said your father protects your mother."

"Not that way. He'd change my report card so Mom wouldn't worry, but an illegal adoption is a whole different category."

Amber said, "Do you think you're my sister?"

Katie sat for a while, looking at Daniel's hair. Then, "I want you to be."

Shivers curled up Amber's spine. "I feel the same."

"So can't we just be sisters?" Katie's head jerked up. "Do we have to prove it with a lab test? There's more to sisterhood than DNA, so why force the issue?"

Amber cocked her head. "You're proposing a lifelong game of pretend."

Katie said, "I never had a sister. It was just me growing up, so I don't know what kinds of things sisters do, but I'm sure they don't compare DNA."

"They might as well," Amber said. "My sister Olivia and I—heck, we'd count how many French fries we had. *She got more than me*! And if Mom got me shoes and didn't get her shoes, or if Olivia got new pencils but I didn't, watch out."

Katie said, "I'll argue with you if you want."

"You have to slam doors," Amber said.

"I can do that too." Katie's eyes crinkled. "I bet your toothbrush is prettier than mine."

"I bet it is, and it's because I'm going to grow up to be a ballerina." Amber laughed. "But over time, wouldn't you want to know? Really know?"

Katie said, "Why?"

"Because the past is written in the present." Amber tucked up her knees and hugged them to her chest. "All the garbage and all the good stuff, it made us. What happens to you if you're always with someone, all the time, and then you're ripped away from them? What happens if your familiar touch is gone?"

Katie looked aside, then said, "Marcus was your soul-mate, wasn't he?"

Amber started.

"I can't be that. No matter where I was born." Katie sighed. "A part of you really did go missing. Maybe me. But definitely Marcus."

Amber said, "Then don't go away again."

The words came out...broken? More broken than she intended, but maybe it was the late hour, the lingering starlessness.

Katie said, "Well, Dad only ordered me not to talk to Maureen anymore. He doesn't know about you."

"Wow," Amber said. "Rebellion at its pickiest."

"I will be able to honestly tell him *that woman* hasn't contacted me again."

"Did the DNA kit arrive?" When Katie nodded, Amber said, "Keep it. If you change your mind, send it in and let us know."

Katie said, "Just promise me you won't ever involve my mother."

What? "Why would I do that?"

"I don't want my mother involved. If anything I do might involve her, I refuse."

Amber raised her hand. "I promise I won't involve her. I will not call her, write to her, send her a singing telegram...nothing."

Katie sighed. "Thank you. I'd better get him to bed. And you get some sleep, too. There are stars out there, and you'll see them again. That's my promise to you."

They disconnected. Amber did a quick sweep of the house to make sure the cat hadn't left anything else around, but before she got back to bed, the phone rang.

Mom. "Come on over to Nikki's house!" she sang. "It's baby time!"

twenty one

Nikki eased herself into the labor tub, and a moment later, she let off a shuddering sigh.

The magic of the liquid epidural. Maureen rubbed her shoulder. "Whatever position is most comfortable."

Nikki murmured, "This." She'd gone onto her knees and was leaning her forearms on the side of the tub, lowering her head. "This is good."

Maureen had pegged Nikki as a naked birther, the kind of woman who disrobed the minute she went into labor and couldn't stand the slightest touch against her skin. Instead, Nikki had met her at the door in a thick white bathrobe, and even now in the tub she wore a pink maternity t-shirt. She kept craving touch. Primarily by Dennis, but anyone would do. Maureen had held Nikki through contractions while Dennis filled the labor tub.

Dennis had a nasty cough, and he looked exhausted. He kept rubbing Nikki's back, but he was much more miserable than new-dad worried.

The bell rang, and Maureen went to let in Amber. "You got here fast."

"I have a siren." Amber was covered in snow. "No, I didn't really do that. But I was already awake, talking to Katie. She's so skittish."

As Amber hung up her coat in the closet, Maureen touched the snow on her hair. "It's gotten that bad?"

"It's pretty lousy, but not horrible if you take it slow. They upped the forecast to eighteen inches. Winter's last hurrah." She shook her head and more snow flew off. "How's it going?"

"She's doing great. Come on."

Amber trailed her to the labor tub. "Dennis, you look like hell."

"That's what I said." Nikki huffed. "But he won't..." She closed her eyes, and then her face tightened and she gripped the side of the tub.

Amber darted up to her and grabbed her hands, kneeling alongside the tub. It was an instinctive movement, but Maureen's heart went to her throat as Amber stayed forehead-to-forehead with her friend, breathing in unison. Nikki breathed with her, shoulders relaxing.

In less than a minute. Nikki looked up, worn.

Amber said, "You were saying Dennis won't go to the doctor?"

"I'm saving my sick leave," he rasped.

Maureen took a flashlight. "Open up." It didn't take more than a look. "That's strep."

Nikki said, "Told you."

Amber said, "But you win, because this is paternity leave, not sick leave." She squeezed Nikki's hands. "How are you doing?"

"Better. This tub is awesome."

Despite being a non-naked birther, it turned out Nikki was not a deep-inside-yourself birther either. Maureen wanted the mom's inclinations to take precedence, and some moms wanted to birth in a cave with the midwife sitting quietly in a corner.

But Nikki craved strength in numbers. Distraction was her thing. Jokes, chatter, back rubs, scented candles, music, lights. Maureen suspected that if the neighbor showed up with a lasagna, she could stay and chat, at least until pushing. Last year, a strength-in-numbers mom had labored dancing to an old Hansen CD. The

248

mom had laughed between songs, "I'm sorry you have to listen to this," and Maureen had replied, "Don't be. It's like a trip down memory lane, and my daughters didn't even pay me to listen back then."

So Maureen sat by as Nikki chatted between contractions and then craved touch and cuddles during. Maureen used a hand-held doppler to check the baby's heart rate every fifteen minutes, noting how well the heartbeat bounced back after each contraction. She tracked the changing shape of the belly as the baby descended, observed how the contractions stayed nice and even. Good progress for a first time mom. By dawn, Nikki was almost in transition.

Meanwhile, Dennis was flagging. His cheeks were flushed, and he looked dead on his feet.

Maureen left Amber with Nikki and brought Dennis into the kitchen. He looked worried. "Is something wrong with the baby?"

"The baby's fine and Nikki's fine." Maureen crossed her arms. "I'm worried about you. Can you get checked out today?"

They ran down the options. His doctor's office. Urgent care. The ER. The Quick-Clinic at the chain drug store in Elmira. "Call your doctor first," Maureen said. "I know you're a big strong guy," she said over his protests, "but you're about to bring a new baby into a house with strep. See the doctor."

He said, "Nikki needs me."

"Nikki needs you well." She pointed to the phone. "Start calling."

Maureen had Amber heat up some chicken broth, and while Dennis drank it, she considered their options.

The doctor's office in Owego said they'd work him in sometime later this week, but they were cancelling all appointments today because of the storm, and they refused to page the doctor. The Quick-Clinic was closed due to the storm. Urgent care had a three-hour wait, and it was a half hour drive even without snow. Nikki needed them here, not hanging out in a waiting room.

Maureen couldn't get hold of Dr. Jacobson. Not being in practice anymore meant he wasn't on call—pretty much the whole point of the exercise.

She went back to the labor tub where Dennis looked flushed on top of his pallor.

Eighteen inches of snow. A newborn in a household with strep. And all because no one wanted to do their damn job. Not the doctors, not the receptionists or the phone service, not the Quick-Clinic. No, as long as they were on their couches in front of their fireplaces, what did it matter if other people suffered? How was this any different than what she herself had experienced, when the system's primary concern was running the system?

So she picked up the phone and dialed Sam, the druggist. "Will you be there?" she asked. "Despite the snow? I've got an emergency."

"I'll meet you," he said. "I wasn't planning to open, but let me know when."

"Fifteen minutes," she said.

Next.

"Amber," she said, "I need you to run down to Sam's Drugs."

She pulled out the prescription pad and said to Dennis, "Are you allergic to anything? What antibiotics do you usually get?"

"He gets amoxicillin," said Nikki. "No allergies."

Maureen wrote the script, then handed it to a frowning Amber. She murmured, "Isn't this slightly illegal?"

"I can write it for Nikki. She's my patient."

Amber said, "And then if your patient's husband takes her medication, the fault is all his?" She shook her head. "I'll be back in a bit."

"Drive safely. And be careful. I keep feeling as if someone's following me."

Amber said, "Well, given the road conditions, it would have to be a snowman. I'll be fine."

Maureen gripped her hand. "Thank you, honey."

Looking down, Amber smirked. "Not a big deal. Doulas are supposed to fetch things for the mom, right?"

She departed.

Outside it kept snowing like crazy. Raymond texted that he wasn't going to work, and later again that the college had cancelled classes. Maureen kept filling her chart and forcing Dennis to drink tea with honey or to gargle salt water. They kept Nikki occupied and distracted, gave her cuddles and kept the tub warm, and when it got tougher, they reassured her she was doing great.

An hour later, Amber returned with amoxicillin and a box of donuts. "I felt bad that he opened just for us, so I had a moral responsibility to buy these. And I passed two cars in ditches. Nikki, you can pick 'em."

"Thanks," Nikki murmured. The contractions had grown longer and closer together, and she'd been struggling to stay on top of them. "I aim to please."

Nikki had entered transition, the intense time from seven to ten centimeters. Her focus narrowed, and now when Amber got face to face with her, while they breathed together deeply and slowly, Nikki struggled to stay relaxed. Maureen told Dennis to take two pills for his first round of antibiotics, just to get a good top-up, and then go to bed. "You'll wake up before Nikki starts pushing," she said. "I promise we'll get you."

Nikki was going deep inside herself now during contractions, but seeming scared. Maureen took a look at the rising snow, wondering how they'd transport in this weather if Nikki decided she wanted to go to the hospital for an epidural. But really, by now, there wasn't time for an epidural anyway. Maybe she had an hour until pushing. In all this snow, she'd take half an hour at least to get to the hospital, and another half hour for the anesthesiologist to insert it.

In the middle of a contraction, Nikki's low moan turned into a whine, and then into a cry. "I can't do this! I can't!"

Maureen squeezed her hands. "Nikki, honey, you're doing it. You're doing fine."

"I can't!"

"Hey, breathe." Amber wrapped her arms around Nikki's shoulders. "Breathe. We're here."

Nikki went limp as the contraction ended. Amber stood and stripped off her jeans.

Maureen did a double-take. "Do you want me to find you a bathing suit?"

"You're not leaving her side," Amber said. "Me neither." In just her bra and panties, Amber stepped into the pool, then knelt beside Nikki. "Okay now. We're doing this together. Ready?"

"No," Nikki whimpered, and Amber tousled her hair. Nikki shifted to hold onto Amber in the tub, and Maureen backed off. Nikki had held Amber during Marcus's funeral, and now at the beginning of her baby's life, they'd reversed. Another contraction came, and Nikki leaned into Amber, but she didn't cry out.

That was the next hour, right there. Other than getting more comfortable, Amber didn't move. Nikki stayed face-into Amber's shoulders, moaning low and deep. *Open* she was murmuring. *Ohhhh-pen.* Maureen had told her to do that, and she was. Mouth nice and slack. Open mouth, open cervix.

And then at some point, Maureen realized it had been several minutes since the last contraction, and Nikki sat up, asked about the snow, then made a wisecrack about Dennis owing her bigtime for sleeping through everything. She asked for half a donut, and Maureen handed her a towel to dry her hands and then the food. She passed the towel to Amber. "Get into something dry and go wake Dennis."

Amber frowned. "But—"

"Wait. Why is it stopped?" Nikki's eyes went huge. "Is something wrong?"

"No, something's right. You're getting a break." Maureen patted her hand. "You're probably complete, so the cervix is out of the way and the baby's not putting pressure on it anymore. But he's going to keep descending, and then you're going to start pushing. You might have as long as half an hour, but probably less."

Climbing out of the tub, Amber glanced at the clock. Maureen didn't need to look: it was just after noon. Amber stripped off her wet underwear, pulled on her t-shirt, and headed for the laundry room. "I'm taking your clothes," she called.

Nikki said, "Sure, but they're all maternity."

Maureen said, "She probably wishes she'd gone for the swimsuit right about now."

Nikki laughed, but mid-laugh her fingers clutched the edge of the tub, and her head jerked up.

Maureen said, "What?"

"I thought...I think my membranes just went." Nikki's voice was shaken. "I felt a pop."

Maureen clutched her hand. "Amber! Amber, get Dennis—now!"

Nikki let out a grunt and flexed her spine backward, coming up off her knees and craning back her head. Maureen put her hand on Nikki's neck. "Try to curl forward. That's it. That's the pushing feeling."

Nikki glared at her, ferocious. "How would you know?"

"I've seen it before." Maureen grinned. "Next contraction, push like we discussed. Long breath, let it out. Push until you feel like stopping, as many times as you want until the contraction ends."

Nikki nodded. Maureen clasped her hand. "You can do this. You're strong."

Amber returned, dressed. Dennis followed her, looking sleepy but better than before. Nikki closed her eyes and curled over herself in the pool, letting out an "Ooh!" as she pushed. It was all involuntary. Nikki needed only to guide the force.

The contraction ended. Maureen got a heartbeat. Great, great. Nikki whimpered, and Dennis cradled her head and shoulders.

"Almost there," said Amber.

Nikki raised her head, then clenched her teeth and narrowed her eyes as she pushed again.

Maureen couldn't tell if the baby was visible. She'd have bet almost, but it wasn't worth putting Nikki on her back just to get a peek.

It went like that for a while, the baby inching up and down with every push, Nikki giving her all and Maureen suggesting other positions to push in. Eventually she had Nikki squatting with her hands on the side of the tub. "Can you feel him?"

Nikki looked at her in confusion.

Maureen said, "He's right there. Touch him."

Nikki slipped her hand between her legs and touched the hard round head just there, just on the verge. Maureen leaned close. "There's your goal. Aim right there."

On the next contraction, Nikki let out a yell, then a shriek, and Maureen watched the head slide out, face-down as it should be, but the cord twice around his neck. She plunged her hands into the pool. "Push again!" she shouted, and Nikki pushed while Maureen kept that head right there on the perineum. His body slid out, over his own head, and he somersaulted over his own cord to arrive face-up in the water.

Maureen unwound the cord as she lifted the baby into Nikki's arms. Dennis shouted, "It's a boy! It's a boy! You did it!"

The baby squawked as the air hit his face, but then he quieted, looking around the room.

Nikki knelt, chest heaving, as Maureen handed her the baby. She dropped back against the side of the tub, baby to her chest, and the tears came.

Maureen checked the clock. 1:14 PM.

Nikki stroked his face. "Are we supposed to cut the cord?"

"Wait for it." Maureen touched his hair. "He needs the rest of his blood."

Nikki said, "But no one else can hold him yet." No, with the cord attached, he could only be with his mother, which was right where Maureen thought he should be.

Dennis beamed. "Look at him. Look at him!"

Nikki was breathing hard, and she reached a hand to Amber. "I did it."

"Yeah." Amber's voice wobbled, and Maureen turned to find her trying to wipe away tears with a tissue, but it was coming apart in her wet hands. "You tell him, he's going to have the best-installed car seat in the world."

An hour later, Amber slipped out to the kitchen to make Nikki something to eat. She hadn't managed to get out of the room before they'd delivered the placenta (she could have lived a long time without seeing one of those) but then afterward it was neat to watch her mom giving the baby a newborn exam. All the prodding, weighing, manipulating—and Mom had talked her way through each step, like "Okay, his hips aren't displaced" while spreading his thighs and bicycling his knees. But now Mom wanted to check that the uterus was clamping down, so with a breezy "I'll see what's for lunch!" Amber had dutifully fled.

She grabbed one of the trays they used for dinner-and-Doctor-Who, then poured milk. And orange juice. Nikki needed Vitamin C, right? She opened a can of chicken noodle soup and started it heating, then looked in the fruit bin. What would Nikki like? Well, let her choose. She set an apple, an orange, and a banana on the tray. Then she made a ham and cheese sandwich (the poor girl needed protein), found a sleeve of Ritz crackers, got a yogurt and a spoon, then put the soup on the tray too.

Nikki had the baby at her breast when Amber walked in, sing-songing, "Lunch time!"

Nikki pointed to Dennis, lying in bed like a brick. "Poor guy."

Mom said, "You worked harder than he did."

"I feel great." Nikki grinned. "Like I want to do laundry and make twenty phone calls."

"And update your Facebook." Amber tried to figure out where on the bed to set the tray: not on Nikki's lap with the baby, but neither on Dennis. "That reminds me: do I need to take more pictures, or were the first thirty thousand sufficient?"

"Shut up." Nikki waved her over. "Here, have a baby."

The baby had fallen asleep. Mom gentled him away from Nikki while Amber set up the tray.

"That's not lunch," Nikki exclaimed. "That's a buffet!"

Amber puzzled over it because it looked so much bigger now than it had in the kitchen. "You burned about five thousand calories giving birth." She shrugged. "I'm reasonably sure you just lost eight pounds."

Nikki rolled her eyes and reached for the sandwich.

Mom said, "More than that. At least five pounds of fluid and a pound of placenta." Mom spread a baby blanket on the bed, then folded a corner, laid the baby down, and wrapped him. She tied the bottom points around the back of the baby's neck. Suddenly there was this expertly wrapped armload, a baby-burrito using his own weight to maintain snugness.

And then, the horror: Mom passed him to Amber.

She knew nothing about holding a baby except that she'd better not drop him, so she stood rigid.

Nikki stopped devouring lunch to say, "Smell him. Isn't that insane?"

Not relishing the scent of icky diaper, Amber dutifully inhaled—and gasped. "It's sweet! He smells sweet!"

Mom grinned. "They all smell that way. Don't be in a rush to bathe him."

"No way. I want to bottle that." Nikki finished the sandwich and reached for her yogurt.

Sure, Nikki would make fun of her for bringing enough food for a thousand people—but she ate like she was famished. Obviously you needed calories to do that kind of work, if not during then afterward.

And then, with the weight and scent of the baby grounding her, and the sight of Nikki eating like a gladiator, Amber realized: there's no way. There was no way someone had stolen Katie from her mother twenty-four years ago. How could there be? Who could walk into a room like this and take a baby from a woman at the top of her game? And who could grab this little bundle of person and walk down the hall to hand it over to some shady black-market kidnapper? Wasn't that against every bit of human nature? To trade in human beings, in human blood and human sweat? No one would do that.

So Katie couldn't be her sister. They should just let this whole pursuit go. Katie was a nice person with a screwed-up family, but nothing more.

Nikki looked up. "Um, about the name. Dennis and I discussed calling him Marcus."

Beside her, Mom froze.

Amber looked right into the baby's face. Eyes closed, mouth pursed, he had a tiny rough triangle in the center of his upper lip. He was peace and potential and fragility all at once.

"I'd rather you didn't," murmured Amber.

"I figured, but I wanted you to know." Nikki looked serious. "We're probably going with Dennis's father's name, but I wanted to see if it fit."

Amber forced a smile. "At least it's not *your* father's name."

Nikki laughed out loud. "Really? Kermit isn't your top choice?"

Amber looked into the baby's face, but she didn't make the retort on her lips. Instead she breathed deep so she would always remember that intoxicating sweetness.

TWENTY TWO

Twenty-four hours after she'd left to assist at Nikki's birth, Maureen returned home. Ray had gone to bed already, but he'd left a note on the table beside a stack of mail. He loved her; he hoped all had gone well with Nikki's baby; he'd used most of the gas for the snow blower so if she wouldn't mind refilling the gas can tomorrow. Oh, and Dr. Jacobson had stopped by.

At the bottom of the stack of mail was a yellow envelope. Thick.

Her hands trembled as she opened the metal clasp, only to find inside it a second envelope, one sealed with string around two paper circles. On it, a post-it. *Sorry I missed your call. Here are your records from Memorial Hospital.*

It took three circuits to unwind the string, and then out slid the printouts, fuzzy the way records were after you converted them to microfiche and then converted them back. But—records. Hers.

At the table, she paged through them all. No details about her pregnancy. These were just the Labor and Delivery Unit's dry recounting of the horror-show that had changed her life's direction. Between the lines she found nothing, no notes to indicate twins. No fundal height, no notes about position (no, there one: vertex. Nothing more.) The records of dilation, drugs given, and so on. Membranes artificially ruptured. Nothing like *11:53, doula climbs into the tub to hug laboring mom. 2:12, ctx 3 min apart, mother dancing to Hansen.*

There was Amber's birth weight and length. Her APGAR scores. Her feeding records and pediatric notes.

Nothing screamed "Stolen baby!" Just another delivery on the assembly line.

Maureen reached the last page with her discharge instructions and thumbed backward until she found a signature. She didn't care about the discharge signature because after the birth, she'd never seen her own doctor again. But back at the actual birth record was that monster's signature. *Anton Vilkas.* The kind of name she'd love to find on a gravestone.

Maureen tossed the papers down only to have something catch her eye. She flipped back through, and then, just above that jerk's signature, was another name. The name of a nurse. Claudine Pratt.

Maureen traced her finger over the name, and as she thought, she bit her lip.

———◦◦◦———

Five phone calls.

Twelve Google searches (but who's counting?)

Two newspaper articles. Well, obituaries.

Three different people-searches cross-referencing the different information from the above.

One midwife friend who said, "Yes, actually."

All that, and one final visit to the website of Dr. Vilkas's practice.

One nurse, located.

"Nailed you," whispered Maureen.

The hell of it was this nurse had stuck by that monster doctor for twenty-five years. Whatever you got paid in the black market baby trade, it must be pretty high. A quarter-century with one doctor, shadowing him through at least two practices: that wasn't normal. In a high-burnout field like nursing, nurses could and did change specialties. Plus, from everything Maureen found, this nurse had been divorced twice (with the resulting name changes), so her attachment to one doctor had outlasted two marriages.

The highway curved up toward the finger lakes, a ribbon lying on the land as Maureen flew over it in her Jeep. The road glistened, but the snow had been plowed off to the sides and sand dumped on the surface. She hadn't told Amber her plan. Really, she hadn't wanted to hear what Amber would have said. *No, Mom, don't.* Or even worse, *Yes, I'm coming.*

Not this time, sweetie. This one was hers.

The one online photo echoed Maureen's memory, a nurse with angular cheeks and long black hair, an upturned nose, and a way of giggling breathlessly when you refused consent but she was going to do something anyhow. The woman couldn't have been much older than Maureen, but she'd bullied her with hospital regulations and "Oh, this is required" when it wasn't actually required. Just that the hospital required the nurse to do it, and therefore she wanted Maureen to capitulate. And at the last moment, the nurse had slapped that mask over her face. Something not recorded in those meticulous records with their neat rounded print.

And now she had her name. Claudine.

Sherry had been the one to connect all the dots. *Wait, this is impossible, but I met a Claudine...* And then working backward, they found it all. Everything. It was scary how much they could piece together online, reconstructing the road map of a life. Amber would be proud.

Maureen pulled off the highway and navigated the streets of Cortland until she reached a narrow little avenue. Whatever the doctor paid this nurse, she wasn't attracting attention with it, that's for sure. She was probably socking it away in an off-shore account, waiting for the day she'd escape to a beach house in Aruba.

Maureen's hands hurt. She unclamped them from the wheel and found a parking spot.

As she looked at the building, she paused. That couldn't really be it, could it? There was "not attracting attention" and there was "living in a hole." Why would you steal babies and sell them if not for the money? And not money in and of itself of course, but spending the money.

Actually, Maureen thought, it didn't matter why they did it. What mattered now was getting the story from her.

The front porch slumped ever so gently, like an old man standing too long in line. She placed her feet with care on the wooden steps, then looked up again at the windows. The lights were on.

Maureen headed through a wooden screen door with flaking paint. It opened lopsided on its hinges. She crept up creaky stairs where the wood gaped between the steps, and on the second floor was a door with a "2" and nothing else. *Well, Claudine, here we go.*

She knocked, then stepped off to the side and waited until the door opened.

Claudine was shorter than Maureen remembered, but as soon as Maureen saw the woman, the heat surged in her head. "Claudine LaBonte?"

The woman's eyes flared, and she tried to slam the door, but Maureen pushed her booted foot into the doorway. "I just came here to talk."

"I'm not talking to you!" The woman shoved at the door in vain. Yeah, go ahead and try. Those boots were designed to climb mountains in the snow so she could deliver babies at any time, any place. The door would break first. "Get out or I'm calling the cops!"

Maureen said, "Please do. I'll have you arrested before you can say *felony kidnapping*."

The woman heaved again at the door. Maureen said, "Why do you do it? How much does he pay you per baby?"

"He's not!" the woman shouted. "He's not!"

"You do it for kicks?" said Maureen.

"He doesn't." The woman stopped, then choked out, "You don't understand."

"Make me understand." Where was this voice coming from? It was the same tone she used during a delivery when the baby was compromised and she needed to act immediately. *Hands and knees, now.* Deeper, designed to cut through a mother's panic. Or the baby-thief's. Fine. It would do.

The woman gave another futile shove at the door, then leaned against it, not trying to shut it as much as for support. "You were the only one. The only one I know of."

Maureen's vision spotted. "What? Why me?"

"Please don't." The woman was crying. "He— If he finds out I talked to you— He already thinks I talked to you."

"How's he going to know?" Maureen said. "Are you also his most convenient booty call?"

The nurse shook her head. "But if you tell him I said anything..."

Maureen waited. "Well?"

263

The door shook against Maureen's shoulder as Claudine gave way to sobbing. The woman gasped for breath, only it wasn't enough, and then Maureen gave the door a quick push. Claudine yielded. By inches, Maureen slipped inside.

The interior was a perfect match to the exterior, furnished with what you'd find at a garage sale. Shoulders slumped. Claudine stood with tears streaming down her face. Maureen took a seat at a round table with four metal chairs. "I'm not talking to Vilkas. I have no reason to."

Maureen said nothing more, waiting for Claudine to get herself together. Finally Claudine moved toward her couch. Tracing a finger on the vinyl tablecloth, Maureen said, "Was I really the only one?"

Claudine huddled with her hands clasped between her knees, staring at the carpet. "He never told me to do it again. I didn't ask. I don't want to know."

"And why'd you do it?" Clearly not for the money.

Claudine groped for a tissue box and yanked on a tissue that split on its way out. She pulled at the other half and tried to mop her face. "He said he'd get me fired for insubordination. He said I'd never work again, and I needed to do what he said."

Maureen said, "You believed him?"

She nodded. "Friends of mine got fired for less. A mom gave birth before the doctor got there, so a nurse caught the baby, but they fired her. They were downsizing, and they'd just as soon fire me. He'd get a lawyer and say it never happened, and I needed my job."

Believe her or not? But hadn't Maureen been pushed around just as much at that age? It had been so easy back then to believe the doctor had authority, especially with the god-like powers they claimed. *If you don't let me check your cervix, I can't guarantee a good outcome.* Because you *can* guarantee it if I do? But at the time, the absurdity had seemed real, in those airless hallways where Nature was the enemy and women her soldiers.

Maureen said, "Why did he do it to me, then?"

Claudine shook her head. "You... He said..."

She shrank in on herself. Maureen said. "Go on. I won't be mad."

Of course, now that meant she couldn't get mad at whatever Claudine said, but she needed the information.

"You were poor." Claudine shivered and glanced up, then back down again. "He said you were too young to raise two, and you had no money. He said the babies would suffer. But he had a friend, another doctor whose wife couldn't get pregnant. And they couldn't adopt because she'd been sick."

Katie. Katie. My baby.

"But if the doctor's wife had a baby, she'd find the will to live. It would make all the difference, that they'd give the baby a better home, a better education, a better life."

Maureen's nails bit into her palm. "Did that make it right?"

No, damn it, don't do that midwife thing, the supportive listening. This woman was a kidnapper, an aide to kidnapping. A monster.

"That made it better." Claudine wove her fingers. "That one at least wouldn't grow up dirt poor."

Maureen said, "We managed. My daughter graduated college. She has a Master's degree."

Claudine said, "Would she have been able to with two?"

They'd have figured it out. They'd have found a way to feed and diaper a second baby, a way to fit more children into one room. Only then, would they have been ready the next year to throw caution to the wind and have Olivia? Would they have had Brendan?

Maureen's voice went soft. "That wasn't your decision to make."

Claudine said, "I didn't make that decision."

She kept her voice low, almost like a breath. "No, you were *just following orders.*"

Claudine huddled tighter over her lap. Maureen realized, Claudine never had children. She'd had two husbands but now was left with no family.

Maureen steadied herself. "How'd you come to work for him? Since he threatened to end your career?"

"The hospital had layoffs. He tracked me down that same day and said he'd make a job for me in his practice."

Maureen said, "To keep tabs on you?"

"He's a good man." Claudine sniffled and got another tissue. "He did it for a friend, to save his wife. He did it to help the baby. He gave me a job. He got in over his head, but he doesn't break the law. He's not a bad man."

Maureen let her babble out the speech she must have told herself a thousand times. How did this make sense, this amoeba of a woman with all her soft parts on the outside? "You were afraid he'll find out I'm speaking to you," Maureen said. "A good man would kill you?"

"No, but... He thought I told you because you requested your records. And so did she. And he had me in his office, screaming, but I never said a thing. I never told anybody, not even my husband."

A shiver climbed Maureen's back. "Nobody?"

Claudine shook her head. "I never wanted anyone to know. Even when I wanted to tell, I was scared to talk. He knew. Nobody else."

And that was it. A whole life wrecked in an instant. It wasn't just Katie who'd lost a future.

There was nothing more to be gained here. Maureen walked to the door.

Claudine said, "He's coming after you."

Hand on the knob, Maureen's throat tightened. "The good man is going to kill me too?"

"He'll make you sorry you looked into this. He'll do anything." Claudine stared at her lap. "Just leave it alone. Please. I don't want to go to prison."

"Look around." Maureen's shoulders sagged. "You're already in prison."

TWENTY THREE

Amber pulled up at her parents' house. The lights were on, but neither car visible.

Scott, approaching with a file folder. A grim, "Come with me." Amber, following with a cold feeling because of his dull eyes. The fear she'd find out protestors burnt down her parents' house. Fear that the County Fire Commissioner was pulling back her job. Mute, she'd let him lead her to an evidence room, where he'd gestured to the desk.

Amber got out of the car, holding a folder. A very slim folder.

Scott had sat across the table from her and first handed her a nameplate: "Colin Allcars." Amber smothered a grin, and he'd said, "I'm getting this dusted for fingerprints."

"Should I ask for an attorney?" she'd said.

Instead he'd laid a thin folder onto the table. "I requested the report on Marcus's death."

Amber climbed the front steps and unlocked the door. Mom wasn't in the kitchen, but from the living room came the muted sounds of a movie soundtrack mingled with unintelligible dialogue.

"I want to go over it with you," said Scott.

Fighting nausea, Amber's first reaction had been, "Why did you do this? Did you think I was lying?"

"I wanted some answers for you," Scott said. "After looking over their report, I agree with you: they did a crap job. And you'd better believe I called back the chief

of police in Binghamton to ask for the rest of the report even though I know full well they never bothered to compile any."

Amber blinked. She couldn't see Scott across the table. *"But why? Why can't you just let him be dead?"*

"Have you?" Scott opened his hands. *"I wanted you to have it. Whether you look at it or not, I wanted you to have even this much."*

Following the sound of the dialogue, Amber found her father on the sofa, remote in one hand and a tablet computer balanced on his knee. He didn't greet her, and she didn't speak while the scene ran. French, no subtitles. A man and a woman stood on a bridge, watching the gulls while having a subdued conversation that sounded simultaneously beautiful and constipated. Everything sounded better in French, even "You had no right to do this!"

"I know I had no right," Scott said, *"but as far as I'm concerned, this is an unsolved crime."*

"My life is an unsolved crime!" Amber rolled back her eyes to stem the tears. *"Do you think you're going to charge in like a hero and solve the unsolvable puzzle? And then what? I thought you wanted to romance me, not bring Marcus back from the dead."*

Scott had gotten a look on his face that stabbed her through the heart, not what she'd expected at all, but maybe he'd thought they would sit there cozy, going over the report line by line. Ah, look, the autopsy said parts of his brain ended up on the opposite wall. *Like some romantic poetry, let's examine this word. Let's see if someone wrote between the lines that the freaking butler did it.*

He said, *"I wanted to help."*

"Then bury him!" she shouted. *"You don't know what it was like! Let it be. You're not Marcus and you can't bring him back!"*

"I wish I could!" he exclaimed. "I can't fight a dead man! I can't compete with someone who died before he did anything wrong."

Amber recoiled into her seat.

Standing, Scott dropped the folder on the desk. "I can't win against a ghost. I can't even get into the race.

Amber said, "I never asked you to compete."

He turned. And she said

Dad paused the movie. Mid-transition, he'd caught the image of a gull's wings as it blended into a car's ignition. "What are you up to?"

"I didn't want to be home. Mom's out?"

Dad nodded. "She's with Olivia. Have you eaten?"

"I'm not hungry." Amber swallowed, looking up at the ceiling. "Scott Stadler—the police sergeant—he requested the report about Marcus. From the Binghamton police. And..."

She froze solid on the seat, closed her eyes and fought to breathe.

Dad shut off the movie, abandoning the room to darkness. "It's hard to read?"

"It's..." Amber's voice wobbled, and she tried to stop the tears.

Dad put his arm around her. "Don't roll your eyes at me, young lady."

Amber melted into his shoulder. "You don't miss a trick."

"They taught them all back when I got a PhD in Fatherhood." He gave a squeeze. "Let's go look at the thing."

"I can't go through that one more time," said Amber. "I can't."

Scott said, "There aren't guarantees."

"There are guarantees." Amber tightened her fists. "I can make sure it won't happen again."

Scott moved back to the table, and he spoke lower. "By living a loveless, lonely life?"

"I'm not lonely and I'm not loveless." Amber looked him right in the eyes. "I've got my family and I've got plenty of friends. I've got my job, and I'm living for that."

Scott said, "But how much are you losing by insulating yourself like this?"

"It doesn't matter," Amber said. "It doesn't matter how much you could win on the roulette wheel if you can't afford to lose what you put down."

Scott only stared, shocked. And then he said, "I always thought you were fearless."

Amber said, "It's better—"

Dad said, "Bring it to the table."

"—to have nothing to lose."

Amber followed with the report.

Dad took it from her hands. "There's not much," she said. "Scott said it was grossly incomplete. They didn't even secure the crime scene properly, which is how Carmen took all his things. I know they never interviewed me even though I was the last person to see him alive, and they barely interviewed her. They talked to the roommate and the landlord, and nothing else."

As Dad opened the pages, she said, "There's factual errors, too. He had a work-study at the university, but they have him doing a part-time job at Burger King."

Dad shook his head. "Binghamton's finest. Is the autopsy report here?"

Amber's mouth twitched. "What there is of it. Practically nothing, like they'd written it before he even got on the slab. Gunshot wound to the temple, possibly self-inflicted. Nothing you could work with. Gun stolen eighteen months before the shooting. Because you know how it is, a guy with no prior criminal record or mental health issues gets suicidal, steals a gun, then waits a year and a half to put a bullet in his brain."

Dad reached for her hand and gave a squeeze. "I'm sorry, honey."

Amber looked down.

Dad held tighter. "You went through hell, but I was so proud of you. You did everything right."

Amber looked up. "What did I do? I collapsed."

"You didn't give up," said Dad. "You took your time, and then you got back on your feet."

Amber said, "That's what anyone would have done. You can't let one bad thing destroy you."

Dad said, "Some people do. But instead here you are."

Scott went back to the door. "I can't win against that."

But then he stopped mid-stride as Amber choked out, "I think you're going to."

Amber glared at her lap. "Yeah, the child-prosecuting much-hated junior assistant Fire Marshal of Tioga County, New York."

Dad chuckled. "That only means you're doing your job right."

Scott stepped back toward her. Amber closed her eyes. He took her hand, then drew it nearer, nearer, and then with his breath warm against her fingers, he kissed them. She trembled, biting her lip, unable to read the silence for what he would do next. Then after a long moment, without another word, he left the room.

Dad patted her hand. "Don't knock yourself. Now here," he said. "Let's look through this again."

TWENTY FOUR

Katie's name looked like a scribble on the FedEx signature line.

Back in the kitchen, she started to open the envelope but then got interrupted by Daniel, who needed a snack. Then milk. But finally she got it out. Two packets? Oh, yeah, one for Maureen and one for Amber.

The results were unenlightening for the price, as Mike had predicted. The Private Investigator had been thorough about detailing all the boring stuff, pulling up information on everyone's public record. Everyone was, reassuringly, exactly who they said: stable women with stable jobs and a longtime commitment to a small community. Moreover, the PI had compiled reasonable guesses at their finances based on some forensic accounting. Amber's paygrade was public record, for example, and he knew what the average professor pulled down at Raymond Brickman's college. No guess what a midwife earned, but he included the reimbursement rate from two major insurance companies and Medicaid. Then he gave the cost of their home when purchased fifteen years ago versus what it would cost today (cheap house, decent equity) and the value of the cars (older models). If this was right, they had no debt and lived within their means.

So, no shakedown here. No attempted blackmail.

It was...odd. But maybe it was real.

Maureen and Amber had this idyllic existence in small-town America. They probably had a Main Street and a Corner Store, and maybe there was a diner where everyone hung out. Life in a town so small that everyone knew everyone else: could that have been hers? Not that this was bad. But what if?

Dad texted her. "FedEx website says it arrived."

Abruptly she wished she'd never mentioned it to Dad. She texted back, "It's here. All boring stuff."

Dad's reply appeared in seconds. "I'm coming."

She replied, "No rush."

Nothing more from him.

She paced. She helped Daniel with a letter puzzle and stacked dishes in the dishwasher. Too soon, the door opened, and in came Dad with his own key. He hadn't even bothered with the doorbell. His eyes were narrow.

"You got here fast."

He kissed her cheek, distracted. "Where is it?"

Katie took the FedEx envelope off the counter, and then, as she reached in, changed her mind and pulled out only Maureen's report.

Dad glowered as he took it from her hand. Katie clutched the envelope, not sure how to hide Amber's report with Dad right here. Maureen... Well, she deserved whatever Dad could throw at her. But how to hide Amber?

Easy. She walked to the trash and dropped in the envelope as if it were empty. She'd fish it out later.

Grimacing, Dad read the report. Katie said, "If she's a lunatic, she's hiding it pretty well."

"She's practicing cowboy medicine," Dad said. "A *homebirth* midwife? She's not just insane. She's criminally negligent."

Katie said, "The state licenses criminal negligence?"

"The state licenses cigarette sales and allows bungee jumping," Dad said. "You can't stop people from making stupid decisions. The best you can do is make it slightly safer to risk their lives."

Well, he had a point there. "The thing is, the investigator didn't find out anything dangerous. She has no history of psychiatric problems, no arrest record, nothing like that."

Dad said, "Except that she seems to have been practicing as a midwife back when it was illegal in New York State, and she's calling you to spout lies about your mother."

Katie fell silent.

Practicing medicine without a license. That was... yeah, that was dangerous. Because what if something went wrong? The studies actually seemed to say it was just as safe for a low-risk woman to birth at home as at the hospital, but what about the times something went wrong? Did you just drop her off at the front door of the ER and pat her on the back?

In the middle of that train of thought, Dad opened his laptop bag and pulled out a portable scanner.

"What are you doing?"

"I want a record of all this. In case she tries to contact your mother directly."

Katie's breath quickened. "Why would she want to do that? Wouldn't Mom already know anything she might tell her?"

No answer.

"Look, whatever is going on, whatever Maureen is trying, who cares? I don't believe that she wants to kidnap my baby," she added. "Someone who delivers babies would be in the perfect position to steal a baby without having to go out of state."

His hand still on the packet, Dad paused. "What did she tell you?"

Katie edged backward, toward the trash can. Her brain fumbled for a way out. "I already told you! That's why I'm so confused by it all. What would she tell Mom?

And why would Mom care? From what you said, Mom doesn't even know about Maureen."

"Katherine." Dad looked right into her face. "What other lies is she telling you?"

Katie stared at the floor. "It doesn't matter, does it? She's not anything to me. She's... She's nobody. A pushy, arrogant nobody who's making women birth in barns because it's a better experience. What more do you want?"

Dad stepped closer to her. "Do not ruin everything for your mother. Do not. She's happy now. She's stable and comfortable, and you are everything to her."

Dad's eyes were hypnotic. She couldn't bear to look up and see him boring through her skull to get at the truth. "How would I do that, Dad?"

Dad said, "I'd do anything to protect your mother."

"I know." Katie nodded. "I've seen it."

Silence. A very long silence.

Finally Katie said, "Maureen doesn't seem likely to contact Mom, anyhow. I happen to know Mom was at Mom's birth, so she knows whatever happened there. How's Maureen going to lie about that? It's not Mom Maureen hates. It's Anton Vilkas."

Dad went back to the report. Katie said, "And for all you're making her out to be a monster, the report would actually make her out to be a nice person if we didn't already know she was up to whatever she's doing."

Dad huffed. "Endangering women is nice?"

Katie said, "Well that one client..." She caught herself before saying "Amber's friend." "She wrote a prescription for the woman's husband because he was sick."

Dad looked up. "Where?"

Katie said, "The last page, the Facebook screenshot."

Dad tore through to the back, then smirked. He fed that page through. "Perfect. Thank you, Kitten. We may be able to get her out of our lives for good."

———◦◦———

Nurse Claudine hadn't left Maureen's mind in the past twenty-four hours. She'd called Amber, though, and told her what the nurse had said.

"She's going to crumble on the witness stand," Amber muttered, "if she fell apart like that for you."

"I don't want to implicate her," Maureen said.

Amber choked. "What?"

"Vilkas is the monster, not her."

Amber grumbled, "Stockholm syndrome."

"Just don't do anything about it yet," Maureen said. "If we can nail the doctor without involving her, I'd rather do it that way. She's suffered enough."

"We're not going to nail the doctor on what we've got," Amber said. "Any competent defense attorney will say memories under anesthesia aren't valid."

Maureen hesitated. "But—"

"But nothing. Remember when Grandma was seeing gremlins?" Maureen bit off a giggle there: her mother had been more irritated that the gremlins were wearing shoes on the bed than that they were clambering over her legs. "And Grandma was awake. So we need testimony."

Maureen bit her lip. "I could say I was awake."

"You cannot perjure yourself." Amber's voice had gone flat. "Perjury is wrong. The whole system runs on honesty, and once we start lying under oath, we lose everything."

Maureen said, "I wouldn't perjure myself. But maybe Katie's DNA will be enough to convict."

To which Amber had only said, "If we ever get it."

Maureen puttered around the house, straightening things, when she felt a prickly sensation. She looked right at the phone, but not with a sense of who would be calling. Instead she had a sense that she wanted to run.

277

The phone rang.

Caller ID read Regional Medical Center, and Maureen took it. That feeling of dread: was one of her clients in trouble? Maybe in the ER?

"Maureen Brickman," said the voice, thin and precise.

Maureen's pulse raced, and her lips went numb. She choked out, "Speaking."

"You need to stop investigating now," said the voice.

She closed her eyes to get her bearings. It could be some obstetrician who'd just lost a client to homebirth. But in general, the doctors were making too much money to care about the odd homebirth client (odd in more ways than one.) So she just went straight for the heart. It was either the doctor or Katie's father. Given her physical reaction, this was a voice she'd heard before.

"Doctor Vilkas."

He didn't acknowledge.

"Are you calling to threaten me?" Maureen said. "Because I'm going to send you to prison."

"I assure you I'll be fine," he said.

Maureen started pacing, forcing herself to keep silent rather than scream into this man's ear—this man who'd seen her every month of her pregnancy under pretext of keeping her safe but all along had planned her harm.

He continued, "You have a patchwork of suppositions and no proof of anything."

"I have twenty-six chromosomes," she said. "DNA doesn't lie. You'll be the one explaining to a judge how half my DNA ended up in Connecticut."

"I'm just telling you, I'm about to turn in my proof to the state licensing board and destroy your career." He sounded so calm, the kind of voice you wanted in your surgeon. That's all an obstetrician was: a surgeon who got very good at one surgery and waited for excuses to perform it. "But if you want to protect your daughter's career, you'll stop this now."

Maureen couldn't hide the smirk. It came out in her voice. "Which daughter?"

"Amber Brickman." He had no right saying her name. Maureen wished she could wash out his mouth with Drano. "If you persist, you're condemning her."

Maureen said, "You always were a coward. Anesthetizing a vulnerable young patient. Forcing a nurse to sign off on your personal felony. How much did they pay for your integrity?" She steadied herself. "Does the money quell the nausea when you look in the mirror and see a kidnapper?" He started speaking, but she increased her volume. "You know what? I know my job, and everyone knows Amber's the best thing ever to happen to this county. She's untouchable."

Vilkas hung up.

Maureen fumbled with the button before finally getting the phone off. Then she stood at the window, eyes closed, and hoped she hadn't just ruined everything for Amber.

TWENTY FIVE

The unmistakable sounds of impact made everyone jump inside the police station: the shriek of brakes followed by the slam of metal, and more slamming, and then silence—followed by the commotion of everyone trying to get to the front door at once. There were cops and firefighters flooding out, when Amber finally got to the parking lot, she found a UPS truck on its side, jack-knifed across the intersection of Main Street and Oak.

"Go!" Scott shouted at another cop, and then took off at a run. Amber sprinted after, although really what was she going to do?

Scott was already giving orders. *You, go direct traffic. You, get those pedestrians out of there. You, call for the ambulance.*

Amber came around the side of the capsized UPS truck and gasped. The truck had blocked her view of the accident scene, but this, this put the deer collision to shame. A pickup had rammed the UPS truck, flipping it, then must have spun and taken out another two cars before smashing into the side of a parked van. In the center of the street lay a body. A pedestrian? No, it was the driver. The driver had gone right through the windshield.

How fast had he been going? And what on Earth was so important in Patmos Springs?

Already an ambulance siren approached, and Amber had no idea what she should do. She ran to Scott.

"Direct traffic," he said. "There!"

She ran to Tillman Street and began directing cars to back around, but she could follow the sounds behind her: the ambulance's arrival, the Fire Chief radioing for more ambulances from Owego, and then—chaos.

As the EMTs approached the driver on the road, a German Shepherd launched from the pickup, growling, to crouch between them and the driver. The dog wouldn't put any weight on one foreleg and had blood matting its fur, but he was still coiled to spring.

One of the cops approached, and the dog lunged at him, snapping, and the cop backed off. The dog staggered back to his master, ears flat. He growled.

Protecting his master.

"We have to get to him!" called one of the EMTs. "There's no time!"

The cop tried again, not backing off, but this time the dog got its jaws into his arm. Todd Longtree and Scott both dashed toward him, Todd with his billy club out. The bitten cop blasted pepper spray at the dog, which got the dog to release, but it only made him madder.

And then Scott, getting close; Scott drawing his gun as the dog launched at Todd Longtree's throat; screams from the bystanders swallowed by the blast of his discharge as he shot the dog in midair.

Amber turned her back, biting her lip and fighting the urge to scream. Scott. Oh, Scott.

The tumult increased behind her. She couldn't look. The paramedics were shouting, and the priest from the Catholic church was climbing into an ambulance (last rites? Here?) and more noises came from the fire department. There was George Tillman handing out bottles of water to anyone involved in the crash or the cleanup. Pedestrians ran up to her asking what had happened, as if they couldn't tell, and some drivers just didn't to turn around, but she didn't want them just to stop and get out of their cars. *You can't help. Just leave. Go some other way.*

Leave. What she should have done in the first place.

The ambulance took off. Another arrived. It was only when animal control came to remove the dog that Amber turned around and realized they had most of it under control. Shortly one of the cops positioned a squad car at the neck of Oak Street where she was directing traffic, and Amber alerted the Fire Chief that she was leaving. She had no role here anyhow. No fire meant no need for a fire investigator.

Scott was working with a single focus, his face hardened. She knew that look. She probably looked that way when she ran.

Back in the station house, she spoke briefly to Rochelle at the desk, then left a post-it for Scott. "Come have some coffee." It was the perfect opportunity to change his nameplate, or at least flip it upside-down, but he wouldn't be in the mood for that now.

Useless. In a crisis, she was useless. She brewed new coffee, what seemed to be her only skill. When Scott returned she'd stay with him, take him for a real dinner so maybe he could forget and he wouldn't bring up that his Dad had a hunting dog and she wouldn't have to say that Scott had no choice in the matter. Then they could forget that tomorrow the newspaper would be all over him just like it was all over her.

But with the papers she could help. As the county's only certified car seat safety tech, she could tell the papers that an unrestrained dog in a vehicle is a danger, that the dog can be thrown around, and the dog doesn't understand the EMTs are just trying to help. It only knows is master is hurt, and the dog wants to protect him.

For now, though: Scott. She'd help Scott. She'd make good on the dinner thing. She'd make reservations at that really awesome Chinese place in Elmira. She'd reserve a movie from the Redbox at the MiniMart, and they'd watch it afterward. Distraction. Conversation.

Amber reached for the phone she'd left on her desk in the hurry, but instead of dialing the restaurant, she saw she'd missed a call from Mom. She retrieved her message, and from the first word, Mom's voice sent her stomach into the basement.

"Amber, sweetie." Somber, stunned. "I need to talk to you. Vilkas called yesterday. He threatened me. I didn't back down. Well, just now, I got a call from the Midwifery Licensing Board. They found out I'd written the prescription for Dennis, so until they have a hearing, my license is suspended."

Amber dropped into her chair.

Mom went on, "He threatened you too, so... so, if there's anything... Just be careful. I love you."

That monster. How dare he go after Mom? Did he even think that would stop her? Discredit her? All Amber had to do was talk to the DA. The Brickmans could be all done with playing nice about encouraging Katie to cooperate on her own. They could just subpoena her DNA and everything would come to light. Everything. They'd put that nurse on the witness stand, cut her a deal if she talked to the jury, and bang. One phone call and she'd force everyone's hand, drag Katie's parents into court, try that doctor for kidnapping, and throw away the prison keys.

And then... What good did that do Mom, if she couldn't deliver babies anymore? When that was all Amber ever remembered her wanting to do?

Run. She'd run three miles this morning before breakfast, but now she wanted to run another three. She'd come back and find out Mom was mistaken. Find out what Vilkas planned to do to her. Find Scott and sit next to him and watch him drink his coffee. And then try to make it better.

Somehow.

Mom's number went straight to voicemail, so she was probably on the phone with Olivia or Dad, or maybe her clients. This would be a nightmare for them if it dragged on for months, proof positive that this "doctor" didn't actually care about women in the first place. Jerk.

But she had work to do, so she pulled out the paperwork from the Spice Hills Apartments fire, and for a moment she hated the Hernandez kid too. She didn't just hate his brain-dead choice to hang out in a laundry room smoking cigarettes and setting fires, and not just his wannabe activist mother or his ignorant friends with more eggs than sense. Him.

The phone rang at her elbow, and she jumped. She took until the second ring to settle herself before answering. "Fire Marshal. Brickman speaking."

Not until she had the phone in hand did she think it might be Vilkas. But really, bring him on. He'd have to be an idiot to threaten a law enforcement officer at her job. No, instead it was a woman. "I'm Jennifer Conrad from the Binghamton Press and Sun Bulletin."

It was probably bad, but always better to sound like it had to be good. "How may I help you?"

"I'm doing a piece on the DelGaudio restaurant fire," she said. "We've got new allegations that John DelGaudio bribed you to find—"

Amber burst out laughing. "What?"

"I take it you deny the allegations." The reporter sounded amused too, for what it was worth.

"Of course I deny the allegations. Would you like a copy of the final report? The one I sent to the State?"

The reporter didn't even hesitate. "Sure!"

"There was no hint of arson. No accelerants, no foul play. The burn patterns led to the dishwashers, and as it turned out, those dishwashers have since had a recall based on my information. I'll email you the report, plus a contact to speak to at the dishwasher company."

"Thank you! Actually, I may do an article about a local fire marshal leading to a national recall. That's a much better story. Have you had any contact with DelGaudio since the fire?"

"He stopped by with cookies last week," Amber said. "But the firefighters ate them all before I got back to the office."

"That's a shame," said the reporter. "I bet they were good."

Amber said, "So what exactly were the allegations? Or do I have to wait until the paper comes out?"

"No, because if it's this flimsy, I don't get a story out of it." The reporter sounded disappointed. "An anonymous tip got called in to the county Fire Commissioner's office, and based on what got called in here, the Fire Commissioner laughed the caller off the phone. It's a slow news day, so I followed up."

About to say, "I can give you a lead on a car crash," Amber stopped herself because the headline wouldn't be, "Pickup Rams UPS Truck." It would be "Cop Shoots Fido." Scott didn't need that.

Instead Amber emailed the report, verified the reporter had received it, and then wasn't surprised when five minutes later she got a call from the Fire Commissioner.

The Fire Commissioner was a brick of a guy, a Fire Chief for twenty years before moving to desk work, and a good friend of the Old Man. She'd seen to the phones on more than one three-hour lunch hour when they'd gone out to discuss business and maybe had actually done so.

"Brickman," chuckled McKenna, "you're pissing people off again."

She grinned. "Means I'm doing my job, sir."

"Absolutely. Today I got two complaints about you. One serious, one not so serious."

Two? Vilkas was busy.

"We got an anonymous tip that you took bribes to find a fire accidental."

"I sent the report—"

"You documented it eight ways from Sunday," said McKenna. "If DelGaudio offered you a bribe, he's an idiot, but fortunately I know he's not."

Amber frowned. "So what's the not-so-serious accusation?"

"Actually, that was it." McKenna sighed. "The other one was that you targeted what's-his-name, the sixteen-year-old kid from the Spice Hills Apartments, because he's Latino."

Amber gulped. "What?"

"It was a formal, yet anonymous complaint, that you're discriminating against Latinos."

Amber said, "Why would I do that? And do I have a long history of charging Latinos with arson?"

"I don't believe it," McKenna said, "but we need to investigate because of the political climate."

Terrific. Amber sighed. "Would it help if I told you my ex-fiancé was Latino?"

McKenna chuckled. "It would have been a better defense if you'd married him."

Her stomach lurched. "You're right about that." Because if she had, she wouldn't be in New York to have this lovely conversation. "Well, what do you need me to do?"

"No reason to get nervous, Brickman." McKenna sounded totally relaxed. Well, yeah, it wasn't his reputation that had been threatened. "I'd never sack someone over the phone. I'd do you the respect of driving over to do it in person."

"Thanks." She bit her lip. "No, really, what do you want me to do? Discrimination is easy to allege and impossible to disprove."

"I'll handle it," said McKenna. "As you said, you've got a track record. Just do me a favor. The report you're writing about him? Document it even more than you did DelGaudio's."

"Will do." A rush of fear shot through her as Scott appeared in the doorway, shadows under his eyes. "Is there anything else I can help you with, sir?"

As Scott approached the desk, the Fire Commissioner said no, that was all, and complimented her work again. "That's the kind of effort that saves lives."

Scott dropped into the chair alongside her desk. Without a word, Amber got him a mug of coffee. Her Avengers mug. With cream. Two sugars. Stirred. She set it front of him, then rested a hand on his shoulder.

He reached his hand to hers. "Thanks. So remember when I said it was awful to shoot a deer?"

She gripped his shoulder. "You had no choice."

"Did I?" He sounded brittle. "Was there *no* other way to get that dog away from my officers? None?"

"Well, no, not even with a sack full of raw meat. He was protecting his master, and he wasn't going to stop." She sat. "You did what needed to be done. You didn't force one of your guys to do it for you." She offered a smile, but staring down at the mug, he didn't see it. "That's bravery."

"Heroism, even," muttered Scott. "Have you got a hamster I can kick?"

He still hadn't looked up. She leaned across the desk. "If the guy cared for his own dog, he wouldn't have let it ride around unrestrained."

"Everyone does it," said Scott.

"Fifty years ago, everyone drove with babies on their laps, too."

Scott said, "And anyhow, that's why we have cops and firefighters. To protect people who do stupid stuff."

So bitter, so dark. Amber wrapped her arms around her waist and looked at the desk. What was there to say? Whenever he closed his eyes, he had to be thinking of that German Shepherd. What were the magic words here? Joke about the paperwork? Everything seemed wrong, but silence seemed *wronger*, so she said, "Any idea what caused the accident?"

"Our reconstruction guy is going over it now." Scott shook his head. "I have no clue. Stupid people doing stupid things."

"Full employment for the police force."

He huffed. "Right until the minute the Chief gets a call from PETA."

Amber said, "He won't fire you. It's just a dog."

He stood, and she looked up, tense. "You know, I thought you'd be sympathetic. Aren't you the Nature Diva or whatever?"

Amber blinked. "What? But—"

"I *shot* someone's *pet!*" Scott's face was white. "Do you think you could drop the Ice Queen persona for five minutes and have half an ounce of sympathy?"

"But—" Her voice broke, and she looked down. Don't cry. Don't cry. "That's not what I meant!"

"Then what did you mean?" He had his voice under control, but a terrible, measured control, like an archer's bow at full extension. "What is *it's just a dog* except a brushoff?"

Amber lowered her head and rolled up her eyes to keep back the tears.

Scott walked to the door. "You know what? I'm done. I'm done with your attitude, your dead lover, your stone tower. I thought there was a heart under the exterior, but whatever. Roll your eyes all you want."

He walked out.

Shaking, Amber sat, frozen. Just sat. But...but she hadn't...but that wasn't...

She followed him out to the front. "That wasn't what I was doing."

"Go easy on the lies, Brickman." He held up a hand. "Actually, don't talk at all. I'm not interested. Go talk to Marcus. At least he won't care about the brushoff."

She snapped, "That's not fair!"

"No," he said. "None of this has been fair. It's been a nice experiment, but it's over."

He walked away, and Amber retreated to the corridor.

Because...

No, no, screw it all. She'd deal with him...well, never, but who cared? She hadn't wanted Scott's attention right from the start, so ta-dah, she got what she wanted. Why wreck it? That was Katie's gig, to run after the people you didn't want to talk to and explain yourself. Who would want to date a cop, someone who would probably get shot someday, and even if he didn't, he was older than she was and men died first and she'd already been the Black Widow. Besides, there was enough going on with Mom and the DelGaudio fire and the Spice Hills residents she was apparently discriminating against because, you know, Fire Marshals tended to discriminate against arsonists. Oh, and Katie, at the heart of all this, Katie who could have saved all of them a boatload of trouble if she'd just stuck the damn Q-tip in her mouth and mailed it off like a good girl.

No, not Katie. This hadn't started with Katie. It started with someone else. And so help her, it needed to end with him too.

TWENTY SIX

The thing about a doctor's office is you don't actually have to have an appointment to see the doctor. They're mortals. They're visible, and you don't get atomized if you fail to leave a propitiatory offering of co-pay at the reception desk.

In fact, after being in a doctor's office once, it turns out you know the way through the waiting room and right into the back.

One nurse did try to stop Amber, and Amber just flashed her Fire Marshal shield, too fast for anyone to notice it was fire and from the wrong county, and then the nurse backed off. She'd gone pale. Maybe it was the one Mom interviewed.

Oh. That would be rich.

"Are you Claudine LaBonte?"

The woman backed up, ready to run.

"I'm not here for you. Show me his office."

The nurse pointed, and Amber said, "The one at the end? Awesome. Go re-inventory the supply closet. I never saw you."

The woman fled into a room.

Amber didn't bother knocking on Vilkas's door. It wasn't as if he'd invite her in.

He looked up, irritated, but as soon as he saw her, the irritation morphed into hatred. "Oh, it's you. Didn't anyone ever tell you going under an assumed name is the most childish trick in the book?"

"Then don't you feel like an idiot that you fell for it?" Amber folded her arms and leaned in the door frame. "What are you trying to accomplish, Vilkas? Because the end is days away for you."

Vilkas said, "I told you and your mother to quit this pursuit. What do you want? To take custody of the Haywards' daughter? She's twenty-four now. She's not your property or your mother's. Let it go."

"I'm not letting go of the truth." Amber's gaze narrowed. "And now you're calling in false reports?"

Vilkas drummed his fingers on the desk.

"Fortunately, the Fire Commissioner and I had a great laugh at your expense." Amber smirked. "The next false accusation you make, you'd better have sworn testimony from the President and the Pope. Because your credibility? It's shot."

Vilkas said, "Oh, I'm not done with either of you. And what about your father? Is he clean?"

Amber stepped in from the doorway. Her fists were so tight the pain shot up her arms.

Vilkas said, "What about Brendan? Your sister Olivia?"

Amber's heart raced. The world was turning into one high-pitched whine.

Vilkas added, "What happens if a doctor calls Child Protective Services on her and her infant?"

Amber's vision had gone white. She rested her palms on the desk, and she lowered her voice. "I will deny I ever said this." She kept her voice low, uninflected. "I will perjure myself if I have to." She looked right into Vilkas' eyes. "But I can burn your house to the ground and no one will ever know." Her hands were shaking, and she pushed harder into the desktop. "You touch my family again and it will look like your stove went up, or your dryer, and the cops will tell each other it was just the street cleaning itself."

"The other one doesn't want you." Vilkas was pale. "If she did, she'd have cooperated by now. What can you possibly offer? Life in a small town? A career delivering babies that narrowly escape with their lives?"

Amber leaned in closer. "Her identity."

"She has one. She's done quite well for herself, unlike some." Vilkas eyed her. "She had a car for her sixteenth birthday and vacations in France, ballet and horseback riding lessons. And you had...?" He paused. "Weekends cutting coupons?"

Amber snickered. "You didn't do it for *her*. You did it for yourself." She turned to the door. "Kidnapping is a class A felony, and there's no statute of limitations. The day they process her DNA sample is the day you need to introduce your patients to the on-call doctor."

Vilkas sounded chipper. "You'll never get it."

"Would I come in here if I didn't have it already?" She looked at him over her shoulder. "I'll get the answers the same way we knew to look for the questions. Because, Doctor, the past is written in the present."

She slammed the door at her back, then stalked down the hallway, pausing at an unmarked door amidst a row of exam rooms. Inside she found that mousy nurse, tears in her eyes, hands at her mouth.

"One thing," Amber said. "Tell me and I'll go. First or second?"

The nurse shook her head. "What?"

"Which one am I? The first twin? Or the second?"

Claudine bit her lip. "First."

"Thank you." Amber turned away.

Claudine said, "And he told me—"

Amber's eyes watered. "It's bad enough you did it. Are you looking to me for forgiveness? I'm never going to tell you it's all right."

Claudine said, "He had me wrap Baby B in a sheet—"

"Katherine." Amber's voice was tight like wire. "Baby B was Katherine."

"—and I brought it to another room as if it was laundry."

"And you became complicit in kidnapping." Amber glared at her. "Just another day at the job, the day you became a felon."

The nurse put her hands on her face. "I'm sorry. I'm so sorry. He threatened me."

I don't care. I don't care what he said, what he did, what he promised. You sold your soul, and for what? The chance to keep your job?

Claudine sobbed. "Do you understand?"

"No." Amber's throat tightened. "I can't."

She left the supply closet, left the hall, left the building. Left the parking lot wishing she knew whose car was whose and could chain Vilkas' car to a tree and then chain Claudine's car to his, so he could keep dragging her all over the place while going nowhere.

Somehow she got back to Patmos Springs, shaking, nauseated, angry, the monologue in her head shifting from one tirade to the next. Nothing was safe. Scott was a jerk and she was well rid of him. Mom was an idiot for writing that prescription. Nikki was a blabbermouth who should damn well have known better than to tell the whole town. Katie was a stubborn hardnose who should just spit in a test tube.

And Vilkas—Vilkas deserved to go straight to Hell, only she didn't believe in Hell either; Hell was just the life you lived when you followed a doctor from office to office in terror, buying your own eternal employment with complicity. Because just as Claudine was protecting her job by staying quiet, so was Vilkas protecting her silence by employing her. Yoked together like an unholy marriage of guilt.

And then, in the middle of all that, Marcus. Marcus who would have steadied her, who would have been able to talk sense to Katie, who would have taken Amber away from all this because together they'd have been in New Mexico, digging for relics and watching the stars.

You don't look at the stars anymore, he'd said in the dream.

She pulled up in front of her house. *Marcus, there are no stars.*

The landlord Mr. B called hello through his window, but she ignored him as she rushed up the steps. She rolled her eyes to stem the tears, but that reminded her of Scott, so then the tears returned stronger. She got inside and dropped onto the couch, and the next minute she was curled around herself, sobbing.

There are no stars. *Marcus, were they ever real? Were you?*

And then she finally thought it: *I hate you. You were such an idiot for trusting your stupid druggie neighbor, and I never should have let you go live there, saving money for a move out west and a marriage that never happened. It was so stupid, and what did it get us? I hate you. I hate you. Where are our stars? What the hell did you do with the stars?*

She became aware of someone paying attention to her. What, was Mom about to call? No flipping way she'd answer the phone right now. But then a tiny touch on her thigh, and another. Four feet. A gentle warm weight on the small of her back, then up to her shoulders, where it settled and sat.

Rocket. Marcus's cat.

The tears stopped. Amber lay, eyes closed, letting the thrum pass through her as the cat purred. For a while, everything else was quiet.

TWENTY SEVEN

Dad banged open the door without ringing the bell, and Katie started up from the dinner table.

"*What* are you doing?" he shouted. "Are you trying to kill your mother?"

"I'm trying to eat my dinner." That was an artificial calm. Her pulse raced, and she took a step sideways, between him and Daniel. Mike wasn't even home because he was working late.

Dad's face was white. "I just got a call from Anton Vilkas. And do you know what he told me?"

Katie glanced at the phone, but what was she going to do? Call the police? *Officer, my dad's yelling at me. He's scary.* Was he being any scarier than usual? He was angry, but he'd never hurt her. Right?

Dad stepped closer. "He told me you've been speaking to Amber Brickman. After I specifically told you not to."

Katie wound her fingers into her sweater. "You never told me not to talk to her."

"She is *deranged*, do you understand? Her mother has an axe to grind, and she's just as unhinged as her mother. She went to Vilkas today and threatened to burn him alive!"

Katie struggled to make her choked laugh look like a horrified recoil. By now she'd read that PI report so often she had it memorized, and Amber was nothing like that. Safety was like her mantra. But boy, Katie could totally see it. Was it bad that her first reaction was to wish she'd been there?

Dad said, "Moreover, Amber Brickman said you were providing a DNA sample."

"What? No!"

"And do you realize what will happen if you do that?"

Katie said, "No, Dad. What will happen?"

It had come out low, so low. Her voice was barely audible.

Dad said, "Quit pretending. I know what they told you."

Katie averted her eyes, and when she did, she caught sight of Amber's report on the counter.

Dad waited. Daniel said, "Mommy?"

"You know what? Why don't you let me and Grandpa talk, and you can finish dinner later." She gave him a cookie. Hello, Mother Of The Year Award Committee? Once again, not winning your award. "Here, have dessert in the middle of the meal."

Daniel giggled. "That's silly."

"Very silly. Go play with your blocks."

Daniel left the kitchen, but the report was still lying there in the open. She couldn't move it or cover it, not with Dad watching.

She stepped to the side, but Dad didn't turn. He said, "Did you send them a DNA sample?"

"No, and I don't plan to." Katie put her hands in her pockets. "But you coming here, telling me they're deranged and trying to steal babies and burn people alive, that's just ridiculous." She bit her lip. "I want to know the truth and why you're lying to me."

Dad folded his arms. "Who do you think you are?"

"You tell me." Katie's voice cracked. "Who am I?"

Dad's eyes flew open. "Don't start that nonsense too. You're my daughter and your mother's daughter, and we raised you. We never asked anything of you."

"No? You never *asked* anything of me. You *told* me what to do. You demand I protect Mom, tell me not to speak to people, order me not to run a Q-tip around my cheek and mail it off to someplace in Vermont."

Dad stepped forward. "Did you? Because that's exactly how it's done. I know which lab you might be talking about, and I'll call them."

"And say what? That your majority age daughter who's been self-supporting for three years had the gall to talk to someone you don't like?"

Dad slammed his hand onto the counter. "You're going to destroy this family! You're going to destroy your mother!"

"Me?" Katie's eyes widened. "Me? I'm not the one who stole someone's baby."

Dad was shaking. "You have no idea what you're talking about. We're proud of what we did! There are no regrets. Anyone would have done the same thing."

Katie gasped. "Proud of kidnapping?"

Dad's eyes glinted. "We *saved* you. You'd have grown up with Medicaid and food stamps and hand-me-down underwear, six to a bedroom in some hole-in-the-wall with young clueless parents."

Katie blinked rapidly. "But..."

"*They* didn't deserve you. Your mother and I were desperate to adopt." Dad's eyes were burning. "But no one would do it because she'd been *hospitalized*," his voice took a mocking tone. "And her anxiety *wasn't under control*, and every agency said no. They didn't have all the medications back then that they have now! But I knew all along that having a baby would save her."

Katie said, "That's not right."

"No, it's not right, but they wouldn't see how much it would help her." Well, Dad missed the point there, but no time to argue. "Anton wanted to get out of that hell-hole of a clinic, deal with real patients and good families, but it costs a mint to start your own practice, and for the first year you're earning nothing, and so often they fail. But then Anton realized what he had in Maureen Brickman, and he called me. A treasure! A treasure, and that other family never knew!"

Katie's throat closed up. "But..."

Dad's voice became passionate, "To get you, we had to move upstate so we could be near where Anton delivered. We had to leave behind all our friends and family, and I had to leave a career I loved in order to spend every damn day listening to people complaining about stomach aches and the texture of their bowel movements. But we did it for you. We gutted our savings account to pay what he needed, but we knew you'd be worth it." So help her, Dad sounded choked up. "It was all for you."

Katie's eyes filled with tears. She couldn't see him, but she knew how he'd look. Focused. Piercing.

"Your mother was *so* happy to have you. It was like a light went on in the house."

Katie bit her lip. Nodded.

Dad gripped her shoulders. "I was right. She needed you, Kitten. Watching you grow up was the best thing that could have happened to her."

Katie closed her eyes. Stop. Stop. *Stop.*

Dad said, "And think of all the people Anton was able to help in his new practice. It wasn't just your mother you saved. You breathed life into his career. And then all his patients benefitted. That's tremendous. How many people can say they've saved so many? Starting with their own mother?"

Katie didn't dare look up.

"That's why you need to have nothing to do with those people. Because it will kill your mother if she thinks she might lose you. You'll send her back into the pit, and you'll never get her out again."

Mom would crumble. All these years, Mom had been afraid of nothing as much as losing her.

Dad's voice was smooth. "Now, what have you told Amber Brickman?"

"Nothing." Katie couldn't raise her head. "I have her information, but I gave her nothing. They sent me a DNA kit, but I never sent it back."

Dad was matter-of-fact. "Give it to me."

Katie went into the bathroom to retrieve the kit. Her hands trembled as she tried to shut the medicine cabinet door, and she battled more tears. She couldn't. She shouldn't. Mom.

She brought it back into the kitchen and stopped. Dad was holding the PI report.

Amber.

No. Not Amber.

Gone was Dad's understanding tone. "Why did you hide this from me?"

"You never asked."

Dad crossed the kitchen in three strides. He snatched the box from her hands. "Enough of this." He ripped open the box and threw the test tube on the tile floor. It cracked, and then he brought down his heel on it.

"Dad!"

At the sound of breaking glass, Daniel ran into the kitchen behind him.

Dad shoved the report into his coat. "I can't believe how you're behaving. I'll ban you from our home!"

Katie stepped between Dad and Daniel. "Do it! And when you do, I'm telling Mom it's you who's keeping her from her grandson, and you who's keeping her from her daughter."

Dad zipped up his coat, Amber's report inside. "Don't you dare."

Katie kept Daniel behind her. "And I'll say, How can he do that to you? How can he do that to his wife?"

Dad lowered his voice. Maybe she should grab the phone after all. "You're destroying her."

"Maybe." She sounded so reasonable, as if saying *Yeah, that soup was too salty.* "Maybe this will finish her off, but you've been destroying her by inches for three decades, all along blaming me. Because she knew. She was afraid of losing me because I wasn't hers. It shouldn't ever have been my job to protect her."

Dad drew a breath, but Katie interrupted. "There's no way I could have done that, so it's no wonder I failed. And it's no wonder you've always been disappointed in me."

Dad glared at her. "Then don't disappoint me again."

He stalked to the door and slammed it on his way out.

Damn. Damn. And he'd taken that report.

Daniel said, "Grandpa was mad."

"He really was." Katie carried Daniel back to his seat. "Finish your dinner while I clean up." She certainly didn't have an appetite anymore. She swept up the broken glass in long strokes, then short ones to get it into the dust pan, and then it went into the trash with a shower of crumbs.

That was it, then. Maureen was right.

And she. And she was...?

It didn't matter. Didn't they say that adopted kids didn't have a "real" mom and dad because the "real" parents were the ones who raised them? Like when her mom brought her home puking from school and gave her Alka Seltzer in a tall glass, or the times Dad helped with her trigonometry homework, or the night her mom waited up for her to get home from prom. The ones who gave their DNA, those were the 'biological' parents, and they...well, not that they didn't matter, because they did.

Maureen had given her life. Maureen and Raymond. Surely that counted for something.

Dad wouldn't ban her from their family. It was just a threat, the old threat. You can't have a semester in London because your mother needs you. Don't say things like that because your mother's already so fragile. No, Dad wouldn't risk the fallout if he kept her from Mom.

And Amber...was her sister. For real. Amber. Her twin. Someone fearless like that was her twin.

Katie helped Daniel with dinner, then washed dishes in a daze. Her phone kept buzzing with incoming texts from Dad, still furious. Endless, endless, the anger. Always the irritation, the disappointment, the fact that she wasn't even good enough to be his daughter.

So Katie turned off her phone.

She got Daniel his bath, got him into warm pajamas. He was everything. She'd already lost one. Daniel was everything. This new baby was everything.

Of course Mom was anxious. If Katie made contact with Maureen, Mom would truly fear Katie would go. Mom would collapse. It was like if Katie thought she'd lose Daniel. No one could withstand that kind of strain. No wonder Mom always held back. No wonder Dad was so protective.

Daniel went to sleep. Mike still wasn't home, so she turned on Skype and tried Amber. Her sister. Her other half.

It took so long that Katie was sure the connection had failed, but then it came on, and Amber looked exhausted.

"Are you okay?"

"No." Amber glowered. "And I wish you'd call off the hounds of war."

Katie frowned. "I didn't know they'd been loosed."

"Trust me, they're gnawing on everything." Amber sighed. "Look, are you going to send that DNA sample?"

For a moment she could see Dad again smashing the test tube with his heel. Katie stared at her lap. "Um...no, because—"

"Oh, come on!" Amber exclaimed. "For crying out loud, why not?"

Amber's eyes were livid. Katie cringed into her chair. "My Dad—"

"Oh *of course* your father!" Amber looked away. "Who wouldn't need Daddy's permission to donate some spit? You don't want to be written out of the will, do you? You're the one who got the ballet lessons and the trip to France and the car on her sixteenth birthday."

"And you got the love!" Katie exclaimed. "Want to trade?"

Amber pulled back.

Katie snapped, "You are just as stubborn as your mother, do you know that?"

"You may be too," Amber replied, "but you don't want to find out. Look," she added, interrupting Katie's protest, "I can't deal with this tonight. Your father and that splendid specimen of a human being Dr. Vilkas are causing no end of problems. They're on a witch hunt for me and causing major professional problems for Mom... sorry, *my mom*...and I can't deal with you too."

Katie's gaze dropped. "I'm sorry."

"Yeah." Amber's eyes were shadows. "I'm sorrier. I'll talk to you sometime."

Her image grew as she leaned toward the computer, and then the call disconnected.

For five minutes, Katie stared at the blank screen.

TWENTY EIGHT

Katie spent the night scared. It helped a bit when Mike came home, but just knowing Dad had her house key, and that Dad was furious… what would he do? Not harm them, but what? Although it did occur to hcr that if he got rid of her, she'd never send her DNA anywhere. Then Mom would grieve, but at least she'd never face her worst fear.

It was ridiculous. Even at three o'clock in the morning Katie knew it was ridiculous. But she couldn't shake it off. A childhood of fear kept pressing her from all sides. She propped a chair into the front door, underneath the doorknob. If Dad pushed his way in, at least she'd hear it go.

In the morning, Mike laughed at her security device, and she sheepishly removed it. But as she got Daniel ready for the day, she considered what would happen if she brought him to her mother. Whether her father would be there. How many texts he might have sent after she turned off the phone. Whether he'd be lying in wait to "talk" to her again.

Tired. She was just so tired.

She said to Mike, "After last night, I don't want them watching Daniel anymore."

Mike said, "Fine by me." He'd been against the grandma-babysitter arrangement from the start. "We just need to line up someone else, and then we're free."

Free. For five hundred a week, they'd be free.

Dad would hit the ceiling, sure. Mom would get weepy. Katie would have to come up with some plausible explanation, maybe that Daniel needed to socialize more, or maybe that another provider could prepare him for preschool entrance exams. They did that nowadays, right?

Mike left for work, and Katie called in sick.

People did that. People called in sick for childcare reasons all the time. It would be fine.

She ought to call Mom and let her know. But that meant calling. And. And she just didn't want to talk to her, knowing now.

How could they? She looked at Daniel and it wouldn't leave her head: how could they?

She took him into the back yard, both of them wearing winter coats, but it was undeniably warmer than last week. The crocus and daffodil bulbs had weathered the snow and put up their heads. The tips of the tree branches had gone reddish, no leaves visible yet but with new growth and tiny buds.

She really needed to call. Mom would start to worry soon. What a mess. No, what a disaster. And then Mom would call Dad, and Dad would do whatever Dad would do. But what would it be?

She powered on her phone. Dad had kept up the texting for hours last night, but whatever. She texted Mom. "Not feeling well. I'll keep Daniel today."

Dad might come anyhow. She ought to go back inside and lock the door, but being outside felt strangely safer. He might not check the yard. Maybe they could hide under the deck.

Yeah, that was real rational. Exactly what you'd expect from a science teacher. Dad wouldn't hurt her. He'd just browbeat her into keeping the secret and brainwash her into thinking it was honorable.

Daniel dug in the sandbox, and Katie wondered what it was like to watch your child while fearing the cops would come. Whether anyone could love a baby the same knowing he could be taken at any time.

No, of course they couldn't. They'd hedge their bets.

She glanced again under the deck, and something caught her eye.

She stepped nearer, and there under the deck lay the broken tree limb that had crashed down during the storm last autumn, but it looked different now. She got close and inspected, and sure enough, just like the branches still on the trees, its tips had gone red.

She pulled off her glove and stroked the branch ends. The broken limb had put out new growth. It was dead, but there was life stored in it.

Life.

Katie's hand went to her abdomen, to the baby growing there. Yes, yes, you do love a baby the same even though he might be taken from you. Maybe you love him even more. Because love is fearless, or at least it should be, and it's unconditional because you give all you have for as long as you have to give it. Even knowing you could lose him, you love. If you don't, the fault isn't in the uncertainty, and the fault isn't in the one you might lose. It's in the one who's too uncertain to love.

Katie blinked hard. She touched the branch, and she froze in place as her phone buzzed. That would be Mom texting back. *What's wrong? Can I help? Are you going to the doctor?*

No, it was too much. She could stay here and live in fear, buried in secrets and the burden of protecting everyone but herself...or go. Just go and be where she wanted to be.

She turned to Daniel. "Hey, sweetie?" She sounded unnaturally cheerful. "Do you want to take a ride?"

Amber's morning consisted of luring out the cat and rewarding his newfound socialization by dumping him into the cat-carrier. He yowled all the way to the Mill Street Veterinary Clinic, where a doctor injected the cat with a thousand vaccinations and then diagnosed the cat with inflammatory bowel disease. He sent Amber home with one furious cat (who at least slunk meekly into the cat carrier) and a tiny vial of Metronidazol plus a bag of low-residue cat food that cost thirty dollars.

"Call me back if he doesn't improve," said the doctor as she checked out. And that made sense because Amber still had some money she hadn't spent.

The cat went back home (and promptly disappeared himself) and Amber drove to work. Scott wasn't around (Fine. That was what she'd wanted all along) and the Old Man had renewed everyone's appreciation of her by brewing something sharp and black and with an octane rating that should run five dollars a gallon.

The Old Man departed for a factory inspection in the northern part of the county, and Amber settled down to look at paperwork that...well, it made a factory inspection seem fun. But as the morning dragged on and firefighters choked down the "coffee" in hopes of a new pot appearing, she learned more about yesterday's crash. Yes, everyone was furious about the dog, meaning the dozen people who'd called the non-emergency line to say the dog was a good dog, and he'd have sat if they'd just talked to him. Meanwhile the cop mauled by the good dog was doing fine after stitches and antibiotics at the ER.

The owner of the dog had died from blood loss and shock plus massive head trauma. Scott had shot the dog to save him, and he'd died anyway.

This job was good. On the good days it was good. On those days it was challenging and forced her to think, and she could help so many people. But today? Today the building felt solemn and Amber felt useless.

She checked the clock. She could keep staring at these papers until one, when she had a car seat inspection in Candor. Until then, pencil-pushing origami sounded like the best she could hope for.

When the desk phone rang, Amber took it with the thought that maybe now she'd have something to do. "Fire Marshal's office. Brickman speaking."

"Amber," said the Fire Commissioner. "I need to talk to you."

Amber's heart went right into the basement, because McKenna sounded grim. Yesterday he'd been amused, but not today. She ventured, "More about the discrimination charges?"

"Actually, no." Yes, he was uncharacteristically somber. "This accusation has teeth."

She felt so cold. "Go on."

"I spoke to Felicia Hernandez today."

Right, the mom of the Spice Hills arsonist. "She's a bit of a bulldog," Amber said.

"Somehow she got ahold of information implicating you in an illegal activity."

Amber blinked. "What?"

McKenna sighed. "Given the nonsense yesterday, I checked this out before calling you. When I get three complaints in twenty-four hours, I generally assume someone got released from the mental hospital and found a phone."

What had she done that looked illegal?

"Your mother's midwifery license was just suspended because she prescribed to someone not her patient, correct?"

Amber said, "She didn't prescribe it to *me*! And it's not illegal to be related to someone with piss-poor judgment."

McKenna said, "But you were the one who picked it up."

Amber's heart pounded so hard she could feel it in her throat.

"Hernandez is alleging that in order to be in law enforcement, you can't be of bad moral character. I need you to tell me," said McKenna, "that you had no idea."

No idea what? No idea that it was for Dennis? No idea her mother was a midwife? No idea that Dennis wasn't the one giving birth?

"I can buy you some time," McKenna said.

"This is insane!" Amber shouted. "Some butt-hurt mother starts a witch-hunt and they come up with *this*? This?"

McKenna said, "Amber, I need you to listen."

"It was snowing like crazy! His own doctor wouldn't prescribe because he was in his pajamas and his office wouldn't page and said they'd see him in three days. The Quick-Clinic had closed because the roads were unsafe due to the snow and therefore they told him to drive an hour to the ER...and did I mention his wife was five centimeters dilated because she was giving birth?" Amber's voice had gotten loud, but worse than loud, it was becoming shrill, and she heard it but couldn't stop. "What did you expect her to do? Let his kidneys shut down?"

McKenna said, "I'm just saying that the law—"

"The law wasn't for that!" Amber was pleading now. She could hear herself and hated herself for it. "Not when a midwife has to deliver a baby and her client needs her husband, and the man's got a fever and can't stay upright."

McKenna said, "So you knew."

"Did you want him to die? Or the baby?"

McKenna said, "You need to get calm."

Amber closed her eyes and struggled to think. She had no defense. Yes it was wrong, but no it wasn't, and if she denied it no one would believe her. Mom was in trouble, but now would Sam the pharmacist get in trouble? Would Dennis? Would Nikki because the script was in her name?

"This isn't fair!" Amber shook her head, as if McKenna could see her. "Why is *this* the law to enforce? When kids are out there playing with fire and their mothers think it's cute? Or when people get shot execution-style in their own beds and the cops rule it a *suicide* because it's less paperwork?"

McKenna said, "I'm not going to keep talking about this over the phone. I'm driving over."

Amber slackened into her chair. McKenna didn't fire people over the phone.

"Brickman?"

"Yes, sir."

"I'll be there in twenty minutes."

He hung up.

She cradled the phone, then sat with her head in her hands.

No. This was all wrong. Vilkas. Mom's need to save the whole flaming world. Dennis for not going to the doctor. It wasn't like anyone even would have thought about how what they were doing would affect anyone else, and Amber knew she wasn't important, but here it was her life burning to the ground.

She pulled her shield from her pocket and set it on the desk. She retrieved her jacket, the one with the Tioga County emblem on it, and hung it over her chair. Then she took her backpack and slipped out the rear door, to the parking lot.

TWenTY nine

Patmos Springs is deceptively far from Danbury, Connecticut. Especially if you begin the journey at nine o'clock in the morning, setting a DVD into the player in the back seat and thinking to yourself, Newburgh is only about forty minutes. If you went north, Albany is two hours. You'll arrive long before lunch. New York State just isn't that big.

And the drive gets further when the two-year-old in the back seat doesn't fall asleep right away, nor at all. He's old enough to recognize every logo in America and asks, as you pass each exit, for McDonalds and Dunkin Donuts and Friendly's and Burger King, although he doesn't yet recognize Wendy's. When you pass over the Newburgh-Beacon Bridge, and he starts off cheering and ends it screaming, then it's time for a break. That's when you check the map to discover you're not even a quarter of the way there.

Patmos Springs is also deceptively far from the Tioga county seat in Owego, in that it takes a Fire Commissioner twenty minutes to get out to his car and drive the fewer than five miles, and in that time, an Assistant Fire Marshal can be long gone from her desk.

McKenna went through the front entrance to the Fire Marshal office, giving Scott a nod as he passed. He reached the office to find it empty, both computers off, the coffee pot dry on the hot plate. As he walked to the back to flip the switch, he noticed Amber's shield on her desk.

He picked it up. "Brickman?"

No answer. He dropped the shield back on her desk and walked out to the front, to Scott. Glancing at the nameplate on the desk (upside-down today) he said, "Sergeant Stadler? I'm trying to find Amber Brickman."

Scott shrugged. "She's not in her office?"

He shook his head. "Can you radio her?"

"Sure." Scott pulled out his handset. "Brickman, you're being paged." Then he hesitated. "Sorry, sir." Then again into the radio, "Brickman, the Fire Commissioner is at the front desk to see you."

Again no answer. McKenna said, "Did she leave?"

Scott shook his head. "I didn't see her go, but there's a back entrance. She sometimes parks there. Hang on."

Two minutes later, he returned. "Her car's in the lot."

McKenna said, "She left her shield on the desk." And when Scott did a double take, he said, "She was pretty distraught when I spoke to her. I think she thought I was about to sack her."

"Why would you do that? She does more work than anyone else in the building. Excepting myself." Scott said into the radio again, "Brickman, the Fire Commissioner is here to see you."

Then he picked up the phone and dialed, frowning. "Okay, this isn't good. Where is she?" He waited a moment, then said into the phone, "Amber, this is Scott. Call back. We're wondering where you are."

McKenna took out his phone and reached the Old Man, who verified that Amber wasn't with him.

Frowning, Scott grabbed the radio. "Dennis, are you in the building?"

"I could be in a minute. I'm about four blocks away."

Dennis was at the McDonalds, to be exact. He'd gone on a search for coffee after the whole *hot pot with a layer of burnt grounds* began to lose its appeal. Without anything more urgent to do, he was spending a few minutes showing baby photos to the manager and forgetting to take back the money the cashier insisted they couldn't accept.

Over the radio, Scott said, "We can't find Amber. And we need to. She was pretty upset."

Dennis waved off the cashier and took his Styrofoam cup, walking onto the street. "I don't know where she could be, but I'll check around."

Back in the squad car, he pulled out his cell phone. "Hey, Nix?" he said when Nikki picked up. "Is Amber with you?"

Nikki sounded tired. "Yeah, she has that work-at-home arrangement, only she doesn't like her home, so she comes to ours. It's so quiet and peaceful with a newborn."

Dennis laughed. "Did you get back to sleep after I left?"

"Yeah, he let me for about an hour."

He said, "Well, I'm looking for Amber."

"Call Scott. She's with him."

Dennis blinked. "He's the one who asked me to find her."

"Well, she texted me about, um, half an hour ago? Said she was going to talk to Scott."

Dennis picked up the radio. "Scott, Nikki says she went to find you."

Scott radioed back, "I've been at the desk all morning, and my eyesight isn't that bad."

Nikki was saying on the phone, "Okay, here they are. Thirty minutes ago I texted to ask about her mom, because I heard on Facebook she's being investigated, and it sounds like it's all my fault, and then she texted me, *My life is a nightmare.* I texted back, *I'm really really sorry,* and then she wrote back, *I need to make amends with Marcus.* But she's upset and I think she meant Scott because, well, you know, Marcus is dead and Scott's the one who's mad at her."

Dennis said, "Nick, I'll call you back." He dropped the phone and turned on the siren.

It was only a quarter mile back to the station house, but he couldn't explain that pressure, the fear—it needed sirens, and it needed that zero-to-sixty jump and then he needed to just leave the car wherever it stopped, and he needed to run into the front lobby.

Rochelle was saying to Scott, "She wasn't in there."

Dennis rushed the desk. "Scott, we need to find her. You said she was distraught? Well she texted Nikki that she was going to talk to Marcus. *Marcus.*"

Scott went white. "Oh, no. No, no, no—"

McKenna said, "What's going on?"

"Yesterday I was pissed at her and I told her to go talk to her dead ex-fiancé. And then she thought you were about to jump all over her too." Scott pointed to Dennis. "I need you to check out Amber's apartment. Just go." Dennis took off. He looked at McKenna. "Can you do me a favor? There's a coffee shop about a block away, called Tillman's. Can you ask if they've seen her?"

Two miles away, Nikki hadn't moved from the phone since Dennis hung up, so she answered on the first ring. "What's going on?" She had that broken note in her voice. "I tried calling Amber, but she's not picking up."

"When she said Marcus, we think she actually meant Marcus," Dennis said. "I need you to call Maureen and see if she's heard from Amber. I'm on the way to check out her apartment."

Nikki said, "Why? You think she's in danger?"

Dennis said, "Hon, she thought she'd lose her job and effectively made a suicide threat, then disappeared. Yeah, I think she's in danger."

In the center of town, McKenna reached the coffee shop. "Mr. Tillman?" He flashed his shield. He already had his cell phone in his other hand. "I was wondering if you've seen Amber Brickman. She's the Assistant Fire Marshal."

"I know who she is." The weathered man looked concerned. "I haven't seen her today."

McKenna dialed. "Stadler? She's not here."

Dennis reached Amber's apartment at just about the time Katie and Daniel's minivan crossed into Binghamton. Holding up the radio, he said, "She's not answering the bell."

Scott said, "Is her landlord home?"

Dennis checked the window. "It's dark. I'm trying the inner door."

Dennis climbed to the landing and banged. "Still no answer."

Over the radio, Scott said, "Kick in the door."

Dennis laughed out loud. "You mean like in the movies?"

"Dennis!"

Shouting, "Police action! Stand clear!" in case Amber was on the other side, Dennis planted a kick right beside the door knob, and the lock splintered. He gave it another shot, and the door banged inward, leaving the dead bolt standing in the wall. "Amber! Amber, are you here?"

"Search the apartment."

"Doing it, Sarge. I don't see her." He looked through the bedroom, checking the closet and around both sides of the bed, then underneath with his flashlight where the cat's eyes glittered. He checked the tiny spare room, then the bathroom, and finally the hall closet. "She's not here. Oh, hell." He stopped in the kitchen. "She left her wallet, cell phone and keys on the table."

Scott's voice pitched up. "What?"

Dennis flipped open the wallet. "Her cash is still inside."

"All units," Scott called into the radio. "All units, respond. 10-56A."

While the units began radioing in, Dennis got a call from Nikki. "What on Earth's going on?" She sounded frantic, her voice wobbling. "Tell me!"

"Amber got in trouble with the Fire Commissioner. I'm not sure for what. She's gone."

"I'm coming over."

"No." Dennis's voice had dropped half an octave. He might as well have said, *Stand back, civilian.* "Nix, you've got to stay there. Right there. In case she comes to you."

"But I can help!"

"You don't know where she is any more than the rest of us do. I want you in place in case she runs to you."

A hard gulp. It sounded as if she were crying. "Okay. But tell me. If anything happens."

"You're listening to the scanner," he said. "You'll hear it the instant I do."

Back at headquarters, Scott pored over a map of Patmos Springs with McKenna and two officers at the desk. He put a pin through the location of the station house, spearing a paper with the time she'd been there. Then another through her apartment, timed ten minutes later. "Okay. She runs about an eight minute mile. She's been gone forty minutes, maybe thirty-five since she left her apartment." He set that at the center of a compass. "Five miles would make this the furthest she could have gotten, running in a straight line." He traced a circle. "But the roads aren't straight, so she's going to be well within this area. Give me some ideas."

McKenna said, "Are we sure she hasn't come back here?"

"Relatively." Scott looked at Rochelle. "Go through the place again, checking the women's locker room and bathroom." He turned to the other rookie. "I want the Nextel phones from the supply closet."

The rookie headed off. Scott said to McKenna, "That will help us communicate off the scanner, in case she's listening. I can't imagine she's trying to avoid us, but we might as well not be broadcasting where we go."

The rookie brought back the box, and Scott handed him one. "Take a patrol car and drive through this area." He circled a bunch of the city streets. "This is her normal jogging route, and I'd half bet she's going through there. If you see people who look like they've been hanging around for a while, ask if they've seen her."

The rookie said, "Any idea what she's wearing?"

"She's got a blue jacket for running." Scott lifted the radio. "Dennis, are you still at her apartment?"

"Trying to get the door back in place, yeah."

"Leave that. Check her front closet and look for a blue jacket."

"It's on the table, with the phone and the keys."

Scott said, "Thanks." He looked at the rookie. "Well, then I've got nothing. Ask if they've seen a jogger."

Rochelle returned, along with three firefighters. Scott said to her, "I want you patrolling here," and he indicated the schools and the main strip. "Do a few drive-bys and keep your eye peeled."

Someone entered the lobby, and Scott looked up to find Maureen. He'd never met her before, but she had Amber's eyes. She rushed to the desk, and he said, "Ma'am, we're doing everything we can. I'd really like you to wait at your home, in case she turns up there."

"I'm not completely stupid," she said. "My son is at the house, and if he sees Amber, he'll call at once." Maureen leaned on the desk. "You need people to look for her, and I'm here. It's not as if you can stop me."

Scott fought a smile. "Well, I see where she gets it from." He gestured to the map. "We're picking the likely places she'd go."

Maureen pored over the map. "What exactly did she say?"

Scott said, "She wanted to be with Marcus." He lifted the radio. "Dennis, how did that text go?"

"Make things right with Marcus, something like that."

Maureen said, "That's not a suicide threat. She had something in mind." She focused on the page. "I spoke to her last night. She wasn't distraught, just worried about my job and upset about the dog."

Scott grunted. "She didn't care about the dog."

Maureen didn't look up from the map. "She was devastated about that poor dog."

Scott blinked. "Why? Did she ever have a dog?"

"No, but she has a heart." Maureen traced her finger over the village of Waverly. "Making things right with Marcus, huh? That means Marcus's mother's house. What was her name...? Carmen. They never got along."

Scott said, "Where does Carmen live?"

Maureen shook her head. "I can't remember the street address, but was in this area, an exit or two down 17."

Scott bit his lip. "I don't think she'd try to make it that far. She's on foot, and she left her keys and cell phone at home."

Maureen started. "Really?"

Scott got the radio. "Dennis, come in to the station house. I have an assignment for you."

Dennis answered by walking in the front door. "Amazing, huh? Where to, Sarge?"

Scott handed him the Nextel phone. "Dial in to the private network. In case she's listening to the scanner."

Dennis said, "Using what?"

"Look, the feds paid for this stuff. We're using it." Scott waved him over to the map. "Mrs. Brickman says Marcus's mother lives out in this direction. Drive down 17C about five miles, then take 17 back up. You'll see her if she's on either road. I'll call Waverly and alert their officers to be on the lookout for her too."

"On my way."

Scott turned on a Nextel phone and handed it to Maureen. "You head out too. Check any locations where you think she might stop. Have you spoken to your husband?"

"She couldn't run all the way to the college," Maureen said. "At least not all at once. She'd take a while."

"Contact him and tell him to stay put at his office in case she does try. And see if he has any suggestions where to look." Scott frowned. "I want everyone where she'll find them if she goes looking. Remember, we're assuming she's solo, but there's nothing to say she didn't hitch a ride."

Maureen said, "She's not stupid."

Scott frowned. "Then that makes this a lot worse, doesn't it? Because what she's doing looks pretty dumb."

Patmos Springs hadn't had an all-points bulletin for fifteen years. The chief of police was a rookie back then, and every July he and Todd Longtree recounted that tale at the department barbecue. None of the current department wanted to miss out on this one, so Scott found the off-duty officers reporting in one at a time. And out he sent them.

After Maureen left, he stationed two officers to different areas of the Susquehanna River, one of them the K-9 handler. He roughed up Cookie just before they put the dog into his vest. "Find her, Cookie. I don't know what to expect. Just in case." And he outfitted the officers with Nextel phones as well.

The chatter over the phones was tense, sober. Scott kept an eye on the clock. He'd only ever seen her do an eight minute mile, but what if she were faster? The possible places only grew as the time went on.

And then, from Rochelle: "Sarge, she was here!"

Scott scrambled for the Nextel. "Where?"

"I'm at the site of the DelGaudio restaurant." Rochelle scanned the area, taking in the burnt remnants of the restaurant now encircled with chain-link fences. "John DelGaudio spoke to her, he's not sure how long ago. But she was at this spot."

Over the phone: "Can he take a guess as to when?"

DelGaudio shrugged. "Maybe...twenty minutes ago? Half an hour?"

Rochelle relayed it back.

"Really?" Scott sounded surprised. "She was moving fast. Did he speak to her?"

"Yeah." Rochelle glanced up the road, in the direction Amber had disappeared. "He's here with some contractors. She was looking over the restaurant site, and when he went to talk to her, she asked if he had a bottle of water. Then she took off again. Up Mill Pond Road, heading west."

"What was she wearing?"

DelGaudio said, "Um...black pants? A grey Nike sweatshirt?"

"Thank you. That's perfect."

Over the radio came a woman's voice. "Did she say anything else?"

Scott said, "Yeah, that would help."

DelGaudio said, "She was breathing pretty hard. I asked if she was okay, and she said yeah, just taking care of loose ends."

Rochelle related this. Scott said over the phone, "Thanks. Take the car up the way she headed, and report back if you find anything."

Back at headquarters, Scott jotted down the time on a small paper and stabbed the location with a pin. He called the two officers at the river. "Come back. She's going westward, or at least she was, and I'm less convinced we have a suicide threat on our hands."

Dennis replied, "I'm not. Sarge, she's running herself to death. She'll just run and run and run until she collapses."

McKenna said, "I was warned about that too."

Maureen said, "I still don't think we should rule out Carmen's in Waverly."

Scott said, "Go to Waverly."

McKenna leaned over the map. "Tying up loose ends might mean the two open investigations: the DelGaudio fire and the Spice Hills Apartments. I'd spoken to her yesterday about malicious anonymous complaints about her behavior at both of them."

Scott frowned. "Spice Hills is….here." In the same direction. He frowned. "Dennis, can you get to the Spice Hills Apartments?"

"Sure, Sarge. That's got to be outside the zone."

"She's pushing like crazy, and she's tying up loose ends. That's nice and dangly. Go for it."

"On my way."

As Scott hovered again over the map, Maureen pulled onto 17-C, also known as the Bike Trail. If Amber were going to try running, she wouldn't run alongside the highway, so this made more sense. As she drove, her cell phone—her actual phone, not the Nextel unit—rang. She reached for it, then gasped at the name on caller ID.

She bumped to a stop on the shoulder, leaving a trail of dust behind the car. Her hand nearly missed the *talk* button. "Katie?"

"Maureen, this is Katie Woodson. I—" A hesitation. "I'm almost at Owego. I wanted to meet with you guys."

Maureen's eyes filled with tears, and she struggled to talk but found nothing to say.

Katie added, "I tried to call Amber, but she's not answering."

"We don't know where she is. She's lost. I..." Maureen struggled to get a grip. "Get off 17 at Owego and take 17C to Patmos Springs. Go straight up the road to the police station. We'll meet you there."

Katie said, "What do you mean by lost?"

"She ran," Maureen said. "She's distraught. She left her badge on her desk and left her cell phone and keys on her kitchen table, and she's gone. We need to find her. In case."

"I'm getting on 17C now," Katie said. "I'm coming."

For whatever good that would do.

Maureen fought the urge to turn the car around and race back to town. Her daughter was there. But her other daughter—her other daughter... "You're about ten minutes from the police station. Just go in and talk to the sergeant at the desk. I'll let them know you're coming."

By the time Katie reached the police station, there was an officer at the door, and he ran to the minivan as soon as she pulled into the lot. Daniel had finally fallen asleep just before Binghamton, so she hauled him out and let him keep sleeping against her shoulder.

The officer said, "Come with me. I don't know if she said anything to you when you spoke to her last, but she's acting erratic, and we're worried about her safety."

"She sounded awful last night. She couldn't even talk to me."

Scott brought her inside. "You look just like her."

"Apparently there's a reason for it." Katie shifted Daniel so she held him against her chest, head to her shoulder. "Of course now is the time he falls asleep."

As Scott gave her a quick rundown, Katie shifted against the front desk so Daniel's weight rested on it.

When he finished, she said, "Back up. She texted her friend that she had to make amends with Marcus. Where's Marcus buried?"

Scott looked startled. Into the radio, he said, "Guys? Where is Marcus buried? Is she going to the cemetery?"

Maureen said, "She has never once gone to the cemetery."

Dennis added, "She says cemeteries are ridiculous. Nikki brought flowers one year, but she wouldn't go."

Katie huffed. "I didn't ask for your opinions. Can't you just tell me where it is?"

Over the radio, Maureen said, "He's in the cemetery on Adams Street."

Scott pointed out Adams Street to Katie. "The cemetery's here. It's beyond the limit of where she could have reached on foot by now, but it's northwest of Patmos Springs. Maureen," he said into the Nextel, "she could be heading that way."

"No, let me go," Katie said. "I've got a GPS, and you're already searching everywhere. If you're right and I'm wrong, I'll just come back."

Scott shrugged. "Sounds fine to me. Keep your eyes on the roadsides, in case she's down. Take this." He handed her a Nextel phone. "It's plugged into the group network, so you can talk to everyone else. If you find her, call immediately."

Daniel stirred only a little when she strapped him back in to the car seat. She turned on the GPS and headed out, keeping an eye on the map and an ear to the radio as she drove through unfamiliar territory, past abandoned houses and leaning barns.

The engine whined as it labored up a hill, but then Katie crested it, and beyond that was all flat. The gas gauge edged down, but she sped up. Her minivan blazed over the road that lay like a ribbon over the surface of the land, farms on either side and one hoped no speed traps, since all the cops were out searching for a woman who looked just like her. She passed a sedan doing 55 and scattered three crows feasting on a road-killed woodchuck. In her head over and over, Katie thought, *Please be okay. Please be okay. You can't do this to me. They stole us from each other. Don't steal yourself from me too.*

Twenty-four years had separated them. A chance interview on the evening news had brought them together. Amber couldn't separate them forever now. How could that be right?

The cemetery came into view, and no one was there.

"Oh, for Heaven's sake!"

She slammed on her brakes at the graveyard, sending gravel skittering over the low headstones and flat footstones. A pebbled road led in a horse-shoe around the lot bordered by a low stone wall. The whole thing was smaller than the McDonalds back in Danbury.

"Guys, she's not here."

"Thanks, Katie." That was Scott. "You might as well come back in."

Katie pulled through the cemetery, but it wasn't as if she'd find Amber hiding behind a gravestone. There just wasn't that much to this place, flat and aged.

Although, wait. Hadn't Amber said Marcus was buried on a hill?

Hills were in short supply around here. Katie glanced at the GPS map, but this was definitely Adams Street, and this was the cemetery.

She scanned up the road, then zoomed out. And there, about a mile back, it said, "Saint Thomas The Apostle Church."

Thomas. The name meant twin.

Katie edged back onto Adams Street and took the road at a more reasonable clip back toward the church, watching the arrow move by pixels down the screen.

South-east. Closer to Patmos Springs. Maybe back inside their projected area. And then, when the arrow and the building almost met, the road climbed. At the top of the hill she found an unmarked road. She turned onto the gravel, stony bits snapping like popcorn beneath the tires, and beyond a clump of trees, a tiny church came into view.

Her heart pounded. She pulled into the parking lot. There, tucked behind the church, was a graveyard. Again, rows of headstones. And among them, a figure.

Daniel still slept in his seat. Katie shut the engine. Then, into the phone, she whispered, although she didn't know why, "Everyone? I have her. Saint Thomas Church off Adams Street. I have her."

She slipped out of the car and left the phone inside. It was so quiet here, the wind hushing through the trees and scooting the clouds with no sound whatsoever. There were dates, engraved names, the silence of sleep, the patience of eternity. She'd found this before at Kieran's grave, but again the quiet reached out to her here, a sense of the numinous.

Katie crept her way through the gravestones to a woman in grey sitting on the grass. A woman who looked just like her.

Amber looked up, and then her eyes widened. "It's you." Her voice was a whisper. "You're here."

"I'm here." Katie sat at her side, and Amber put her arms around her. Katie buried her face in Amber's hair, and for a long time, neither of them said anything at all.

THIRTY

Maureen parked alongside two police cars, a minivan, and a black sedan. Actually, she didn't park: she stopped, and she slammed the car door hard enough that even thirty feet away, Amber's head turned. "Mom!"

"I could kill you!" She stalked over. "What did you think you were doing?"

"I thought I was going for a run!" Amber's eyes were wide. "I had no idea you guys would go looking for me!"

"You left your office!"

"Yeah, because McKenna has this habit of firing you to your face, since that's so much more personable." Amber folded her arms even as the Fire Commissioner laughed out loud. "Screw that. He can fire me by Post-It note. But I wasn't thinking clearly, and when I changed into my sweatshirt, I forgot to grab my cell phone and keys. I didn't realize until I locked myself out, so I thought, whatever, and just went running." Her eyes were wide. "I'm sorry! I had no idea."

Maureen grabbed her and hugged her, and as soon as Amber was in her arms, it was okay. Amber was so solid beneath her touch, so very there. All this trouble because she'd changed into Marcus's sweatshirt. She'd only wanted to be with Marcus again. Not forever, but just a little.

Amber whispered, "I didn't think anyone would notice I was gone."

Not even notice? Like not noticing the sun went out?

McKenna said, "I'm sorry for causing all this trouble, Mrs. Brickman. I wasn't on my way to fire her, but I thought the conversation would be better handled in person."

Dennis huffed. "Well, I'm not sorry at all. I got a chance to kick in a door!"

Amber's eyes flew wide. "You kicked in my apartment door?"

Dennis nodded. "Splintered the lock right off!"

Amber flung up her hands. "My landlord is going to blow a gasket!"

Dennis said, "Not as much of a gasket if you were dead and couldn't pay your rent."

Maureen said, "How did you think you were going to get home, anyhow?"

"I don't know," Amber said. "I always got home before."

It was infuriating—her just standing there after causing all this trouble, *Ma, I didn't do anything wroooong!*, and it made Maureen just want to scream. "And what are we doing here? You told me she buried him in the cemetery off Adams Street!"

"We *are* in the cemetery off Adams Street!" Amber swept her hands around. "The church is *off Adams Street*. If I meant the Adams Street Cemetery, I'd have said *The cemetery* on *Adams Street*, since for some reason, they put the Adams Street Cemetery *on Adams Street*."

Behind Dennis, Katie choked on giggles. She had her son on her hip, and as she struggled so hard not to burst out laughing, there was something of brilliance in her expression.

As Maureen met her eyes, Katie gasped, "You two totally deserve each other."

Amber burst out laughing, and then Katie gave it up too. The toddler on her hip was looking around, doing the "social laugh" thing without knowing why.

Maureen stepped toward her, and Katie forced a smile. "Sorry. I mean, it's good to finally meet you. In person."

Maureen said, "But why? What are you doing here?"

This time the smile was real. "Amber wanted my DNA. So I brought all of it."

Amber laughed again. "Including the DNA you left in him?"

Katie nodded. "It's the only responsible thing to do."

Dennis snickered. "You know, they make test-tubes for that."

"Thank you." Maureen's throat was tight. She'd thought she was losing one daughter—and now both of them, both of them were right here. "I'm just so glad you came."

Katie reached for Maureen, who held her tight, so tight. "I don't know what's going to happen with this. We'll just have to figure it out." She turned to her son. "Danny, you need to meet someone. I want you to call her Grandma Maureen."

———◦———

Amber's first act as Daniel's aunt was to climb into the back and re-attach his car seat while Katie stared in horror. She wouldn't let them leave the church yard until she had that seat in tight enough that they could have airlifted it with just a hook through the five-point harness.

Katie decided to stay for three days, so Maureen cleared out an unused bedroom. Katie's husband seemed more amused than bothered by her absence. He had Daniel on a wait list for three daycares and was looking into a fourth. Meanwhile, Katie called in absent from work. "I'm three hundred miles away," she said. "Call it personal reasons."

Maureen took advantage of her own "days off" to bring Katie to a few tourist spots, some scenic drives (a lot of scenic drives, actually, since going anywhere pretty much required them). Brendan came for a visit. Ray stayed home as much as possible, and together they went through the family photo albums, sharing histories and telling stories, giving Katie a guided tour through the generations they could remember and an entry-point into her history.

More tensely, Maureen broke up the days with several phone calls (and finally a phone conference) with the State Office of Professional Medical Conduct. After submitting copies of Nikki's records as well as a letter from Dennis, they determined her to have "acted outside the scope of her profession." Due to the extenuating circumstances (the storm, the fact that her client was giving birth during the action) the board gave her a probationary period of one year and didn't issue a fine. Maureen spent the next afternoon calling back her clients. Nikki sent flowers and another apology.

Given the board's decision, there were no consequences for Dennis at all. That left Amber, who had also asked for a three-day leave of absence.

She, the Old Man, and McKenna had a closed-door meeting after which McKenna declared that retrieving medication didn't impugn her moral character. "Accessory to improper prescription isn't exactly a disciplinary code," he said, "but exercise better judgment next time, okay? Especially when you know someone wants your head on a plate."

Amber didn't look away from her telescope as Katie said, "He's going to be a little bear tomorrow. This is so far beyond his bedtime it's not even funny."

How did you calibrate this thing again? They'd only used this model a half-dozen times, but Amber remembered it was fairly similar to the first scope. She identified a couple of stars and helped the telescope triangulate its position. It was too early in the year for night-insect sounds, but she could hear cars and the wind in the trees. The shadow of Daniel was outlined with a half-dozen glow stick bracelets, necklaces, and one around his head. "Does he know what Saturn is?"

"Oh, sure. He knows the names of all the planets."

"Well, then let him see it." Amber hit a button, and the telescope began swinging through a long arc. "If he gets tired, can he go lie down in the car?"

"What kind of mythical two-year-old do you think he is?" Katie grinned. "That would never work."

"Oh. Well, no, I wouldn't know. Okay, come here." She pointed out over the nose of the telescope. "See that? Follow those three stars in a row, and then down? That's the Big Dipper."

Katie repeated this to Daniel, pointing them out. "That's a pretty neat constellation, right? It looks like a spoon."

"It's actually not a constellation," Amber murmured. "It's called an asterism."

"And he's going to know the difference because...?"

"I don't want to be getting him in trouble when he tests for the most exclusive preschools. Anyhow, if you follow it this way," and she gestured off to the side, "this is an actual constellation. It's Leo." She punched a few buttons in the telescope's controller, and it adjusted itself. She checked through the scope, then had Katie look. "See that whitish star? That's Regulus. It's one of the stars in Leo."

Katie had Daniel look through the viewfinder and explained it all again. Amber showed her the outline of Leo, and Katie asked if Daniel could see the lion in the sky. Then Amber programmed another code from her notes, and the telescope hummed as it swung around. "Now we're looking at a bright orange star called Arcturus."

Daniel said, "It's funny that stars have names."

"Better than numbers," Amber said. "Or should I call you Boy Number Seventy-Eight?"

He giggled. Amber located another star. "This one's called Spica. It's two and a half times dimmer than Arcturus, and it's part of the constellation Virgo."

Everyone took a turn at the viewfinder. Katie said, "Is this what you and Marcus did? You spent the night doing a guided tour of stars?"

"And shivering, yeah. Or being devoured by mosquitos." Amber chuckled. "That's why we were looking forward to New Mexico. At least we wouldn't have to worry about freezing to death. But when it's really cold, it's actually easier to see because of the atmospheric conditions. I'm glad we got one cloudless night while you were here." Amber programmed the computer again. "Okay, Dude, here's the big show. You know the planet Saturn?"

"Saturn has rings," said Daniel.

"It totally does." Amber looked through the view finder. "You know how the stars we looked at were just circles? Well when you look at Saturn, it's going to have ears."

Katie held Daniel up to the view finder, and he laughed. "Saturn has ears!"

"Those are the rings. They sure confused Galileo," Amber said. "He thought they were moons, but then they disappeared when Saturn turned so the rings were edge-on toward the Earth."

Katie said, "He's not going to get that."

Amber held out her notebook so it was broadside. "You see this?" Daniel nodded. She turned it so he was looking at just the edge. "See how narrow it gets? Well, the rings are really thin, so sometimes they couldn't see the rings. And then," she turned the notebook again, "they'd come back. But it didn't mean the rings weren't there, only that you had to wait a long time to find them."

The glowstick-festooned Daniel played in the dark beside his mother while Amber turned a page. "Okay, this is totally cool. Hang on."

Hang on indeed. It took about five minutes, with Katie rubbing her gloved hands and Amber wishing she'd worn more than just Marcus's sweatshirt, for Amber to get the image she wanted. And then she stepped back and showed her.

Katie said, "What am I looking at? It's like a figure eight."

"It's a double star," Amber said. "Twins."

Katie looked up. "Really?"

"Really. I have a list of them, but this one's a true binary star. STF-1423."

"That is so cool!" Her voice had ticked up for the first time. "Are there more of those?"

"Bunches." Amber adjusted the scope to another one in Leo. "This is an orange and red pair."

They went through a few more star twins. Katie said, "Why is there a haze around the stars? Is it just not a very clear telescope?"

"You mean why don't I give you Hubble pictures?" Amber chuckled. "It's a light pollution problem. Even way out here. Actually, open that metal case. There's a bunch of filters, and I'll show you how they can help."

While Katie opened the case, Amber craned back her neck to take in the dome of the sky. So beautiful. She hadn't been out in this for ages. Well, almost four years. But this had been here all along, waiting for her.

You were right, Marcus. The stars are here after all.

Katie handed her the largest of the filters, and Amber shook off the reverie. "That's a Barlow lens. Watch what it does. First take a look without it." Then she fitted on the lens. "Now take another look."

Katie drew a sharp breath. "It's bigger."

"It doesn't really get clearer, though. Grab another one."

They experimented with the different filters, different colors. Daniel climbed back up into Katie's arms, the glow-sticks shifting as he moved. "Isn't this amazing?" she whispered.

"Which one is Heaven?" Daniel asked.

Amber said, "They all are."

Katie looked at her. Amber looked down. "Maybe. All of them, together."

"I like that. Okay, Danny-boy, down you go." She got down on one knee in the grass and pulled another filter from the box. "What does this one do? It's got its own case."

Amber just caught sight of a square box and was about to say, "What is that?" when Katie opened it by a pair of hinges—and something glimmered.

"Oh no," Katie whispered.

She turned to Amber and handed it up to her.

A ring box. Inside, a tiny round diamond.

At first Amber wouldn't take it. Then, shocked, she reached for the box, velvet against her leather gloves, and just stared.

Standing, Katie whispered, "Put it on."

Amber pulled the glove off her left hand and slipped on the ring. A tiny point of light glinted on her finger.

He'd done it. That idiot had done it. Marcus must have gotten a part-time job and saved up and never told her, and he'd been waiting for a good stargazing night to ask her to fetch the right lens, and she'd have found it just the way Katie had, and...

Yes, she thought. *Yes, I'd have married you.*

His last gift to her. Out there under the stars.

Katie wrapped her arms around her. Amber closed her eyes and let the stars hang overhead for a long time.

———◦○◦———

Maureen grabbed the phone as she moved toward the door. It rang in her hand as she watched the headlights crawl up the driveway, but she wasn't sure who.

"Maureen?" said a gentle voice. "This is Dr. Olson, Olivia's doctor. Nothing's wrong," she said with a laugh, "but I wanted to give you a call."

On the driveway, two figures got out of Katie's minivan, and Maureen watched them detaching Daniel from his car seat.

"What's up?"

"I just wanted to let you know one of my patients turned her breech baby using one of your techniques," said Doctor Olson. "She thought I was nuts, but it worked, and last night, she delivered."

Maureen blinked. "Really? That's—what did you have her do? The cold peas on the top of the abdomen?"

"I had her rock on hands-and-knees for about half an hour with headbanger music playing through a pair of headphones against the top of her belly." The doctor laughed out loud, as if even she couldn't believe she was saying this. "I pointed out that it was less painful than an external version and had no co-payment or medical side effects. Other than looking ridiculous." Maureen laughed too. "She felt the baby flip after twenty minutes, and that night she went into labor."

"Wow." The girls were coming up the walk, one of them holding Daniel. "Thank you for telling me." Maureen hesitated. "Since I have you on the phone, I was wondering... Would you consider being my backup physician?"

A hesitation, and then, "I'd be honored, Maureen. Not just because you'd trust me with your patients, but because I know you've had bad experiences with doctors, and it's hard for you to forgive."

Hard to forgive. Hard to get past having your life ruined. Except...except had it been ruined? Hadn't she gotten here despite all that? Or had she gotten here carrying this heavy load, and now it was time to put it down?

Doctor Olson added, "But I have one request."

Maureen tensed. Talk about trust and forgiveness, but here was the kicker, where the Medical System started talking: not taking smokers? Screening out healthy women because some chart somewhere said they weren't healthy?"

Doctor Olsen said, "I want to attend a homebirth. Even if I just sit in a corner and watch, and if that's all right with you and your patient. I want to see you in action. I have a feeling you have a lot to teach me."

Maureen had never heard angels sing. But at that moment, she wondered if she had.

She let the girls in the front door, Amber hauling a sound-asleep Daniel and Katie rubbing her chilled fingers. Maureen promised to call Doctor Olsen in the morning to hammer out the details, then got the doors for Amber and Katie, turning on lights strategically so they could get Daniel into bed without waking him. They went back downstairs, still silent, Amber with her hands shoved in her pockets.

A new backup physician. A backup physician as wonderful as Doctor Jacobson. A doctor who understood birth as a partnership.

Head reeling, Maureen settled in the kitchen where Ray had a kettle on. She touched Katie's shoulder as she walked by. "It's been great having you two here. I wish you didn't have to go home."

Amber was holding her left hand in her right, staring at the table top. "What are we going to do about things?"

Maureen glanced at Katie, who looked somber and a little stunned. Amber had said she wouldn't mind having Doctor Vilkas go up the river (Maureen wouldn't mind either, but she also wouldn't mind if the doctor drowned midstream) but Katie's concern was understandable: what would happen to her mom and dad?

Katie said, "I want to call my parents."

Her parents. They'd always be that. Meanwhile Maureen and Ray were still Maureen and Ray, and they might always be. Biology alone didn't replace your entire childhood.

Amber still had her hand clutched to her chest, as if she'd gotten a burn. "You want some privacy?"

Katie pulled out the phone. "Actually, I want you here."

Maureen said to Amber, "What's the matter with your hand, honey? Did you get hurt?"

Amber showed her the ring. Maureen gasped.

Katie looked up from the phone. "It was hidden in the telescope box."

Amber pulled back her hand and wrapped her fingers again around the ring.

Maureen's heart pounded. Marcus. Oh, poor Marcus. Such a good kid.

Abruptly Katie straightened. "I'm here. I'm okay."

The Brickmans fell silent while Katie sat, her eyes smoldering. She mm-hmmed a few times, and then,

"Dad? You've said all this before. I want to talk to Mom. Put Mom on the phone." A hesitation, and then, "Dad, put Mom on the phone or I'm hanging up."

She hesitated, and then she hung up.

Amber snorted. "Good for you."

"It's not going to last." Katie winked at Maureen. "But I'm finding my backbone."

The phone rang. She answered. "Dad? Put Mom on the phone." She waited a moment and then hung up again.

Amber said, "How many times will this go on?"

Katie smirked. "I don't know. I've never tried before."

It rang a third time, and when Katie picked up, she said, "Mom?" and then waited. Then, "Thanks. I wanted to talk to you."

Maureen let out a sigh. That might not have ended well.

Katie said, "And did Dad tell you why I did that?"

Maureen's hands hurt—she'd clenched her fists, but it wasn't anger. It was tension. She relaxed her jaw the way she told her laboring moms. Breathe deep.

Katie was staring at the table top. "I love you too." She was hurting: her every motion right now screamed of pain, and Maureen couldn't help herself from touching Katie's hand. Hurting because even if these people had lied to her, they were her parents. She still loved them. She was supposed to.

Katie said, "But Mom, listen... Dad said you got me in order to save you. I can't do that. I grew up knowing that if only I did everything right, you'd be fine, only you weren't because how could I do that? How could a five-year-old do that? A ten-year-old? And all along you kept telling me that you'd lose me. You'd lose me if I went away to college. You'd lose me if I married Mike. But you can't keep me. Even if I was your biological child, I'm not a sacrifice for you. I can't save you."

Katie hesitated. She looked at Maureen, then at Amber. "I don't know," she said.

And then suddenly she burst out laughing. She covered the phone. "Dr. Vilkas fled the country."

Amber's eyes widened. "Someplace without an extradition treaty?"

Maureen murmured, "Oh, his poor nurse."

Amber snorted. "Ma, are you nuts?"

Well...the poor woman had lived in fear for twenty-four years. Sticking close to that jerk was all Claudine had known. In a perverse way, by setting her free, he'd made her more lost.

Katie was saying, "No, I don't know what happens now. I mean..." She glanced at Amber. "I haven't given them a DNA sample. After what Dad said, and after what they found out on their own, we didn't think we needed it." A pause. "I know you don't want that. I don't want that either."

She nodded a lot while speaking. Amber had always stayed unnaturally still on the phone, as if decoding at a distance what her eyes couldn't see. Katie would have been more like Olivia, lying on her back swinging her feet in the air while chatting with friend after friend.

"Mom..." Katie sighed. "You realize what you did? They say it's a felony."

Felony. Not that it was wrong, but that the government thought it was wrong.

But Katie's eyes were tearful. "You know I don't want that. But it's not my choice, is it? My twin is in law enforcement. I don't know whether she's mandated to report it."

Amber murmured, "For that matter, Scott's even more in law enforcement. He may have reported it already."

Katie looked miserable. "That's not my fault. They found me. It's not like I went looking for them."

Maureen extended her hand. Katie glanced at her, and she furrowed her brow.

Come on.

Katie said, "Mom? Hang on. I think...um, Maureen, my biological mom, she wants to talk to you."

Maureen took the phone. "Hello? Mrs. Hayward?"

"Hello." The voice on the other end sounded timid. No, not timid exactly. Fragile. This note wasn't the defeat she'd heard in Claudine's voice, but something else.

Maureen said, "Why are you hounding Katie? She did nothing wrong."

Mrs. Hayward didn't respond.

"You and your husband, you've been on her about keeping your secrets. Is that fair to her? Why should she sacrifice her identity to protect you? Parents are supposed to protect their children, not the other way around."

Mrs. Hayward said, "You're taking my daughter away from me."

Maureen's vision whited out. "You took *my* daughter away from *me*."

Silence.

"All those times you were afraid of losing your daughter? You did that to me." Maureen's fist clenched in her lap. "You took your worst fear and inflicted it on someone else. And you want to blame that on Katie too? When she's been nothing but a good daughter to you?"

Maureen's fingers crushed into the phone, and she wondered what series of denials would come next, always an infinite train of excuses. Heck yes in the morning she'd be marching down to the police station and filing a report. They'd subpoena Katie's parents' DNA—they'd subpoena Katie's if they had to—and they'd put Nurse Claudine on the witness stand, and if the pair of them went to prison, it would still be less than they deserved.

Katie's eyes filled with tears. Amber reached for her hand. "It's okay," she mouthed, and Katie nodded.

Maureen was about to speak when Katie's mother said, "I'm sorry."

Maureen stopped.

"I wanted a baby. You're right. You're right to be angry. I should never have done that."

Maureen closed her eyes.

"She's been a good girl. She was everything I ever wanted, and you had two of them, and they told me you wouldn't even know, so what was the harm, and I needed to believe it. We gave her a good home. I gave her my best. I'm sorry." Now her voice sounded like tears. "Whatever happens, just... She's always been such a good kid. Don't give her any trouble."

Maureen couldn't open her eyes. She kept her head down, toward the table.

Ray put his hand on her shoulder.

Maureen whispered, "Do you love her?"

Katie's mother sounded broken. "Of course I do."

Maureen said, "I forgive you."

Amber got up from the table and walked to the door. Ray just kept his hand on her shoulder.

"I forgive you. I'm not going to call the police. You don't have to leave her behind or leave the country. Whatever happens to your relationship, that's up to her. She's got to deal with the lies you told her all along," Maureen said, "but I'm not calling the cops."

Across the kitchen, Amber said, "You're letting them get away with it?"

Mrs. Hayward said, "I'm sorry."

Maureen said, "I know you are. Here, I'm giving the phone back to your daughter."

Katie took the phone into the living room. Ray put his arm over Maureen's shoulders.

Amber sounded upset. "And that's it? They get off just like it was nothing?"

Maureen exclaimed, "What good is it going to do? Sure, we could send them to prison. She's sorry. She's had to live with the fear of losing Katie for the past two decades, and her husband is adamant what he did was right. Sending him to prison wouldn't change that."

Amber said, "But—"

Maureen stood. "Hear me out. They're not going to go try it again with another baby. They had their shot. So what's the point?"

Amber said, "Justice."

Still less than they deserved. Maureen said, "Justice? They could never possibly make it right! If they stayed in prison forever, they'd still never make it right."

Amber folded her arms. She was still wearing Marcus's sweatshirt.

Maureen's shoulders slumped. "And honey, where's the justice for Katie? How is she going to live her life knowing she's complicit in sending her mother to prison?"

Amber said, "Closure, then."

Maureen stepped closer. "Sometimes, sweetie, we don't get to have closure. Sometimes the best we can get is understanding." She crossed the kitchen to Amber and took her hands, inadvertently brushing the engagement ring. "We can't go back and get what we should have had. You always tell me the past is written in the present, and you're right. We use that to solve the mysteries. But then what do we do with it?" She gave Amber's hand a squeeze. "Sometimes the best we can do is carry it forward to make a better future."

The next morning, Amber approached Scott at the desk. He glanced at her without a smile. No expression, really. It stank. "I didn't get a chance to apologize to you for scaring you last week." She looked down. "It wasn't my intention at all."

Scott nodded. "I understand. I got an explanation from Dennis."

Nothing more. Well, now was a great time to go down in flames. Amber leaned against the desk. "Katie went back home this morning. I'm going to drive out there in a couple of weeks and meet her husband. I don't know if I want to meet her *parents,* but it might happen."

Scott frowned. "Are you here to write a really long report?"

Amber rubbed the fourth finger of her left hand. She'd taken off Marcus's ring last night. Tucked it away, nestled it in her jewelry box. There it could remain like the stars, but not for everyone to see during daylight. "Actually, if you can believe it, we're not pressing charges."

Scott's demeanor changed for the first time. "Really? And here I've been looking up exactly how many forms I'd be filling out to get an arrest warrant in another state."

Amber found herself smiling in response to the beginnings of his smile. "That stinks. I know how much you love paperwork."

"It wasn't even the paperwork I was looking forward to as much as the inevitable media circus when they realized Patmos Springs was on the map. Although it would have been fun to get to know my peers in the FBI." He frowned. "Why not?"

"Because." Now Scott was looking right at her, and Amber braced herself. "Because sometimes people screw up your life, and you can't just stay pinned down forever."

Scott smirked. "You guys have been reading fortune cookies?"

Amber nodded. "They give me the lottery numbers, and I've learned to speak Chinese, too." Her hands were beneath the desk, and he wasn't looking directly at her. "But yeah, we're pretty much letting them get off scott-free."

Scott said, "I resent that. I'm not *free*."

Amber reached into her back pocket. "Which reminds me, I owe you a dinner."

She handed him the Olive Garden gift card he'd turned down.

He looked irritated. "This again?"

"I treated you badly. I'm sorry. And I have this too." She pulled out a second Olive Garden gift card. "It turns out they were twins, separated, and they were supposed to be together."

He gave a surprised laugh. "And—?"

"And I think you're supposed to take someone," she ventured.

Scott looked thoughtful. "I'm probably supposed to take some kind of diva." His brows furrowed. "A mad running woman who reassembles puzzles and picks up prescriptions in her spare time."

"And cleans up after her cat, yeah. Something like that." She handed him the pair of cards. "Good luck finding her."

She got almost to the corridor before Scott caught up to her. "Excuse me, ma'am." He laid a hand on her arm, and Amber's heart thudded. "I'm afraid you're a person of interest to me, and I know a flight risk when I see one."

She met his eyes, and he smiled. She looked at the floor, but not fast enough that he missed her grin.

Just then the door slid open, and someone stepped inside. Scott turned, and the person glanced at the nameplate on the desk. "Um...are you Officer um...wait, really?"

Amber bit her lip as Scott stalked to the desk, where the nameplate now read *Dorkface*. "I'll go get him for you," Scott said, then turned toward Amber. "And you, young lady, you're coming with me."

Acknowledgments

Special thanks to my early readers: Sarah Begg, Chris Smith, Laura Maisano, Normandie Fischer, and Roseanne Wells.

More thanks is due to a number of fire professionals who don't want to be named but gave me advice about what exactly a Fire Marshal does, and more specifically about Fire Marshals in New York State. They shared from their incredible experiences and helped me avoid many stupid mistakes (although I'm sure I forged ahead and made a number of different ones.)

And finally, thank you to Stephen for helping me with the stargazing information and finding my twin stars, as well as defining an asterism.

Thank you so much for reading *Half Missing*! Please consider leaving a review at Amazon or Goodreads (or both. I'm not picky.)

If you'd like to hear from me when new books appear, you can check out http://www.janelebak.com or http://www.facebook.com/JaneLebakAuthor.

I've also got other books, but if you liked *Half Missing*, I'd suggest this one next:

Lee loves her life in New York City: unattached, works as an auto mechanic, and can see her guardian angel. She's like a big kid in a playground, and so what if she has a teensie problem with telling the truth?

But now she's fallen in love, only the guy thinks she's someone she isn't.

Sometimes the truth doesn't make you free: sometimes, it just makes you miserable.

—

Thanks again for reading my story, and I hope to hear from you!